Star Born

BEN BARRY

Edited by Amy Draemel

eBook ISBN - 979-8-9897820-0-0
Paperback ISBN - 979-8-9897820-1-7
Case Laminate ISBN - 979-8-9897820-2-4

To my children, Leo and Caroline, thank you
for always asking me to tell you stories.

1

The Calamity

Torrell couldn't believe his eyes and his mouth hung open as astonishment fully set in. "Ten of them? There are more fools than I realized," he muttered to himself. His second thought was, "How did they become so powerful?" This one, however, was left unsaid as it weighed heavily on him. He already knew the answer and his resolve strengthened as his anger grew. Torrell turned back to his friends and they saw the serious look on his face.

"So, do you think they'll still let us into the party if we don't have any invitations?" Michael asked playfully, trying to insert some gallows humor to lighten things up.

Torrell shook his head slowly and replied, "The party is bigger than I expected, but still rather exclusive." After pausing for a moment, he returned to his worries and finally let the question that was itching at the back of his mind out, "The amount of power they are channeling… I didn't even know that was possible!"

"Well now I've gotta see this," Ciara chimed in. "Besides we didn't come all this way to just hang out in the hall. We might as well get in there and start mixing it up." This made Leila chuckle and suddenly the cold that had been emanating off of her turned into intense heat.

That heat washing over him triggered Torrell to make the decision he had been debating quietly to himself. "OK, we're going to play this just like we discussed yesterday. Go for the priests first. There are ten of them instead of six like I expected. He has brought more Star Borns over to his side than I realized and it is clear they have stolen cores to make themselves even stronger." he said as the power and commitment in his voice increased.

"Ciara calls the shifts as usual. I will go after Warwick as soon as I see an opportunity," he finished. Then, without another word, Torrell ran into the cavern and the rest of his team followed his lead as they quickly fanned out around the large room.

Almost immediately, they were under attack from hidden guards, but not from the priests who were completely absorbed by the ritual. Huge columns of fire raced toward them and they began moving in unpredictable patterns, just like they had practiced in training for the past several months. The tactic worked and the attacks consistently missed, giving them time to find the guards' hiding spots. The fatigue that had built up from just getting to this moment melted away, replaced by an intense focus.

Ciara spotted a fire thrower and called out in the short hand language they all learned to speak, "Heat! Forward! Low, right!"

Phoebe and her target saw each other at the same time and his hands were enveloped in flames as he charged up a large fireball to throw at her. She immediately sent a huge blast of wind at him that pushed the ball back onto him, engulfing him in his own flames. With a satisfied grin, Phoebe joined the shifting pattern again.

Leila then seized an opening to attack one of the priests and launched herself headlong at her target, an icy fog emanating from her hands. Ciara noticed what she was doing and that she had not seen the concealed guard at the base of the pillar the priest was standing on. She yelled, "NO!" Unfortunately, Leila didn't hear her and the guard sent a large rock directly at her that caught her on her right jaw. Ciara continued to watch as her friend crashed into a wall hard and tumbled down to the ground, finally laying motionless.

Then, out of the corner of her eye, Ciara saw Torrell appear right next to the guard, placing his hands on either side of his head. She looked away, knowing what would happen next as he drained all the energy from the guard. When she turned back a few moments later, she only saw the gray husk of what used to be a young man and Torrell was nowhere to be seen.

The remaining four members of the unit spent several minutes moving around the cavern, trying to find any remaining guards, but the room seemed to be lightly defended. Clearly, Warwick was so arrogant, he thought there was no chance anyone would make it this far. Ciara decided to take a risk and called the group back together at the far end of the cavern. When they were all together, she spoke in a low tone even though she knew the priests wouldn't be able to hear her in their focused state.

"Torrell, you need to guide us here since you're the only Star Born with us. While those priests seem to be completely vulnerable at the moment, as soon as we break their trance I am pretty sure they are going to be way more dangerous than the two Elementals they had guarding them," she said.

"We are going to have to take as many of them out in one

concerted attack as we can. I recognize a few of those Star Born priests and know their capabilities. They have been training with Warwick since the beginning and will be very hard to beat," Torrell replied.

"The ones I know are all on the right side," he pointed, identifying each one. "They need to be taken out at all costs. Michael, I know you swore you would never do it again, but I need you to empty them."

Michael's face changed from calm determination to fear and panic immediately. Tears welled up in his eyes and he shook his head vigorously. With a shaky voice that was difficult to understand, they all heard him say, "No, no, no, no, no… I promised Greyson I would never… You can't ask me to do that again… It was a d-d-d-different time in my life… I learned to be better!"

Torrell placed his hand on Michael's chest. Ciara and Phoebe followed suit and placed their hands on his back and head. Then Torrell said in a gentle voice, "Greyson made the ultimate sacrifice to get us to this point. You were both here to make sure Saul grows up in a world that allows him the freedom to choose his path. I know this is a big ask, but it must be done."

With that, the group waited quietly while Michael struggled with his thoughts. Finally, he nodded and then stepped back to collect himself so he could prepare for what would happen next.

Torrell then turned to Phoebe and asked, "How many do you think you can take out with an air whip?"

Phoebe took a moment to think about it and then replied, "Probably two or three, depending on what kind of angle I can get."

"OK, that's helpful. I think we can work with that," Torrell confirmed.

Then Torrell turned to Ciara, but before he said anything

she held up her hand and said, "Don't worry about me, I've already been working on something and I think it's ready. You have Warwick, right?"

Torrell raised an eyebrow and opened his mouth to say something, then thought again and just nodded. With that, Phoebe rose into the air, Michael ran toward his assigned priests, and Ciara headed into a tunnel off to the left the rest of them hadn't noticed.

Once he saw that Michael and Phoebe were in position, Torrell walked steadily toward the altar. When he was several paces away from the ring of pillars, he closed his eyes and began the internal preparation he needed to fight Warwick. He confronted all of the feelings roiling inside him - the anxiety related to his friends placing so much trust in him, the guilt that he didn't do more to avoid this day, and the deep sadness from seeing friends fall while fighting alongside him. These all began to melt away and he felt the connection to his powers grow dramatically.

He opened his eyes and looked for a signal that Ciara had started the attack and he didn't have to wait long. He heard sounds coming from the small tunnels and passageways connected to the large cavern that were too small for humans, but just the right size for other creatures. At first it sounded like the soft rustling of leaves, but it grew much louder in a matter of seconds and he saw a black cloud of bats shoot out of several openings that immediately enveloped a priest. He fell off his pedestal and his connection immediately severed.

The rest of them knew this was it and Michael placed his hands on the ankles of two priests. They looked down at him suddenly, but it was too late for them as he pulled every ounce of moisture out of their bodies. Their skin pulled tight around their bones and their joints as water rippled around Michael's arms and torso. Their connections both disappeared as they too fell off their respective pedestals.

Phoebe spun incredibly fast, and upon reaching full acceleration, she reached out an arm holding her hand like a knife blade and suddenly stopped her rotation. The air along her hand and arm condensed and traveled incredibly fast toward the priests. When the shock wave hit three of them, they each cried out in agony as they were launched off their pedestals and crashed on the ground in a twisted heap.

Meanwhile, Torrell concentrated his attack entirely on Warwick, racking him with bright blue bolts of energy. He saw this was having the desired effect as the beam that Warwick was sending through the round oculus in the cavern's ceiling started to flicker.

The remaining four priests broke their trance and Torrell noticed one of them turn toward Michael. Making a split second judgment call, he directed half of his attack at the priest, temporarily incapacitating him. Without missing a beat, Michael turned the water rippling around him into a concentrated blast at the priest, lifting him off his pedestal and slamming him into a nearby wall. However, Michael didn't have a chance to see what happened as a large glowing sphere hit him from the side. He didn't utter a sound as he slumped onto the floor and ceased moving. Torrell saw his side was charred black and knew he was beyond saving. Trying to remain in his calm, connected state, he again directed the full force of his attack on Warwick.

Phoebe was busy dodging attacks from the remaining three priests. They were coming fast and furious and she could barely get out of the way before another was headed her way. Out of the corner of her eye, she saw Ciara emerge from a tunnel with a thick carpet of rats and mice following at her heels. With a flick of her index fingers, the mass of rodents split into two columns and surged toward the closest of the three priests, who began to scream as she was immediately enveloped and suffocated by the small animals.

This attracted the attention of the last two priests and they combined forces, sending two energy orbs at Ciara that were impossible to dodge given her position. Without thinking, Phoebe dove through the air so quickly that Ciara could barely track her movement and she intercepted the energy orbs. She dropped to the floor and looked up at Ciara as the light slowly faded from her eyes. Her hair drifted down to the floor and pooled limply around her head like a broken halo.

Ciara, safe for the moment, looked down at Phoebe and let out a primal scream of anger while summoning all of the animals nearby to attack the remaining priests. Bats, rats, mice, and even salamanders amassed around the two priests. They bit and tore at the priests who managed to fend them off for a while, killing swathes of them with blasts of energy and charging their bodies. However, there were just too many of them and Ciara had whipped them up into a frenzy so violent the priests eventually succumbed.

With the final two priests' connection severed and Torrell's continued attacks, Warwick finally broke his trance and ceased the ritual. He looked around and saw the damage Torell and the others had done.

"It's over. Call off your army and let's begin the process of healing our people." Torell said.

Warwick's eyes darted back and forth, surveying the battle he missed and assessing how he had miscalculated his enemies. Torrell noticed a twitch near Warwick's mouth and how his hands were trembling. He felt the waves of anger emanating from Warwick and sensed something was building up inside him. Anticipating an attack, he created armor covering his forearms and shins, intending to send back whatever attack that came.

The attack came, but not in the way he anticipated, as Warwick sent powerful bolts of energy at Ciara. Her eyes opened wide and she collapsed on the ground as her core rose out of her body and started flying quickly towards Warwick. Witnessing such a brazen and forbidden attack on the young woman he had long thought of as his daughter, the last of Torrell's restraint vanished. He unleashed every last available bit of energy in his body at Warwick, concentrating a blast on the center of his chest. Ciara's core evaporated in the air as Warwick dropped to one knee, breathing hard and clutching the amulet hanging around his neck.

Torrell ran across the space between them and jumped up onto the altar, standing over Warwick. Then he asked with deep sadness in his voice, "Why?! You knew her since she was a young girl!"

Warwick laughed maniacally and his hands began to disintegrate. Torrell frantically reached into his jacket before Warwick could travel away. He pulled out a large vial with intricate inscriptions all over it, removed the stopper, and aimed it at Warwick. The particles started flowing into the vial and Warwick screamed, powerless to stop what Torrell was doing. He made guttural noises as if he was struggling to find any way possible to escape. However, after about a minute, there was nothing left of Warwick.

Torrell replaced the stopper and set the vial on the altar, bowed his head and breathed deeply. Then he saw an ornate book next to where Warwick had been standing. Moving slowly and carefully like a man much older than his years, he bent down and picked up the book. He ran his fingers across the familiar symbol on the cover and felt the lock disengage. He was about to open this book that he hadn't seen for decades, when he started to feel vibrations under his feet.

The vibrations grew stronger and he heard a low rumble around him. He noticed the rats and mice began to scurry out of the cavern and then he knew he should be doing the same. He ran back the way he came in as the rumbling and shaking grew. He reached the passageway, running as fast as he could, but the air felt like it was thick and viscous, making his movements feel slow and clumsy. The book was glowing and it lit his way enough to avoid tripping over rock outcroppings and other obstacles, but the shaking was so severe that pieces of the ceiling started falling and some hit him painfully on his shoulders and back.

He came around a corner and saw the light from the cave entrance, which was enough for him to decide to make one final push. As he emerged, he didn't stop running, heading down the slope while the shaking turned into a very strong earthquake. He didn't dare turn around because he knew those precious seconds might be the difference between life and death.

When the tremors were so strong that he could no longer make any real progress moving away from the slope, he finally turned around to see a large crack form in the middle of the mountain that spread rapidly. As he stared wide eyed and mouth agape, part of the mountain slid off, leaving a shear wall in its place. Then, just as fast as it started, the tremors abated and finally went away.

Exhausted, Torrell continued down the slope and when he reached a clearing, he could see his allies chasing Warwick's scattered forces. Without his power feeding them, they were not able to continue the war. Feeling his legs give out from under him, he collapsed on the ground and sobbed, mourning the friends he loved so much who gave their lives for this moment.

2

The Bookshop

Sunlight peeked through the shades, the sounds of his parents moving around in the kitchen, and the smell of cooking bacon roused Leo from his sleep on Saturday morning. He had just been in the middle of a vivid dream, but it was fading so fast that he couldn't remember any of the details. He slowly turned onto his back and reached his hands above his head as far as he could and pointed his toes the opposite direction to get the maximum stretch he could manage across his body. Slowly relaxing back into his cozy bed, he debated in his head whether he wanted to wake up or keep dozing for a while. It was his birthday after all and he had the whole day free to do whatever he wanted with his friends.

Just as he made up his mind to doze a bit longer, he heard his dad call up, "LEO! Bacon is ready!"

Leo immediately opened his eyes, jumped out of bed, grabbed a book off his bedside table and ran down the stairs as fast as he could, skipping the last three and landing with a loud thump in the kitchen entryway. Leo's dad was standing there holding a plate piled with scrambled eggs infused with sriracha and soy sauce, sourdough toast, and three extremely crispy strips of bacon. It was Leo's favorite breakfast and he took the plate while sauntering in a silly walk over to the counter to dig in.

"I don't know why you like bacon like that..." his dad remarked.

"You mean cooked?!" Leo retorted.

"Ben, he has a point." Leo's mom chimed in. "Chewy bacon is just uncooked and gross."

His father sighed deeply and threw a few more strips in the skillet as Leo began to chuckle at the sick burn from his mom. He opened his book to where he left off the night before and began to read, but then his dad dropped a bright red envelope on top of the page he was reading.

"Bubbe and Papa dropped this off earlier while you were sleeping in. They thought you might want to have it before you start your day," his dad explained.

Leo tore it open and there was the usual sweet and sappy card from his grandparents. The cover had an old famous painting of flowers and when he opened it a gift card dropped out onto his lap. He scanned the message they wrote, something about how big he was getting and whatnot and grabbed the card to see what it was. His parents jumped a bit when he let out a very loud yelp of glee. He now had $50 to spend at his favorite bookshop and it just so happened there was a book he *had* to get that day.

He looked up at the clock on the microwave and saw it was just past ten in the morning. How did he sleep this late? He never slept past eight... Shrugging that off, he was even happier because the shop was already open so he could go there straight after breakfast. He ran to the game closet to grab his phone and sent a message to his closest friends, "HEROES ASSEMBLE!"

He walked back to his plate and started taking bites again as the replies immediately started coming in.

"Leo, we never agreed to that being our secret message to meet up," was the first message from Meimei.

"Yeah, Leo, I thought we decided it was going to be something in another language," Ania added.

"I don't even like superhero movies," Stella chimed in.

"Take that back! Those movies are epic!" Aran interjected indignantly.

"It's your birthday, you can use whatever secret message you want," Caroline said definitively.

Leo grinned, he knew he could always count on Caroline. "Exactly! It's my birthday, so let's say that's the message for today!!" he wrote. Then he added, "Twenty minutes! Be there! I'm gunna make it rain!"

Leo's phone was inundated with gifs from his friends making fun of him and he engaged with the banter for a few more minutes while he finished his food. Then he ran up to his room, threw on his favorite pair of sweatpants with the big holes in the knees and a tie dye t-shirt from last year's camping trip, and tied a sweatshirt around his waist even though he knew he probably wouldn't wear it.

He ran back downstairs and called to his parents, "Heading to the bookshop!"

"TEETH!" his dad replied.

Leo groaned, took his shoes back off, and headed to the bathroom to brush his teeth as fast as he could. Then he bolted back to the front door, shoved his feet into his shoes, and called to his parents "Bye! Love you! Yes, I have my phone!"

"Home by five!" his mom yelled back, "The family is coming over for dinner!"

They heard Leo yell back, "Got it!" as the door slammed shut behind him.

It was a warm day and the scents of the neighborhood around him created a comforting sensation inside him. He headed right and started walking down the sidewalk, wondering what the next book in the series he was reading would be like. He had been checking almost weekly and it still hadn't arrived. He turned a corner on autopilot since he knew this route so well and was jolted out of his thoughts by someone calling his name. Caroline came running up from behind him as he was turning around to see who it was.

"I was waiting for you and you walked right past me!" she admonished.

"My bad… I was totally zoning out," he replied sheepishly.

"It's all good, what were you thinking about?" she said with genuine interest.

"I was wondering what will happen in the next book. They better have it today," he said with barely contained excitement.

"You're obsessed!" she chided him, but he knew she wanted to read it just as badly as he did.

"Well the last book was so good! I mean it was dark, right? But so good! I started rereading it last night and I am totally sucked in again," Leo bubbled.

Caroline nodded in agreement and was about to reply when she saw Aran walking on the other side of the street. He was easy to spot because he was decked out in his usual uniform - shorts, classic rock band t-shirt, and a wide brimmed hat that looked like it was out of an old western and had enough dirt and dust on it to add authenticity. She called out to him and he turned, waved, and cut across the street to join them.

"How much do you want to bet Leo immediately checks for the next book?" he said to Caroline.

"Am I that predictable?!" Leo exclaimed.

"YES!" they answered in unison. Then, "JINX! 1-2-3-4-5-6-7-8-9-10!"

"Really, guys?" Leo said with annoyance.

Caroline and Aran looked back at him with their best "who me?" expressions. Then Aran said, "Wait a second, you jinxed me at school on Wednesday! Now that you're 12, you think you've outgrown it?!"

They all started to laugh and Leo replied, "Well, I am older and clearly more mature than you."

"Oh, no you didn't!" Aran exclaimed and then the conversation devolved into the three friends sarcastically arguing why they each thought they were more mature than the other two. They were still on the topic when they arrived at the bookshop and saw Meimei, Ania, and Stella waiting out front.

Meimei had a very serious expression when she handed Leo a wrapped present and said, "Happy birthday," in a monotone. Leo took it and, based on the weight and size of it, he instantly knew it was a book. Of course it was, his friends knew that was the best kind of present for him. Then a little tickle at the back of his brain made him suspicious. Meimei's seriousness, everyone was staring at him, something felt off.

"Wait a sec, is it?!" Leo's voice squeaked as he asked, but not one of them replied. He felt the nervous energy coming off his friends and immediately tore the wrapping paper off the gift. With bits of paper now lying at his feet, he stared at the cover of the book he had been waiting a year to read. He raised it above his head and started doing a happy dance and sang an excited song as his friends all lost their composure and laughed hysterically.

"Do you know how hard it was to keep that book from you?" Meimei asked.

"Huh?" Leo responded as he stopped his dancing and singing.

"It's been out for over three weeks! We asked Mr. Novickas to hide all the copies he got so we could get you one for your birthday," Meimei explained. "We had to promise him we would each buy copies."

"You didn't..." Leo said with a mixture of confusion and awe for their thoughtful and frustrating trick.

"Of course we did!" Ania retorted as she walked into the bookshop. "I checked and all of our copies are at the front counter. Who's ready for a bookfest?" she continued.

All the friends went in, bought their copies, and then settled into the corner by the cooking and travel sections since they knew there was less traffic for them to block. They were all in their happy place reading quietly, surrounded by the musty smell of used books and hearing the soft conversations in the shop, when Stella suddenly gasped. The rest of the friends were startled out of their reverie and Caroline asked, "What?"

"Have you guys reached page sixty-eight yet?" Stella answered.

The rest of them shook their heads since Stella was a very fast reader. Leo was a close second and he said, "Give me a second, I'm just a few pages away." He plowed through the next pages as quickly as he could and then looked back at Stella with a wide eyed, startled expression.

"No way... I thought she was dead, right? I mean, she died two books ago!" Leo said.

"Maybe not?" Stella asked, suddenly unsure of her memory.

"No, I am positive she died." Leo said firmly as he got up. "I'm sure they have a copy of that one here, let me go check."

He walked across the back of the shop to the fantasy section and looked along the shelf, quickly finding what he was looking for. As he flipped through the book, he was distracted by a strange glow coming from the slightly open door of Mr. Novickas's office at the end of the aisle. Leo looked up from the book to get a better view and, as he stared, curiosity overcame him. He started walking toward the office and, with every step, the glow got a little brighter.

When he reached just a few paces from the door, it suddenly opened wide and Mr. Novickas was standing there looking around frantically. When his eyes landed on Leo, he said, "What the…" as if he was coming out of a deep sleep and his brain was just starting to turn on.

"What are you doing here?" he asked Leo.

"I was looking for this book and then I saw that light in your office…" Leo replied as his voice trailed off.

Mr. Novickas seemed lost in thought as he muttered softly to himself and the seconds ticked by. Leo began to feel a bit uncomfortable and started to turn and walk back to his friends.

"Sorry," Mr. Novickas suddenly said as he shook his head slowly, "I just didn't expect this right now. I mean, at least not here… Listen to me… I am not making any sense…"

Leo continued to turn and took a step away when Mr. Novickas began to speak again.

"Leo, do you by chance have a moment? I want to show you something," he asked.

Leo hesitated for a moment. While he was extremely curious about what was in the office and he trusted Mr. Novickas, something about this moment made it feel very important and he didn't want to say the wrong thing. He turned back and slowly nodded and Mr. Novickas stepped aside so Leo could enter the office. He peered in and saw a relatively small room that sat between the shop and the storage area in the back. There were bookshelves here too and they were covered with volumes that looked very old. There were ornate leather bindings and embossed lettering for titles and names that Leo was familiar with, but hadn't read yet. Here and there, leaning against the rows of books on different shelves, were unframed pictures of people.

He barely registered most of this because on Mr. Novickas' desk was a large book that covered it almost entirely and was glowing brightly. Leo felt drawn to it and stepped all the way into the office.

"Could it be?" he heard Mr. Novickas mutter as he took a few steps to position himself alongside the desk. Then he asked Leo, "Would you mind placing your hand on this book?"

Leo felt the hairs on his arms standing on end and a slight shiver ran up his spine, but, oddly, he wasn't worried at all. He took two small steps forward and slowly placed his hand on the center of the book. When he did this, the latches on the cover suddenly open with a loud click and the cover began to open. Leo removed his hand to allow it to continue and a moment later he was staring at the first page of the book. It was covered in symbols he couldn't read, but they looked intricate and hand drawn.

"You're a Star Born…" he heard Mr. Novickas whisper with awe.

"Did you say Star Born?" Leo heard and he turned quickly to see Aran standing in the doorway.

Mr. Novickas looked just as flustered and confused by the additional voice in the conversation as Leo and replied, "Uh… Listen… I was in the middle of something and this is all quite unexpected…"

Leo's mind was then flooded with questions and, as he opened his mouth to start asking them, Mr. Novickas held up a hand.

"I know you're probably confused and want to know what this is all about." he said to Leo, his voice was now commanding and clear. "That's perfectly reasonable and I can explain everything, but I'd like your parents to be with you when I do that."

Leo cocked his head to the side, completely dissatisfied with what Mr. Novickas said.

"I know… This is not what you want to hear, but please trust me that it's for the best," Mr. Novickas said in a soothing tone.

"C'mon Leo," he heard Aran say as he tugged on Leo's arm. "I was coming to get you, we all want to go get some lunch."

Leo slowly turned to leave the office and he heard Mr. Novickas say, "Come back around 8 o'clock after I have closed the shop. I'll leave the door open for you all."

Leo walked back to where his friends were all sitting and it was all he could do to put one foot in front of the other. He knew Aran was saying things to him, but he couldn't process anything. He kept thinking about the feeling in his body when he touched the book. It was like all of his senses were turned up to the maximum. He could feel every inch of his skin and how his shirt touched some parts of his back and not others. He could hear the slight scuffling of Mr. Novickas' shoes on the floor as he watched Leo. He could smell that Daphne, the woman working at the front counter, had packed a turkey sandwich with mustard for lunch that day and it was sitting in a paper bag on a shelf in the storage room. Even more than all of that, it felt *really* good. It was like he was connected to the book and he wanted to go back to the shop right then, grab the book, and run all the way home with it.

Leo began to emerge from his fog and found himself sitting

at Zachary's pizza several blocks away from the bookshop with a huge slice of pepperoni in front of him. His stomach did a flip and he realized that he was famished, so he reached down, grabbed the slice, and started taking big bites while pieces fell on his lap, the table, and his plate.

"Look who's back with us!" Caroline said warmly.

"Slow down, dude! That's deep dish, you can't just shove it into your face like that!" Aran chastised him while chuckling.

Ania took the slice out of his hands, placed it on his plate, and then handed him a fork and knife as well as a stack of napkins. Leo was still too hungry to be concerned about the mess he made and proceeded to finish the slice. He then asked for two more and easily put them away. His friends alternated between staring at him and making fun of him. He heard Meimei say, "It's like he's going for some kind of record…" and he finally leaned back to begin cleaning himself up.

As he picked the bits of cheese and meat off his pants, he asked in a casual way, "How long was I out of it?"

"It's been almost two hours," Caroline responded. "You were like a zombie. When we left the store, we had to steer you all the way here. Then you just sat there and stared into space while we ate."

"Yeah, I tried everything to snap you out of it," Aran chimed in. "I mean, I flicked your nose, yelled in your ear, shook you really hard. I even sang your least favorite Rush song!"

"There is no Rush song that I like," Leo responded sardonically.

"Exactly!" Aran agreed, unfazed by Leo hating on one of his favorite bands.

As Leo decided whether or not he wanted to dial up the snarkiness, Stella walked back to the table and told everyone they had to settle up because the restaurant was closing until dinner time. They all divided up the bill and headed out, spending the rest of the afternoon walking to all of their favorite haunts around town.

The entire time, Leo's thoughts wandered back to the book in Mr. Novickas' office, but he kept them at bay and enjoyed his ideal birthday. When four o'clock rolled around, he said his goodbyes and began heading home for dinner.

3

Decisions

After leaving his friends and being alone for the first time since he left the house, Leo became aware that something didn't feel "right." As he was thinking about it, it occurred to him that wasn't the word he was looking for. It was just that nothing felt the same as it did this morning. The after effects of touching the book were still with him and his senses were heightened as he walked back through his neighborhood. All the colors seemed to be just slightly more vivid. The greens of the Monterey pines were a bit brighter and the smells were more complex, like he could pick out the individual components of the potpourri surrounding him.

Not only that, but everything was tingly. That was the only word he could think of to describe it. He stopped for a moment in front of a small house he had walked by countless times and never took much note of. It had a series of beds filled with different flowers, ferns, grasses and other plants. He looked at each one and, as he focused on it, he could discern the tingle felt different.

A bright orange California poppy caught his attention and he walked over to it. Focusing on it, the tingle felt warm and fast for some reason. His curiosity grew and he reached out to touch it. His fingers grazed the petals and the sensation grew dramatically, radiating up his arm and into his chest. Overwhelmed by the moment, he immediately pulled his hand back and the sensation returned to the more muted level he felt before. He did this a couple more times with the poppy, feeling the sensation magnify and dissipate as he touched it and let go. Then, he experimented with some of the other plants, experiencing how each felt slightly different. The one he liked the most was a jade plant that felt cool and calming to him.

As he was about to try another plant, he felt a different sensation entirely. It was nothing like the plants and when he looked around he saw an older man who had been walking his dog standing across the street and staring at Leo with a perturbed look on his face. Leo sheepishly waved and hurried away, wondering how long the man had been watching him.

He arrived home about ten minutes later and when he shut the front door he heard his mom call out, "Is that you, Leo?"

"Yup, I'm home!" he replied.

"Can you give me a hand?" she asked him and he walked around the front stairs to the kitchen where he saw his mother had been cooking up a storm. Mixing bowls were piled up in the sink, an apple pie was cooling on the counter, and she was in the process of putting vegetables in a food processor.

"Whatcha making?" he asked.

"Bolognese!" she answered with a grin.

Leo's mouth immediately started watering. He loved any form of pasta, but bolognese was probably his favorite.

"Dad made fresh noodles?" he probed and his mom gave

him a knowing nod. Leo pumped his fist in victory. Even after his massive lunch, his stomach growled audibly and his mom giggled softly.

"What can I do to help?" he reminded her.

"Oh yeah, can you empty the dishwasher? I am making a bit of a mess and folks will be here in about thirty minutes," she replied.

"Alriiight…" he said, disappointed in his assignment, and got to work pulling out glasses from the top rack.

As he worked, something nagged at Leo, like he had forgotten something important. Then he heard his father call to them from the backyard where he was running their dog Astro around, asking "What time is it?" This jogged Leo's memory and he froze.

Leo turned to his mom and said in a serious and urgent tone, "I need to talk to you and dad *right now.*"

She looked at him with confusion and concern, then they heard his dad call out, "Hello? Time check?"

Leo called back with a little too much frustration, "Just come inside dad! I need to talk to you guys!"

His mom put down her knife and wiped her hands on a dish towel as she walked around the kitchen island to stand next to Leo. She rubbed his back and was asking him, "What's going on, honey?" when his dad came inside and joined them in the kitchen with an annoyed face. That quickly changed when he saw Leo's agitated state and the concerned look on his mom's face.

Leo gently shrugged off his mom's touches, guided her over to one of the stools under the counter, and then he gestured for his dad to take the other seat. He took a deep breath and then said seriously, "Look guys, something happened at the bookshop today…"

"Don't tell me you made a mess in there again. If there's

another ice cream incident, you know you'll be banned!" his father said in a joking way, trying to lighten the mood.

Leo rubbed his eyes with the palms of his hands in frustration. His dad never missed an opportunity to bring up 'the ice cream incident.' He thought it was a cute story, but Leo found it embarrassing just how many times he had heard his dad tell it. When he was about four years old, his parents had taken him to get ice cream down by the shops. It was his first time getting a cone, just like his parents, and he was super excited. They would always walk down the street eating their ice cream and then stop in the bookshop before heading home. This time, when they got there, his parents weren't quick enough to stop him as he ran into the shop and he had gone down a whole aisle dragging his cone along the bindings of the books before they caught up to him. It was a huge mess and everyone at the shop knew him as the ice cream kid for years after that.

"Dad, not now, this is important," Leo snapped and his dad furrowed his brow, confused by what had gotten Leo so riled up.

"I don't know how to explain this to you..." Leo continued. "I mean, I don't understand it myself!"

"It's OK," his dad said, "Just take it slow."

"Alright... I met the crew at the bookshop and we all got copies of the new book. We had been reading in our usual corner for a while when I wanted to look something up in one of the prior books in the series. As I was doing that, I saw a strange light coming from Mr. Novickas' office."

Leo paused, shaking his head and leaning on the counter. The feelings were strong in him again and he was finding it hard to focus. Then his mother started stroking his hand and that pulled him back into the present.

"Guys, it was so weird... That light! I just felt like I needed to see what it was, but, when I got close to the office, Mr. Novickas opened the door all of a sudden with a crazy look on his face! When he finally focused on me, he invited me in and showed me this huge, glowing book on his desk."

At this moment, he saw his dad look over at his mom, but she didn't return it and continued to look directly at Leo. When his dad turned back to him, Leo continued, "He asked me to put my hand on it and, when he said that, it was as if that was all I wanted to do. I don't think I could have held myself back! I didn't have an ounce of control… So, I did it. I put my hand on the book and it was like I was supercharged! It was the most amazing feeling…"

Leo trailed off and stopped speaking, lost in the memory of that feeling. Then his dad pulled him back again saying, "Leo, what did the book do when you touched it?"

Leo's heart began to race as adrenaline coursed through him. He pulled his hand away from his mom and leaned toward his father saying urgently, "How did you know the book did something?!"

His father looked at him with sympathy and said gently, "I think we can help explain if you tell us what the book did."

Leo took a couple moments to collect himself and then said, "The book was locked… When I touched it, the lock opened and then the cover began to move too. How did it do that?! The book opened itself, guys!"

"Did Mr. Novickas say anything, Leo?" his mom asked.

"Yeah, he called me a Star Born… What does that mean?" he replied.

This time, when his dad turned to look at his mom, she met his gaze and it was clear to Leo they knew what was going on. His mom turned back to Leo and began, "Listen, Leo… The rest of the family is coming over soon and…"

"No, mom! I need to know what this is! I can't wait hours until you guys and Mr. Novickas can explain it to me when it's more convenient for you!" Leo yelled, suddenly consumed with uncontrolled anger that surprised him.

His dad immediately stood up and came around the counter, pulling him into a tight hug and pressing Leo's head into his chest. Leo tried to resist it at first, but he relaxed into the hug with tears of frustration welling up in his eyes.

"Mr. Novickas wants us to come to the shop tonight?" his dad asked and Leo nodded into his chest.

"Did he say what time?" his dad probed further

"Eight o'clock, after he closes up. But that's hours away and…" Leo began to pull away and complain again.

His dad pulled him back into the hug and said warmly, "I get it buddy. I know you don't want to wait, but it's only a few hours and then we will make everything clear. Just know, your mom and I went through it too and we will help you. This is a really good thing! We are very excited for you!"

Leo looked up at his dad, "You can't even give me a quick hint right now?"

His dad laughed deeply in a way that always made Leo grin. It gradually abated to a lighter chuckle and then he looked back down at Leo and said, "Be patient. Besides, this bolognese is not going to cook itself and your mom has made a huge mess in the kitchen. I mean, how can one person use this many things to cook a simple meal?"

"I'm not hearing that, Ben!" his mother interjected. "Half the stuff in the sink is from your fresh pasta! Now get out of my way and clean all of that up before I force you to eat leftovers while the rest of us have an amazing dinner."

Leo's dad raised his hands in surrender, chuckling again, and rolled up his sleeves to start scrubbing while Leo emptied the dishwasher. They happily worked this way together for a while, humming along to the music playing on the stereo. Astro suddenly woke up from his seventh nap of the day and ran to the front door as Leo's grandparents let themselves in.

"Hi everyone! Where's that birthday boy?!" called his grandmother as she walked into the kitchen followed by his grandfather holding a nicely wrapped gift. He handed it to Leo who proceeded to rapidly open it as Astro weaved his way between everyone's legs in his excitement.

"Sneakers! I totally wanted these!" Leo exclaimed as he gave bear hugs to both of them.

"Well, we saw your shoes when we came over a few weeks ago and noticed they are almost as holy as your pants there, Leo. We figured it was time for a new pair," his grandfather poked in his normal way of showing affection. Leo returned the comment with a face mixed with mild annoyance and silliness.

Not long after that, his aunt, uncle, cousins, and Bubbe and Papa arrived. "The whole fam damnly is here!" quipped his grandfather as everyone gathered around the dinner table. They all tucked into the hearty meal of pasta and salad, showering the chefs with praise throughout the meal and taking turns getting seconds.

Near the end of dinner, his cousins Finn and Lucy turned to him and asked, "So, did you get the latest book?"

"Oh my god, yes!" he answered. "I've only just started it, but it already has a major twist I wasn't expecting."

"Well then, you're going to like our gift!" Lucy beamed as Finn handed it to Leo. He tore open the paper and his jaw dropped while he took a deep breath.

"They made a game based on the series?!" he said, unable to take his eyes off the case he was holding.

"I thought for sure you would know about that," Finn said in a somewhat teasing tone.

"No! I don't know how I missed this! Mom, can we go play this for a while?" Leo said, tearing his eyes away from the case to give her his most cute and pathetic face possible.

"OK, but just for a little while, we still need to do cake and then we have to head down to meet Mr. Novickas," his mother answered.

"You're meeting with Mr. Novickas tonight?" Papa asked as Leo noticed the rest of the family's faces shifting from showing pleasant enjoyment of the evening to confusion.

"We'll explain while they play their game," Leo's dad answered and, while Leo was very curious to sit in on this conversation, his desire to play the game won out and he ran off to the den with his cousins.

After a short while exploring the game and dying five times, Leo and his cousins heard his mom call out, "Cake time!"

"Just in time," said Finn, "I was about to die again. This game is good, but hard!"

"Yea, no kidding!" said Leo as they all got up and headed back to the dining table.

Sitting in his place was a cake with twelve candles burning and his family broke into song. On the final note, Leo managed to blow out all the candles just barely, letting out the last bit of his breath.

The cake eating part of the evening was a bit rushed as it was getting close to the time when he and his parents needed to meet with Mr. Novickas. His family members began to say their goodbyes and Leo felt his stomach begin to clench up. All of the questions he was able to ignore for the past few hours flooded his mind again.

Leo took the last stack of dishes into the kitchen and rolled up his sleeves to start rinsing them off when his mother said to him, "Let's leave those until later," and took his hand as they walked to the front door. Nobody said a word as they put their shoes on, walked to the car, or as they were driving over to the bookshop. Leo felt jittery and noticed his hands were trembling slightly.

As they walked into the store, the familiar jingle of the bell alerted Mr. Novickas and he called to them, "One sec, I'll be right out!" A few moments later, he appeared from the aisle that led to his office and beckoned them with his hand to come back saying, "Amy, would you mind locking that door?" Leo hesitated to take a step as his feet felt glued to the floor and then he felt his father's hands on his shoulders, gently guiding him forward.

When they reached his office, Mr. Novickas turned to Leo's parents, shook his dad's hand and gave his mom a warm hug. Then he put his hand on Leo's shoulder and said, "Well, I didn't expect this to happen so soon, but here we are, right?" Leo looked over to his parents and saw awkward grins on their faces. His dad was rubbing his head over and over like he usually did when he didn't know what to say.

His mom fidgeted with her wedding ring and broke the silence "Star Born? Really? I mean, has this ever happened to the same tribe so soon after discovering one?"

"I haven't heard of anything like it," Mr. Novickas said.

"Adam, are you sure Leo is a Star Born?" his dad asked.

"Positive. One-hundred percent. The test is simple, he was able to open the book. That's all it takes," Mr. Novickas answered solemnly.

"That's all the test is? Opening a book? I mean, our tests were way more involved than that!" his father said incredulously.

"Ben, you know better than that." his mom said. "Each type has its own path."

"Hey guys, time to include me in this conversation here. I can't understand anything you're saying," Leo interjected, his voice dripping with frustration and anxiety.

"Good point, Leo… Good point… Why don't we all grab a seat and begin explaining things to him," Mr. Novickas said as he pointed to the small, uncomfortable chairs that were arranged in a close circle in his cramped office. As they all sat down, their knees were almost touching.

"I have been giving this talk for many, many years, Leo, and every time is different," he said. "There is a lot of information to take in and you are going to have a hard time believing some of it at first. Just ask as many questions as you want and we will take all the time you need."

Leo just gave a shallow nod. He was so nervous, he wasn't even sure he would be able to make a sound if he tried to speak.

"Leo, the world has a lot more going on in it than you realize," Mr. Novickas began. "In fact, it has more going on than most people realize. The first thing that we need to help you understand is that everyone on earth has powers," and he noticed the color begin to drain from Leo's face. He caught Amy's attention and nodded toward Leo.

When she saw Leo's state, she rubbed his knee and said, "It's OK, stay with us now…"

"Most people don't even know they have abilities, I prefer to call them that, because they are mostly very weak and extremely undeveloped. It wasn't always this way, but, unfortunately, it has been since ancient times. There was an event that led to people forsaking their abilities and eventually banning their use entirely. We'll talk more about that another time, but I want to try to get through the basics first," Mr. Novickas paused for a moment, looking at Leo expectantly. Leo realized Mr. Novickas was waiting for him to acknowledge he was ready to continue and nodded his head again.

"Your family is part of what we call a tribe. The tribes were formed by people who wanted to maintain their abilities during those dark times when most of the world turned away from them. Today there are many tribes around the world and we work to preserve the traditions around our powers. We also find people who develop stronger powers and train them to use those powers responsibly. You have to understand, it can be very dangerous if someone develops their abilities without guidance," Mr. Novickas explained gravely.

"Remember that tsunami in Japan a few years ago, Leo?" his mother chimed in.

"Yeah, that was horrible… You're telling me that it wasn't caused by an earthquake under the ocean? A *person* actually caused that?" he asked incredulously.

"Yes, that was a horrible mistake. We found him too late and no matter what we tried, we couldn't teach him how to maintain control. We had taken him to a remote island to try again and in the midst of using a new form of training, he unleashed all of his power in one massive blast that formed a huge tsunami…" she trailed off, shaking her head.

"These are very rare occurrences, Leo." Mr. Novickas assured him and he paused to make sure the words sank in with Leo. When he's satisfied that Leo was ready, he continued, "Let's pick up where we left off. We refer to ourselves as The People of the Books as much of our knowledge is passed down in three different volumes. Earlier, you saw a copy of the Book of Star Born. There are two others, the Book of Earth Born and the Book of

Moon Born. Most people are Earth Born and there are many different kinds that you will learn about. Occasionally we find a Star Born or a Moon Born, but they are very rare. In fact, some tribes don't have either one in their communities."

"That's what you heard me asking about when we arrived," his dad said, joining the conversation. "Our tribe has been lucky compared to many because we have always had a Star Born, but usually there has only been one for each generation. A number of years ago, a Star Born emerged and she replaced one who had passed away not long before."

"You probably don't remember Mr. Anderson," his mother added and Leo confirmed that with a shake of his head.

"Well, it is very uncommon for a tribe of our size to have two Star Borns in the same generation," Mr. Novickas said as he took the lead in the conversation again. "It is also uncommon for their powers to emerge so close to their twelfth birthday. While this is common for most Earth Born, it usually takes a bit longer for the other two types."

"So, I'm a Star Born and all of you are Earth Born?" Leo asked, finally feeling like his jitters were subsiding.

"That's right!" Mr. Novickas said encouragingly. "Your parents are what we call Elementals. Your mom can control anything with water in it and your father controls stone, soil, and metal. They are also two of our tribe's Elders who are responsible for teaching newly emerging Elementals."

"So who is the other Star Born? Will they be my teacher?" Leo asked with growing interest and excitement.

Mr. Novickas took a deep shuddering breath and suddenly looked deeply sad. Leo even thought he saw his eyes had become teary as they all waited for Mr. Novickas to collect himself. He rubbed his eyes and finally looked up and behind him to the books on the wall, clearly uncomfortable making eye contact.

"She's no longer with us…" he began with a slight quiver to his voice. "As your mother pointed out earlier, sometimes when people emerge, they are extremely powerful and struggle with control. This hadn't been a problem during most of her training, but she was so promising and her teacher rushed her development…"

"Remember that big earthquake about five years ago?" Leo's dad asked.

"I can't forget it. I made you guys follow the preparedness checklist that I brought home from school," Leo responded warily.

"Again, it wasn't an earthquake. She lost control and did some serious damage to the town. We were lucky, there were only two casualties and we were able to clean things up enough to hide the evidence of what happened," his dad finished.

"Wait, she died during training?!" Leo asked anxiously and his father nodded.

"Who was the other person who died?" Leo asked with even more urgency.

"Her teacher," Mr. Novickas said as he looked directly into Leo's eyes. "He was a very powerful Star Born, but nobody could have survived that release of power."

Then Leo remembered a photo that caught his eye when he was in Mr. Novickas' office earlier and his senses were heightened from the book. He got up and reached behind his mom for the photo with its corners curling. On it was an image of a young woman dressed for hiking with a big smile and the Golden Gate Bridge rising behind her. Leo showed the picture to Mr. Novickas and said, "This was her, right?"

"Yes, her name was Maranda," Mr. Novickas replied with a bit of awe in his voice. "It never ceases to amaze me how sensitive a Star Born can be… How did you know that was her?"

"It just felt right to me. I don't know if I can explain it better than that," Leo replied simply.

"Ben, does this convince you now?" Mr. Novickas asked, turning to Leo's dad.

"Yeah, I think I was already there before. I was still just trying to process all of this myself. It has been a bit of a whirlwind afternoon!" Ben said.

"So who will train me if there isn't a Star Born in our tribe?" Leo asked, looking around at all the grownups in the room for some direction.

"Well, you're getting a little bit ahead of yourself," Mr. Novickas said a bit more sternly than Leo expected. "Being a part of the tribe is a decision you have to make for yourself. We prize free will very highly and nobody can be coerced to be a part of the tribe or learn to develop their powers. But to answer your question, I would begin your training."

Leo's face contorted in confusion and he finally asked, "How can you teach me if you're not a Star Born?"

Mr. Novickas laughed deeply and then he said, "Well, I have seen a lot of stuff and known many people over the years. I have been privileged to count several powerful Star Borns as close friends and they have passed some of the basics along to me. You should know I am a Biologic, which means I am connected to living things. My particular specialty is the human body and I can heal most ailments as well as prolong life. This includes my own… Leo, I should tell you, I am nearly four hundred years old and I have been taking care of that copy of the Book of Star Born for the past two hundred years."

This hit Leo like a ton of bricks. Four hundred years! He knew Mr. Novickas was older, but not *that* old. He didn't look a day over fifty-five! His wife didn't look that old either, did that mean she had the same powers? A whole new batch of questions flooded his brain.

"Leo…" His mother's voice broke through all the noise and he blinked a few times, finally focusing on her face. "Mr. Novickas asked you an important question."

"I'm sorry, can you ask it again?" Leo mumbled.

"I know this is hard, Leo, but we need you to decide if you want to begin your training and join our tribe," Mr. Novickas said gently.

This was all so much to take in… Powers! He had powers! This was something he had imagined so many times after watching superhero movies. Then his mind turned darker and he remembered Maranda. His powers were also dangerous and could not only kill him, but also others. Just the thought of potentially killing someone sent him spiraling deeper. What if he wasn't strong enough? What if he caused a disaster? Would they take him to some remote place for safety? He began to breathe hard and he could feel his hands getting clammy as well as drips of sweat rolled down the side of his head.

Leo finally looked back up, meeting Mr. Novickas' gaze and said, "If I say no… What would happen?"

"Tomorrow morning, we will take you to meet another tribal leader," Mr. Novickas began. "Her specialty is the mind, a very delicate power to master. She would work with you to help you forget about all of this. You would not remember this conversation or anything about the tribes or your powers. Your parents would also be tasked with monitoring you until you grow up. At that point it would become the responsibility of the broader tribal community to share the burden."

Not as bad as Leo expected, but not great either. He then mustered the energy for his next question, "Have any of my friends joined the tribe?"

This brought a wide smile to Mr. Novickas' face, "As a matter of fact, yes! Amy, would you like to answer his question?"

His mother took his hand and continued where Mr. Novickas left off, "Well, you should know, I am training Stella. I mean, given how much time she spends swimming, it's no surprise that she is a water Elemental." Leo nodded knowingly and laughed softly.

"Ania is a form of Biologic that we call a Verdant. She is quite gifted with plants! Meimei is a Physic - they can manipulate natural laws to their benefit. I think she is studying levitation at the moment… Oh! Aran also expressed early for an Earth Born when he was eleven. He's a Caretaker and has a deep connection to animals. I have to tell you, many of my closest friends are Caretakers. They just seem to be so warm and affectionate!"

Leo's mood was much brighter now hearing about his friends and he waited expectantly for his mom to continue, but it seemed that she was finished. "What about Caroline?" he asked.

"Well, she doesn't turn twelve for a few months, so we aren't sure yet," his dad answered. That made sense to Leo and he didn't pursue it any further. Then he turned back to Mr. Novickas.

"Why did I feel so different after I touched the book? I mean, would my powers have developed if I had never touched it?" he asked.

"Excellent questions, Leo!" Mr. Novickas seemed to be getting excited. "The book does awaken your powers a bit when you first start the process, but the effects are usually short lived and it is only with practice that you will be able to maintain them. If you didn't have contact with the book for a few days, the effects would largely wear off. Now I have a question for you."

"OK, shoot," said Leo.

"You've always been a sensitive person, right? Ever since you were a little kid?" he asked and Leo nodded his head again, this time with a bit more energy.

"Well, that's a pretty consistent trait for Star Borns. It is a great strength as they are able to feel things before they are expressed. It is also a weakness as that sensitivity can be overwhelming at times," he finished.

This really touched Leo deeply. There had been times, especially lately, when he felt so emotional. He could feel when his friends were frustrated with each other and about to argue and it actually hurt him inside. In fact, at that moment, he could feel all the nervous anticipation from his parents and Mr. Novickas. It was becoming a bit too much for him and he was starting to have trouble focusing again.

"Can you give me a little while to think by myself?" he asked them and they all quickly agreed, filing out of the office. Leo could hear them talking softly in the shop while he pondered what direction he would take. The dark thoughts and fear from earlier were still with him, but there was also a mix of hope and excitement to share this with his closest friends. He was surprised at how quickly he was able to come to a decision and, when he opened the office door, he found them standing right there.

They all turned toward him and he said, "I made my decision." Then he walked back to his chair and they all joined him. He reached out to take his mom's hand and said, "OK, I would like to join the tribe. I need to understand more about myself and do not want to turn away from that."

He felt his mom squeeze his hand in support and his dad reached out to muss his hair. Then he heard Mr. Novickas clear his throat to say, "Then your training begins now."

4

PAIN

ANIC IMMEDIATELY RETURNED and Leo suddenly felt like he couldn't breathe as he saw his parents stand up. He stared at them while they all talked, but he couldn't understand a thing they were saying because the words,"I'm not ready!" were screaming in his head over and over. Minutes ticked by and he was frozen on his chair, not breathing or making a single sound.

His vision clouded around the edges and he felt very dizzy as his brain struggled with the lack of oxygen when he felt a new sensation on his right hand. It startled him so much that he immediately took a gasp and turned his head so he could see what it was. Staring back up at him was Mr. Novickas' dog, Scout, who was licking his hand. "Has he been here all this time?" Leo thought, breaking the cycle of anxious thoughts. Then another series of thoughts followed quickly behind it, "Of course he has been here... He's always here... I mean, as long as

I can remember he has been here… Wait, how old is Scout? Is Mr. Novickas extending his life too?"

Scout stopped licking Leo's hand and this brought him out of his silent internal dialogue and back into the moment. He noticed it was very quiet in the office now, so he looked up to see Mr. Novickas and his parents staring at him with curious expressions.

"You doing all right there, buddy?" his father asked, but Leo didn't know how to answer and stayed silent.

His mother stepped forward and leaned down to give him a kiss on his cheek. Then she said, "Give us a call when you are done and we will come pick you up."

These words were what finally kicked Leo's brain back in gear and he asked incredulously, "Training starts now?"

Mr. Novickas gave him a kind smile and said in a soft, rumbly voice, "It's very important to start your training as soon as possible after you have made your first connection with the book. When you wait too long, it can make the process much more… difficult."

"But it's, like, past nine o'clock!" Leo said in a squeakier voice than he intended.

His father sat back down next to him and leaned forward, touching his forehead to Leo's and then said, "Mr. Novickas is your elder and in charge of your training. This is a very important relationship for you now and the first step is to establish trust and belief in his guidance."

"But why can't you guys stay?" Leo asked quietly, his voice shifting from squeaky to trembling.

"Because this first step must be done on your own," Mr. Novickas replied. "And I can answer your next question for you too. You heard me correctly, *on your own*. I won't be present either. Well, I mean, I'll be here in the store, but not with you as you take this first step. It must be done in your own way and completely of your volition. I can't guide you at all."

Leo felt his dad pull his head back and looked up as he stood again. Their eyes met again and Leo gave his dad an imploring look. His dad returned the look with a wink and mouthed the words, "You can do this." Then Leo watched as his mom and dad made their way out of the office and he sat there alone with his thoughts while Mr. Novickas let them out of the shop. Mini waves of frustration, anger, fear, and resignation washed over him as he thought, "What kind of training is it if I don't have anyone guiding me through it?"

He had the urge to find the back door and run away, but then his stubbornness kicked in. He straightened his back, grabbed the sides of the chairs tightly, took a deep breath, and said to himself, "I made a decision, let's do this."

"Good! That's the spirit!" Mr. Novickas boomed over his shoulder as he entered the office again, startling Leo.

As the hairs on Leo's arms settled back down, Mr. Novickas came around to face Leo and said, "Listen, I know this is all very confusing and I wish I could make it easier. As you heard your mom say, 'Each type has its own path.' You also know I am not a Star Born, so this is a very uncommon arrangement. I can assure you though, I have learned enough to start the training and I have done it once before. I believe you can do this… Don't ask me why, because I wouldn't be able to explain it. I just know it deep inside."

Leo sat silently for a few moments and finally nodded his head and asked, "OK, what do I have to do?"

"Well first, I need you to help me clean up and move these chairs back out of here," Mr. Novickas said and Leo smiled widely in response.

Leo followed Mr. Novickas' instructions and took the familiar old wood chair his mom had been sitting on back to the children's reading area and when he returned to the office, he found Mr. Novickas standing beside the desk waiting for him.

"The Book of Star Born contains the collective learnings of everyone who has come before you and is learning right now," Mr. Novickas began. "That's right, you heard correctly, it is being updated even now as we stand here together. The number of copies of this book is a closely held secret that not even I know, but they are connected somehow. As Star Borns learn about their abilities, the books capture this knowledge for others to learn when they are ready. Learning from this book will be one of your most important tasks in the coming months."

"But, Mr. Novickas, I…" Leo started to say before he was cut off.

"I'm sorry, Leo, from this point on, I can't answer any of your questions or provide any more guidance. All I can do is set your task before you, which is that you need to learn to read this book," Mr. Novickas said firmly.

"What?! How am I supposed to do that?!" Leo shouted and immediately regretted it.

Mr. Novickas' eyes flashed wide open in surprise for a brief moment and then returned to his normal relaxed gaze. "I'll be in the back doing inventory. You can come and find me when you're done," he said and then he walked out the other door to the back storage room leaving Leo by himself again.

Adrenaline was coursing through his veins and he felt jittery and antsy, unable to sit down. He paced back and forth, taking deep breaths to gradually calm down. His eyes scanned the office, taking in more of the details. He picked up different pictures scattered around the shelves and saw various scenes from

Mr. Novickas' life. A shot of him with his wife in London, a black and white photo of him in a dense forest surrounded by what Leo assumes are a group of friends, and a small portrait that looked very old with the paint cracking in various parts and showing a serious looking woman. His eyes eventually came to rest again on the picture of Maranda and he began to ponder again if he would be strong enough to complete his training.

"Well, there's only one way to find out…" he said to himself and he returned to the desk, sitting down on the worn rolling desk chair.

Leo placed his hand on the book and the energy flowed through him again as it opened to the first page. He stared at the intricate symbols, but he still could not decipher what they meant. He looked at each one closely, trying to find clues to what would unlock it. He traced the graceful curves and hard corners with his finger, wondering whether it required some kind of physical touch to give him the power to read it. He felt the coarseness of the paper, but there was no indentation where the writing was made. He also noticed the book looked like it was recently made even though he knew it was older than even Mr. Novickas. The pages were bright white and there wasn't a scratch on the cover.

The inspection of the book, however, brought him no closer to understanding the characters on the first page. So, Leo decided to look in the back for a glossary or some kind of way to start on a translation. To his surprise, the back few pages were completely blank and when he released them the book turned itself back to the first page. He tried again, flipping through the first twenty or thirty pages of the book, but those pages were blank as well and the book again turned itself back to the first page.

"What the…" he said to himself and then repeated this

trick several more times. When he was finally satisfied this was a dead end, he leaned back in the chair and stared at the book. It occurred to him that he should check the cover and excitement returned as he leaned back over the book examining the inside front cover. He couldn't find any discernible markings or clues, so then flipped all of the pages to expose the back cover. Again, he couldn't find anything but the rich leather and intricate metal filigree encasing the cover.

Leo closed the book again, examining the symbols, lock, and decoration on the front. Everything looked very intricate and meaningful, but he had no idea how to interpret anything he saw. He tried to flip the book over to examine the back, but it was extremely heavy and it took all of his strength to move it less than an inch.

"DAMMIT!" he shouted as he shoved the office chair back and stood up. He walked to the other side of the office and stared angrily at the book. With the energy coursing through him again, his senses were heightened and he could hear the ticking of the wall clock over the door to the front of the shop. He glanced up at it and noticed it was almost midnight. With this realization, fatigue began to drag him down and a small worry creeped in that Mr. Novickas may have been wrong about him. However, he pushed the thought away immediately and stomped back to the book.

Opening the book once more, he felt every part of it, dragging his fingertips along the surfaces to see if there was something he could feel that may not be visible. Eventually, he wondered if the key was inside the book, so he dug his finger into a seam on the cover. The next thing he knew, a huge amount of energy was coursing through that spot and he was launched several feet back from the book and landed on his butt.

Slightly dazed, he said, "Note to self, don't try to damage the book…"

He rubbed his eyes and checked himself to make sure he wasn't hurt. Realizing everything looked OK, he sat back down in the chair and scooted it back up to the desk. Feeling tired and stuck, he put both of his hands on the book and wondered to himself, "What do I need to do?!" However, no answer came to him and he was overcome with the urge to close his eyes and put his head down. He followed this feeling and allowed his head to slowly droop down as his eyelids grew heavy. He found a place for his head directly in the center of the first page, between his hands, just as his eyes closed entirely.

Leo was finally able to relax and let all the tension and energy out of his body. In the back of his mind, he half noticed that as he did this the parts of his hands and face that were touching the book began to feel warmer. This encouraged him to let go entirely and he released the last bit of his energy. For a few moments, he was deeply relaxed by the comforting warmth that seemed to be traveling down from his hands and face to his arms and back. All the events from the day, being up so late at night, and the comfortable feeling flowing through his body caused him to drift off to sleep.

It seemed as if he started to dream immediately and he found himself in a desert. The sun was beating down on him and all he saw for miles around him were sand dunes. He looked all around for some shade as sweat began to drench his hair and clothing, but he didn't see any shelter. He knew he couldn't just stand there, so he tried to start walking down the face of the dune into one of the small valleys to hopefully find a sliver of shade, but his foot wouldn't budge. The heat from the sun only grew and his skin started to burn badly, but no matter how hard he tried, he couldn't take a step.

The pain from the heat grew to an intolerable level and Leo cried out in pain. At that moment, he suddenly woke up and realized his dream was just interpreting what he was experiencing in real life. His head was still laying on the book, which was now glowing so brightly he had to squint. It was also painfully hot and he struggled to pull away from it, but his hands and face were stuck to it. He tried to call to Mr. Novickas for help, but no sound came out.

The brightness and heat continued to grow and his skin felt like it was on fire. He grit his teeth and shut his eyes tight, trying to breathe through the pain that is now spreading throughout his body. Images formed in his vision even with his eyes closed and a part of him recognized they looked similar to the characters in the book. He also heard voices speaking in different languages echoing in his head. The cacophony grew louder and this added to the pain he was experiencing.

Leo lost track of time as the images ran fast across his vision and blurred together. He was certain that he had made some grave mistake and the book was going to kill him. Strangely, he was not afraid of that, he just lamented that he was going to be an embarrassment of a Star Born who died trying to learn to read a book. This caused him to chuckle and he was startled to hear himself for the first time since this ordeal began. Then he started noticing the pain had dissipated significantly and was continuing to fade from every part of his body except for his head where he felt a massive headache forming.

He opened his eyes and confirmed he could see again. The book had returned to its normal level of glowing. He wiggled his fingers and he watched as they released from the book without any pain. He turned the palm of his left hand to face him, expecting to see blackened skin, but it looked completely unharmed.

Taking a deep breath, he slowly raised his head and removed his other hand from the book, without the slightest hint of injury. He rubbed his face and only felt clammy skin as the last traces of his ordeal evaporated. Leo glanced at the wall clock again and saw that it was now almost one in the morning.

"Try reading it now," Mr. Novickas said from behind him and Leo was startled so much he fell out of the desk chair.

"Have you been there the entire time?!" Leo exclaimed as he stood up and turned to face Mr. Novickas.

"No, just the past few minutes. I noticed it was much dimmer in here and figured the process was nearly finished," Mr. Novickas said casually.

"You KNEW the book was going to do that to me?!" Leo spit back.

Mr. Novickas sighed, pulled the desk chair to him and sat down heavily. He ran his fingers through his hair and then looked Leo directly in his eyes. "It's a different process for each Star Born, but one consistent thing I have been told and have now seen twice is that it's always extremely painful. The book is effectively downloading knowledge into your brain and then programming it how to use it. I know that sounds strange, it's just the best way I have heard it described…"

His anger dissipated quickly and Leo slowly turned back to the book and looked down at the first page. What was once complete gobbledygook to him was now as clear as the book he was reading with his friends earlier that day. He read it out loud to Mr. Novickas:

You are Star Born and your eyes have now been opened
Trust these pages to guide you and pass your knowledge to
others through them

Be the guiding light for your community
Commit to sharing your gift for the betterment of all
Your journey begins here

Turning back to Mr. Novickas, Leo saw a warm smile on his face and heard him say, "Very well done! I knew you had it in you!"

"What happens now?" Leo asked.

"Now, you go home and get some sleep. Come back here again on Monday after school. I want to make sure you enjoy what's left of your weekend." Mr. Novickas answered.

Feeling fatigue set in fully, Leo nodded absentmindedly with half open eyes and turned to walk out of the office. He wobbled a bit and then felt Mr. Novickas steadying him.

"Not that way," he heard Mr. Novickas say, but it seemed far away. "Let's go out the back and I'll give you a ride home. I'm not sure you'd make it out of the shop before finding a spot to spend the night."

Mr. Novickas guided him through the storage room and to his car, shutting off lights along the way and locking the door behind them. As soon as he sat down in the passenger seat, he let his eyes close and fell into a deep sleep. He didn't even feel his dad gather him out of the car and carry him up to his bed.

5

INDUCTION

Opening his eyes slowly, the first thing Leo became aware of was that he was in a long corridor. It was dimly lit, but he couldn't tell where the light was coming from. The ceiling and the walls seemed to be painted with the same dark charcoal color. He looked around and could see clearly enough that each side had doors facing each other that were evenly spaced apart. It appeared the corridor was extremely long because it went off into the distance without a single bend or turn along the way. He stood there pondering for a few minutes, trying to figure out what he wanted to do. He had the urge to call out, "Hello?!" or "Is anybody else here?!" Then he thought back to all the movies where he yelled at the main characters for doing something so naive and foolish. He had no idea where he was and figured it wasn't the best idea to advertise his presence when he didn't know who was going to hear him.

He took a step to the door closest to him and leaned his

head closely to it, listening. He heard two voices talking, one sounded really raspy and the other one was quite deep. They were really agitated, perhaps even arguing, but he couldn't make out what they were saying. He wanted to get a little closer so he could listen better, but he knew it was probably a bad idea and quietly moved down the corridor a bit to listen to a door on the other side.

This time he could hear sound coming from it well before he got to it. When he was standing right next to the door, it occurred to him that it sounded like pounding water, like he was standing at the bottom of a waterfall. He put his hand on the door and felt a strong vibration coursing through it and wondered if the door was actually holding back a massive amount of water that was pounding against it. This door didn't seem to be any better of a choice from the first one, so he continued on down the line.

He stopped at several more doors and heard a variety of different things on the other side. One sounded like a jungle with various insect and animal noises echoing around, while another one sounded like it was along a coastline where he heard seagulls and large ship horns calling out. He came upon a door that didn't seem to have any threatening noises on the other side, perhaps just a soft sound of wind blowing. When he touched the simple door knob, however, it was frigid and he snatched his hand back from the stinging sensation.

Wondering if he would ever find a way out of this situation, he continued to walk down the corridor trying to remember how he even ended up in this place. Suddenly, he felt a strong sensation as he was passing yet another door. He paused and tried to understand this feeling. It wasn't unpleasant, it just felt like something he should pay attention to and explore a bit. He turned toward the door and inspected it, but found nothing unique about it. It had the same white trim, black paint, and glass door knob that every other door had along the way. He leaned his head closer, listening carefully, but didn't hear anything on the other side. Unsatisfied, he put his ear on the door and still didn't hear anything. He also didn't feel any vibrations or extreme temperatures.

Standing up straight again, he scratched his head while he decided what to do. He knew he was going to have to open a door at some point since there didn't seem to be anything else he could do in this place, but how did he decide which door to open? He felt around in his pockets to see if he had anything to help him, but there wasn't anything there. Not even the random granola bar wrappers he forgot to take out when he got home after hanging out with friends. Figuring this was as good a door as any to open, he put his hand on the knob and turned it as quietly as he could. When he was sure he had turned it far enough, he then slowly pushed the door open just far enough so that he could peer in and close it quickly if he didn't like what he saw.

As he scanned around slowly, he could tell it was a mostly dark room. He could make out the shape of some familiar objects with the little bit of light that was there. A desk, some book-shelves, and another door on the far wall from him. Then he saw in the middle of the room a young woman sitting in a large, leather chair. Next to it was a small side table with an old lamp on it putting out just enough light for her to read. He noticed a sheaf of papers in her hands and she seemed to be concentrating intently on it.

Leo pushed his head further through the small opening he had made in the doorway to get a better look at the woman and he was surprised to see she looked a lot like Maranda. Suddenly excited, he opened the door all the way and one of thc hinges made a soft creaking noise. The woman heard that noise and looked up to see where it came from and now Leo was able to get a full look at her. It was absolutely Maranda.

Immediately wanting to go talk to her, Leo took a step into the room and as he did so he saw her expression change suddenly. Her eyes opened wide, she shook her head, and held out her hand telling him to stop. Trying to react quickly, Leo started to lean back and try to pull his foot back, but in his excitement he had taken a large, confident stride. Though his foot should have been meeting the floor of the room, it found nothing but air and Leo felt himself begin to fall. He struggled to right himself, but this just made him tumble forward, completely out of control. He fell head first into the dark space and when his momentum turned him onto his back, he looked up and saw Maranda peering over the ledge and staring down at him.

Leo landed hard suddenly, took a deep gasp of air, and opened his eyes wide to find himself in his room again. He was tangled up in the blanket and sheets from his bed. So much so that he could barely move his arms and legs. He struggled for a few moments, but he quickly realized that he was stuck. Then he heard a soft knock on the door and it opened a crack. He heard his dad say softly, "Leo? Are you up?"

"Not exactly." Leo answered and his dad opened up the door the rest of the way to see the predicament.

"I heard a thud. You must have been having some crazy dream!" his dad said as he knelt down and began to loosen the fabric enough for Leo to help.

"You have no idea…" Leo said and he finally pushed the rest of the mass off of himself.

"Wanna tell me about it?" his dad asked.

Leo considered a moment and then said, "Naaa. At least not right now."

"OK, that's fine, but dreams can be…"

"…powerful tools to help us understand the world around us," Leo finished the adage his father had been saying for as long as he could remember. "I appreciate it, dad. We can talk about it later," he continued, trying to avoid hurting any feelings.

"Alright, well, I just finished making some waffles if you're hungry," his dad moved on.

On the mention of food, Leo's stomach did a flip and he immediately felt famished. He tried to jump to his feet, but his legs were unsteady and he toppled back to the floor. His father caught him and then helped to keep him steady as he tried to stand up all the way. His legs were trembling slightly and he looked at his father with a confused look.

"You had a big night last night and must have used a lot of energy. Let's get some food in you," and his father led him slowly downstairs to the kitchen, depositing him in a stool at the counter.

Leo's mind wandered as his dad moved around the kitchen, making familiar noises that were comforting and helped him shake off the edgy feeling that lingered from the dream. It had been such a vivid experience and even now he could remember all the details from the dream. He could never do that before with a dream. In fact, usually the harder he tried to remember a dream when he woke up, the faster it would leave his mind. The image of Maranda looking down at him as he fell was etched into his mind now. The initial concern she showed when he stepped into the room recklessly was no longer there. Just a calm resignation and, upon further examination, Leo remembered she even had a bit of a smirk.

Leo was pondering what meaning this dream could have, but his mind was not cooperating. He had a dull headache in the back of his head that he knew meant he needed food soon or a bout of "hanger" would ensue. As if he could sense the urgency, a few moments later, his dad pushed a plate with two large, golden waffles in front of Leo. They were drenched with maple syrup and Leo's mouth watered so much he almost drooled. He grabbed his fork and began to tear off hunks of waffle, shoveling them as fast as he could into his mouth and barely chewing before going back for another big mouthful.

His dad just leaned on the kitchen island behind him, watching the carnage in front of him. Leo took the last bit of waffle on his plate and looked up at his dad with eyes that said, "That's all you're giving me?" Then his dad reached behind his back and produced a large bowl filled with blueberries, strawberries, and raspberries. He deposited the bowl in front of Leo as he removed the syrup covered plate and could barely get his hand out of the way before Leo speared his fork through a large strawberry. He walked over to the fridge, filled up a tall glass with milk, and then left that in front of Leo as he cleaned up the kitchen. He heard Leo slowing down, looked over, and laughed uncontrollably.

"Whaaaa?" Leo said with the last of the berries still filling his mouth.

"If you could see yourself right now!" his dad said between guffaws.

Leo smiled sheepishly, swallowed, and then asked his dad for a napkin. His dad tossed one to him from across the room and, after Leo wiped his face, he leaned back in his chair feeling satisfied.

"Wanna tell me about last night?" his dad asked.

Leo took a deep breath and looked down at his hands, "I don't know how to explain it…"

"Give it a shot," his dad encouraged.

Leo gazed back up at his dad and said, "I was connected to the Book of Star Born, dad. I mean really connected. It downloaded knowledge into me!"

Leo's dad just nodded his head with a kind smile on his face.

"You don't look surprised," Leo said suspiciously.

"Well, I haven't really heard of one of the books downloading into a person before, but I have heard plenty of strange stories about people's first sessions with their respective books," his dad said matter-of-factly.

"Dad, everything feels different now."

"Tell me more," his dad encouraged.

"I mean… I can feel you. Well… I mean… I feel your abilities," Leo said haltingly as he felt his brain clicking back into gear.

"Really? What do I feel like?" he dad asked with genuine curiosity.

"Heavy…" Leo responded.

"What do you mean, heavy?" his dad prodded.

"I mean, you feel like a huge weight on that side of the room. Like there is no force that would be able to move you unless you let it. But it's not just that. There's a strength to that weight. It's as if I know you could crush even the strongest structure without much of a thought…" Leo said as he trailed off feeling a bit uncomfortable.

His dad walked back across the kitchen, leaned over the counter, and took Leo's hands. "That's pretty amazing, Leo. I've never heard my abilities described to me the way I feel them inside myself."

"Really?" Leo said hopefully.

"I've only really known one Star Born before, but I do know you all are pretty sensitive. I have no idea how you process those feelings, but I have to say this is a very special moment for me to experience, seeing you with these abilities for the first time," his dad said with a quiver in his voice. Leo also noticed how the feeling of his dad's power changed as he became a bit emotional.

Not knowing what to say next, Leo asked, "Where's mom?"

Shaking his head clear, his dad answered, "Oh yeah, she's training Stella this morning. They should be done soon. As a matter of fact, I hope you don't mind, but we arranged for some of your friends to meet up at Ania's house. We figured you might want to talk about things with them."

"That's great! Thanks, dad!" Leo said excitedly. "When can I head up there?"

"Actually, any time now probably works," his dad answered with an odd look on his face.

Leo cocked his head to the side because he knew this look well. What had he missed in what his dad had said? He racked his brain for a moment and then it occurred to him.

"Some of my friends?" Leo asked.

"Good. You were paying attention. I need to make sure you really understand what we are going to talk about next," he said seriously. "You can only talk about your abilities, experiences in training, or ANYTHING related to the tribe with other members of the tribe. This is really important, Leo. It's what keeps us all safe. Many times people have tried to take advantage of these powers. We have successfully hidden ourselves, only to repeat some of the darkest periods of history when someone discovered us."

"Like what, dad?" Leo asked with trepidation.

"Wars for one, but let's not get into that right now. This is your first day being a part of the tribe, you should enjoy it. There is plenty of time to understand the responsibilities that come with your powers," his dad said with the same serious tone.

"So which friends are off limits?" Leo asked, not really wanting to know the answer.

"There are a few who haven't discovered their powers because they aren't old enough yet and some who may not develop strong enough powers to begin their training. The one I think you'll find the hardest for now is Caroline," his dad said gently.

This hit Leo like a ton of bricks and what little excitement he had about spending the day with his friends learning about their powers was suddenly gone. Caroline was one of his closest friends. They had grown up in the same neighborhood, shared the same babysitter before they started preschool, and had basically seen each other almost every day of their lives when they weren't on vacation or something similar.

"Look, Leo, I know it's hard to keep things from people you care about," his dad said as he saw how much Leo was struggling with the rule. "There are some friends I have that are very close, but I can't share this part of me with them. Let's just be patient and see whether Caroline's powers emerge around her birthday like you. It's only a few months away after all."

This calmed Leo down a bit. He began to brighten and said hopefully, "Sure, it's only a few months." He then went silent for another minute or so trying to build back his excitement from before, finally asking, "So, who will be at Ania's house today?"

"Just like we talked about last night. Aran, Meimei, Stella, and of course Ania. They're all still pretty early in their training, but I'm sure you'll have plenty to talk about," his dad replied.

Leo nodded and then slid off of his stool. He paused for a moment and noticed his legs were now firmly beneath him again, then he said, "I'll go get ready."

"Sounds good," his dad answered, returning to his normally, cheery demeanor. "Just give us a call if you're not going to be back for dinner. I have a feeling you guys are going to be hanging for a while."

Leo smiled in agreement and then headed up to his room. A short while later, he walked out the front door and, on autopilot, began to go his usual route to Ania's house before stopping himself. That route would take him right past Caroline's house. A knot formed in his stomach as he slowly turned around to take the long way. With each step, the knot loosened a little bit and he was able to think about everything he wanted to talk about with his friends. He started trudging up a steep path that carved a route between the closely packed houses in their town, but he didn't feel winded at all because his excitement had taken over again. When he reached the top, he ran the rest of the way to Ania's house.

Even before he arrived, he could hear them arguing in the backyard. He grinned when he picked up a bit of what they were saying and realized they were debating the latest season of one of his favorite shows about heroes who piloted powerful robotic lions and could combine them into a giant super robot warrior.

"C'mon, you really think the green one is best?!" he heard Meimei ask incredulously.

"Let me guess, you like the red one," Ania spat back.

"Actually, as the foremost expert on this topic, I have to correct you both. The black one is the best," Leo said as he rounded the corner of the house with a big grin on his face.

All of his friends jumped to their feet and rushed over to greet him. Aran gave him a warm hug, Ania a playful shove, and Stella initiated their secret handshake with him that he could barely remember since they had come up with it in second grade. Then Meimei put her hand on his shoulder, looked straight into his eyes and said, "You OK?" Leo's smile faltered a bit, but he recovered quickly and nodded his head firmly.

They led Leo over to a small circle of heavily used camping chairs and Aran jumped in first, excitedly asking, "So you found out just last night?!"

"Yeah…" Leo answered with wide eyes. "It has been a little crazy trying to absorb all of this…"

"So, what are you?" Ania asked, jumping straight to the point as always. "None of our parents would tell us."

"Wait! I wanna guess!" Meimei jumped in. "You're an air Elemental and can manipulate our farts!"

This made the whole group erupt with laughter, even Leo. Settling down again, they all looked at Leo expectantly and he said quietly, "I'm a Star Born." He watched confused expressions form over all of their faces, with Ania's being the funniest because her jaw had actually dropped and her mouth was so wide that she looked like a cartoon character.

Stella broke the silence first, "You're the first non-Earth Born any of us have met!"

"Yeah, I mean, they told me a little about the different types when my powers first emerged, but we have only really met other Earth Borns," Meimei chimed in.

"You can do stuff with energy right? Can you charge my phone? It's almost dead," Aran quipped, bringing the mood lighter again.

"Ha Ha… Very funny," Leo responded with feigned annoyance.

"Seriously, Leo, we don't know much about Star Borns. What can you do?" Stella asked earnestly.

"Well, I only know a little bit so far," Leo began as his friends leaned forward a little bit, listening intently.

"Since yesterday afternoon, I can sense the different energies that flow through everything. I mean… I can sense the energy flowing through that tree over there," Leo said as he pointed at the large tree that had been the home of at least three forts over the years and now had a big swing hanging from it.

"I can also sense your powers and…" Leo continued, but he was cut off by Ania.

"Pause please!" she interjected. "You can sense our powers?"

"Well, yeah," Leo answered simply.

"So you're some kind of power detector and can sense if someone has them?" She asked, trying to digest what he was saying.

"It's not just being able to sense whether you have powers," Leo responded, searching for the right words. "I mean, each of you feels different to me."

"You can tell what kind of powers we have?" Ania asked incredulously.

Leo thought for a moment and then responded, "Yes, I think so."

After a brief pause in the conversation, Meimei then asked thoughtfully, "What do I feel like?"

He turned to focus on her, slowly examining and processing what he saw. Then he met her gaze and said, "It's interesting, you are so different from what my dad feels like. It's as if you're constantly shifting from lightness to heaviness. You're constantly moving even though you're just sitting right there. The coolest part for me is that I can see these tiny particles swirling around you… No wait, that's not the right word… Orbiting! They're orbiting around you!"

He watched Meimei lean back in her chair with a grin on her face as she thought about his analysis. Then he heard Aran say, "DO ME!" So Leo turned to him and repeated the process, but this time it came much faster.

"Oh, you're hot and wild!" Leo began. "Your energy is raw. I mean, it's so pure! It feels as if you could leap around this yard like a cat, but totally gracefully. Also, bizarrely, that crow on the electrical line up there seems to be paying a lot of attention to you…"

"Ah, that's Gertie. She's been hanging with me for the past few days," Aran answered casually.

Knowing he now had to assess everyone, Leo turned to Stella and a wide smile spread across his face.

"What?" she asked.

"Your power feels familiar and comforting. It's a lot like my mom, which makes sense since you're both water people. Somebody said you're called Elementals, right?"

Stella nodded.

"You don't feel exactly the same as my mom though," he continued. "You *do* feel different. Like… Both of you feel cool and vast, kinda like an ocean feels, I think. The big difference is that my mom feels really calm to me whereas you feel like one of those surfers who is riding a huge wave."

"Woah…" Stella whispered.

"Sorry…" Leo said softly and then he started gnawing on his lower lip, worried he had said something wrong.

Then Stella started talking again, "It does feel that way sometimes… surfing a giant wave and trying not to fall off and be slammed down as it crashes into the shore."

"It doesn't feel like you're about to fall off to me," Leo said reassuringly. "Honestly, it feels like you know what you're doing and you feel excited by it."

"Training was really good today, I think I was getting the hang of a couple things," Stella said warmly.

Feeling more secure that he was on the right track, he turned to Ania and she gazed back coolly. "You are strong and immovable…" Leo began, but was interrupted by Aran who said, "I could've told you that without being able to sense her powers." Everyone chuckled knowingly except for Ania who shot a look at Aran and they all grew quiet pretty quickly.

"You feel rooted to the ground," Leo continued. "Like you could withstand even the strongest force like a hurricane or tornado."

"I'll accept that," Ania said approvingly with a firm nod.

"I'm not done yet," Leo corrected her and she glared back, daring him to say another word. This just emboldened him and he continued, "All living things feel to me like they have a particular rhythm. All of you have a unique rhythm, the plants in the yard, the animals around us. I can feel their individual rhythms if I focus on them. What is really cool right now is that I can feel the plants near you have changed their rhythm to match yours"

"What?" Ania asked with her brow furrowed in confusion.

"All the plants by you have adopted your rhythm. The rose bush right there, the tree over in the corner, even the patch of grass under your chair. All the same as your rhythm. It's like they are all waiting or listening to you. Ready to act when you call for them."

"I wonder…" Aran muttered and then Leo saw Gertie take off from the wire and glide down to land on Aran's shoulder. "What does Gertie feel like to you?" he asked Leo.

"She's sharing your rhythm now!" he said excitedly. "This must be part of your powers and how you connect to other living things!"

"Right?!" Aran said as he gave Leo a high-five, disturbing Gertie and sending her back up to the wire.

"That is so cool," Meimei added. "Every day feels like a new discovery! I mean, I know we're probably not actually discovering anything that hasn't been known before. It's all new to us, though!"

"Well, every second is a new discovery for me right now," Leo said self-deprecatingly.

"True!" Meimei said, realizing how all of this must have felt for him. "There is so much we need to share with you. Actually, we should probably start with what to expect from training. It's no joke, Leo."

"Seriously," Ania added, "I am so tired after training, I usually fall asleep at the table during dinner."

Then Ania's eyes went wide and she said excitedly, "Oh yeah! I can't believe I forgot to tell you all! Last night I fell asleep and my head dropped right into my plate. I mean *just* like in a TV show or something. I had so much mashed potato in my hair that my mom just sent me to take a shower right away."

The whole crew erupted in laughter and, when the last few giggles poured out, Stella turned to Leo and began to explain what they had been experiencing in training so far.

"So, we have to go to training almost every day after school," she began. "You know how I always say I can't hang out because I have swim practice?"

Leo nodded.

"Training! I haven't been to a swim practice in months! At first I was really bothered about it, but after the first month of training I was able to use my abilities to swim way faster than anyone in the Olympics. After that, it didn't seem as fair or challenging anymore."

"Focus, Stella," Meimei nudged.

"Yeah, yeah… Anyway, they started us all out on what we now know is very simple stuff, but it was so hard at first. I mean,

Aran told us they had him listening to Natalie's parakeets for a whole week until he could understand a simple conversation they were having."

"It's true!" Aran said. "A whole week and when it finally clicked, I realized they had basically been complaining about how creepy it was that I kept staring at them for hours."

"That's not even the best one," said Stella. "They had me trying to roll a single water droplet along the top of a table."

"No…" Leo said in disbelief.

"If I'm lying, I'm dying," Stella swore. "Heck, they had Ania growing blades of grass and Meimei had to bend a spoon without touching it."

"Actually," Meimei jumped in. "I found out my dad convinced my teacher, Leslie, to play a trick on me. Turns out there was some dude back in the day who claimed he could do that with his mind. They thought it was so funny, but I'll find a way to get them back…"

"They do try to make it fun," Aran said. "They have some games we play as we are learning new things. Sometimes they will also pull in other members of the tribe who have mastered a particular skill to work with us. There are actually quite a few Caretakers in our tribe, which I have been told is usually more common in rural or remote areas."

"When one of us started our training, we kind of disappeared for a while," Meimei leaned in. "Remember that camping trip I went on with my family a few months back? It was just the start of my training."

"I was wondering about that…" Leo responded. "I mean, it was weird you were pulled out of school for a camping trip."

"Yeah, well, expect your life to revolve around training for a while. We'll miss you!"

"C'mon, Meimei," Stella chastised. "It's intense, but we still have time for other stuff. I mean, we have been able to hang out a bunch, right?"

Meimei shrugged and then nodded begrudgingly.

"So, who is going to be your mentor?" Ania asked.

"Mr. Novickas," Leo answered.

"Huh?" Ania responded in confusion. "He's a Biologic. Is there not another Star Born in our tribe?"

"No. I mean there was, but she died."

"Died?!" it's Aran who was now asking the confused questions.

"Yeah… Her name was Maranda. She lost control of her powers and blew up part of town a few years ago. They told everyone it was an earthquake."

"That wasn't an earthquake… whoa…" Aran leaned back in thought.

"But wait, what does Mr. Novickas know about being a Star Born?" Ania asked, trying to figure things out.

"You know what? Quite a bit it turns out. I have a feeling he knows way more than we would ever expect."

"Yeah, that dude is old, it would make sense that he knows a ton," Ania confirmed.

"So… what was it like for you guys when you had your first session with the book?" Leo said to the group.

"What do you mean?" Meimei asked.

"Like, when you started your training and connected with the Book of Earth Born."

"Oh, none of us has been allowed to touch the book yet."

"So how do you wake up your powers?"

"They just kind of woke up on their own," said Stella, not understanding Leo's line of questioning.

"You're saying one day you woke up and your powers were just there?"

"Well, yeah, kinda…" Stella responded. "I didn't know I had them, but I was at swim practice and about mid-way through I created a small wave in the pool while racing my friend Vivi. It was actually kind of lucky that my coach is part of the tribe and recognized what happened."

"Yeah, I thought I was going crazy because I was hearing voices all the time," Aran added. "Turns out it was mainly our cats…"

"What did you mean 'connect' to the book, Leo?" Ania asked with a penetrating squint.

"My powers didn't just emerge. The Book of Star Born woke them up when I touched it at the book shop yesterday."

"So that's what was happening in Mr. Novickas' office!" Aran exclaimed.

"It also explains why you were in such a daze afterwards," added Meimei.

"Exactly, I had the weirdest walk home after I left you guys. Then I went back with my parents last night and met with Mr. Novickas. He told me about Maranda and gave me the choice if I wanted to start my training. When I agreed, my parents left and then he had me sit with the book to figure out how to read it. You have no idea how hard I tried, but I couldn't figure it out! Then, when I finally just gave in and stopped trying so hard, I was able to connect with it and it started downloading knowledge into my brain…"

"Downloading into your brain?!" Stella asked incredulously.

"Yes, that's how Mr. Novickas explained it. It was excruciating! I mean I basically passed out afterwards from the experience.

But, suddenly, I was able to read the book. It was as if the book was writing itself for me…"

"I hear that is what the Book of Earth Born is like too," Stella said with a bit of awe in her voice. "Once we are far enough in our training, we will have time with the book and it will change itself based on who we are and our powers."

"So what did the book say?" Meimei asked.

"I don't think I am supposed to say," Leo replied hesitantly and Meimei shrugged casually letting him know it was OK.

"Well, your first day of training is the best!" Stella jumped back in. "I didn't want to stop practicing with your mom. I think I even made her pretty late for dinner."

"Speaking of which, I'm STARVING!" Ania shouted.

"I could eat!" Aran said cheerfully.

"You can always eat," Leo said playfully and they all laughed.

"Let's see what my dad has bought, I bet we have a few bags of gyoza," Ania said and they all headed inside.

6

Back to Basics

"Furyurmph!" Leo shouted when he heard his alarm blaring from across the room. He was actually trying to yell something much worse that he definitely would have gotten in trouble for if his parents had heard him and the pillow hadn't been over his head. He chucked his pillow at the alarm and missed it badly. Not only that, but the alarm was much louder now that the pillow wasn't dampening the sound.

He threw off the covers somewhat dramatically and stomped across the room to turn it off. He briefly considered crawling back into bed, but he knew that would just prolong the inevitable. Then he saw his new book sitting next to the alarm clock and remembered that he set it there to motivate him to get dressed and down for breakfast so he could read a few more pages before school. He had stayed up a little too late the night before trying to finish it and was just about twenty pages shy. As usual, the only reason he stopped in such a crazy climax was because he could barely keep his eyes open and had read the same page at least four times.

He slowly shed his pajamas and picked out a t-shirt and some sweatpants from the pile of unfolded laundry on the floor. When he was finally dressed for the day, he dragged himself downstairs and began fixing himself some breakfast. All of his muscles felt clumsy and he made a racket pulling out a bowl and glass. He reached into the pantry for his favorite cinnamon squares cereal and saw they were completely out of them. Morning hanger overwhelmed him and he yelled, "MOM! We're out of squares! Should I add it to the list?"

"Yup, I know! I already have a whole shopping list for later today!" she answered with an annoyed tone from the dining room table where she was working on her computer. "Have some of those honey nut O's. You used to love them, I don't know why you don't anymore…"

Leo emitted a frustrated grunt, pulled out the O's, and poured himself a huge mountain in his bowl. He walked over to the fridge to get some milk and orange juice, then noticed they were out of those too. He turned to his mother in exasperation.

"We don't even have any milk?!"

"On the list!" she replied as she stood up and walked through the kitchen and then up the stairs.

He rolled his eyes and slid into a counter stool. He stared at his mound of cereal contemplating just how bad the day was going to be and if he should have just gone back to bed, when Astro walked over and squeezed himself between Leo's feet and the cabinet. Some of Leo's hanger broke and he decided to pet Astro while shoving big spoonfuls of O's into his mouth. By the time he was half-way done with his breakfast, his mom came back holding some papers and her usual mug of tea.

Just as Leo was about to reach for the book to start reading, his mom said, "Now don't forget, after school you have to go straight to the bookshop for training with Mr. Novickas."

A rush of adrenaline flooded Leo's senses and he was suddenly very awake. In his morning stupor, he had completely forgotten today was his first day of training. He took another spoonful from the bowl and noticed he could barely get any cereal into his mouth because his hand was shaking a bit. His mom noticed too and said, "It's totally normal to feel nervous."

Leo put the spoon down and thought quietly for a moment before saying, "I'm not… I am actually just really excited I think."

His mother came around with a big smile and planted a big kiss on his forehead. Then said, "C'mon, if you finish up quickly, I can probably drop you off at school on my way to work."

Leo took a deep breath, steadied his hand, and then proceeded to finish his breakfast. His mind was racing and he barely remembered to pack his lunch and load up his backpack. As they were walking out the door, he realized that he did in fact forget to brush his teeth and decided to not alert his mother to the oversight.

He usually arrived at school just as the bell was ringing to start the day, but this time he was actually early and happened to have beaten most of his friends there. He looked across the yard to their usual hang-out spot and saw Caroline sitting by herself reading her copy of the book. For a moment, guilt prickled at the back of his mind for not being able to share everything that happened over the weekend with her. However, he tamped the feeling down quickly and walked across to sit with her.

"What part are you on?" he asked as he slid his back down the wall to sit with her.

"They have recruited the ancient dragon leader to the cause

and are amassing in the mountains," Caroline said, not even looking up from the book.

"Ah, that's a really good part. I love the moments in a story right before a big battle."

"Mmhmm…" she said, barely acknowledging his comment and letting him know that she wasn't going to stop reading until the bell rings.

Soon after, his friends trickled into the yard one by one and gathered around Leo and Caroline. Aran was the last to arrive and, when he saw Caroline reading the book, he said, "Oh! I finished it last night! Don't you love how she ended the book? I never saw…"

"QUIET!" Caroline said firmly as she interrupted Aran. "If you give away a single thing about this book, I will make you eat it one page at a time." Then she returned her gaze to the book.

"She told *you*!" Meimei said.

"I would've said the same thing," Leo affirmed warmly, respecting the love of a good book. Aran returned the comment with a friendly smile, acknowledging he almost committed a cardinal sin.

Not long after that, the bell rang and they split up to go to their different classrooms. Leo, Aran, and Caroline filed into theirs and grabbed their usual seats off to the side. Their teacher, Mr. Blankfeld, walked in a minute later with messy stacks of paper loaded from his arms and trapped under a big, bushy salt and pepper beard. He tried to place them carefully on his desk at the back of the room, but as he walked away they all saw the stack slough over and add to the mess that was already there.

As he walked to the front of the classroom, he hooked his thumbs in his suspenders and said in a voice that is way too energetic for a Monday morning, "So did you all have an eventful weekend?"

This triggered Leo's excitement from earlier and his mind began to race, thinking of what his training might be like later on that day. He had no idea what to expect, so he imagined learning to do things out of a comic book, like shooting lightning bolts out of his fingertips and sucking electricity from a power outlet. He was so immersed in his thoughts that he didn't notice when Mr. Blankfeld called on him because it was his turn to read a short story he wrote for last week's assignments. Aran gave him a strong shove and he was jolted out of his thoughts. He looked around in confusion and Caroline pushed his folder in front of him saying, "Let's hear your story, Leo!"

He recovered quickly and pulled out some sheets of paper. As he walked to the front of the class, Mr. Blankfeld said, "Are you with us, Leo? I can ask someone else to go if you're not ready."

Leo shook his head and said, "No, I'm good." Then he began to read his story. As usual it was set in an imaginary world and he got so into the assignment that he had written several pages instead of just one like most of the class had done. When he was done, he looked up to scan the classroom and to his surprise everyone seemed to be paying attention. Nobody zoned out like they usually did. He looked over quickly to Caroline and Aran and they nodded their approval with big smiles on their faces.

"Well, that was quite a tale!" Mr. Blankfeld said in his permanently excited voice. "It looks like it's time for art class, but when we get back we can try to finish up with the rest of your stories."

The brief moment of pride was replaced with a deep sense of malaise. Art class was his least favorite time of the week. It wasn't because he didn't think it was valuable, he just could never make anything look like he intended. What made things worse was that Aran was a gifted artist and Leo would always find himself wishing he could soak up just a bit of that talent.

Today was even harder for him because he just couldn't focus on the project, no matter how hard he tried. He would keep returning to his daydreams and then rush to catch up when Caroline smacked him upside the head to focus again. By the end of the lesson, what was supposed to look like an octopus resembled something closer to an umbrella and he was just relieved that it was lunchtime.

Leo and his friends regrouped at their spot and Meimei regaled them with a story about the crazy computer her brother built from scratch. He even included a virtual reality headset that made everyone in the family nauseous when they tried using it. In fact, her mother insisted Meimei actually turned green and they had to pull the headset off before she made a mess of her brother's room. Everyone had a good laugh at the story, except for Leo who was deep in his thoughts again. He didn't even notice when Ania stole half of his lunch. While she wasn't very hungry, she still ate everything.

He continued to muddle his way through the day with either Caroline or Aran dragging him back into the present to make sure Mr. Blankfeld didn't notice anything. When the final bell of the day rang, Leo let out a small yelp and shoved everything into his backpack. He pushed into the clump of kids trying to leave the classroom at the same time and, when he emerged, he ran across the schoolyard.

He heard Meimei yell sarcastically, "See ya, Leo! It's been great hanging out with you today!"

He turned around to wave while running backwards and plowed into a couple of younger students. His friends began laughing at him, but it barely registered. His only thought was to get to the bookshop as fast as possible. He took every shortcut he knew, leaping over fences and cutting across lawns. When he finally stormed through the door to the shop, he was sweating and out of breath. His hair was tangled and sticking to the sides of his face.

"You OK, little man?" D'Vonte asked him from the front counter.

"Huh?" Leo said, turning quickly to the voice he heard.

"You don't look so good…"

"Wha?" Leo said, looking at himself and realizing why D'Vonte might be concerned. "Oh… No, it's OK. I'm fine. I was just in a rush… Is Mr. Novickas around?"

"Yeah… I think he is over by the detective novels."

Leo immediately set off across the shop to look for Mr. Novickas. D'Vonte just shook his head with a slight grin on his face and went back to a stack of books in front of him. When Leo turned down an aisle on the far side of the shop, he saw Mr. Novickas at the end of it shelving a stack of books he was holding. As he neared, Mr. Novickas looked at him and raised an eyebrow.

"Did you run here?" he asked.

"Uh… yeah… I guess I am kind of excited to start today?" Leo replied uncertainly.

"Well, you're a little earlier than I expected. Help me shelve these books."

Leo reluctantly took a stack of books that Mr. Novickas gathered from the cart and began to walk around the shop putting the books in the correct sections. He knew the shop so well that he returned to the cart soon after and picked up another stack, impatiently trying to get through this chore so he could get to what he came to do. When he came back to the cart again, he noticed it was now empty and Mr. Novickas wasn't there. Frustration climbed up his back slowly and made him feel hot until he heard Mr. Novickas call him from behind. Leo turned and saw him leaning out of his office door, beckoning him to follow.

When Leo entered the office, Mr. Novickas gestured for him to close the office door. As he pushed it, Leo noticed the door was rather heavy and it slid closed with a low clunk from the latch. Suddenly, the room was much more quiet, the noises from the shop reduced to unintelligible voices and muted scuffles of shoes on the old floor boards. Leo turned back around and watched Mr. Novickas as he reached between two books on the bookcase immediately opposite his desk. He heard a thud and then the entire set of shelves softly pivoted out a few inches. Mr. Novickas pulled on the wooden frame to open the secret passageway fully and Leo saw a set of stairs that twisted down into the darkness.

"After you," he said to Leo casually.

Leo stepped forward, peered down into the darkness, and glanced up at Mr. Novickas with trepidation. Mr. Novickas' eyes widened suddenly as if he just had an idea and then he reached across Leo to push a button on the wall. Suddenly, soft lights illuminated the staircase and Leo could see they went down for quite a ways. He took a deep breath and began the descent, hearing Mr. Novickas close the bookcase behind them.

After a few flights of stairs, Leo noticed the walls shift from what you would normally find in a basement into a smooth rock-like surface. There were bits of micah and other shiny materials embedded in it, giving off a glittery shimmer as the light caught them. When he finally reached the bottom, he found himself at the end of a short hallway that led to a huge cavern made of the same stone from the stairway. As he walked in, he was immediately struck by the scale of it. It was so large, it looked like it could fit the entire school yard in it and still have some room to spare.

Leo looked around and noticed it was pretty much empty, with just a few bookcases and rolling glass panels on the wall to his left. There was also a small desk and chair set up in the middle of the room. Mr. Novickas came around him from behind and simply said, "C'mon!" walking directly to the desk.

Leo followed and when he got closer, he could see the Book of Star Born glowing softly on the desk. Nervousness prickled across his skin and he breathed slowly to try and calm himself.

"You know, your dad created this space," Mr. Novickas said in a teacherly way. "He is a really gifted Geologic, I must say. It takes a deft hand to make mineral compounds like this. I honestly haven't seen anyone else able to create anything quite like it in all my years.

Anyway, this is where you will begin your training and I must insist that you not use your abilities anywhere but here for the time being. These walls have been designed to dissipate the effects of your abilities. We have no idea how strong they will be yet and you almost certainly do not have the necessary control yet to wield them safely. Do you understand what I am saying?"

Leo nodded quickly.

"I mean it, Leo. You can't use your abilities anywhere else. Not even a little bit." Mr. Novickas said sternly.

"I get it!" Leo responded in an impatient tone.

"Good. Now have a seat and start reading."

"What?" Leo asked with incredulity.

"You heard correctly. Sit down and start reading the book," Mr. Novickas said in a matter of fact tone.

"But… I thought this is the start of my training…"

"It is."

"I'm not even going to learn a technique or something?" Leo asked plaintively.

"First you need to read, then you will practice," Mr. Novickas said, his tone softening.

Leo looked down at the hard, wooden chair and then glanced back up at Mr. Novickas before sitting down. He placed his hand on the book to unlock it and, as he focused on the first page, he heard Mr. Novickas begin to walk back out of the cavern. When the steps faded away and it was completely silent, he finally let out a long breath and slouched into the hard back of the chair.

Staring at the first page of the book, he saw the familiar writing. He read "Your journey begins here" over and over again. All the excitement and distraction from the day was gone and he felt completely deflated. Realizing he was starting a pity party for himself, he shook his head a few times, leaned over to the book, and turned the page.

He watched as writing quickly cascaded across the page, forming sentences and paragraphs. When the book had finished writing itself, it then added some flourishes and decorations around the edge of the page.

"Nice touch," Leo said aloud, as if he was talking with the book.

As he read from the top of the page, he had the eerie sense that his casual comment was right and the book was actually starting a conversation with him.

You are infused with raw emotions. In many ways, these emotions are a source of strength for you, but you must learn to control and eventually master them. Fear, anxiety, anger, and joy. All of these serve a purpose and can be harnessed in the right ways. They can also overwhelm you and cloud your mind, rendering you unable to summon your powers or control them when the need arises. Your first skill to master is meditation.

Leo's heart raced and he rubbed his eyes with the heels of his hands, thinking to himself, "Oh my god… I'm connected to this book for real…" He noticed the words started to rewrite themselves and the new sentence he read landed like a ton of bricks.

Your heart rate is too fast. Begin by focusing on trying to slow it down beat by beat.

Leo jumped up from the chair so fast, it slid back a few feet and then tipped over, landing on its back. He paced around the table for a minute, muttering to himself, "Oh my god…" over and over again. Breaking himself out of the cycle, he finally walked over to the chair, tipped it upright, and dragged it back to the desk. He plopped back down into the seat and then closed his eyes to focus on feeling his heart. It was beating almost as fast and hard as when he did the mile run test in gym class last spring and he pushed as hard as he could to beat Ania even though she had a growth spurt and was several inches taller than him.

He directed all of his thoughts toward slowing his heartbeat and noticed it slowed slightly, but he was still nowhere near a calm rhythm. That word, "rhythm," resonated in his mind and made him think of the metronome sitting on the piano at home. He thought of the soft clicking as it set out the slow steady pace he was supposed to practice. Then he placed his hands on his thighs and started tapping a steady, slow rhythm with his right index finger. With his mind, he tried to slow his heart down to match the tapping and over the course of a couple minutes it gradually slowed to the same beat.

A deep sense of satisfaction enveloped Leo and a grin appeared on his face for the first time since entering the bookshop. He slowly opened his eyes and looked back down at the page and he noticed some of the words began to change again. A whole section at the bottom of the page had rewritten itself. Leo began to read the next section and it outlined a basic meditation technique that involved him relaxing each muscle in his body one at a time, starting from his toes and then moving up his body. He spent the next half hour practicing this, noticing his mind would sometimes wander and he would have to pull his focus back to the meditation. By the end of it, his body was so relaxed he felt like he might just slide right off his chair.

Leo slowly moved his arms to wake them up a bit and then sat back up fully. Returning to the book, he started the next section and the calm he was feeling almost immediately ebbed away.

These basic techniques are important to master in stressful situations. You must learn to do them quickly and without any warning. Now place your hand on this page and you will practice returning to a calm state as quickly as possible.

Leo hesitated for a moment. He had a feeling this next part was not going to be very comfortable. Looking around the cavern, he braced himself and then gently rested his hand on the book. His vision began to cloud around the edges almost immediately and he looked down to see the floor of the room starting to disappear. As it vanished around the desk, the table tumbled down into a deep rocky abyss below along with the book, its pages flapping as the air pushed through them. Then it was his turn and he fell rapidly with the chair underneath him since he had a death grip on it. He screamed at a much higher pitch than he expected or would ever admit to his friends, feeling the drop sensation overwhelm him.

He closed his eyes to remove one of his senses and tried to

hold back the panic that was building inside him. This helped a little and so he started to slow down his breathing, relaxing his fingers and letting the chair move away from him as he felt the acceleration of his fall building and the rush of air whipping all around him. He decided to open his eyes to assess his options. Looking around him, he saw walls of jagged rock surrounding him and there was really no way to slow himself down. However, instead of this scaring him more, it seemed to calm him and he began to accept his predicament.

Leo relaxed further and found himself able to spread out into a position he had seen skydivers do in movies. He tried moving his left arm and the shift in the way the air flowed around his body caused him to lose control and tumble toward the rocky walls. He quickly spread his limbs back out into the stable position and tried more subtle changes in the shape and position of his hands. He quickly figured out how to move around and glide through the air and, just as he began to have a little fun, he felt a strong tug at his belly button. The next thing he knew, he found himself back at the desk in the cavern with his hand still on the book.

Leo fell out of his chair gasping for breath and feeling nauseous. He remained crouched on all fours for several minutes waiting for the sensations to dissipate. When he finally felt ready, he got back into the chair and looked down at the page. It still just ended with, "Now place your hand on this page and you will practice returning to a calm state as quickly as possible."

With a little less trepidation this time, he placed his hand back on the book and he recognized his vision clouding at the edges this time. A moment later, he found himself trapped in a display that he recognized from the Oakland Zoo. He was standing face to face with a grizzly bear and it was immense. However, this time, he wasn't scared because he knew it was just practice. He heard some murmuring and looked around to see lots of people staring at him with faces showing shock and fear. A mother with two children off to the right called out, "Someone find a staff member! They need to get that boy out of there!"

Leo chuckled a bit and waved his hand to assure her he was absolutely fine. He didn't know why he did this since she wasn't real, but he figured it was good to play along with the simulation. He turned back to the bear and it huffed at him loudly, shifting its weight across his paws and looking agitated. The noise grew from the spectators and that seemed to rile up the bear further, but Leo remained unconcerned. He looked around to see what fun things he could do in this scenario, so he didn't see the bear pick up its giant, front right paw and swing it at him. When it connected, his shoulder erupted in pain and he was knocked off his feet.

He heard several screams from the onlookers as he grabbed his shoulder. It was hanging limply at his side and he was unable to move it without extreme pain. The bear took a couple steps forward and roared at Leo. He pushed himself back a few feet as fast as he could, no longer sure if he was actually safe in these simulations. He began to stand up and realized this was a bad idea almost immediately as the bear took another swipe at him. Leo braced for the impact, but it didn't lessen the pain that radiated across his side and back.

Back on the ground again, he felt dampness on his shirt and looked down to see he was bleeding heavily from several gashes on his arm and upper chest. He heard individual voices from the people who had turned into an audience for his mauling.

"I can't believe this is happening…" a man with a deep voice said.

"Is anybody going to do anything?" said a teenage girl with a quiver in her voice.

"How did that boy even get in there?" an older lady asked.

Then Leo heard much more closely a voice off to his left say, "Do exactly as I say. Don't turn to me. Stay calm and lay down slowly on your stomach. Spread your arms and legs out slowly, then play dead."

Leo did as he was instructed and he listened to the big breaths from the bear. His heart was racing again and he could feel his shirt getting more saturated with each beat. He began to practice the technique to slow his heart, tapping his toe on the inside of his shoe to set the rhythm. A bit easier this time, he was able to bring his heart rate down much more quickly and he listened for more instructions from the voice he was assuming was one of the zookeepers.

"RUBICON!" the voice called out.

"What?!" Leo asked.

"Not you! The bear! Keep quiet!" the voice chastised.

"Rubicon! What are you doing to the poor boy! Get away from there!"

Leo stayed quiet and listened. For a moment, there was no movement and it sounded like the spectators were all holding their breath. Then he heard the bear shift its weight and turn toward the zookeeper. Suddenly, the bear let out a deafening roar and Leo risked a peek to see it rearing up on its hind legs. He saw the zookeeper now too and he was a short distance away, standing his ground. The bear let out another huge roar and then returned to all fours showing the same menacing behavior at its new target.

"Get up as slowly and quietly as you can," the zookeeper called to Leo and he continued to follow the instructions.

"There's a door about twenty paces behind you. It's a clear and straight shot. Don't turn your back on the bear, just slowly back your way to the door."

"What about you?" Leo asked.

"Are you crazy?! Don't worry about me, just do what I told you to do!"

"He's going to come after you next!" Leo said a bit too loudly and he noticed the bear register him again.

"Look, get out of this enclosure now!" the zookeeper commanded and he started to wave his arms slowly and whistled to get the bear to focus only on him.

The bear stalked slowly toward the zookeeper and Leo shook his head. He couldn't let the bear attack someone else and he resolved to do something about it. Then Leo dug his shoes into the soft ground and launched himself at the bear, plowing his good shoulder into its side. Just as he made contact, however, he felt the tug against his belly button again and he was yanked back into reality. The transition this time was only slightly less jarring because he could still feel the intense pain from the injuries he sustained from the simulation.

Checking to see if there was any actual damage and feeling relieved when he found none, he looked at the book again and was frustrated to see it had not changed this time. The instruction to place his hand on the page was still the last line of text. He debated with himself, trying to decide if he should do another simulation or if he wanted to call it for the day. Eventually, his stubborn side won and he took a deep breath as he returned his hand to the page.

This time, he found himself back in the dim corridor from his dream the other night. He was standing in front of the door with the two voices, except this time he could understand what they were saying.

"I've heard reports they found him…" he heard the raspy voice say.

"How credible are your sources?" asked the deep one.

"Very, we can trust them."

"This is definitely an interesting development."

"Do you think the time has finally come when we can come out of the shadows?"

"Perhaps, but I need to make contact with him first to see if he is ready to join our cause."

"How will you do that? I am sure he will be well protected."

"You know none of that will hinder me, but maybe we can skip all that trouble. He happens to be listening to us right now," the deep voice replied with an amused tone.

Leo took a few steps back and pressed himself into the doorway on the opposite side of the corridor.

"What the heck is going on?!" he whispered to himself and as if to answer he heard the voices much more clearly.

"How is it possible he is listening to us right now?!" the raspy voice asked with a combination of worry and awe.

"He's in the Connector," was the simple response.

"How would he have access to the Connector so soon?! He was just discovered!"

"I don't know. It's a most intriguing development, isn't it? Why don't we find out?"

Leo stared at the door with wide eyes and sweat beading on his forehead. He noticed the doorknob turning slowly and he realized that he had two choices - begin running down the corridor or face whomever was on the other side of that door. He then heard a doorway open down the hallway and footsteps racing toward him. Realizing this probably made his decision for him, he pushed himself into the middle of the corridor and prepared himself to face whomever was on the other side of that door. A wave of calm descended upon him as the door began to open and then quite suddenly the tug at his belly button happened again and he was jerked back into the cavern again.

This time he was not alone when he arrived, Mr. Novickas was standing in front of the desk looking surprised.

"Where were you just now?" he asked Leo, his voice tinged with a mix of worry and curiosity.

"What do you mean?" Leo responded in confusion.

"You were just staring at the wall and mumbling to yourself for at least five minutes. You didn't respond when I said your name. You only came out of that kind of trance when I shook you really hard."

"I was practicing," Leo said slowly. "The book was giving me simulations to practice relaxation techniques."

"What do you mean *simulations*?" Mr. Novickas asked, curiosity winning out over worry.

"The book was putting me in stressful situations and I had to use the techniques to return to a calm state. They were so lifelike, you wouldn't believe it… The first one I was falling into a deep pit below this cavern. Then the second one I had to face a grizzly bear at the Oakland Zoo. The last one was the strangest though… I was in something called the Connector…"

"Did you just say you were in the Connector?" Mr. Novickas asked in disbelief.

"Well, that's what the voices behind the door called it. Just looked like a never ending hallway to me, though."

"Can you describe it a bit more for me, Leo?" Mr. Novickas probed and Leo laid out the details he could remember.

"It's so weird the book created that simulation," Leo remarked. "I had a dream about that hallway the night the book downloaded into me."

Mr. Novickas didn't reply and it appeared he was lost in

thought for a minute or so. Then he said, "This is probably a good time to stop for the day, Leo. Why don't you run home so you're not late for dinner."

"But wait, you're not telling me something," Leo complained.

"It's nothing, don't worry about it. We can talk about it another time. Come back again after school tomorrow so you can continue to practice your techniques."

As Leo stood up, the book closed itself and Mr. Novickas led the way back up the stairs. When they reached the top of the stairs and stepped into Mr. Novickas' office, Leo decided to ask one more question that he had been thinking about all day.

"So, since you're training me now, should I start calling you Adam?"

Mr. Novickas smiled widely and began to laugh, then he answered, "Let's keep it to Mr. Novickas for now, hot shot." He pushed Leo gently out of the office and closed the door behind him before Leo could protest.

Leo walked slowly to the entrance and, when he stepped outside of the shop, the sun was already starting to set. He made his way home and, by the time he arrived, he was famished and couldn't even think about training anymore.

The next day felt much more normal for Leo. Those first training jitters weren't there and he was mostly able to ignore the persistent questions about the simulations and Mr. Novickas being so cagey at the end of the session. It was only at the end of the school day that he started to pick it apart at all and that was actually at the prodding of Aran. Leo was just finishing packing up his backpack when Aran came over.

"Hey, mind if I walk with you to the bookshop? I am meeting my mentor there, he wants to do a bit of a field trip with me today," Aran said.

"Sure, wouldn't mind the company, actually. A field trip sounds fun, I doubt I'll get to do a field trip any time soon…" Leo said, only slightly sullenly.

"Hey, it's not all it's cracked up to be. Last time, he had me standing in a field summoning birds, squirrels, and butterflies to hang out on me. I swear he was just trying to make me look like a fairytale princess or something to amuse himself," Aran said jokingly, making Leo laugh.

"By the way, now that we are not within earshot of the innies, how was your first day of training?" Aran asked.

"What did you say? The innies?" Leo asked.

"Yeah, innocents, folks that don't know about their abilities," Aran answered matter of factly.

"Don't tell me people actually use that term," Leo said incredulously.

"Naa… But wouldn't it be cool if we did have a secret name to refer to them?" Aran said cheekily.

"Should've known," Leo sighed. "Training was alright I guess. I basically just read the Book of Star Born and practiced meditation techniques."

"Really? You didn't do any target practice with chi balls or something like that?" Aran asked with astonishment.

"Nothing like that. Seriously, I just read the book and followed its instructions."

"Bummer…" Aran said. "I would've thought you'd get to do a couple interesting things. I guess there is something to be said for starting slow."

"Yeah, I guess so," Leo agreed.

"Oh, I almost forgot to ask, did you see Ania at the bookshop yesterday?"

"No, why would she have been there? Didn't she have training after school too?"

"Oh my god, this is too good a story to not share, but you have to promise to not let on that you know it, OK?"

Leo nodded and said, "Of course!"

"Ania's training didn't go so well yesterday. She had a special trainer come down from the university up in Davis. She was supposed to teach Ania how to increase the growth rate of some more complex plants. In the process, Ania overdid it a bit and, get this, she turned green," Aran said excitedly.

"NO…" Leo said with astonishment.

"Totally! And that's not all! She also sprouted some branches on her arms and back. At least that is what I heard my parents say last night when they thought I was asleep," Aran said with a sneaky smile.

"Is she OK? Did she reverse it?"

"Yeah, she's fine now, but she needed help reversing it because she was so out of sorts she couldn't do it herself. They had to take her to Mr. Novickas eventually."

"Wow…" is all Leo could think to say as they finally arrived at the bookshop.

They saw Caroline's dad standing out front, focusing on his phone. He looked up when Aran said, "Hey, George."

"Finally! We gotta get moving! You're ready to go, right?" George asked.

"Yeah, of course. Please don't tell me we are going back into the park to commune with small animals again," he said in a slightly snarky tone.

"Nothing like that. We're late. Gotta head to the Oakland Zoo to help out with a bear there. It was all over the news yesterday. A kid got into the enclosure and the bear attacked him.

The really strange part is they haven't been able to find the kid. There was no sign of him after they got the bear away from him. Anyway, now the bear is all riled up and they can't manage to sedate it. We need to connect with it together to help it calm down. It can be really hard to do it by yourself when large mammals are in this kind of state."

Leo's stomach dropped when he heard this and he only mustered a weak wave when Aran said goodbye. He was still processing the revelation that the simulations may actually be real when he knocked on Mr. Novickas' office door a minute later and barely said a word as he was led back down into the cavern. They stopped at the desk and chair, just like the day before, and Mr. Novickas said, "OK, read up! I'll see you in a few hours."

Leo dropped his backpack on the floor heavily and sat back down in the hard, uncomfortable chair. He opened the book and turned back to the second page where he'd left off, but the book turned itself to the next page. This page had already been written, none of the words flowed onto it like the day before, and it began with instructions on how to clear his mind.

You are young and your mind is wide open. While this will help you learn, openness can sometimes lead to distraction. Removing distractions is one of the most important skills for a Star Born to learn. The exercises here will teach you the first techniques on how to do this.

The book then layed out several steps for clearing his mind and he practiced them for the next hour. Thankfully, the book didn't prescribe anything like the day before and he actually became very good at it quite quickly. However, he also found it terribly boring and he groaned loudly when he turned to the next page and saw that it was providing instructions on how to fall asleep in almost any situation.

As you generate actual energy, there are only two ways you can replenish it when you use it. The first is eating and, while there is no training necessary for this, some foods contain more energy than others. The second is sleeping. As you develop your abilities, sleeping will become one of the most important activities that you do.

"C'mon…" he said to himself. "I have no problems sleeping."

As if on cue, the book began to rewrite itself again and most of the text disappeared beneath the passage he just read. The only words that remained were:

Sleep now.

"What? Right here?!" he asked the book, but nothing happened.

Leo shrugged, slid off the chair, shifted the contents in his backpack to make it a more comfortable pillow, and then layed down. He closed his eyes, but he couldn't shut off his mind. It was full of frustration and annoyance. His friends practiced real skills with their mentors and trainers, but he just sat in a cavern reading a bossy book.

He tried some of the relaxation techniques from the day before and, while he got close to drifting off, inevitably his brain turned back on. Finally, he conceded that he may have something to learn and sat back in the chair. Without him uttering a word, the page rewrote itself with instructions on three techniques for falling asleep rapidly. He read through them carefully and practiced each. The first two techniques worked well for him and he took two fifteen minute power naps, waking both times feeling refreshed. The third one made less sense to him because it seemed to be most useful in situations that are very distracting. The stark cavern was anything but distracting.

He noticed several words appear at the bottom of the page:

Place your hand on the page.

"Not again," he thought, but he did as he was instructed and suddenly the room was filled with very loud music. It wasn't one loud song either, but several overlapping with each other. One was clearly heavy metal, the second sounded like a classical symphony, and the third was one of the songs he played to annoy his parents sometimes. He practiced the third technique five more times before he was finally successful at falling asleep.

When he woke up, Mr. Novickas had appeared again and was standing over him with a wide grin.

"Enjoying your training?" he asked mirthfully.

"I can't say that I am..." Leo responded sullenly, letting out some of his frustrations.

"Something tells me you have more to say," Mr. Novickas prodded.

"Look, I get the importance of these techniques and all," he began and he felt anger that hadn't been there before suddenly rise up out of him. "But every single one of my friends was able to do something at least a little interesting with their abilities right at the start of their training. I mean, what can I do at this point? Oh, I can open a locked book, meditate, and fall asleep in a loud room. Can't we mix in something interesting along with all the boring, tedious stuff?!"

Leo saw Mr. Novickas was very quiet and he wondered if he had gone too far.

"You think you know better than the thousands of years of learning contained in that book?" he asked pointedly.

Unable to back down when he knew he should, Leo retorted, "Are you kidding me?! Sometimes you need to reassess things to make sure they keep up with the times!"

"I see…" Mr. Novickas said tersely and he took a long pause before finally saying, "Fine. I'll see you here tomorrow. Same time. Same place. Don't be late." Then he stalked back up the stairs leaving Leo by himself.

Feeling guilty and angry at the same time. Leo snatched up his backpack and walked out on his own. His anger had barely diminished when he arrived home and he shoved large forkfuls of leftover pasta into his mouth without uttering a word to his parents over dinner. When it was time for bed, his anger continued to swim through his mind and he eventually needed to use the third sleeping technique that he had learned earlier in the day.

When he woke up the next morning, his anger had diminished somewhat, but he still felt Mr. Novickas was not being fair the day before. He enjoyed the distractions at school that day and managed to not have a cloud hanging over him, but, at the end of the day when it was time for him to head to the bookshop, he couldn't help feeling extremely nervous about what might unfold next.

When he arrived, Mr. Novickas was not in the shop or in his office. So, Leo opened the secret passageway and made his way down to the cavern. When he got there, he saw Mr. Novickas waiting in the middle of the room, standing behind three of the glass screens on wheels he had noticed the first day. The desk, chair, and Book of Star Born were nowhere to be seen.

"So you think you are some kind of genius," Mr. Novickas said, practically spitting out the words. "Or maybe that's not it. Maybe you think your ancestors were fools who didn't have the benefit of all the things we have today."

"Listen…" Leo began to answer.

"I didn't say you could speak!" Mr. Novickas interrupted, shouting him down and the anger from the day before boiled inside Leo again.

"You are so damn arrogant! I mean, I always had a feeling you were a spoiled brat, but now I know for sure that you are. I was a fool to think you could be trained as a Star Born. I wish I had erased your memory of the book instead of starting you on the path. In fact, maybe I should do that now. I mean it'll be a little hard to deal with some of the memories and you might have some side effects, but nobody will really care and I will have done a service for the tribe."

At this point, Leo was breathing hard and seething with anger. If it were possible to shoot daggers out of his eyes, they would have been flying freely. Then Mr. Novickas said something that cut deeply, "You're not special, Leo. You're just so terribly ordinary and you'll never amount to anything."

"What would you know about being special?!" Leo yelled and waves of energy erupted from his body. They lashed the ceiling and walls where they were absorbed and the only sign of the barrage was maybe a little more twinkling from the glittering fragments inside it. The waves also barreled into the glass panels in front of Mr. Novickas, but he was completely protected and the energy simply ricocheted and scattered, eventually being absorbed by the rock as well.

Leo collapsed on the floor, panting and feeling weak. Mr. Novickas walked around the glass panels and knelt beside

Leo. He handed him a granola bar and put his hand on Leo's shoulder gently. Then he said in a kind tone, "A Star Born who cannot control their emotions is extremely dangerous. Before you can use your power, you must practice what the book is giving you. It senses the turmoil inside and knows these are the lessons you need first."

Leo put the whole granola bar in his mouth and chewed as best as he could, trying to get it into his system as quickly as possible. When he finally swallowed, Mr. Novickas helped him to his feet and said, "I think that's enough for today. Head on home and I'll see you tomorrow."

As he walked home, the experience of losing control weighed heavily on him. He began to beat himself up, questioning how he could have been so naive. When he finally walked into his house, his mom saw him as she crossed the foyer and she turned to say hello. As she opened up her arms to give him a hug, Leo began to cry hard. It was the kind of cry that you sometimes need when you've been through an intense experience and he certainly had been through many of those this week. His mom just held him as he let all the emotion out and when the sobs finally abated into sniffles, she led him into the kitchen and sat him down at the counter.

"You're having a week, huh?" she said and all Leo could do was shrug.

"Wanna talk about it?" she asked and he shook his head slightly.

"That's OK," she said and she came around and rubbed his back. Then she reached for something at the end of the counter and handed Leo a harness and leash.

"Go take your dog for a walk, he has been missing you."

Leo took it and rounded up Astro, then set off on his walk.

He meandered around the neighborhood, not really having a set route to follow. Eventually he found himself in front of Caroline's house and decided to ring the doorbell. A moment later, she was standing in the doorway with a big smile and, when she saw his expression, she just held up one finger to tell him to wait a second.

"Mom! I'm going on a walk with Leo!" she yelled and they both heard, "OK, but not too long!" in response.

When they reached the sidewalk, Caroline was the first to say something.

"You've been busy this week! I've barely seen you outside of school."

"Yeah, sorry about that. My parents signed me up for a karate class," he replied, feeling guilty for lying to her again.

"Don't worry about it!" she said brightly. "Is it fun at least?"

"I don't know yet," he replied. "It's pretty hard actually."

"Well if anyone can figure it out, it's you," she said encouragingly and the pureness of her support started to lift the weight from the day a little bit.

"Oh! Guess what! I finally perfected my chocolate cupcake recipe today!" she shared.

"But you already had the best ones I've ever eaten," he said doubtfully.

"That's nice, but no. I added nutella frosting to them. Huge improvement! I'll give you a few to take home."

More of the weight lifted off Leo's shoulders and he smiled for the first time in the past two days. They continued their walk and talked about all the fun things he hadn't been able to think about that week. When he finally returned back to his house he felt so much better.

❦

The next day Leo woke up and resolved to follow the book's guidance. He made a silent promise to himself and knew he would redouble his efforts to master its lessons. He arrived at the cavern that afternoon with a determined look on his face and Mr. Novickas simply nodded and stepped aside as Leo headed down to the cavern.

Over the next two months, Leo learned numerous skills to focus his mind, relax his body, and deal with different stressors. Occasionally, the book created more simulations that were so real he couldn't imagine they weren't, but still something told him he didn't understand what was happening fully. As he progressed, these simulations became less frequent and Mr. Novickas or another member of the tribe tested him in different ways. At first, he struggled with these challenges and, more often than not, failed to navigate them. However, steadily, his skills and confidence grew.

Then one day, after a particularly grueling session with Mr. Novickas, he managed to maintain his focus and return to a relaxed state consistently over the course of hours of various challenges. At the end of the session, Mr. Novickas smiled as Leo guzzled the last of the water in his glass.

"What?" Leo asked as he wiped his mouth with the back of his hand.

"You're ready," is all Mr. Novickas said.

"Ready for what? I should probably head home soon, my whole family is coming over for fondue tonight. I still don't get it, but my mom and aunt really love it."

"It's time for you to practice with your abilities," Mr. Novickas said and Leo nearly dropped his glass.

"Are you sure?" he asked with trepidation.

"Leo, you're ready."

"But I think I could work a bit harder on the third level focus techniques," Leo said even more anxiously.

"Leo, you won't lose control easily. You're ready."

"You're sure?" Leo asked with a little hope in his voice and Mr. Novickas nodded firmly.

Leo took a big breath and said, "OK, then. What's next?"

"Go home and rest up. I need a couple of days to set things up and you deserve a break. You've been doing some great work, Leo, I'm very proud of you."

This filled Leo with more happiness and satisfaction than he could have imagined, but he just gave a simple nod, picked up his backpack, and turned to head out of the cavern.

7

Boot Camp

"I WIN!" CAROLINE SCREAMED triumphantly and Leo, Aran, and Meimei tossed their cards down.

"I don't get it," Meimei complained. "How are you so good at this game? I mean, if you calculate the probability that you could win all four games, it would be super low."

"What can I say? My kittens just don't explode," Caroline responded with a cocky swagger.

"Do you research strategies to beat us so badly in your free time?" Leo asked.

"Nope, it is just a gift. Wanna play again?" Caroline said with a wide smile.

"NO!" the others yelled back at her and she pretended to take offense.

"What a dreary weekend we're having," Aran lamented as he gazed out at the rain drenching Caroline's backyard.

"I know… Have any of you looked at the forecast to see when we will get a sunny day?" Leo added.

"It's supposed to rain all week," Meimei answered.

"Ugh… This is making me depressed," said Aran.

"Guys! Rainy days are awesome! I have been waiting for months to have a rainy week," Caroline said cheerily.

"Stoooopppp, Caroline! I can't handle the happiness! All my energy is draining away," Aran moaned as he slid off the couch and landed in a heap on the floor.

"Oh well, I guess Aran is dead now," Caroline said sarcastically as she stood up and started walking to the kitchen. "Does anyone else want ramen?"

"Your words have revived me!" Aran yelped as he jumped to his feet raising his hand.

Leo and Meimei started to laugh as they headed into the kitchen because Aran continued the dramatic flair as he started to cook for everyone. He spun around the kitchen and tossed ramen packages in the air, catching them behind his back most of the time. Finally, with a flourish, he presented each of them with a steaming bowl of soup and sat down at the dining table to join them.

"So, Leo, are you heading to the bookshop tomorrow after school?" Meimei asked and immediately realized her mistake when Leo shot her a look.

"Oh! I have been meaning to go there to pick up a Spanish to English dictionary. My mom signed me up for a class that starts next week. Mind if I tag along?" Caroline asked.

"Sure… No problem…" Leo responded hesitantly and Caroline looked at him with a raised eyebrow.

"You don't have to sound so enthusiastic," she said. "I can go another time if you like."

"No, no, no!" Leo backpedaled quickly. "I didn't mean it

that way. It's just… Mr. Novickas heard from my parents that I am trying to earn some extra money and he said I could help unpack boxes and sort books." The lies were coming easier and that made Leo feel even worse.

"What are you trying to earn money for?" Caroline asked suspiciously.

"Just a new video game," Leo answered as casually as he could.

"You got a job to earn money for a video game?" Caroline questioned, clearly skeptical.

"They're just so expensive… I mean, even when I try to buy them used, it would still take four months of allowance. I just don't want to wait that long."

"Yeah, I hear ya," Caroline said, seeming to accept the explanation, but maybe not entirely.

"Look, we can head there together, I just probably can't hang out since I will be in the back storage room most of the time," Leo continued.

"That's fine! It'll be nice to have company on the walk over," she said brightly, clearly deciding to move on and the tension in Leo and the others dissipated.

❧

The next day, Leo and Caroline set off for the bookshop together after school. He was actually glad to have her along for the walk because it helped to distract him from the nervous itchiness that had become more intense as the day went by. It was the first day that he would be practicing with his abilities and the fact that he had no idea what to expect was the source of his discomfort.

When they arrived, Mr. Novickas was at the front counter and he greeted them.

"Oh hey, Caroline! Hey, Leo!" he said as he shot a brief look that Leo understood immediately.

"Hi!" Leo said. "Caroline is here for a Spanish to English dictionary. My parents said you have some boxes you need help unpacking?"

Mr. Novickas immediately understood and replied, "Oh, I can help you with that, Caroline." Then he said to Leo, "Why don't you go and head on back. I'll show you what to do in a few minutes."

Following his cue, Leo waved goodbye to Caroline and walked back to Mr. Novickas' office. He closed the door behind him and then opened the secret passageway. Once he shut the door, he ran down the stairs as fast as he could and when he arrived in the cavern it looked completely different. There were targets lined up on the far wall and various machines along the right wall too, but he couldn't tell what they did. In the center of the room were numerous pedestals with different objects on them. The familiar items from the first couple of months were still there too. The desk, chair, and glass screens were all clustered around the bookshelves on the left side.

He set his stuff down by the desk and began to wander around, examining all of the new equipment more carefully. He started on the far side, looking at the targets closely. They seemed to be standard archery targets, but different. They were filled with gray insulation and the material covering them felt heavy duty and slick. He walked over to the machines when he saw Mr. Novickas appear at the entrance.

"What do you think?" he asked Leo warmly.

"It's a lot of stuff! I was wondering why you needed all that time to set up, but now I understand."

"Yeah, it's not as complicated as it looks, but I have been

keeping it in storage for a while and I had to make sure some of it still works. Thankfully, I only had to make a few repairs."

"So where do we begin?" Leo asked nervously.

"Let's go see what the book wants to assign you today," Mr. Novickas responded.

When they reached the desk, Leo placed his hand on the book and the familiar energy that coursed through him was immediately calming. The book's pages turned rapidly and then finally settled on a new page. At the top, Leo read the words "Energy Armor" and a ripple of excitement cascaded from his core down his arms and legs.

"What does it say?" Mr. Novickas asked, snapping Leo back into focus.

"The first section is titled, 'Energy Armor,'" Leo told him.

"Oh, good! I was hoping it would start you there. It's one of my favorites because each Star Born's armor has a different appearance. It is totally unique to that person," Mr. Novickas said excitedly. "Why don't you read the section while I go set some things up for you."

Leo leaned over the book, not wanting to sit down, and began to read rapidly:

Covering your body with energy armor is an advanced skill and will take time to master. You will start by covering only your arms or legs. If you prepare properly, you will be able to defend most attacks.

"Ok, ready?!" Mr. Novickas called out. He had wheeled one of the machines across the room and Leo realized it was a pitching machine like they have at batting cages.

"You're not going to launch baseballs at my head are you?" Leo asked half seriously and half jokingly.

"Well, I would recommend you don't let them hit your head," Mr. Novickas said completely seriously and when he flipped the switch the machine started to hum. He picked up a large metal basket and loaded the machine. Then he looked to Leo and simply nodded his head as he pushed a button on the side. Immediately, a baseball came flying at Leo and it whizzed over his head as he dropped to the ground.

"Nope, that's against the rules." Mr. Novickas chastised. "You are supposed to use your armor to deflect the balls. Also, I would prefer that you not disintegrate them, please. They are all I have at the moment, but I have some more on order that should arrive next week."

Leo stood back up and faced the machine, but, before he could set himself, Mr. Novickas pushed the button again and a ball came flying at him. This time Leo didn't duck, but he also didn't know what he was supposed to do to "prepare" his body. So, he just turned slightly and the ball slammed into his shoulder. He yelped due to both the shock and pain that was more intense than he expected.

"Hey! That can really hurt me!" Leo yelled at Mr. Novickas, rubbing his shoulder and knowing he would likely have a big bruise there soon.

"What part of *use your armor* do you not understand?" Mr. Novickas asked.

"How about you teach me a bit before launching hard projectiles at me?" Leo snapped back.

"You learn faster by trying right away," Mr. Novickas said as his hand moved back over to the button. "Plus, this is more fun!" Then he pushed it again.

Leo had a feeling that Mr. Novickas was going to do that, so he was already moving to position himself and tamping down his frustration. Then he remembered one of the focusing exercises he learned recently where he practiced feeling his internal energy and moved it around inside his body. Within a fraction of a second, he decided to direct all of his energy into his arms, imagining it covering them. With a sudden flash, turquoise energy ballooned from his shoulders down to his wrists and Leo raised his arm just as the baseball was reaching him. He watched as it scorched when it touched the energy, then it caught on fire, and finally it turned into ash falling to his feet.

"I said DON'T disintegrate the balls!" Mr. Novickas called out, but Leo barely noticed. He was just staring at the rippling waves of energy encasing his arms.

"How about you turn it down a bunch of notches so training doesn't just last twenty minutes today?" Mr. Novickas continued.

"Huh?" Leo said, feeling a little loopy.

"You're dialed up to a ten right now. How about going for a three?" Mr. Novickas coached.

"Oh… Sure…" Leo responded and then he closed his eyes and focused on taking some energy out of the armor. Just as he felt like he had it dialed in correctly, he felt another baseball slam into his gut, knocking the wind out of him. As he gasped for air, he heard Mr. Novickas say, "Who closes their eyes in the middle of being attacked?"

Leo's anger flared for a moment and he noticed the armor flicker. He regained his composure quickly and the armor returned to its steady, flowing state. Except now, it was not as voluminous as before. It was tighter around his arms and the movement reminded him of miniature waves. He heard the machine launch another ball and he looked up to protect himself with his left forearm. When the ball made contact, it careened away, smashing into one of the bookcases and knocking over some of its contents.

"Sorry!" Leo called out.

"Don't worry about it! There's nothing super precious in this room that we can't replace pretty easily. Except for the Book of Star Born, of course. I don't think a baseball can hurt it, though."

Mr. Novickas then launched a rapid succession of balls at Leo, turning the machine constantly to shift the angle of attack. Leo steadily got the hang of timing the balls and knocking most of them away with just one smacking into his thigh and another grazing his ear. As he connected with more of them, he could feel a slight bit of pressure where the ball touched his armor, but he knew he was completely protected and he found the feedback helped him to know how to direct the ricocheting balls. A few minutes later, Mr. Novickas raised his hands and yelled, "Time to reload!"

Leo powered down his armor and walked around the cavern picking up balls and tossing them in the metal basket that Mr. Novickas had set out. Then they returned to their stations and Mr. Novickas called out, "Batter up!" However, this time, he suddenly aimed the machine down and Leo recognized what's happening and formed the armor around his legs. Deflecting the balls with his legs proved a bit more challenging and he struggled to reposition himself quickly enough to deflect them let alone direct them where he wanted them to go.

The barrage suddenly stopped and Mr. Novickas said, "Nice! Go ahead and take a break. Grab some water and read the book a bit, I'll gather up the balls."

Leo nodded and as he walked back to the side of the cavern he felt a bit of exhilaration having finally used his abilities. It felt more natural than he expected, kind of like things that were always there were starting to click into place. He reached his backpack, pulled out a water bottle and guzzled down most of it before pausing to catch his breath again. Then he looked down at the book and read more of the section that had now appeared after his first couple of rounds with Mr. Novickas.

Leo was proud to see most of what he did was how the book explained the process of generating armor. There were also some additional tips for how to be more exact in the energy levels he used to create the armor and how to change the armor's shape. This intrigued him and he powered up his right arm, focusing the energy around his hand into a rough shape resembling a hammer. "Cool…" he whispered to himself with a bit of awe, and then he powered down again to keep reading.

The section was much longer than the ones he studied before and it covered a great deal of detail on things he should consider when using his armor. Some of the risks it warned of were interesting, including that it could conduct electricity unless he developed the skill to insulate it properly. The book also noted that maintaining it while also generating attacks or amplifying Earth Borns was an advanced skill and should not be tried without extreme care because it could harm an untrained Star Born. He made a mental note to ask Mr. Novickas about amplifying Earth Borns later and then he read the final paragraph in the section.

> *You have more power inside you than you realize. More than you could possibly use to even create full body coverage for an entire day. Parts of your armor can also be charged or removed rapidly with basic practice. This will become less necessary as you master more advanced skills.*

Leo stepped back from the desk a few paces and began powering up and turning off his armor quickly, starting with his arms, then moving to his legs, and finally shifting between all four. He heard Mr. Novickas call out, "Looks like you're ready for another go!" and Leo felt a bit of excitement as he jogged back over to take his position.

Before he even got there, however, he saw Mr. Novickas turn a dial on the top of the machine and then flip a switch next to the button he used to fire the balls at him. The machine erupted with a rapid succession of balls and Leo barely got his left arm covered in armor before the first one hit him and he felt a slight sting from the impact. The same thing happened when he deflected another ball right after with his right arm and he realized that Mr. Novickas had turned up the force of the balls dramatically. A nervous sensation sat in his gut as he scrambled to shift his armor rapidly between his limbs just fast enough before a ball hit an uncovered spot.

He found himself suddenly off balance as he leaned back dramatically to buy a fraction of a second as one bounced off his shoulder when he noticed a ball headed straight at his chest. He knew immediately that he couldn't twist himself into a position where one of his arms covered that spot in time, so he imagined a circle of shiny metal armor where he thought the ball was going to hit. As it pounded into that spot, he completely lost his balance and landed hard on his butt. Another ball whizzed over his head and he saw Mr. Novickas quickly turning the machine off. Leo started to stand up, rubbing his chest and Mr. Novickas walked over quickly.

"How did you do that? Did the book teach you how to do that?" he asked Leo with deep curiosity.

"What? The quick armor shifting? Yeah, that was in the book." Leo responded, confused by the tone of Mr. Novickas' voice.

"No, you made a focused shield in the center of your chest. It was different from the rest of your armor. Not the bluish green color, it was more deep purple and it looked spikey like a cactus."

"I dunno," Leo answered simply. "I just reacted quickly because I didn't have time to prepare."

"You don't understand, Leo. That isn't supposed to be possible. Your energy color and texture is kind of like your fingerprint. It is unique to you and a Star Born only has one, but you have now demonstrated two. Not only that, but they are very different. I have never heard of this before... I'm going to have to reach out to the Council for guidance..."

"What's that?"

"It's a group comprised of senior leaders from across the tribes. It is very secret, I can't explain more than that."

Mr. Novickas looked away, muttering to himself and Leo was familiar with it enough now to know it was just the way he thinks. Leo took the opportunity to process all of this new information as well and a thought popped into his head so he decided to satisfy his curiosity.

"OK..." Leo said, getting Mr. Novickas' attention. "So... What did Maranda's armor look like?"

Mr. Novickas cocked his head to the side and furrowed his brow, then he asked slowly, "Why are you asking about that?"

"You said each Star Born's energy is unique, I was curious what hers was like."

"Hmmm... Well, I guess I would describe it as a deep yellow... Almost golden. It was also totally smooth and joined together like lots of square, rectangular, and triangular panes of glass were surrounding her... It has been a while since I thought of that..."

"She sounds powerful," Leo said softly.

"She was," Mr. Novickas responded solemnly. "It's why I never understood how we lost her. She was one of the most amazing Star Borns I have ever seen..."

Leo knew this was a sensitive subject for Mr. Novickas and felt ripples of sorrow flowing off of him, so he decided to change the subject quickly asking, "The book mentioned something about amplifying Earth Borns. What does that mean?"

"The book mentioned that already?" Mr. Novickas asked, returning from his thoughts.

"Yeah, just briefly."

"Hmm... How to explain amplification... " Mr. Novickas began. "Think of it this way. You can lend your energy to an Earth Born so their abilities are stronger. That's why it's called amplification. The amount you lend to them is directly related to how much stronger they get. At first, when you learn how to do that, you have to be touching the Earth Born and even then it is *extremely* dangerous. I mean, you could kill them, Leo. Don't go trying this with your friends, do you hear me? Remember, they have to be able to accept the energy you are giving them.

"Over time, though, you will be able to share your energy over greater distances. If you get really good, you can share your energy with other Star Borns or even combine your energy with another Star Born to amplify an Earth Born. Even more important, you have to take your energy back eventually and when that time comes you need to be very careful because you can easily take an Earth Born's energy along with your own. If you do that, you will permanently weaken them and, if you take too much from them, it is another way to potentially kill them."

"OK... Wow... There was more to that than I expected... I think I'll stick to armor for now," Leo said as he thought about how risky his powers could be.

"Sounds like a good plan."

"So what's next?" Leo asked.

"I think this is a good stopping point for today. We can pick back up tomorrow. Also, make sure you bring some snacks and a lot of water. Training is going to be much more physically demanding from here on out."

"OK, got it. By the way, I didn't get to finish reading the section earlier, is it possible for me to take the book home so I can study things a bit more?"

"No. The book stays here," Mr. Novickas said sternly and this made Leo bristle a bit, but he let it go and just nodded. Then he crouched down to pack up his backpack before heading home.

Later, after having dinner and finishing his homework, Leo decided he needed to try to take some notes on what he had learned that day to help him remember and practice. He headed back up to his room, grabbed a notepad and pencil, hopped on his bed, and started jotting things down. After a short while, his eyelids started to get heavy and he dozed off a few times. Each time he woke up, he tried to reread what he had last written down and pick back up with his notes. However, it was a losing battle and eventually he fell asleep sitting with his back leaning against the wall.

The next morning, Leo woke up lying in his bed, wrapped up in his covers. He didn't remember going to bed and when he saw the pad and pencil placed carefully on his side table he knew his parents must have taken care of him. As he laid there for a minute or so, he felt his body starting up and soon felt energized. He tossed off his covers and hopped out of bed, then shed the stale clothes he was still wearing from the day before. Once he was ready for the day, he headed out of his room, but as he was padding down the stairs quietly in his socks he could tell something wasn't right.

He could hear that his parents' voices didn't sound chipper like they normally do in the morning. Instead, they sounded strained, like they were arguing about something. When he rounded the corner at the bottom of the stairs, one of the floorboards creaked loudly and they immediately stopped talking. As he walked into the kitchen, his mother put on a big smile and walked over to him.

"Hey there!" she said as she pulled Leo into a big hug. "Training must've worn you out yesterday. We found you passed out in your room at 8:30 last night."

"Yeah, I kinda noticed I was dozing off a few times…" Leo said hesitantly.

"I have a feeling that might happen a bit more frequently now," she said with a knowing grin. She reached into a cabinet and pulled out a bowl and a glass, handing both to Leo. He then went about gathering the pieces of his breakfast and thinking about how tense their voices sounded just a minute or two before.

"Hey, what were you guys talking about just now?" Leo asked pointedly as he sat down at the counter, not able to contain his curiosity or think of a better way to approach the subject.

"Oh, it's just something I was reading about in the news that kinda riled us up," his dad answered breezily, but Leo could feel bits of anxious energy shedding off him and knew he was not telling the whole truth. He was not entirely sure how he knew this, but Leo decided not to probe any further. He figured he would have to be patient and pick a better moment to find out more. So, he finished his breakfast, occasionally participating in the idle chit chat his parents started up to cover their prior conversation and eventually headed off to school as usual.

Later that day, when he arrived at the shop, he used the keypad code Mr. Novickas gave him a few weeks before to let himself in the back door and headed straight to the cavern. During his walks to the shop, Leo had developed a habit of clearing his mind as a preparation for his training. So, his senses were finely tuned to pick up an anomaly while he descended the stairs. It was nothing more than a slight itch under his skin, but he knew he needed to listen to it. Nearing the bottom of the stairs, he powered up the armor on his arms and legs for good measure. He knew he probably shouldn't expend this much energy, but he didn't want to take any chances given the lessons Mr. Novickas taught him the day before. Stepping through the doorway to the cavern, he was immediately met with a barrage of projectiles flying at him. Baseballs were flying at him at even faster speeds than before along with heavy bean bags and what he found out quickly were paintballs.

Leo moved as quickly as he could to deflect everything coming his way, knocking them back as hard as he could. He learned quickly to not do that for the paintballs when several of them splattered all over his face and clothes. Shifting his energy to various parts of his body to try to protect himself as best he could, he saw different colors erupting in those spots. Mainly it was the spikey purples from the day before, but he also noticed some deep, lumpy greens and even some smooth bubbles of red.

Despite his best efforts, however, some things made it through his defenses and each impact was painful. After what felt like an eternity, but in fact was only a couple minutes, Mr. Novickas exhausted his ammunition and Leo heard him clapping and laughing loudly.

"Nice job! Nice job! I guess you *were* listening to me yesterday! How did you know I was going to ambush you?" he asked jovially.

"I could feel something was off as I came down the stairs," Leo replied between panting breaths while rubbing a sore spot on his side.

"I was hoping the walls would numb your senses a bit more, guess we did your focus training a bit too well, huh?" Mr. Novickas commented as his smile shifted to a look of moderate concern. "I got you good there, I can sense it. Let me have a feel." He placed his hands gently on Leo's side, but it still made Leo wince with pain.

"OK, yeah, I'm going to have to take care of this one. Let me check for anything else that needs attention," he said, guiding his hands over different parts of Leo and making mental notes as he went. Finally, satisfied he had checked everything thoroughly, he looked Leo directly in his eyes and said, "This shouldn't hurt too badly, but it might feel a bit uncomfortable." Then he closed his eyes and Leo felt warmth emanating from Mr. Novickas' hands. It spread deep inside him and a dull ache grew in multiple parts of his body. It transitioned to a strong throb that steadily got harder to tolerate and Leo had to begin an advanced meditation to tolerate the excruciating feeling. When Mr. Novickas finally opened his eyes, the discomfort ebbed away quickly.

When Leo stood up, he couldn't feel any of the injuries he had sustained earlier and the only sign of the attack was the splattered paint all over him. He looked around and shook his head at the huge mess all around him, then dropped his backpack and started to pick up a few balls and bean bags.

"Don't worry about that for now. Go ahead and study for a little while so I can set up for the next practice session," Mr. Novickas instructed and Leo gladly walked over to the desk. He pulled out a granola bar, opened the wrapper, and took a bite as he placed his hand on the book. He watched the familiar routine of the flipping pages moving to where he would begin to study and noticed many more pages were turning than he would expect. In fact, the book went well past where he left off the day before. When it finally settled on a page, there were a number of drawings and diagrams accompanying the usual text. Leo read the first section:

Energy bending is an advanced skill and most Star Borns do not have the opportunity to try it, let alone master it. As you have been informed, each Star Born has a pattern or a fingerprint as it was described to you. This is usually static and will not change for the lifetime of a Star Born. In addition, your pattern usually guides the types of specialties you can develop with your abilities.

However, it is possible to change your pattern temporarily or permanently by bending your internal energy. Developing this skill is beneficial because it opens a wider variety of skills that you will be able to master. You have already demonstrated that you are flexible enough to energy bend. Now you must practice holding your energy in different patterns to take advantage of those specialties. This section explains in detail how to do this.

Leo spent the next hour reading about the steps to energy bend and testing the techniques on the backs of his hands. Every time he changed his energy, it felt different, like an additional sense was heightened. He enjoyed the different feelings and got wrapped up in his practice, so much so that he didn't notice when Mr. Novickas walked up behind him and observed what he had learned to do.

"So you have learned how to start energy bending?" he asked Leo thoughtfully.

"What?!" Leo said a little too loudly, nearly jumping out of his skin with surprise.

"It looks like you have gotten pretty good at that since yesterday," Mr. Novickas teased.

"How long have you been watching?" Leo asked suspiciously and then with an intense look also asked, "You know about energy bending? Why did you act like you didn't?!"

"Chill out…" Mr. Novickas admonished, waving him off. "I just learned about it earlier this morning when I received a message from the Council. They were actually stumped at first because it has been many generations since there has been a Star Born who can energy bend. They spent much of the night researching to find out about it. This is a good thing, Leo! They might want to send a Star Born to work with you personally!"

The idea of having a Star Born mentor filled him with intense feelings of excitement and anxiety at the same time. Over the past months, he had finally begun to feel more comfortable with his abilities. He also felt like he was finally getting to know Mr. Novickas better and it was a relationship he had come to value greatly. He knew he would learn much more quickly with a Star Born guiding him, but he didn't want to do that if it meant he couldn't work with Mr. Novickas anymore.

"Leo?" Mr. Novickas prodded. "You still with me?"

"Uh… yeah… sorry…" Leo responded.

"I asked you if you could show me a bit more of what you have learned."

"Oh… sure," Leo said tentatively at first and then with a flash of nerdy glee he erupted with all the information he had absorbed from the book so far.

"At first I really had to strain to change my energy a little bit, but the book showed me some techniques to make it easier. Also, look at these diagrams, they are really helpful!" Leo gestured at a space in the middle of the book and Mr. Novickas squinted, shook his head, and smiled ruefully.

"Those make no sense to me, Leo. The book is only for Star Born."

"Ah… sorry!" Leo said, furrowing his brow and thinking about how to explain what he had learned. Then it came to him and a big grin erupts on his face.

"It's all about patterns," he explained. "When I bend energy, I am consciously changing my natural pattern. At first, I sensed different energies as kind of separate frequencies, as if everything was humming a different note. Now that I have practiced bending a bit today, I can sense more of the pattern and play with it. What really helped was remembering how my friends' energies feel. Just now I was bending my energy towards those feelings. I am not sure what it does really… I mean, it looks cool, right? All the different colors and stuff… The book said I can develop different specialties through bending, but I haven't gotten to the section that tells me how that works."

Mr. Novickas sighed deeply, but didn't say anything.

"Am I making sense?" Leo asked.

"Yes. Completely. I am just trying to think of a practical way for you to explore this ability…"

"Let me read a bit more and see what else I can learn," Leo suggested.

"Sure," Mr. Novickas affirmed. "I'm going to clean up some more, just holler when you find something that might help."

On that note, Leo looked back to where he left off in the book and he saw the next section was titled, "The Link Between Energy Bending and Amplification." Leo's heart began to race as he remembered Mr. Novickas' warning from the day before. The potential risks of amplification made him want to steer clear of it, but the excitement about potentially being the first Star Born in a long time to energy bend was too exciting to ignore, so he continued to read.

Energy bending and amplification are related abilities as both rely on your ability to be sensitive to Earth Born energy patterns. By bending your energy to mimic an Earth Born's pattern, you unlock abilities that align with that power. For example, patterns can increase your speed, sensitivity, the force of your attacks, and the strength of your defenses. Similarly, by understanding Earth Born patterns you are better able to modify the energy you give them to amplify their abilities. This will also help you safely control the amount of power you give them and take back from them.

Leo read several more pages that covered how to sense Earth Born energy patterns in minute detail. So much detail, in fact, that it was the first time he had felt bored reading the book and his eyes grew heavy. Shaking his head to stay awake and yawning, he forced himself to finish the section and turned the page. When he saw the next page was blank, he sighed, realizing the book was telling him he couldn't go further until he mastered what it had just given him.

He stood up and looked around for Mr. Novickas and didn't see him anywhere. Figuring he probably went back up to his office, Leo packed up his stuff and headed up the stairs to find Mr. Novickas and brief him on what he learned. When he came through the hidden doorway, Mr. Novickas swiveled his desk chair around to face Leo and looked at him expectantly.

"Well, I think the book really wants me to learn more

about Earth Born energy patterns," Leo said with a mild hint of annoyance.

"You don't seem too happy about that," Mr. Novickas probed.

"Well, I mean, I was patient and worked so hard on my focus and meditation so I could get to the cool stuff we are doing right now. It just feels like I am taking a step back…"

"Ah, I see," Mr. Novickas said with a knowing smile. "Don't worry, I think we can find a way to make this both challenging and fun. Can you do me a favor and let your friends know they will be joining you for training on Friday afternoons? I'll let their teachers and mentors know about this change too."

"Wait… what?" Leo said, unable to process what Mr. Novickas was saying due to the rapid shift from feeling dejected to elated.

"You heard me right," Mr. Novickas responded without missing a beat. "Now get out of here, I have order forms to fill out."

❦

Leo ran the entire way home, wrenched the door open when he arrived, kicked off his shoes, and leapt up the stairs to get to his room as fast as possible. He dropped his backpack and slammed the door behind him before grabbing his phone from the dresser and typing out a message to his friends.

"You're not going to believe this! We're going to start training together!" he wrote and then started pacing around his room waiting for replies. He didn't have to wait too long for a bubble to pop up on the screen showing that Meimei was typing something. Then he heard a knock on his door.

"Yeah?" Leo asked, not taking his eyes off his phone.

His dad opened the door and asked, "Everything OK?"

"Yeah, why?" Leo said somewhat annoyed that his dad was distracting him.

"Well, you left the front door wide open, ran up to your room, and then slammed your door. Not the usual thing you do when coming home."

"Oh, sorry!" he said genuinely. "I am just excited! Mr. Novickas is going to have me start training with my friends!"

"That's great!" his dad said warmly. "Dinner is in fifteen minutes. Be there or be square."

Leo looked up from his phone, glared at his dad, and then rolled his eyes in dramatic fashion. His dad just started chuckling in response and closed the door behind him. As if on cue, Leo's phone started vibrating violently with an onslaught of texts.

"We get to come to the bat cave?!" Meimei wrote first.

"No way! I've been curious to check out your powers!" Aran chimed in.

"What kind of training are we going to do?" Stella asked.

"Do we have to?" Ania asked sarcastically, throwing in several poop emojis for good measure.

The thread quickly devolved into a series of gifs and random quotes from shows before Meimei finally focused the group again.

"So when is this training starting?" she asked.

"I think on Friday," Leo answered.

"Friday, like three days from now?" Stella asked.

"Yeah, I think so," Leo confirmed.

"But I was going to hang out with some venus fly traps that day," Ania threw in, ignoring Meimei's attempt to keep things practical.

"Do you have ANY more details?" Meimei asked.

"Not really. Mr. Novickas just said to let you know and he would talk to your teachers and mentors."

"LEO! TIME FOR DINNER!" his dad called up.

"Gotta go! Dinner!" he wrote to the group.

"Wait! I haven't thought of my witty comment yet!" Aran complained.

"If we waited until you thought of one, we would be here all night," Ania wrote.

"BURN!" Stella exclaimed.

The phone continued to buzz as Leo tossed it on his bed and ran downstairs.

Leo was worried the next few days would drag as he waited for Friday to come, but both Mr. Blankfeld and Mr. Novickas kept him very busy and the time flew by. His project on the Pyramids of Giza was due at the end of the week and he barely had time to work on it. At the same time, he was being put through his paces in training each afternoon. Mr. Novickas had started to use a variety of machines and other kinds of equipment to further develop his skills with energy armor. Not only was it exhausting, it was also dangerous, and Mr. Novickas had to heal him twice on Thursday when various items made it through Leo's defenses.

Finally, Friday arrived and the entire group was full of excitement all day. Leo managed to make it through his presentation on the pyramids, but it took a great deal of effort to stay focused. Even then, he almost forgot to cover a whole section he had prepared on hieroglyphics. The same happened for Aran, who did his project on Ancient Greece and forgot to talk about his model of the Parthenon until Mr. Blankfeld reminded him.

During lunch, Caroline was baffled at what was going on with her friends. Nobody was talking and Ania hadn't tried to steal anyone's food.

"So, guys, my birthday is coming up and I was thinking of doing a movie night," she said.

"Cool," Stella said, clearly barely paying attention.

"I found a great documentary on Led Zeppelin," she continued and Aran just stared into space. Now she was sure of it, there was definitely something going on. Aran had lectured the group on the virtues of Led Zeppelin at least twice in the past month and she had left the door wide open for him.

"What is going on?!" she yelled at the group.

This jolted everyone out of their daze and Leo was the first to respond, sensing how agitated Caroline had become.

"What do you mean?" he said.

"You guys have been like zombies all day! I mean ALL of you!"

"No we haven't!" Meimei said defensively.

"Really?!" Caroline snapped quickly. "You forgot to hand in your math homework. You NEVER forget to do that. It's like the first thing you do on Fridays. I sometimes wonder if you're worried it will explode in your backpack if you don't hand it in as soon as you walk into class."

This made Ania chuckle and Caroline shifts her ire.

"Did you notice you're wearing two different shoes today? I bet you didn't. Isn't one of those your sister's?"

For once, Ania didn't have a witty comeback.

"Look, it's been a long week," Leo started to try to calm Caroline down.

"Don't try and tell me you're all tired from completing your projects and stuff," Caroline growled, refusing to be soothed. "We all had the same amount of work to do and you are the only kids in class acting like this. Something is going on and none of you are telling me. I've had a feeling about this for a while now, but I haven't made a big deal about it. Now I am just fed up! Somebody better tell me what's going on or I'm out of here!"

The group was gobsmacked. Aran's jaw had actually dropped and a piece of his sandwich was hanging precariously out of his mouth. Nobody knew what to say and the longer the silence lasted the more the tension increased.

"Nothing?!" Caroline finally said, her voice quivering and clearly on the verge of tears. She started to throw parts of her lunch back into her bag quickly.

This finally broke Leo's mental block and an idea popped into his head.

"Wait! Stop!" Leo said and Caroline paused.

"Look, you're right, we have been keeping something from you," he said and he could feel all of his friends' eyes drilling into him.

"Why? I thought we tell each other everything…" Caroline replied, her eyes filling with tears.

"Because it is a surprise," Leo said as if he was revealing a long held secret.

"A surprise? For me?" Caroline asked, brightening a bit, but still on her guard.

"Well, yeah," Leo said somewhat annoyed. "Your birthday is coming up right? We've been working on something for a little while, but there are few things we can't agree on. I guess we can just tell you…"

"No! No, don't do that," Caroline said quickly. "I'm sorry for assuming something bad. I just haven't seen much of you all lately and it has felt like maybe you were intentionally excluding me or something…"

"We would never do that!" said Stella, now with her own tears in her eyes.

"Right!" Meimei jumped in, but still not sure what to say since she was the worst liar in the group.

"Sorry, Caroline, I guess we aren't the super skilled secret agents we thought we were…" Aran said, contributing to the ruse. Caroline shook her head confirming that fact.

"OK, forget everything I said. I will ignore your weird behavior from now on," Caroline said, clearly buying into the story they were creating.

"Great because I don't think Aran has the ability to behave normally," Ania said, finally joining in.

"Hey! I resemble that remark!" Aran responded with mock hurt in his voice. Then he turned to Caroline and said, "By the way, did I hear you mention something about Led Zeppelin?"

"NO!" Everyone said in almost unison and the rest of lunch was filled with the usual banter.

8

Training Gets Real

AT THE END of the day, Leo and his friends made their way separately to the back door of the bookshop and Mr. Novickas guided them down to the secret cavern. Leo was the last to arrive since he walked home with Caroline to try and make up for how they had made her feel. He immediately noticed a few things that he hadn't expected. First, not only were his friends there, but also their teachers. Second, Mr. Novickas had removed a lot of the equipment from the cavern again. Instead, there were just a few stations around the room aligned with each of his friends' abilities, including a large water tank, several large cages with various animals, some pots with exotic-looking vines, and a number of bins filled with things that seem to have been gathered from a junkyard.

"Is that an alligator?" he heard Meimei ask anxiously.

"Yeah, and he's really grumpy too. He thinks that cage is a big downgrade from where he was living before," Aran said seriously.

"OK, I think we can get started now," Mr. Novickas called out, refocusing the group. "All of you have progressed enough in your basic training that we feel you are ready to start using your abilities for next level tasks. During these Friday sessions, you will often be presented with a problem or puzzle and we will expect you to solve it together as a team. These tasks will get steadily harder to solve and you will have time limits to complete them. Finally, once we feel you are ready, these challenges may sometimes involve some form of combat."

This comment caught Leo and his friends by surprise and they immediately started talking excitedly to each other about what a battle would look like.

"QUIET DOWN, KIDS!" Mr. Novickas yelled, staring at each one of them in turn. "Yes, I know that sounds exciting, but, trust me, combat is something that should be avoided as much as possible. It is significantly more dangerous when you have people with strong abilities attacking each other."

"Sheesh, is it so wrong to be at least a little excited to mix it up a bit, finally?" Ania muttered.

"Ania, you better listen or you will be working in the green house for the rest of your life," Mr. Novickas snapped and there were no more interruptions after that point.

"You will notice that your teachers and mentors are here with us. They will be observing you and making sure nobody dies if you make a big mistake. Yes, you heard me right, I said 'dies.' We are going to be putting challenges in front of you that will test the control you have over your abilities. In addition, you will all be working with a Star Born for the first time and that brings its own set of dangers. So, you will listen carefully and follow our instructions. These observations will also inform your training sessions throughout the rest of the week when you are working independently. Any questions before we get started?"

After a short pause, Stella raised her hand and Mr. Novickas nodded at her.

"Are you sure we are ready for this?"

"Yes, we are all sure," he responded in a much more calm and gentle tone. "You have been doing very well and it isn't often we have a new group that is already so close like you all are. That gives us an opportunity to do this kind of training because it requires trust and cooperation. These are things that aren't always easy for twelve year olds."

He looked at the other kids with raised eyebrows and asked, "Does anyone else have a question?"

Ania raised her hand.

"Is this a real question or are you just going to say something sarcastic because I snapped at you before? If it's the latter, put your hand down."

Ania slowly lowered her hand.

"OK, on that note, how about we start on your first challenge? Amy, could you give me a hand?"

Leo's mother stepped forward with a tray of glasses and she had each of them take one. Then, without so much as a twitch from her, the group saw all of the water rise up out of the tank and splash across the floor.

"Your challenge," Mr. Novickas continued. "Is to fill each of your glasses with water and then make your way from the entrance to the opposite side of the cavern without touching the floor. You cannot spill any of your water, you must proceed across the cavern together as a group, and if any of you break your glass you will have to repair it and start over again. You will have one hour."

The group immediately huddled together to map out their plan. Meimei looked at Stella and said, "If we're going to do this in an hour, you're going to have to get that water into our glasses."

"Piece of cake," Stella responded confidently.

"Alright, that's one step covered, how are we going to get across the floor without touching the floor?" Aran asked.

"Well, I could do some really cool stuff with those vines over there," Ania said. "But I am not sure I can pull it off."

"Alright, keep thinking about that while we get started. I'm pretty sure we're going to need every minute of that hour to get this done," Leo said warily.

Stella stepped away from the huddle, focused intensely on the floor, and a stream of water rose up to fill her glass slowly. When it was full, she looked over to Meimei and nodded her head up signaling to hold the glass for her to fill it. Meimei followed her lead and watched the water fill her glass, but, suddenly, the water flowed out of Stella's glass again and spilled back onto the floor.

"What the heck?!" Stella yelled.

"Remember your instructions!" Mr. Novickas called from across the room.

Simmering with anger, Stella closed her eyes and took a moment to calm down. She then returned to filling Meimei's glass before refilling her own. Again, the glass emptied and spilled onto the floor, except this time it was Meimei's.

"C'mon!" Stella shouted in exasperation and glaring at Amy.

"What are we doing wrong?" Meimei asked.

"There has to be a trick," Leo said softly, barely loud enough for the rest of them to hear.

"What?" Aran asked loudly.

"If there is one thing I have learned, it's that Mr. Novickas likes to trick me," Leo said more clearly to the group.

"So what's the trick on this one?"

"He gave us a hint about the instructions, can anyone remember what he said?" Leo asked, growing confident that he is on the right path.

"We have to fill our glasses and cross as a group. We can't spill or break our glasses either," Meimei said.

"Oh no…" Stella said gravely and they all looked over to her in confusion.

"We have to do everything as a group…" she said.

"I'm not following you," Leo responded.

"We have to do everything together at the same time. Not one at a time. I have to fill all the glasses simultaneously…" she clarified and they heard a quiver in her voice.

"OK, so you just have to create five of those water fountains," Aran said flippantly.

"Do you have any idea how hard it is to control a stream like that?!" she snapped at him.

"Alright, remember, this is supposed to help us trust each other and collaborate. Let's not get frustrated with each other," Meimei counseled, trying to defuse the tension.

"You got this, Stella," Leo said encouragingly. "Here, let's just put all our glasses down here in front of you and we will give you some space to focus. We should probably help Ania anyway, she's staring so hard at those vines over there I am worried the pots might explode."

This made Stella chuckle and Leo gathered up the glasses for her. She then sat down on the wet floor and focused on the glasses as she started to create several tiny streams of water from the floor before they splashed back down.

"Alright," Meimei said, turning to Ania. "Whatcha got?"

"Well, I know I can make those vines grow rapidly, I practice with them all the time. I was thinking we could walk on them to get across and not touch the floor," Ania said while biting her nails.

"That's a great idea!" Meimei agreed.

"Well, I can grow them rapidly, but not that distance in an hour and not enough so that we can all cross at the same time," Ania said dejectedly.

"Why don't we just have Leo supercharge you?" Aran asked casually.

"What?!" Leo responded anxiously.

"That's what you do, right? Boost our powers? Just give her a boost so she can grow the vines faster and thicker."

"He has a point," Meimei said.

"I'm liking this idea…" Ania said with a wide grin.

"No, no, no…" Leo disagreed firmly. "You guys don't know how dangerous it is! I mean, I could kill Ania! There's got to be a different way to do this…"

"Twenty minutes have elapsed!" Mr. Novickas said as if on cue.

"C'mon, Leo, that's the whole point of this. We are supposed to practice together and that means you learning to boost us," Aran encouraged, trying to build up Leo's confidence.

"Amplify," Leo corrected.

"Huh?"

"It's not boosting. It's called amplification."

"Boost. Amplify. Whatever. Just do it to Ania please?"

Ania stood up, took Leo's hand, and led him over to the vines. She turned to face him, looked into his eyes, and said, "It's OK, we have a bunch of people watching to keep us safe. Let's give it a shot."

Leo was caught off guard by Ania's sensitivity. He knew she

really cared about her friends, he was just used to her expressing it with sarcasm and jokes.

"OK, I guess you're right…" he said reluctantly. "Show me how you will do it."

Ania knelt down and placed her hand at the base of a vine and suddenly it began to spill down the sides of the pot. While she did this, Leo paid close attention to how her energy felt. She then pulled her hands back and looked up at him. He nodded and stepped back a couple paces and glanced down at his hands. A moment later, they were encased in amber armor with spirals and swirls embedded throughout it.

"Cool…" Ania said with a bit of awe.

"What is that?" Aran asked from over Leo's shoulder, startling him and the armor disappeared.

"I'll explain later," Leo said quickly, then he leaned over and placed his hands on Ania's back.

"Ready?" she asked and Leo nodded. He aligned all of his energy to her pattern and then started to feed it to her little by little.

Ania felt a tingling in her back and her heart began to beat faster. She reached down and placed her hands back on the vines. Not used to the increased power of her abilities, the energy rushed out of her and the vines erupted from the planters. Roots cracked the sides and spread across the wall. Leaves as large as dinner plates unfurled as the vines blanketed the floor. The sensation for Ania was at once overwhelming and exhilarating. She began to laugh uncontrollably and this caused the vines to spread even more rapidly, with the first tendrils reaching the teachers on the other side of the room.

"ANIA! Remember your control!" one of the teachers Leo didn't recognize called out.

The vines' spread slowed and the group watched excitedly as Ania thickened the coverage over the floor. Soon, they could only see small bare patches here and there, with the rest of the floor covered with a thick carpet of rope-like vines.

"That felt amazing!" Ania said excitedly as she lifted her hands from the base of the vines that had widened to the size of a small tree.

"Wait a moment," Mr. Novickas said softly right next to Leo's ear and placed his hands over Leo's. "Don't disconnect from her just yet. You need to reclaim your energy slowly. Focus on the difference between your energies so you don't accidentally pull in some of hers."

Leo wasn't really surprised by Mr. Novickas suddenly being next to him. In fact, he kind of expected it and felt bolstered by his presence. Leo took a deep breath, closed his eyes, and started to draw in his energy. Ania let out a small cry of discomfort and Leo's anxiety spiked.

"That's normal for the first time being amplified," Mr. Novickas said soothingly. "It feels like something is draining out of her, but think of her being an overfilled water balloon and you are letting a little bit of pressure out so it doesn't burst."

Leo refocused and continued to pull his energy in and soon he sensed something nearing that was familiar to him, but not his. Taking the last little bit of his energy back, he opened his eyes and looked up at Mr. Novickas. He saw a big grin and was filled with pride as Mr. Novickas stood up and walked back to the other teachers.

Ania, Leo, and Aran rejoined Stella and Meimei to see how progress was going on the water glasses. They saw that Stella had managed to create five narrow, separate streams and managed to fill the glasses up to about half way.

"How much time do we have left?" Aran called out, pacing and staring at the glasses.

"Ten minutes!" was the response.

Clearly this just stressed Aran out even more because the pacing increased and he started to run his hands through his hair over and over. The minutes ticked by and the jitteriness of the group increased, especially when "FIVE MINUTES!" was called out and the glasses still had a little ways to go. Despite all the fidgeting and grumbling from her friends, Stella didn't break her concentration and the streams remained steady.

Finally, just as "ONE MINUTE!" was called out, Stella leaned back and said, "There. Done."

Each of the kids carefully picked up their glasses and then they all lined up at the edge of the vines. Looking at each other, Meimei nodded and they all walked carefully, making sure they placed their foot in the center of a leaf with each step. They felt each second tick by and struggled against the urge to start running across.

"Thirty seconds!" Mr. Novickas called out as they reached the half-way point and a couple of them wobbled a bit, placing their hands over their glasses. They continued to make steady progress and, near the other side, Aran suddenly got his right foot hooked on a thick vine. He gasped as he began to fall and lost his grip on the glass of water. He caught himself and looked up quickly to see the glass hovering in the air and the water quickly flying back into it.

"Get up!" Meimei said urgently and Aran jumped to his feet, gripping the glass firmly.

As they took their final steps off the vines, they looked over to Mr. Novickas and he said simply, "Ten seconds over." All of their shoulders slumped with the thought they would have to repeat the challenge.

"Not too shabby for their first time!" one of the other teachers said cheerfully.

"Indeed," Mr. Novickas agreed with a satisfied look on his face.

"Good enough to not repeat it?" Ania asked with a bit of hope in her voice.

"I suppose so…" Mr. Novickas answered and the group brightened, grinning at each other. "BUT, you'll need to help us clean up a bit."

"Deal!" Aran said quickly and everyone chuckled.

The group fanned out around the room working on breaking apart the vines and returning the water to the tank. Without a role, Leo watched from the side and marveled at how skilled the teachers were with their abilities. He also felt a swell of emotion seeing his friends there with him. Up to this point, everything he had been studying felt so solitary and working together made him feel more connected to them than ever.

"Alright! Bring it in!" Mr. Novickas called out and they gathered in the center of the cavern.

"Let's do a little debrief," he continued. "You did really well for your first challenge together. That one was pretty simple, but it…"

"Simple?!" Aran blurted out. "I'm just glad I didn't have to let that alligator out of his enclosure…"

"Yes, simple. As I was saying… It was a good example of how we expect you to work together to solve each challenge. No matter what, we will be designing these challenges to play to some of your strengths as well as where you need to develop further. For example, Stella, you had never practiced managing that many complications at the same time."

"And you did marvelously," Amy said warmly.

"Indeed," Mr. Novickas agreed. "The point is, we want you to come prepared for anything. To do well in these challenges, you will need to listen carefully to your teachers and coaches throughout the week. There may be details that will be particularly important when we come together on Fridays. Now go ahead and give us some space, we need to have a conversation about next week."

The kids started to step away and then Aran caught sight of The Book of Star Born. He ran over to it and stared at the intricate pattern on its cover. Leo walked up behind him and grinned.

"Pretty cool, huh?" he said to Aran and the others gathered around too.

"Yeah…" was all Aran could respond with at first. Then he looked up at Leo and said, "What was that you did with your hands right before you boosted… I mean amplified Ania?"

"Oh that? I was trying to make sure I had sensed Ania's energy right. So, I created armor with her pattern to see how it felt."

"Armor?! You can create energy armor?!" Aran asked, flabbergasted.

"So far, that's all I can really do…"

"Well, not the only thing," Ania chimed in, reminding him that he had amplified her earlier.

"I guess you're right," Leo said with a bit of a grin forming.

"What was that like?" Stella asked Ania.

"OMG… Amazing!" Ania said, suddenly more animated than they had ever seen her. "I felt soooo powerful. I could sense things in the vines down to their molecular level. They responded to me so easily, I barely had to think about it…" Then her expression shifted to something darker.

"What's up?" Meimei asked with concern.

"I'm just remembering the feeling when Leo had to take the energy back. As amazing as it was to have all that power… Losing it felt really bad. The only way I can describe it was that I felt like I was shrinking… Even now, I still miss the feeling of all that energy coursing through me."

This caused the group to grow quiet, processing what Ania had shared. Finally, Leo broke the silence and asked Stella, "What's a complication?"

"Oh! That is how many things you are controlling at the same time. It is a really nerdy term, I think it has something to do with watches," she answered brightly.

"Is it just me who's starving right now?" Aran said, clearly not paying attention to the conversation.

"That I can help with," Leo said confidently and he reached into his backpack, pulling out two handfuls of granola bars.

"Woah! Why are you carrying all that food?" Aran asked.

"What can I say? Boosting is hard work," Leo said with a wink.

"Alright, kids! Time to pack up!" they heard Amy call over to them and they waved an acknowledgement.

"Oh, real quick," Leo said urgently. "We need to think about what to do for Caroline's birthday. It's gotta be good, I feel like we dodged a bullet today."

"Don't worry, I have the perfect idea," Aran said confidently.

"A Zoso t-shirt is not the perfect idea," Ania said, glaring at him.

"To you, maybe," Aran retorted.

"I think I have an idea," Meimei interjected and turned to Ania and Aran. "It's not a t-shirt."

The group continued to rib each other as they grabbed their stuff and started up the stairs from the cavern.

When Leo arrived at the cavern on Monday afternoon, he noticed it had been transformed again. All the equipment from Friday was gone and everything was back the way it had been before. Then he saw Mr. Novickas sitting by the desk and shelves, reading a paperback book. Leo walked over and set his backpack by the desk. Mr. Novickas looked up and gestured to the Book of Star Born saying, "Time to get reading. Let's see what the book thinks you need to work on next."

Leo sat down in the hard wooden chair and opened the book. The pages turned rapidly and then settled where he last read about sensing energy patterns. He turned the page and the familiar sight of the book writing itself unfolded again. Leo began to read before the writing reached the bottom of the page and he was immediately riveted. This was what he had been waiting for since that first discussion in Mr. Novickas' office with his parents, creating energy attacks. Diving in with both feet, he devoured section after section, rereading some in an effort to start memorizing them. As he was finishing a detailed explanation on how to form and throw an energy orb, suddenly a large hand blocked his view. Blinking several times and looking up, he saw Mr. Novickas staring at him with a raised eyebrow.

"Lemme guess, you were reading about energy orbs," Mr. Novickas said.

"How'd you know?"

"Well, you've been reading for over an hour and a half and you didn't even hear me when I tried to get your attention while sitting right next to you. I figured it must be something like that. It's the first really cool thing for a new Star Born to practice because it is in every comic book or manga you read."

"Huh… Makes sense…" Leo said as his eyes began to drift back to the book in his eagerness to read more.

"Nope! Reading time is over!" Mr. Novickas quipped, turning Leo's chair away from the desk. "Let's go do some target practice."

This was probably the only thing Mr. Novickas could have said for Leo to willingly walk away from the book and they walked together to the opposite side of the cavern.

"Give me a hand with these," he said to Leo and gestured to the three large targets along the wall. They moved each one in turn to the center of the cavern, setting them in a small semi-circle, and then they took a few steps away to face them.

"OK, show me what you've got," Mr. Novickas said matter-of-factly.

Leo took a deep breath and recalled some of the guidance from a section he read multiple times:

Just as you pass energy into another vessel when amplifying an Earth Born, to create an energy orb you will need to create the vessel you are filling. It is easier to start small and then increase the size of your vessel with practice.

Leo then looked down at his hand and imagined a marble sitting in the center of his palm. Focusing intently, he could actually feel the smooth surface of the marble, even though he could not see it. Then, just as he had done with Ania a few days ago, he passed some of his energy into the marble and he watched it suddenly turn turquoise. Then it turned quickly to white before it expanded slightly and dissipated into the air.

"Good, but too much energy. Fill it more slowly and focus on detailed control," Mr. Novickas coached.

Leo had already figured this out based on what he had read and he formed another marble immediately. Then he filled it as slowly as he could and saw his energy fill the small orb over the course of several seconds. When he felt a crackle of electricity on the surface, he abruptly stopped adding energy and stared at his first energy orb with awe.

"Are you just going to stand there and admire it all afternoon or do you want to throw it?" Mr. Novickas joked.

"Oh… yeah," Leo responded sheepishly. Then he set himself, cocked his arm, and threw the marble at the center target. It flew through the air much more quickly than he expected and erupted on the top right corner of the target, leaving a small singe mark.

"We're gunna have to work on your aim," Mr. Novickas needled.

"Hey, first energy orb here. Cut me some slack," Leo bantered back.

"Yeah, yeah… Everyone wants a trophy…" Mr. Novickas grumbled playfully. "Do that a few more times and see if you can get the hang of it. Ultimately, you should feel comfortable form-ing the orb without having to focus so much of your attention on it. That is going to take a lot of practice and the first step is to be able to form a sphere consistently without over-filling it."

Leo spent the next half hour forming marble-sized energy orbs and, when not breaking them, throwing them at the targets. After a run of about ten orbs where none broke and he started hitting the actual targets instead of the edges, Mr. Novickas asked him to stop and take a break.

"OK, looking pretty good there," he said encouragingly. "How are you feeling?"

"Great!" Leo said quickly before realizing he was being asked for a more thorough assessment. "Well… It's coming much more easily for me with the repetition. It's still taking a lot of focus to not overfill them."

"I can see that, but I need to know how you're feeling," Mr. Novickas prodded.

Taking a moment, Leo stepped out of his thoughts and just felt the sensations in his body. He realized that his hands were trembling slightly and he was feeling a bit light headed. He had thought that was just the excitement, but he now realized how drained he felt. He teetered a bit and Mr. Novickas steadied him, then handed him an apple.

"Let's go sit down so you can eat that and we can talk," he instructed, guiding Leo carefully back to the desk. When they were settled, he continued, "This is when it becomes really important to be in touch with your body and how you are feeling overall. Initiating energy attacks will drain you and, the longer you keep it up, the more dangerous it can be. Think of it this way, when you amplify someone, you get to take some of the energy back eventually. When you are making armor, you are shifting energy around your body and not releasing it. But when you initiate an attack, you are drawing down your reserves and the only way to replenish them is to eat or sleep. When you get wrapped up in the moment, it can have dire consequences. A Star Born without energy won't survive."

Leo absorbed the gravity of those last words while finishing up the apple, already starting to feel better. Seeing that Leo was taking his guidance seriously, Mr. Novickas nodded and said, "That's enough for today. Make sure you eat something before you get here tomorrow and bring more snacks just in case."

"Dude! Do you know how much food I have in my backpack right now?!" Leo countered, opening it to show Mr. Novickas.

"Uh… wow… Ok, you have enough snacks. What are you

doing walking around with that much food? Your backpack must weigh a ton!"

"You have no idea, I think both of my parents have been stuffing it with food and I can't get through it fast enough. I tried to hide it in my room, but they must be sneaking in when I am sleeping to replenish it."

"Well, you will go through it much more quickly now, so it'll get lighter," Mr. Novickas reassured him and Leo looked at him with fake skepticism as he started to leave.

⤴

For the next few days, Mr. Novickas and Leo worked together to refine his control and grow the size of his energy orbs. By the end of practice on Thursday, he was throwing orange-sized balls at the targets and consistently hitting them from much further away. Leo had never been much of a baseball player, but he reckoned that he would be a pretty good pitcher by the time he finished this period of training.

The next day, the group assembled again for their Friday training session and the set up was the same as the prior week. However, this time, there was also a large table and just enough chairs for each of them in the middle of the room. Assuming they were meant to sit at the table, they all picked a spot and sat down without a break in their conversation. A few minutes later, Mr. Novickas appeared at the entrance and walked straight over to them. He then placed a jigsaw puzzle box on the table and jumped immediately into their instructions.

"You all need to complete this jigsaw puzzle in the next two hours under the following conditions. First, you can't touch the pieces with any part of your bodies. Second, all of you need to participate and use your abilities in some way. Third, the puzzle cannot be damaged in any way. Finally, we are being firm on the timer and there will be no grace period. If you don't complete it in two hours, you will do this again next Friday. Does everyone understand?"

Each of them nodded, feeling confident.

"Very well, your time starts now."

Stella immediately reached for the box, but was startled when she heard Mr. Novickas snap, "I said you can't touch the puzzle."

"Not even the box?" Ania asked in honest confusion.

"You all nodded when I asked if you understood the challenge," Mr. Novickas answered cheerily.

The next two hours unfolded with periods of deep frustration and then outright hilarity. It took the group at least five minutes to just open the box and dump out the pieces onto the table. They quickly realized that Meimei was their best asset for this challenge since she was able to levitate the box and lift the lid off eventually without any ripping.

Then they began to follow basic puzzle strategies like flipping all the pieces and spreading them out on the table as well as organizing all of the edge pieces. This turned out to be one of the funniest activities because, while Meimei was still able to help the most, Aran enlisted the help of two small parakeets to do a lot of flipping. It was hard for the rest of them to not just sit back and giggle while watching the birds hop all over the table.

Stella and Ania also found innovative ways to move pieces around and get them into the right spots. They were all really good at puzzles, so creating the picture wasn't the hard part. It was the delicate control they needed to exert. Stella created fine ice sticks that moved with the tips of her fingers and Ania found a way to use the roots of a small sapling to direct the pieces in the way she intended.

Unfortunately, none of them really needed to be amplified to do these things and Leo was largely left to focus on puzzle strategy and finding pieces for the others to move. They finished with about five minutes to spare, but it didn't feel like a victory since they hadn't met all the conditions. Resigned to doing the task over again the following week, Meimei finally let the teachers know they were finished.

"Can you please bring it over here so we can check your work?" George, Aran's teacher, answered.

The group looked over to Meimei and she furrowed her brow due to the nerves she was now feeling, but she focused on the completed puzzle. The edges started to rise, but the center stayed put and they all anxiously asked her to stop what she's doing.

"How're we gunna do this?" Stella lamented.

"Could you make another huge leaf like last week so we can slide it on?" Aran asked Ania.

"The leaf wouldn't be strong enough…" she responded flatly.

The mention of sliding triggered an idea for Leo and he turned to Meimei, asking her, "Could you slide the puzzle and keep it together?"

"Sure, that's pretty straightforward, but how's that going to help us?"

"It'll be clear in a moment if I get this right," he assured her.

Then Leo recalled how Mr. Novickas described Maranda's armor. He said it was flat and angular, which made Leo wonder if he could shape his armor to mimic her pattern without having felt it before. He took his knowledge of energy patterns from sensing his parents, friends, and even the teachers to construct what he thought would work. Then he powered up the armor and golden panes erupted, encompassing his arms and legs. His friends stared at him, mouths agape, while he removed the armor from his legs and reformed the armor around his arms into a large flat surface between his hands. He then placed it next to the edge of the table where they had been working.

Realizing it was her turn, Meimei slid the puzzle onto Leo's armor. Then, they all followed Leo as he made his way carefully to the teachers. George stood up to inspect the puzzle and the group waited for his verdict.

"Looks good!" he said finally. Then he held up his hand for a high-five and Leo looked down, unable to figure out how to respond.

"I guess you have your hands full," he said, winking at Leo.

The next couple of weeks felt like a whirlwind to Leo and his friends. Not only did they have their next round of big projects to complete for school, but each of their training regimens had intensified. Mr. Novickas combined what Leo had been practicing and set up scenarios where he had to manage his armor and attacks at the same time. Barrages of attacks persisted until Leo could disable each machine by hitting targets next to them. As the sessions proceeded Leo became much more skilled, but he still got injured regularly and each practice often ended with Mr. Novickas healing him.

While the pace of their learning increased dramatically, their next Friday challenge was significantly harder. They were tasked with retrieving a flag that was protected with a variety of defenses, each requiring them to combine their abilities to pass. The first time, they tried to complete it by sheer brute force with Leo amplifying their abilities. When this didn't work, they tried a strategy of splitting up into two smaller teams, which also failed spectacularly. It took them another two tries the following week to just barely solve it and it was largely thanks to some new techniques Meimei and Stella had just learned that week.

That night, when they were all home and winding down, Leo's mind started wandering as he watched a movie with his parents. He registered the characters starting to sing happy birthday and he was suddenly struck with panic because of the realization that tomorrow was Caroline's birthday. He leapt to his feet on the couch and vaulted over the back, making a beeline for his phone upstairs. His parents looked at each other in confusion, then shrugged and continued with the movie.

"Meimei! Tomorrow is Caroline's birthday, please tell me you did actually plan something!" Leo frantically typed out to the group chat. Then he paced back and forth waiting for her to write back. After a few minutes without a reply, his anxiety picked up a bit further and he began to hop onto his bed, then off, then back on, over and over again. Finally, when his muscles burned with exertion, he heard the soft vibration sound come from his phone and he grabbed it off the end of his bed. However, it wasn't Meimei who responded, it was Caroline.

"Very funny, Leo," she wrote. Then she sent a gif of a famous actress rolling her eyes.

Leo was frozen, staring at his phone screen, heart racing and unable to reply. How could he have been so careless as to not check which group chat he was writing to? He tried to think of what to say, but his mind was just filled with, "Oh no, oh no, oh no…"

Three dots appeared on screen, showing that Caroline was writing again and Leo threw the phone on his bed as if it was suddenly hot and burning his hands. Then he started to back up until he was wedged between the wall and his dresser, sinking to his knees and covering his face with his hands.

His phone vibrated again, but he stayed huddled, unwilling to see what Caroline wrote. Then his phone vibrated several more times with a slight lull before suddenly erupting with messages. Curiosity overcoming deep guilt and embarrassment, Leo slowly went back to his phone and unlocked it as it continued to buzz. He saw there were now 32 unread messages and he clicked on the icon and scrolled back up to where he left off.

"Wow, Leo, you're actually holding the joke this time! Didn't think you had it in you. I am actually curious what you guys have planned for tomorrow since you said it was going to be so good," Caroline had written.

Then, Leo saw the rest of his friends had jumped in to cover his tracks.

"Right?!" Aran had chimed in.

"Never thought I would see the day," Ania wrote.

"What ARE we doing," Stella asked, inserting a thinking emoji at the end.

Meimei then joined the conversation with, "Don't give Leo any more high-fives or his head is going to explode." Then added, "Seriously though, I was going to text everyone earlier, but my mom surprised us with a trip to her friend's ramen restaurant and I just got back. Meet at my place tomorrow. 1:00 pm and don't be late!"

"Got it!" Stella wrote back first followed by thumbs up from Aran and Ania.

"Are you going to tell me what we're doing?" Caroline wrote, then sent another gif of a cartoon character running around a room searching for something.

"Nope, it's still a surprise," Meimei said.

Caroline just sent another gif of a profoundly disappointed

toddler collapsing on the sidewalk and the rest of the group started sending more gifs to each other.

As Leo read through all the messages, his heart rate slowly decreased and he finally decided to jump back in after Aran sent a gif of a rock band shooting off fireworks from the ends of their guitars.

"Oh yeah, tomorrow at 1:00 pm. How could I have forgotten?" he wrote with a wink.

"Duuuude! Well played!" Aran wrote.

"OK, that was legit," Meimei acknowledged and she sent a message just to him saying, "That was close!"

Leo responded with a gif of a famous actress nodding her head quickly with wide eyes and then they jumped back over to the group conversation until one by one their parents told them to get off their phones.

❧

The next day, they all arrived at Meimei's house and Caroline was so excited that she could barely hold still. Aran came over to Leo soon after he arrived to ask him if he meant to send the text that started everything the night before and Leo's eyes went wide and he just shook his head quickly. This just made Aran laugh loudly.

Meimei then let her parents know they were heading out and led them down the street. They all continued to chat as usual, except for Caroline who was glancing around constantly to see if she noticed anything amiss. Finally, Meimei signaled them to stop in front of Stella's house.

"OK, we're here!" she said brightly.

"Stella's house? You had us meet at your place to go to Stella's house?" Caroline asked in confusion.

"Of course, I had to throw you off the trail," Meimei said with a sly grin.

"Wait, is this what I think it is?" Caroline asked, clearly getting even more excited.

"I think so," Stella said warmly. "My mom set up her studio for us. We can use it for the rest of the day. You can use anything in there!"

Caroline started to hop up and down, excited feelings radiated off of her so much that Leo couldn't help but smile and feel giddy too. Artwork had always been Caroline's happy place and it dawned on Leo why Meimei had been so confident in her idea. They all walked around the side of the house and over to the studio in the backyard. Jennifer was waiting for them and everyone gathered around.

"OK, I have stuff for ceramics, painting, drawing, beading, and I could also scrounge up a few other things if you're looking for something else," she said as the kids walked in. Leo went straight for the pottery wheel and started to get set up. Meimei and Ania walked over to a couple of canvases on easels in the corner. Stella and Aran went over to the shelves and picked out several sets of charcoals and oil pastels. Caroline headed over towards Leo and picked out a large plate that Jennifer had sitting on a shelf above the wheel.

"Could I glaze this?" she asked Jennifer.

"Sure! I have been wondering what I wanted to do with that for a while anyway."

The group got to work and the studio was filled with idle chatter. Occasionally, each of them took breaks from their work to check out what the others were doing or to get one of the snacks Jennifer had set out, except for Caroline. It was as if she was in a blissed out trance, creating an intricate pattern filling the entire plate with a careful selection of colors and fine brushes.

As it got later, many of them finished up what they were working on and they gradually gathered around Caroline, marveling at what she was creating. They had grown to expect amazing artwork from her, but this had to be one of the most impressive things they had ever seen her create. She didn't even notice the group surrounding her, until she put the finishing touches on the plate and leaned back in satisfaction.

"Nice work…" Stella said from Caroline's right shoulder, startling her.

"Oh! Uh… Thanks!" she replied as if slowly returning to the world.

"Hey everyone! It's getting kinda late now, you should wrap it up soon," Jennifer said from the doorway.

"I think we're all done now," Meimei confirmed.

"Oh great!" Jennifer said as she came in to survey everything they had been working on. "Don't worry about taking your pieces home today," she said to them. "I will let Stella know when they are ready for you to pick up. Leo and Caroline, I can fire your stuff in the kiln tomorrow."

The group all started to file out of the studio when Jennifer's eyes settled on the piece Caroline had been working on and they went wide with recognition.

"Caroline?" Jennifer said to get her attention. "How did you come up with this design?"

Leo sensed a spike in tension and anxiety from Jennifer and he turned to see what was going on.

"You know… It's something I remembered seeing recently. I think it was in a book or something we got from my grandma's house. I'm not sure if it is exactly the same, but it kinda feels right."

Jennifer just nodded and Leo felt her slowly relax before saying, "That makes sense, I hear she collected a lot of stuff."

"You can say that again!" Caroline affirmed. "Her house was full of stuff. Some rooms you couldn't even get into without moving some boxes. Her art books were amazing though. I can still sit for hours just looking through them."

"I know exactly what you mean," Jennifer said warmly.

On that note, the kids disbursed, satisfied that Caroline had a great birthday.

The next week, everyone waited to hear what Caroline's abilities were, but there was no news by the time they gathered for their next Friday challenge. Everyone was clearly distracted and they struggled with even basic coordination of their abilities as they tried to help a rat navigate a maze filled with various deadly obstacles. When the rat was almost cut in half by a swinging blade, Mr. Novickas stopped the challenge and walked over to the group.

"What is going on with you all?" he asked, clearly very frustrated. When nobody even looked at him, let alone provided an answer, he turned to Leo with a questioning look.

"Well, Mr. Star Born? Care to shed some light on this?" he asked.

Leo hesitated briefly and finally decided to share what they had been whispering to each other all week long.

"We are wondering why we haven't heard anything about Caroline's abilities," he said, and Mr. Novickas' face immediately softened a bit.

"That's why you all almost got this poor guy killed three times?" he said to them as he picked up the rat and they all nodded.

"OK, listen," he said, then took a deep breath. "I really shouldn't be telling you all any of this, but we haven't detected any abilities from Caroline yet. This happens from time to time and you all know it can take a while longer for some people's abilities to express themselves. At this point, if she has any abilities, they are extremely weak and won't likely ever be strong enough to begin her training."

He waited a little to let his comments sink in before he continued, "I know you're probably upset with this news because of how close she is to you. I'm sorry to be the one to share it with you, too. Let's skip the rest of today's session and we will reconvene next week."

As he walked away from them, Ania sank to the floor and crossed her legs. Then she looked up at the rest of the group and said, "Sit down so we can talk about this!"

"This sucks…" Aran said dejectedly and Leo could feel the rest of them were in the same defeated state. However, he was filled with defiance.

"We have to tell her," he said with intensity.

"Tell her what?" Meimei asked, clearly not following his line of thought.

"Everything. The tribe, our abilities, the training. Ev-er-y-thing."

"We were forbidden to speak to anyone not in the tribe, Leo. You know that!" Stella said with a mix of surprise and fear.

"I know and I don't care. She is one of our best friends and we have been keeping the biggest secret from her. She should know."

"That is crazy…" Meimei said, shaking her head.

"I agree," Ania said.

"Thank you! Now, how can we convince Leo this is a bad idea?" Meimei asked, staring up at the ceiling.

"No, I agree with Leo," Ania clarified.

"You do?" Leo asked, confused that someone was actually taking his side.

"Yeah, I do. I think that rule is dumb. There are people outside the tribe who can be trusted. You can't just assume everyone is bad and we know how good Caroline is."

"I agree too," Aran said, emboldened by the strong stand Leo was taking.

"Guys! There are rules for a reason!" Meimei pushed back.

"Yup and we are going to break this rule for a good reason," Leo retorted.

"I think I am in too," Stella said softly and Meimei glared at her intensely.

"OK, I think that settles it. Let's go," Leo said.

"You're going to tell her now?!" Meimei asked, shifting her gaze from Leo to the teachers across the cavern.

"No." Leo answered as if she said something crazy. "We gotta figure out how to tell her. This news nearly made my head explode when I first heard it. We all had people tell us who have experience doing it. We need to figure out the right way to tell Caroline."

This seemed to placate Meimei for the time being, but Leo could sense she was still deeply uncomfortable with the idea. He stood up and walked over to grab his backpack, so the others followed suit. Then they all left the cavern together and quietly made their way back to their homes.

᰾

Over the next several weeks, training intensity continued to ratchet up. Mr. Novickas and the other teachers clearly felt they should get over the news about Caroline quickly, but they still took opportunities to share ideas on how to tell her. Fortunately, the group was able to regain their focus and they made steady progress with the Friday challenges.

On a Wednesday after school, Leo made his way slowly to the bookshop, feeling the sun warm his skin, and he tried to sense if more freckles were forming on his face. When he finally arrived and made his way down to the cavern, he felt something familiar. Meimei was there, too. He was absolutely sure of it, her pattern had become very familiar to him. He peered into the cavern carefully and saw Mr. Novickas and Meimei standing in the middle of the room surrounded by plastic bins and chatting.

"Is it safe to come in?" he called from the stairs.

"For now!" Mr. Novickas said brightly and Leo dropped his bag as he walked to join them.

"Hey," he said to Meimei as he reached them and she responded with the same flat greeting. Things were not great between them since he convinced the group they needed to tell Caroline and there was now a consistent iciness to their interactions.

"So what're you having us do today? Fight each other?" Leo asked jokingly.

"Yup!" Mr. Novickas answered simply.

"Wait, what?" Leo said, caught off guard.

"You guessed right. You are going to fight each other. You can use whatever tools or techniques you have learned. I will be here to make sure nobody gets hurt."

"I'm not going to fight my friend," Leo said and crossed his arms.

"I'm game!" Meimei said brightly and Leo looked at her with surprise and hurt.

"Look, something's going on between the two of you," Mr. Novickas said. "All of the teachers can see it when you're working together on Fridays and it is affecting how well you can learn the lessons we are teaching you. Enough is enough. You're going to work this out of your system. Now go get ready."

Leo felt flushed with anger and resentment, but he knew this would not serve him well in a battle with an increasingly powerful Physic like Meimei. So, he walked to the far end of the cavern, began a series of calming exercises, and then completed a quick meditation that he learned recently to increase the power of his attacks .

"Ready?" Mr. Novickas looked to Meimei and several sharp metal discs rose up from the bins and started to orbit around her.

"I'll take that as a yes," he said seriously. "Leo? You ready over there?"

"Yup!" he called back and his arms and legs were immediately enveloped with flowing armor.

"OK, give me a second to get out of the way and then I'll say "go." If you hear me say "stop," you cease the fight immediately." Then Mr. Novickas walked over to the bookcases, turned around, and yelled, "GO!"

Meimei immediately launched the spinning discs at a frighteningly fast speed at Leo and he moved his left arm to block them. However, he had put a large amount of energy into his armor and, when the discs reached him, the metal began to melt. He heard the hiss of metal droplets hitting the cold cavern walls behind him and quickly dialed it down a few notches.

Meimei didn't wait for him to reset before she launched another volley at him consisting of old bicycle gears, screws, and sections of metal pipe. He batted the objects away towards the sides of the room, feeling the rapid impacts against his armor and realizing just how hard it was going to be to beat her. The next attack began and this time he could see the air was full of objects that were all headed toward where he was standing

He started to dart in an unpredictable pattern around the room, which required Meimei to switch the directions of the projectiles and slow them down significantly. This bought him a little time to consider what he should do when he heard Mr. Novickas yell, "LEO! Stop dancing and fight already!"

Realizing there was no way around it, Leo began to aim the objects he parried away directly back at Meimei and she had to drop to the floor as two full soup cans flew through the spot she was just occupying. He then launched an energy orb at her that scorched the bottom of her ponytail. She grunted with frustration and then redoubled her attacks, rapidly picking materials and launching them in different ways at Leo. Banking them off walls and the ceiling. Even rolling them across the floor.

Leo struggled to keep up with the attacks and focused all of his attention on trying to sense what Meimei would do next. He could feel her pattern shifting as she adjusted to the different materials she was manipulating. It was as if she could understand the atomic make-up of each item and used that knowledge to make it become the most effective weapon possible. Without noticing, he bended his armor's energy into a form that best addressed her abilities. He found a way to make it repel materials based on how she was sensing them, but she was adjusting so quickly he was constantly scrambling to avoid the impact of a large piece of wood, plastic, or metal before it collided with his head.

Leo hoped she would run out of ammunition soon, since the

battle felt like it had been one of the longest he had ever experienced. However, he then realized that she could continue to manipulate all the objects that had already been launched at him before. It was as if she had a never ending supply and he knew he had to figure out a way to penetrate the curtain of objects that surrounded her soon or he would lose badly.

Shifting his armor around his body as he weaved his way around the room and launched energy orbs, he saw that he was keeping her on her toes. He also noticed she was formulating a new strategy and knew it was now or never. So, he decided to barrel directly at her like a juggernaut. Focusing intensely on her, he saw her eyes narrow and nostrils flare and it dawned on him right away that he made a grave error as a wave of debris rolled toward him.

He felt the intensity of the moment and knew the only safe spot in the room was right behind her. As a pencil lodged in his shoulder and he felt the spike of pain, he saw the tips of his fingers begin to disintegrate. In the next moment, everything went black and several seconds went by before light flooded his eyes again and he was looking at Meimei's back. He heard Mr. Novickas yell, "STOP!" before he threw up and passed out.

When he came to, Meimei and Mr. Novickas were looking down on him and he felt the cold floor of the cavern on his back. Then he heard Mr. Novickas say to Meimei, "I think he's awake."

"You OK?" Meimei said to Leo and he heard the genuine concern in her voice.

"I think so…" he replied, wiggling his fingers and toes. Then, turning his head to look around, he saw the floor of the cavern was covered in debris. He remembered the pencil lodged in his shoulder and rubbed the spot, but it was no longer there.

"Already healed that," Mr. Novickas said, clearly still worried.

Leo began to sit up and they made room for him. He scanned

his arms and legs, patted his chest and back, then reached up to the ceiling for a big stretch to get his blood moving as he tried to focus his muddled thoughts.

"Um… How did I end up over here?" he asked them.

"You teleported. Did the book teach you to do that?" Mr. Novickas probed.

"No… I'm not entirely sure how I did it…" Leo said as he relived the vivid memories of the moments right before he disappeared.

"How is this possible?" Mr. Novickas wondered aloud. "I've never seen or heard of a Star Born doing anything like that…"

"Yeah, you disintegrated right in front of me…" Meimei said with a shaky voice. "I'm so sorry, I didn't hold anything back… I mean, I was so angry… I can't believe I put you in that much danger."

The sorrow radiating off Meimei touched Leo deeply and he reached out to hold her hand. He looked right into her eyes and said, "Friends fight sometimes, it's OK." Meimei nodded in response, clearly holding back tears.

"Leo, I need you to think about how you were able to do that. This is really important," Mr. Novickas said insistently.

Leo stood up and started walking around the room, replaying each step of the battle in his head. When he reached the spot where he disintegrated, it was as if he had a connection to this particular spot and an idea popped into his head.

"I think it has something to do with energy bending," he said as he turned towards Mr. Novickas.

"Tell me more."

"Meimei was coming so hard at me and I was struggling to anticipate her moves. I thought that if I bent my energy in a way to counter her, that I would be able to keep up better."

"Yes, I remember when your armor shifted."

"Right, so when I did that, I could sense her connection to every object she manipulated. I mean, that's amazing, Meimei!"

"You could sense that? How?" Meimei asked, even though she already knew most of the answer.

"Let's not go down that path right now," Mr. Novickas said, guiding the conversation back to what he wanted to know. "Leo, what does this have to do with this new ability to teleport?"

The intensity in Mr. Novickas' voice made Leo nervous. Something told him this was an important moment and he needed to be very careful with what he said next. He trusted Mr. Novickas completely, but he had a feeling that he should steer the conversation away from the potential discovery of a new, important ability. A wave of guilt washed over him, because he knew that he was about to start lying to someone he deeply respected and he wasn't exactly sure why.

"What I am trying to say is that I think I connected with Meimei's power. Maybe I was borrowing it or something? I mean, it doesn't make sense that I could do that without any training otherwise," he said.

Mr. Novickas grew quiet for a moment and then started the mumbling that Leo knew signaled intense thinking was happening. Meimei shot a questioning look at Leo and he just gave her a quiet nod to let her know this was normal.

"That actually makes a lot of sense," Mr. Novickas replied finally, clearly relieved, and Leo's guilt only intensified. "Let's try to avoid doing that again for now. Those types of abilities take a lot of work to master and are very dangerous. One thing is for sure, though, you have gone beyond my knowledge and experience. It's time for me to send for your new teacher."

9

GABRIEL

WHEN LEO ARRIVED at the cavern the next day, Mr. Novickas was nowhere to be seen. He walked over to the Book of Star Born and next to it was a note in familiar chicken scratch handwriting that said:

> Our practice sessions are canceled going forward.
> You will pick up with those again when your
> new teacher arrives in a couple weeks. In the
> meantime, you are to still come here every day and
> study. You may not try any of the more advanced
> techniques without proper supervision. If you
> need anything, come up to the store and find me.

"Well, that's just great…" Leo said to himself as he dropped down heavily into the chair. He had been making so much progress and was looking forward to learning more. Everything felt like it was clicking into place and he understood more about himself than ever before. In fact, he had come to the realization that starting his training was the best thing that ever happened to him. Now he felt abandoned and alone in a secret underground cave.

Not interested in starting a pity party for himself, he decided to just get on with studying. Placing his hand on the book, it seemed to light up more brightly than usual and the pages turned furiously until well over half the book had gone by. Leo was nowhere near this far in the book and he turned a few pages back to see the pages were covered with text and drawings. From prior experience, he knew the book was telling him he was ready for something way more advanced and he wasn't surprised to see the heading on the page the book had turned to:

Traveling

It is a misconception to think that Star Borns are able to teleport, when in actuality they are traveling along the energy Earth Borns or other Star Borns are emitting. A Star Born aligns their pattern with the energy they are traveling along and converts their body to that energy. To do this safely, the traveler must be able to maintain focus on their end point as well as a deep connection to their own unique pattern to reconstruct their body. Errors or lack of focus can lead to catastrophic results.

"Maybe this isn't going to be so bad after all," he thought, and he spent the rest of the afternoon reading the section very carefully. It wasn't very long, just about five pages, but most of the sections he had been studying were at least twenty pages. In fact, the basic meditation section was at least forty pages. However, while this section was short, it was packed with very technical information and it took several read-throughs for him to even understand some of the concepts it was explaining. By the time he felt like it was all starting to make sense, his eyes felt dry, he had a crick in his neck, and he realized it was time to head home.

As he walked out the back door of the shop, he wondered how he was going to be able to practice traveling while keeping it a secret. His mind was mush from hours of studying and he went on autopilot, making turns and walking down the familiar streets of the town. Finally, he stopped and became aware that he was standing in front of a door, but it wasn't the one to his house. Instead, he found himself at Meimei's and his finger had already rung the doorbell.

Emily answered the door and looked at Leo with confusion.

"Hi," he said simply to her.

"Hey there, Leo, it's kinda late to stop by. Shouldn't you be home having dinner?"

"Yeah… I just finished practice and was walking home," he said, still not sure why he guided himself there. Then the lightning bolt hit him and he realized why he subconsciously made his diversion. "Could I speak to Meimei real quick? I promise it won't be long."

"Uh… I guess so…" Emily agreed, hesitantly and Leo could sense feelings of concern emanating from her. Then she took a step back and called for Meimei. A minute later, she appeared at the door and Leo could tell immediately that she had been crying.

"You OK?" he asked and she just shook her head as another tear ran down her cheek.

"Is this about yesterday?" he probed gently.

"Mmhmm…" was all she could get out.

"You're still beating yourself up," he said softly as he now understood all the confused emotions he was feeling coming from her.

"I disintegrated you with my abilities, Leo!" she said with fresh tears appearing. "I know you think you did it, but my teacher and Mr. Novickas explained it to me during my training today. My abilities connect to things at the atomic level and I was so focused on tearing you apart that I did it at the most fundamental level."

Then Meimei covered her face with her hands and turned to go back inside, but Leo reached out quickly to grab her shoulder.

"No, they're wrong and I know that for a fact," he said with enough conviction that it caused her to pause and put down her hands. He could still tell she wasn't convinced though.

"Listen," he continued. "It's called Traveling and the Book of Star Born taught me about it today. I actually traveled along your energy. It's really complex, but it makes a lot of sense now that I have both read about it and experienced it."

"The book told you about this?" she asked, starting to calm down and believe what he was saying.

"Yup!" he said encouragingly.

"Is that why you came over? To tell me that?"

"Well, yes, but also to ask you to help me practice it."

"Are you kidding me?!" she said, shaking her head vigorously.

"Look, I can't practice it without a partner and I already did it with you, so it makes sense that I start working with you on it. I get that you are nervous… Heck, I am too! This is just something I need to do and you're the best choice to help me with it."

"Since when did you get this way?" Meimei asked.

"What way?" Leo replied, not understanding and starting to feel a bit prickly.

"So sure of yourself. You weren't always this way before," she said thoughtfully.

"Oh… yeah…" Leo said as he ran his hand through his hair back and forth. "I think I have been feeling it grow ever since I started training."

"I like it," she said and grinned slightly, then she simply said, "OK."

"OK, what?" Leo said, not following again.

"I'll do it, but we start slow and I want to be careful."

"Agreed," Leo said excitedly and then just as quickly looked serious again. "Um… Also, I don't want Mr. Novickas or the other teachers to know about this. I have a feeling this just needs to be something our crew knows about."

Meimei furrowed her brow and stared at Leo for a moment, then said, "OK, I think I understand what you mean. Let's make a plan to start on Saturday. We can figure things out at school tomorrow."

Leo smiled widely again, it felt like Meimei was starting to return to her normal self.

"Cool, OK, I gotta get home before my parents kill me," Leo said and then called to Emily, "Sorry again for stopping by so late!"

"Where do you think you're going?" she called back. "Get in here and have some dinner. I let your parents know you're here."

Never one to pass up a dinner cooked by Emily, Leo immediately stepped back inside, dropped his backpack, and kicked off his shoes as he hurried over to the table.

⁓

That weekend, Leo and Meimei found a secluded spot in the cemetery that was overgrown with weeds and had old rusting machinery that probably hadn't moved in at least a decade. Leo spent the better part of two hours trying to replicate what happened in the cavern, but was completely unsuccessful. Over and over, he reviewed his notes from the book, but nothing happened when Meimei used her ability and he matched her pattern.

It was Meimei who figured out he was overthinking things and he needed the intensity of the moment to focus his efforts. Unfortunately, she didn't inform him of this revelation when she sent an old lawn mower hurtling towards him. Alarm rose up in him momentarily before instinct and his practice from the past couple of hours kicked in. He managed to travel out of the way right before it hit him and he found himself on a mound of gravel about twenty yards away. When he was finally done vomiting from the exertion again, he stormed over to Meimei.

"What the hell?!"

"That was great! You did it!" she said encouragingly, ignoring his anger.

"You LAUNCHED a lawn mower at me!"

"Yeah, you needed to focus and I figured there was something that we were doing in the cavern that helped you do that. Mortal peril was the missing ingredient!"

The chipper attitude and the fact that she had a point caused Leo to pause and think for a moment. Then he started pacing back and forth trying to work out how it felt when he traveled the second time and whether he would only be able to do it if his life was in danger. Finally, he walked over to his notes and flipped through them for a minute while Meimei tapped her foot impatiently. A particular phrase he wrote down made it all come into focus for him:

Think of traveling as a magnet. One end repels while the other attracts. The location you are in needs to change to the repeling end while where you want to travel becomes the attracting end.

"OK, I think I have an idea that won't get me killed," he said finally.

"Alright, what did you come up with?"

"I want you to exert yourself as much as you can. I mean lift everything that you can around you or something."

"How is that supposed to help?" she asked skeptically.

"I need your energy radiating off of you as hard as possible. I'm a noob at this and need all the help I can get."

"Alright, here goes!" she said and suddenly a mass of debris rose up around her. She even levitated an old stump with all the dirt clinging to it.

Leo felt bathed in Meimei's energy and he focused on bending his pattern so it matched exactly. Then he focused his entire mind on the spot of ground right next to her and made it feel like it was pulling him towards it. The familiar sensation of his body disintegrating wrapped around him and then suddenly he was standing next to Meimei feeling like he was going to hurl again. Meimei yelped and then everything she was levitating came crashing down, making a huge racket.

"Holy crap, Leo!" she said.

"One sec…" he said, taking some deep breaths. Meimei took a few steps back, but relaxed when she saw the color return to his face. "OK, I'm cool now."

"We better get out of here pretty quick, I bet someone is going to come and see what made all that noise," she suggested.

"Good idea," Leo agreed, and they ran out of the cemetery, parting ways at the corner.

❧

Leo and Meimei reconvened their training the following weekend and made huge progress. After a few hours in the cemetery again, Leo was able to travel without feeling sick to his stomach each time. Meimei also learned how to enable his travel by coordinating how she manipulated her energy with the timing of his jumps. Soon, they agreed they would be able to bring the rest of the crew into their secret.

After school on Monday, Leo rushed out of class waving goodbyes to his friends as he started to run down the hill to the shops. He was anxious to get back to the cavern to continue studying a section he found the week before covering an advanced technique on pattern matching. It was called "The Spider's Web" and it seemed to involve a deeply coordinated team that included multiple Earth Borns and at least one Star Born. Leo had no idea why he would ever need to use it, but it sounded so cool he wanted to nerd out on it for the afternoon.

When he arrived at the cavern, however, he wasn't surprised to sense a new visitor since it had happened so many times before. The sensation he picked up from the visitor as he descended the stairs, however, was very different from what he was used to and he immediately guessed it might be his new teacher. A prickle of excitement ran down his arms and he rushed the rest of the way down to the entrance.

As he stepped through the doorway, he saw Mr. Novickas speaking with a tall, well dressed man with completely white hair even though he seemed to be no older than his father. The other thing that Leo noticed was the man's hands seemed to be glowing with bright green energy. The hairs on the back of Leo's neck stood on end and he immediately powered up the armor around his arms. Suddenly stopping his conversation with Mr. Novickas, the man turned quickly and launched three large energy orbs directly at Leo. Crossing his arms in front of his face to take the full impact of the attacks, Leo was shoved violently back into the stairwell.

This was not Leo's first rodeo with surprise attacks. He often felt like it was Mr. Novickas' hobby. So, Leo rushed back into the cavern with two grapefruit-sized orbs charged in his hands. The well dressed man seemed ready for this and easily followed Leo's movements, but he made no attempt to power up any of his own armor yet. It was as if he was sticking out his chin and saying, "Take your best shot!" So, Leo stopped running, set himself with a wide stance, and cocked his hand behind his shoulder to throw one of the energy orbs. Instead of doing that, however, Leo dropped the ball and, just before it hit the floor, he kicked it hard at the man's left leg. Then he darted away while trying to see if he landed a blow.

The man had to quickly yank back his leg to avoid getting hit and it was clear he was caught off guard since he seemed to be teetering and trying to regain his balance. Leo took the opportunity to throw his other energy orb at this point and this was when the man finally charged up his armor.

Now clad head to toe in green spikes, the man looked like a glowing Christmas tree and Leo could see he had the guy's attention. A fierce battle erupted as they launched a constant stream of attacks at each other. The man always seemed to know where Leo would be next and nothing Leo did found its mark. It was all he could do to dive out of the way and try to regain his footing quickly enough to launch a counter.

As the battle dragged on, Leo began to feel the effects of the exertion and it got harder and harder to keep up. He saw the man stretch out the armor on his left arm into something looking like a long whip. He then swung it at Leo, wrapping it around his legs and causing him to fall over. He heard the man chuckling to himself, which pushed Leo's stubborn button hard. He wasn't sure why he did this, but he grabbed hold of the energy whip and channeled a big burst of his energy into it like running electricity into a wire.

The visitor let out a loud yelp as the burst shocked him hard and caused him to drop all of his armor. Leo's satisfaction was short-lived, however, because he saw the fury in the man's eyes and he knew the next attack was going to be brutal.

"Don't you think that's enough, Gabriel?!" Mr. Novickas called out from the side of the room and Leo saw the man's face immediately change from pure anger to a big smile.

"You always ruin all my fun, Adam," he called back and then walked over to Leo, reaching out a hand to help him up.

Frustrated and tired, Leo didn't accept the hand and pushed himself slowly to his feet, looking at Mr. Novickas and Gabriel warily. Not even noticing a potential slight, Gabriel pulled his hand back and said to Mr. Novickas, "You've done a good job with this one!"

Then he turned to Leo with a softer expression and said, "Please don't be angry. I know that wasn't the best way to meet someone for the first time. I just needed to know how much you have learned so far and that was the most efficient way. I can assure you, I have never seen a new Star Born of your age able to keep up with that kind of attack."

"You call that keeping up? You knew everything I was going to do before I did it!" Leo said in exasperation.

"Well, I have been doing this for a long time and have some practice training new Star Borns, so I guess I had a big advantage," Gabriel conceded.

"So, what do you think, Gabriel? Will you stick around for a while and train Leo?" Mr. Novickas interjected.

"He's very promising and I would like to say yes, but to be sure I need to spend the day with him tomorrow, if that would be OK."

"I have school tomorrow," Leo said, hoping to find a way out of a whole day with someone he was pretty sure he didn't like.

"Don't worry about that, Leo. I'll work it out with your parents tonight. Try to be here by 8 o'clock," Mr. Novickas said.

"Why don't you head home now and I'll see you tomorrow. Thank you again for an engaging session, I truly enjoyed it!" Gabriel said warmly to Leo.

❧

The next morning, Leo was woken up by his mom gently singing, "Good morning to you!" and gently rocking him back and forth like she did when he was little. He smiled and began to do his usual morning wake-up stretch when he felt every muscle protest as if he had run a marathon the day before. Recalling what he went through and the fact that he needed to go back for more, the smile faded from his face and he began to brood.

"What's with that sour expression?" his mom asked.

"Ugh… I can't believe I am saying this, but can I go to school today?"

"Oh, come on," she prodded him.

"I'm serious! Why can't I just train with Mr. Novickas?"

"This is a big deal, Leo. Some of the most accomplished Star Borns have trained with Gabriel."

"I don't care, the guy's a jerk."

"Hey now, we didn't raise you to form an opinion of a person like that after only one time meeting him."

"He attacked me, Mom!"

"He was assessing you. There wasn't any danger."

"Easy for you to say, you weren't the one fighting him."

"Get dressed and come downstairs for breakfast. We can give you a ride down to the shop if you like," she said, clearly ending the discussion and walking out of Leo's room.

He dragged himself out of bed and slowly dressed as he tried to warm his muscles up enough to not feel every single slight motion he made. It took him longer than it should have, but by the time he was downstairs he felt more awake and ready for the day ahead. He moved around the kitchen gathering his breakfast and then sat down next to his dad at the counter.

"So, I hear you're not too keen to go work with your new teacher today," he said with a raised eyebrow to Leo.

"I'm going to give it another shot. Mom already got to me," Leo replied, his voice dripping with resignation.

"We just want you to be excited. He is the most senior Star Born across all the tribes. He must think there is something special about you if he came all the way here to work with you."

"I get it, Dad," Leo said and then shoveled a spoonful of cereal in his mouth, hoping his parents couldn't tell how anxious he was.

When he was finally ready, he wanted to walk down to the bookshop in order to collect himself, but his parents insisted on driving. He felt the strong vibes of pride they were trying to mask and it just set him more on edge. He got lost in his thoughts and didn't become aware of his surroundings until he was standing in the doorway to the cavern. He looked around and didn't see anyone, so he walked in further. Everything seemed to be the same except the hard wooden chair he usually sat in at the desk and the big cushy chair from the reading area in the shop are sitting in the middle of the room. He walked over to them and dropped his backpack.

"Ah good! You're here!" Gabriel said from right behind him.

Leo whirled around and charged up his armor. For the first time, it covered his entire body.

"Wait a moment! That is hardly necessary!" Gabriel said with a warm smile, looking Leo up and down and nodding in acknowledgement of Leo's display of power. "There will be no battles today, it will be a completely different kind of assessment."

Leo's armor rippled and pulsed briefly before slowly receding back into his core. Then Gabriel gestured to the chairs and said, "Please, take a seat."

Gabriel took the cushy chair and Leo slowly lowered himself into the wooden one so they were seated facing each other. Gabriel then leaned forward and placed his hands on top of his knees with both palms facing up.

"Today, we will be looking inward to see what you have developed so far. You're going to place your hands on top of mine and close your eyes. I will need you to relax as much as possible and remain open throughout this assessment. There may be times that it feels uncomfortable, but let me assure you there will be no danger."

Leo's hands shook a bit as he placed them on top of Gabriel's.

"It's OK, Leo, this is a very standard activity and I have performed it countless times," Gabriel said in a reassuring voice and Leo finally began to relax.

"OK, let's begin," Gabriel said after a few moments of complete silence.

A pleasant warmth spread across Leo's skin, not unlike when Mr. Novickas healed him. Then he sensed something new inside him, Gabriel's presence. He could feel it moving around, pushing against different parts of his energy and moving them out of the way as if he was searching for something specific.

Leo was fascinated by the process at first and felt like he was beginning to understand his abilities better. When Gabriel "touched" a part of his energy, he seemed to pass on some knowledge of that to Leo. However, as Gabriel searched deeper, it began to feel uncomfortable and Leo had the sense that something was wrong.

He felt Gabriel reach out toward a part of his energy that felt like it's the center of everything. A deep sense of fear took hold of him and what had been a mostly pleasant experience now felt like a complete violation. He wanted Gabriel to stop and began to resist, but this just made Gabriel push harder as if he was hungry to reach this part of Leo.

As he felt Gabriel about to reach his prize, Leo gathered all of his strength and determination and he visualized himself pulling Gabriel out of his body. The next moment, Leo opened his eyes and gasped for breath, drawing big lungfuls of air in as quickly as possible. He looked across to Gabriel and saw sweat covering his face with parts of his perfectly coiffed hair sticking to his forehead.

"How did you…" Gabriel began to say with a hoarse voice before stopping and collecting himself for what started to feel like a really long time. Finally, he looked down at his watch and when he spoke again he was back to his charming self.

"Look at the time! We have been going for quite a while, want to grab some lunch?"

Leo just nodded warily and followed Gabriel's lead as they both rose and headed for the stairs.

"Adam tells me there is a good Japanese noodle place nearby that you and your friends like, shall we go there?"

"Uh… sure…" Leo replied noncommittally, but his stomach let out a deep growl and gave him away.

As they walked, Gabriel asked him questions about school and his friends as if he was a favorite uncle catching up after a long time apart. Slowly, Leo began to relax a bit and the deep distrust for Gabriel softened slightly. When they got to the restaurant, Gabriel looked around and threw up his hands.

"Well, you're going to have to guide me here. Despite my travels, I tend to be a bit pedestrian in my food choices," he said to Leo with a sheepish grin.

"Ok!" Leo said excitedly, completely forgetting any concerns now that he was in one of his happy places. "This restaurant serves a noodle soup called udon. You can look up at that board and choose what kind of meat you like and then they let you pick a bunch of fun things to put on top. You HAVE to get the crispy tempura flakes!"

"You're the expert, I'll follow your lead!" Gabriel replied and they jumped into the line.

When they arrived at their table, they had two trays filled with large bowls of soup and plates of fried shrimp and vegetables. After several minutes of silence while they gorged themselves, Gabriel put down his chopsticks and looked at Leo seriously.

"I'm sorry for that experience, Leo. It can be a very difficult process to understand a Star Born's abilities and you happen to be a complicated case. I mean that in a good way, so please don't be concerned."

"Complicated how?" Leo asked, curiosity getting the better of him.

"Well, most Star Borns are relatively weak. They usually can amplify an Earth Born a little bit, but are not able to try some of the advanced techniques and abilities that Adam has told me you demonstrated. Often, when we do find a stronger Star Born, they struggle to control their abilities and become a danger to themselves or their tribes."

"You're talking about Maranda."

"Indeed…she was one of the most promising students we had seen in a number of years and one of my colleagues worked very hard to help develop her control. We thought he had been successful, but it turns out our efforts were not enough and we lost two Star Borns… Did you know she was about to come to London to study with me?"

Leo shook his head.

"Losing a single member of a tribe is a tragedy. The two of them could have accomplished great things…" Gabriel said with a voice cracking slightly with emotion.

"Do you think I will be able to learn to control my abilities?" Leo asked with trepidation and Gabriel looked up with a warm smile.

"Yes. I do," he answered confidently. "I have seen enough at this point to know that staying here and working with you for a while is the right course of action. That is, of course, if you'll have me as your teacher."

This took Leo aback. He had forgotten that everything needed to be his choice and had assumed Gabriel would either choose to work with him or not. Gathering himself, he answered, "Ok, let's give it a shot."

"Excellent! Now enough with this seriousness, let's go have some fun and blow stuff up," Gabriel said gleefully.

They headed back to the cavern and spent the afternoon working on Leo's attacks. He learned to change the nature of his energy orbs, making them hard and dense so they did more damage or springy and bouncy so they could ricochet off walls and objects. He practiced on a series of targets that Gabriel set up and they both laughed as the stuffing from one of them erupted spectacularly when Leo hit it with a beach ball sized attack.

When they took a break, Leo found himself next to the screens that Mr. Novickas usually stood behind to protect himself. He could see an intricate pattern etched all over the frame and it reminded him of something he had seen recently, but he just couldn't place it.

"What are these markings?" he asked Gabriel. "Are they words?"

"You'll have to ask a Moon Born and good luck getting an answer. They are very secretive."

"Why?"

"Because while we have abilities that allow us to do amazing things, they can control when our abilities work. The Moon Borns around the world can control the outcome of any endeavor the tribes undertake. As a result, many have tried to control them and sometimes hunted them when they didn't align themselves with the dominant power at the time."

"Hunted them? People from the tribes wanted to kill Moon Borns?"

"This was before there were tribes, in the time after The Calamity. But I thought we agreed: no more serious stuff for the rest of the day. We can cover this another time. Now, let me teach you how to make your armor elastic so you can bounce around the room!"

The remainder of the afternoon was some of the most fun Leo had in months. It was also clear that having a Star Born teacher would accelerate his learning. By the end of the day, Leo realized his parents were right and he had been too quick to judge Gabriel. Now he just had to brace himself for the "I told you so" jokes coming from them. His parents could be so juvenile sometimes…

10

Seeing a Ghost

Leo sprinted across the street just before a car barreled through the intersection. He was panting and his shirt was soaked, but he didn't want to be late for training this afternoon. He thought to himself, "How does Mr. O'Reilly know to hold me after class every time I have somewhere to be? I swear, that's *his* special ability…." He just knew that if he arrived late, Ania was going to have that smug smile on her face and make some kind of quip that he would have to admit is really funny and he was going to make darn sure that didn't happen.

Squeezing between two joggers, he looked up and saw the sign for the bookshop. He checked his watch and it said 2:58, two minutes to spare. His heart leapt and he thought he had made it in the nick of time. Unfortunately, as he was trying to get through the door, he got stuck behind two older gentlemen who seemed to be in no hurry to get into the store and were very

175

interested in some news about a new bike lane that would take up all the parking spaces by the shops.

"Excuse me…" he said, but they showed no sign of hearing him.

"Can I get through?" He said a bit louder and the only change was they started talking about the new medication one of them was taking.

Leo reached his breaking point and plowed into the space between them, pushing hard until he finally made it into the shop. He started walking briskly to the back and heard one of them say, "That is the weird kid I told you about who I saw staring at those flowers!"

Once he was through Mr. Novickas' office and past the secret door, Leo tore down the stairs, skipping the bottom flight entirely with a huge leap. He ran into the room and as expected all of his friends had arrived before him. And there was Ania, smirking with her arms crossed.

"Two months of intensive training with the most senior Star Born in the world and you still haven't learned to tell time?" she said, drawing out the words so the full amount of snarkiness could be felt.

"Burn!" Aran shouted with encouragement.

"Hey, I'm fashionably late," Leo responded coolly, trying to hide his frustration.

"Holey sweatpants and an old NASA t-shirt are hardly fashionable," she dug further.

"She's on a roll!" Aran yelped, hopping from one foot to the other in glee.

Leo turned and started walking to the desk to drop his bag and grumbled to himself, "It's not like you're up on the latest fashion trends…"

"What was that?!" Ania called after him and he just waved dismissively at her.

A few minutes later, Gabriel and Mr. Novickas joined them and Leo's friends all turned to check out the mystery teacher they were finally meeting for the first time.

"Greetings, everyone!" Gabriel said warmly to the group. "I'm so happy to meet you all. I understand you have trained together before and your teachers found this helped to develop your abilities more quickly. As I think you all know, this is not the traditional way we usually train and I am hardly a traditional person, so I figured you may be able to teach me something new!"

"It's about time someone recognizes our brilliance," Aran said with full bravado and Mr. Novickas shot him a look that quieted him immediately.

"That's the spirit!" Gabriel responded, then a mischievous look washes over his face and Leo knew what this meant all too well. Before he could warn his friends, however, Gabriel started launching low-power energy orb attacks the size of tennis balls at all of his friends. Leo rushed to start helping them, but Gabriel held up a hand quickly as a warning to stay put.

Aran, with all of his cockiness, was the first to fall when two orbs bounced into his stomach and shoulder in rapid succession, knocking the wind out of him. He was left groaning on the floor, tucked into a ball. Of course, he never really had a chance to use his abilities since there were only humans in the cavern.

Ania, Stella, and Meimei fanned out, dodging attacks as best they could, but still getting grazed consistently. Leo saw the burn marks on Stella's arms and Ania's cheek. With each hit, it was like he felt it on his own body. He knew what those burns were like since he had sustained many of them during his sessions with

Gabriel. He felt itchy all over with the frustration of having to watch his friends fight while he just stood there and watched.

It wasn't looking good as the battle progressed and he continued to see his friends struggle to keep up with Gabriel's attacks. From his safe vantage point, he had so many ideas of what they could do, but he knew judgment is quickly clouded when you're in the thick of things. Meimei was the first to get creative when she levitated the desk and started to use it as a shield.

"Yes, Meimei!" Leo called out and Gabriel silenced him with a cold glare.

However, Leo's shout of encouragement had already caught Ania's attention and she worked her way around the room steadily to get behind Meimei for some cover. She was also at a disadvantage, not seeing any plants in the room, and she was becoming exhausted from dodging attacks. Prior to seeking cover behind Meimei, the burn marks were rapidly increasing up and down her arms and legs as she struggled to stay ahead of Gabriel's next volley.

Since two of his targets were now harder to hit, Gabriel concentrated a bit more on Stella and Leo saw she was sweating heavily from the exertion. Then he witnessed something astounding, Stella dragged her hand across her forehead and the sweat flowed over it in the form of countless tiny droplets. She ducked to avoid an energy orb that would have hit her square on the nose and then coalesced the droplets into five marble-sized frozen spheres. She flicked five frozen droplets at Gabriel and they flew toward him at a crazy velocity. Leo watched Gabriel spin and pull up a shield over his left arm to block most of them, but two ripped through his nice blazer.

"When did she learn to do *that*…" Leo muttered to himself.

Meimei took advantage of the moment and charged forward

with the desk as a battering ram. Ania hung back, hesitant to get closer to Gabriel, and that was when she noticed Mr. Novickas placing a small potted plant no bigger than his hand on the floor next to him. He took a few steps away and then winked at her. While Meimei and Stella had Gabriel's full attention, Ania flowed all of her energy into the plant and it exploded out of the pot, rapidly crossed the short distance to Gabriel, and twisted up his legs and torso. Gabriel toppled over and landed hard on his shoulder as his arms became wrapped up too. In a sudden turn of events, Leo's friends had bested the most powerful Star Born in the world and he could hardly believe his eyes.

"OK, OK! I yield!" Gabriel called out with some laughs thrown in for good measure.

Meimei and Stella stood down and Ania loosened the tendrils so that Gabriel could extricate himself. When he was out fully, Gabriel got up and turned to Mr. Novickas.

"No fair, Adam. You helped them."

"I hardly think you were fighting fair yourself," Adam retorted.

"Good point," Gabriel conceded and gave a small bow.

"Come on over, kids, let me take a look at your wounds," Mr. Novickas instructed.

As she was waiting her turn, Ania looked over to Leo and said, "You could've warned us he might do that."

"You were too busy judging my sense of style for me to tell you," he responded with a big grin and Ania just rolled her eyes. Leo took in a deep sigh of satisfaction as he walked over to Stella.

"Hey, when did you learn to launch those ice pellets like that?" he asked her, unable to hold back his curiosity.

"Honestly, that's the first time I've ever done that. Your mom has been showing me how to attract small amounts of water to each other. I was just so desperate out there trying to keep from getting hit that I kinda improvised. The sweat was stinging my eyes and it occurred to me that I could use that since there was no other water in the room. When I looked at him to see what he was doing next, I saw he was sweating too and I figured I could maybe attract my sweat to his. I am surprised how well it worked, I can't wait to tell your mom about it!"

"You're next, Stella!" they heard Mr. Novickas call out.

"Thank goodness! These burns are killing me!" she lamented.

Leo saw Aran get up from the chair where Mr. Novickas had been treating him and he walked over, trading places with Stella.

"Well, I wouldn't say that was the most fun Friday session," Aran said as he tugged back on the well worn hat he wore every day.

"Yup. Welcome to my past two months," Leo responded half jokingly.

"Seriously? You have to do that a lot?"

"At least a couple times a week. It gets more fun as you learn to defend yourself better. He always creates the possibility for you to do something, it's just rarely obvious at first."

"Well, I clearly have a lot to learn," Aran said humbly. "At least he is less serious than Mr. Novickas. He's actually pretty funny."

"Totally, but don't let him know you think that. He'll get an even bigger head. That confidence is no act."

"OK, everyone, gather around please!" Gabriel said brightly and they all came together in a circle at the center of the room.

"Well, that was fun, wasn't it?!" he continued, taking in all of their skeptical faces. "Well, maybe a bit more fun for me than it was for you. I promise it will rarely be that way going forward. I did learn a lot from you today and can now understand why Adam here has been speaking so highly of you all. So, next week please come prepared to get dirty. That's all I'll say for now, I hate to ruin surprises! Now, go enjoy your weekends!"

On that note, Gabriel strolled out of the cavern and the group all looked at Mr. Novickas with perturbed faces. He shrugged and said, "I gave up trying to understand him a long time ago. Just know he's really good at whatever he does." This response was good enough for the group and they gathered up their things to head home.

❧

After peaking out of Mr. Novickas' office door to check if the coast was clear, the group spilled into the shop and they made their way to the front. Leo was the first to spot Caroline at the counter purchasing a book. She didn't notice them yet and he tried to back peddle, but the rest of the group made a commotion as they ran into his back and let out loud complaints.

Caroline turned toward them and her expression changed from benign curiosity to deep hurt in a matter of seconds. Leo felt the intense confusion and despair inside her as she struggled to take in that her friends had been cutting her out of their activities again.

"Hey, it isn't what you think…" Leo started to say and, just like in every movie when someone said that line, he stood there frozen as Caroline held up her hand to stop him from saying anything else. Then she teared up and ran out of the shop.

"What's going on? Why did everyone stop suddenly?" Aran asked from behind them, clearly unable to see what had just happened. This thawed Leo out and he immediately ran after her. However, after sprinting a couple of blocks, there was no sign of her. He knew where she went though and he jogged back to the shop to gather the rest of the group.

After a short walk, they arrived at Caroline's house and her mother, Camille, was waiting for them on the front porch. She gave them a warm smile and came down the steps to greet them.

"Let me guess, she saw you all together at the book shop," Camille said.

"Yeah… We weren't careful enough. It's been only me there for the past couple of months and we were out of practice," Leo confirmed.

"Well, it was bound to happen sometime, right?" Camille commiserated. "It's great that she has friends like you all who care about her and come over right away."

"Thanks, but we feel like horrible friends right now…" Stella said.

"Don't. That's not necessary. Just go try to cheer her up if you can. She's up in her room."

The group started climbing the stairs to the front door, but stopped as Camille started to speak again.

"I do feel it is important to remind you to not mention any-thing about the tribe to her. I know you want to make her feel better and that would be the most straightforward way to explain why you were all together, but it's the last thing you should do."

"I don't understand. You're her mom. We're her friends. Practically everyone she knows is in the tribe. Why does it have to be a secret with her?" Leo complained.

"Do you think I don't wish I could tell her about this whole other part of my life that she has no idea about?" Camille asked him with a raised eyebrow. "This is to protect her as much as it is to protect the tribe. Can you imagine if someone found out she knows about us? She doesn't have any abilities to protect herself!"

"We get it…" Meimei said as she placed her hand on Leo's shoulder, telling him to let it go even though he didn't want to.

They all continued to climb the stairs and made their way to Caroline's bedroom. They found the door closed and looked at each other, acknowledging how serious the situation seemed to be. Caroline's door was never closed. She loved hearing the noises of her family moving around in the house as she read or worked on a piece of artwork. She was never bothered by being interrupted and was truly happy when a friend appeared for an unplanned visit.

Stella took a step forward and knocked on the door softly, but there was no answer. She glanced over her shoulder with a doubtful look, but Ania whispered loudly that she should knock louder. Stella followed the guidance and knocked on the door like a police officer with an arrest warrant and it startled the group. However, they were still greeted with silence.

"Caroline, please let us in, we can explain," Meimei called through the door.

Nothing from the other side.

"C'mon, Caroline, we have the book you bought," Aran said, trying a different approach.

The silence on the other side of the door was deafening.

"Caroline…" Leo said softly right next to the door because he could feel her back holding it closed from the other side. "Please… We can't stand the thought that we hurt you…" The intense feelings of guilt began to overwhelm him and it only got worse when they all heard her start to sob on the other side of the door.

"It's been a long day and I'm sure she's tired," Camille said from the end of the hall. "She'll probably feel better tomorrow after she lets some of these feelings out. Why don't you all head home and I bet she will text you all tomorrow morning."

Taking their cue, they all filed out of the house feeling worse than when they had arrived and the next day they all stayed close to their phones waiting for a text that never came. By the time Sunday evening came around, Leo couldn't stand it any longer and he sat down at his desk, pulled out a piece of blank printer paper, and began to write.

> *Dear Caroline,*
> *I'm so sorry. We just happened to all be at the book shop. It wasn't planned at all.*

Leo scratched the words out haphazardly and then balled up the sheet of paper. He simply couldn't lie to her. It felt like a betrayal. He pulled out another sheet of paper and started again.

> *Dear Caroline,*
> *There's something you should know. Everyone you know is part of a secret group of people who have super powers, but you don't have any and we aren't supposed to tell you about it.*

"Nope!" he said loudly and balled up the second sheet of paper. He remembered just how hard it was for him to understand this world he never knew about before encountering the Book of Star Born. Reading about it in a letter from a friend you thought was cutting you out was hardly the best way to learn this kind of news. He leaned back in his chair trying to think of what he could say, listening to the second hand on his wall clock tick slowly. He crafted several different starts to the letter in his head, each one not feeling quite right. Finally, he decided he just needed to start writing again. He pulled out a third sheet of paper and proceeded to spend several hours writing and rewriting until he could hardly keep his eyes open.

That night he had a fitful sleep. Multiple times, he dreamed that he was in the Connector again and Maranda was far down the hallway, beckoning him to her urgently. However, each time he started running towards her, he felt like he was yanked out of the dream suddenly. The last time he was yanked out, it was his alarm waking him up and it took all of his will to drag himself out of bed to turn it off.

Despite the brain fog from lack of sleep, when he saw the letter he wrote to Caroline sitting on his desk, adrenaline kicked in again and he woke up fully. Leo rushed through his morning routine and got to school extra early so he could make a pit stop in their classroom to drop the letter on Caroline's desk before he headed to the usual pre-bell hangout spot. As his friends arrived at school, they all talked softly while keeping an eye out for Caroline, but she never appeared. When the bell rang and they made their way into their classrooms, however, Leo and Aran found Caroline in her seat looking like she had been crying all weekend. Her eyes were puffy and red and she wouldn't look at them as they sat down around her. Leo also noticed his letter was wedged into one of her books, clearly she hadn't looked at it yet.

At lunchtime, after finishing his food, Leo walked around the school yard in the sun. The fresh air lifted the heavy feeling from his chest slightly and he paused to close his eyes and take a deep breath. Suddenly, he felt someone plowing into his back with all of their force and he was barely able to get his hands out in front of him just before his face plowed into the asphalt.

"You certainly have a way with words, Leo," Caroline said right in his ear. "I guess I forgive you, but you owe me lunch this weekend." Then she pushed herself up on his back, knelt next to him, and then rubbed her hands all over his head, creating a staticy halo of hair.

After Caroline ran back towards a group of their friends playing four square, Leo stayed on the ground for a minute, letting the heavy feelings drain out of him fully until Aran came up and said, "You taking a nap or something?"

"Naaa… Just needed to take a moment," Leo replied.

"I get it, that was a pretty crappy weekend. Did you say something to her? She seems to be right back to her old self."

"I think I will keep that between me and her," Leo said as he rolled onto his back and reached out a hand for Aran to help him up.

Later that day, Leo had a comparatively light training session in which Gabriel seemed just as tired and way more cranky. When Leo was unable to copy Gabriel's energy pattern on demand, he abruptly walked out of the cavern without saying another word. Leo decided he had enough as well and made his way out of the shop through the back door. He didn't want to head straight home though and began to wander around town, turning down streets randomly, lost in his thoughts.

Ultimately, he found himself standing at the edge of the park behind the library he used to go to every day after school when he was in third and fourth grade. He smiled to himself, remembering all of his favorite hiding spots and the time he got a bad poison oak rash when he was playing tag and fell into a big bush. Despite his fatigue and all the frustrated feelings from earlier, he felt really content and sat on a nearby bench, watching the other kids play basketball, hit tennis balls against a wall, and go as high as they could on the swing set.

After a while, he noticed the colors shifting in the sky as the sun started to set more quickly. Many of the kids began to pack up and head home, but Leo felt no need to leave yet. Something told him this was where he was supposed to be and he continued to sit there as his mind wandered and the shadows grew longer. He caught himself nodding off to sleep a couple times and laughed at himself, realizing that was probably the sign to leave.

As he stood up, he felt a strong shiver run down his spine and he went from relaxed and content to wide awake and on guard. He scanned the park intensely, recognizing the feeling of another Star Born. When another stronger shiver hit him, he instinctively turned to look at the deep shadows under a small group of trees across the park from him. He could make out the shape of a person standing there and, while normally he would find that creepy, he somehow knew he was not in danger.

The person in the shadows took a few steps forward and Leo continued to stare intently, trying to make out their shape even though they were still thoroughly concealed. He could already tell it wasn't Gabriel because the person was significantly shorter. Leo started to walk slowly across the park, directly toward the mystery person, and this spurred them to take a few more steps forward so they were just barely out of the shadows.

Leo stumbled and stopped, his mouth open wide, barely able to believe what he was seeing. He blinked a few times, but nothing changed the scene. He was staring at someone who looked exactly like Maranda. A completely intact, not disintegrated, Maranda. She looked so much like the picture in Mr. Novickas' office, but with a completely different wardrobe and a huge traveling backpack slung over her left shoulder. Leo was sure it was her and he started hurrying across the park.

"How…" he started to say as he got closer, but he felt another strong shiver and he noticed she did too because her eyes grew wide with worry. Immediately, she retreated quietly into the trees without saying a word. Leo looked around the park, but it appeared he was the last one there. He walked back over to his backpack and, as he picked it up, he heard Gabriel's voice behind him.

"Well this is interesting, you disappeared from training earlier and now I find you here all by yourself in this park."

"Disappeared?" Leo asked with a hint of annoyance. "You walked out in the middle of our session!"

"I did, but just to get a little bit of air and a drink of water. I didn't sleep well last night and I could tell I was getting too frustrated."

"Uh yeah… Couldn't you tell I was exhausted too?" Leo replied, feeling all of the frustration from earlier returning.

"Honestly, I couldn't at the time, but I understood when you left. I get a little *insensitive* when I am tired. I'm sure you can relate."

Gabriel's comments made it hard for Leo to keep up the one-sided argument, so he decided to just let it go and leave.

"Well, anyway, I think I'll head home now. It's getting dark," Leo said as he turned to start his walk.

"What are you doing here alone?" Gabriel asked, making it clear he was not done talking to Leo.

"I don't know, I just wandered around and found myself here," Leo answered honestly.

"That's interesting, I found myself wandering here too after I left the bookshop. Why do you think we were both drawn here?"

"I have no idea," Leo answered and this was largely true, but he had a theory.

"Really… How long have you been here?"

"I'm not sure, at least an hour? What's with all these questions?" Leo asked, starting to feel even more uncomfortable.

"Apologies, Leo. I have just been around long enough to no longer believe in coincidences," Gabriel answered bluntly.

"What do you mean by that?"

"You and I were both pulled to this location."

"Pulled? No, I just wandered here," Leo said incredulously.

"No, you were pulled, as was I. Only another strong Star Born would be able to do that. At first, when I saw you here alone, I thought it was you who pulled me here. Clearly you are strong enough to do that, but I didn't think you had learned that skill yet and I can see now that I was correct. So this leads me to believe there is another Star Born nearby."

"What? How?" Leo asked in confusion.

"Not to worry, Leo. You're completely safe with me. I'll escort you home."

"I'm sure I would be fine getting home by myself," Leo protested.

"I'm afraid I must insist. If there is another Star Born here, I would know about it. However, I do not and this means we need to start taking more precautions."

Gabriel led Leo out of the park and he followed quietly, not sure what to say and his head swimming with information. Maranda clearly "pulled" him to the park and it was also clear she didn't intend to pull Gabriel there. He made a note that he needed to find the time to research this skill as soon as possible, though there hadn't been much time to look at the book since Gabriel had been keeping him very busy. Also, why would Gabriel know if there should be another Star Born here? Even more curious, why would another Star Born want to harm him?

"Here we are!" Gabriel said, pulling Leo out of his thoughts. He looked around and noticed they were outside his house.

"How did you know where I live?" he asked Gabriel.

"I make it my business to learn about my students, of course!"

"Well… Thanks… I guess I'll see you tomorrow," Leo said, not sure he liked the answer Gabriel provided.

"I will have to let Adam know about this, I'm sure you understand that. There will likely need to be some additional precautions for the time being. At least for tomorrow, I'll meet you at school to escort you to the bookshop."

"Is that really necessary?"

"Alas, I feel that it is," Gabriel said in a consoling way.

Leo let out a deep sigh and dropped his head, turning toward his house.

"Goodnight, Leo," Gabriel said warmly.

"Yeah… Goodnight…" Leo replied as he closed the front door behind him.

11

MAKING CONTACT

FTER ALMOST TWO weeks of lock down, Leo and his friends started to go stir crazy. They were escorted to school by their parents, to training by their teachers, and then picked up afterward by their parents. Everyone was starting to get sick of each other and, after a coordinated effort from the kids consisting of badgering, haranguing, and arguing, their parents finally agreed to let them all meet up at Ania's house on Saturday to get some space.

As usual, Leo was the last to arrive and the perfunctory ribbing ensued, but he was grateful that it was rather brief because they all wanted to get down to the main topic everyone was dying to discuss since they couldn't speak openly at school.

"OK, do any of you know why we are being babysat constantly?" Aran asked bluntly and they all looked at each other shaking their heads and shrugging except for Leo. This did not go unnoticed and they all stared at him expectantly.

"What?" he said with the most innocent look he could muster.

"You're the worst liar in the world, don't even try it," Ania reprimanded.

"Look, I have an idea, but it probably…" Leo started to say.

"EHHHHHH!" Aran interjected like Leo gave the wrong answer on a game show.

"Cut it out, guys!" Leo said plaintively.

"No way, you know exactly why we've been cooped up for two weeks and you owe it to us to explain," Ania demanded and the others nodded in agreement.

They all then sat silently, staring at Leo expectantly for a long time until he couldn't take it anymore.

"Fine!" he shouted and they all grinned.

"Great, what did you blow up?" Meimei asked.

"I didn't blow up anything. They're looking for someone who shouldn't be here and they think this person might be dangerous," Leo started to explain and then immediately interjected. "But I don't think she is!"

"Wait, you know who they are looking for?" Stella asked.

"Yeah… And I want to find her first," Leo said with determination.

"You want to look for a dangerous person everyone in the tribe is searching for?!" Meimei asked rhetorically.

"Yes," he said, looking her directly in her eyes. "And I want you all to help me."

"Am I understanding correctly that you know who they are looking for, but they don't?" Meimei dug further.

"Yes." Leo answered simply.

"How are you so sure?" Meimei asked, confident he was going to provide a weak answer.

"Because it's Maranda," Leo answered with a hint of attitude.

"Maranda?! The girl you told us about who blew herself up?" Stella asked apprehensively.

"Well, it looks like she didn't actually blow herself up, but yes."

"But… how?!"

"I don't know yet and that's why we need to find her."

"And how are we supposed to do that if we are under constant observation by the Stasi?" Ania asked sarcastically.

"The what?" Aran asked.

"Weren't you paying attention when we learned about the Berlin Wall coming down?" Ania chastised.

"Guys! Focus!" Meimei said, pulling everyone back together again.

"Well, that's a good question, Ania. I've been thinking about it and I have a plan…" Leo began.

"No, no, no! We just need to ride this out for a couple more weeks. They won't be able to keep this up for much longer," Meimei said forcefully.

"Let him explain his plan before you dismantle it in a very rational way," Aran said in a serious tone that belied the fact that he always loved a caper.

Giving a side glance to Aran, Leo continued, "I had the same idea, Meimei. How could they keep this up indefinitely? It's the way Gabriel has been behaving in training that makes me think he won't give up the search and will keep us under lock and key. It's like he thinks Maranda is a mortal threat to all of us, but particularly him. Not that I think he knows it's Maranda. He just knows it is another Star Born and he seems to think the fact there is another one here who he doesn't know about is why they are dangerous. But getting back to my idea. It's actually pretty simple, I think we should challenge Gabriel to a battle."

"I was on your side, but you lost me, buddy," Aran said, throwing up his hands.

"You saw how we barely beat him last time and that was only because Mr. Novickas helped us. Gabriel wasn't even using all of his abilities," Stella said with a quavering voice, clearly still traumatized by the experience a bit.

"I think we should do it," Meimei said quietly.

"Exactly! Listen to Meimei," Aran said, about to rest his case and then catching himself. "What? You're agreeing with him?"

"You want to demonstrate that we can take care of ourselves if we are together, right?" Meimei said, turning her undivided attention back to Leo.

"Right," he answered confidently.

"You really think we can take him in an honest fight?" Aran asked incredulously.

"Well, I don't think we will ever get an honest fight from Gabriel. He always has some kind of trick up his sleeves. But yeah… I think we could take him," Leo said with a big smile.

"Can we do the battle in the university greenhouses?" Ania asked excitedly. "I have so many wonderful ideas running through my mind now."

"That's a good point, we need to make sure we all have the chance to use our abilities if we are going to have a chance at this," Meimei said.

"Ok, I like where this is going, I owe him for all those burns he gave me…" Stella said intensely, starting to get into the right frame of mind.

"Am I the only sane one here for once?!" Aran complained.

"Looks like! Who would've thunk it?" Ania said, slapping him hard on the back.

"OK, it's settled, we're going to challenge him for the right to our freedom," Leo declared.

∾

The following Friday, everyone assembled at the cavern as usual. This time, all the teachers escorted their students there and seemed to have decided to stay for the session. The group huddled together, whispering their final thoughts on the plan while they waited for Gabriel to arrive. When he did, he got straight down to business.

"OK, the plan for today is…" he began.

"Actually, we have a different plan for today," Leo interrupted.

"Excuse me?" Gabriel asked with a healthy dose of annoyance.

"We have a different plan," Leo said a bit louder.

"I like the initiative and we can discuss your idea for a future session later, but I'd like to get started on what I had planned."

"We're sick of being chaperoned. We want our lives back," Ania chimed in.

Gabriel shot an exasperated look at Mr. Novickas and then replied, "That is a safety measure."

"We can protect ourselves," Meimei jumped in.

"Now wait a sec. You all are very new members to the tribe. I have seen the confidence of youth cloud better judgment. You all need to trust that we have your best interests at heart with the precautions we have been taking," Mr. Novickas said as he joined the argument.

"Leo told us you think there is a dangerous Star Born here. Let us challenge you to a battle. If we win, it proves we can protect ourselves," Meimei said, not accepting Mr. Novickas' explanation.

"Not a chance…" Mr. Novickas started to answer.

"Actually, Adam, I like this idea," Gabriel interrupted.

"You can't be serious!"

"If you can beat me, which is highly unlikely, we'll lift the restrictions," Gabriel agreed with the group.

"Gabriel. Over here. Now." Mr. Novickas growled.

Gabriel gave the group a big smile and held up a finger to indicate they should wait a moment for them to discuss. He and Mr. Novickas proceeded to have a heated discussion. At first, they couldn't hear anything that was being said, but Mr. Novickas began to raise his voice as he became more irate. Finally giving up on any chance of keeping the debate private, he yelled, "I cannot condone this! Their parents entrusted their safety to us!"

"You well know we don't have time for this!" Gabriel shot back.

"Don't go there! You already assured me we would not rush their training!"

"They are the ones requesting this! Let them prove they are ready! You haven't always coddled your tribe…"

"How dare you!"

"Adam! Set your terms to make it safe enough, but it's clearly time to take off the training wheels!" Gabriel said and he walked away, making loops inside the cavern while Mr. Novickas stared at him and stewed.

The group just about gave up after the stalemate lasted for at least fifteen minutes while Mr. Novickas caucused with the other teachers. He finally emerged from the huddle and called out to Gabriel who was leaning on the other side of the room tossing an energy orb from one hand to another.

"FINE! We have figured out how to make this happen."

Gabriel caught the energy ball in his left hand and it melted back into his palm, then he gave a slight fist pump of victory as he walked briskly across the cavern. The kids converged on the same point to listen to the terms.

"First," Mr. Novickas counseled in the sternest voice any of them had heard, "I am the referee. What I say goes and the teachers will enforce that. If either side oversteps, we will shut this down. We will also configure the cavern to create something closer to a real world environment."

"Aren't you overcomplicating this…" Gabriel protested.

"What's the matter? Afraid of a fair fight?!" Mr. Novickas snapped and Gabriel's face flushed with anger as he forced himself to not respond.

"So do we get a say in any of this?" Aran boldly asked.

"No," Mr. Novickas said coldly. Then he looked around to the rest of the group and said, "We need some time to set up, go upstairs to the storage room and wait there. I'll have someone bring you some food shortly. You better have more of a plan than just issuing a challenge. This is one of the stupidest things I have ever seen in my life."

On that note, Mr. Novickas turned away from them to speak with the teachers and they correctly interpreted that he had dismissed them. They all walked toward the stairs to exit the cavern and heard, "You too, Gabriel. Go find someplace else to be. Come back around seven, we should be ready by then."

Gabriel threw up his hands in frustration and climbed up the stairs with the rest of them. However, instead of joining them in the storage room, he strode out the back door and let it slam behind him. Leo pulled out his phone to check the time.

"OK, it's four thirty, looks like we have two and a half hours until go time," he said.

"Good, that'll be plenty of time for us to go over our plans in detail again," Meimei replied.

"We've been through the plan a ton of times! Let's just chill and read! Look at all the books we have to choose from back here." Ania complained.

"Ania, get over here and be a team player," Stella said in an uncharacteristically commanding tone.

"OK… sheesh…" Ania conceded and the group sat in a tight circle, discussing their plans in hushed tones.

❧

Two and a half hours went by much more quickly than they expected and they had barely finished half of the pizza that Emily brought them when Gabriel opened the back door and stepped in with a flourish.

"Challengers! I trust you are well prepared for our battle!" he said with so much bravado the group giggled despite their nervousness.

"Where have you been all this time?" Leo asked.

"I went back to the restaurant you took me to and ate many fried things. As you know, it is important to fuel yourself with only the best foods before a highly strenuous activity," Gabriel replied, continuing to lighten the mood of a room that had been very serious just a few minutes earlier.

It didn't last, however, because Leo's mother appeared a moment later and just said, "We're ready." Then she turned around the way she came without waiting for them to follow. Leo knew his mother well and could tell she didn't like what was about to happen without even having to sense the emotions radiating off her. So, he was the first one to stand up and start heading back down to the cavern. The rest of the group quickly followed, with Gabriel bringing up the rear.

They were surprised to see the room completely transformed. When Mr. Novickas said "a real world environment," he really meant it since the room now resembled a small park. There were several copses of trees, with branches scraping the ceiling and some laden with fruit. A large, shallow pond had been created in the center, with broad lily pads scattered across the top. A myriad of birds flew between their hiding places, making a loud racket of squawks and tweets. There were even several large boulders placed randomly in the midst of the thick bushes and plants that covered much of the floor. The teachers were all standing behind a line of Moon Born screens set up along one side of the room. None of them looked happy about what was going to happen next.

Most of the group started milling about, finding different elements that excited them. Leo hung back, scanning the room on high alert. A few yards behind him, he heard Gabriel chuckling and muttering, "This ought to be fun…"

"Begin!" Mr. Novickas shouted without warning and it caught everyone, but Leo, off guard.

Most of his friends whirled around in confusion, trying to get their bearings. Leo, however, turned rapidly and dug his feet into the soft soil covering the floor. He pulled his forearms together and created a large shield in front of him to cover as much space as possible. Seconds later, Gabriel's first attacks slammed into him with much more force than he had ever experienced. It pushed him back a couple feet, creating two grooves in the ground, but his shield held and it was just enough time for the rest of them to get their wits about them.

"READY?!" Meimei called out to the group and one by one they called back in the affirmative while Leo continued to fend off attacks Gabriel was attempting to get past his shield by banking them off the ceiling. When Leo heard the last of them answer, he dropped his shield and the entire group unleashed a coordinated and vicious attack on Gabriel. The air was full of items that would tear apart or crush any normal human, including a large boulder, a column of pond water, several thick vines, a scurry of squirrels, and two dense energy orbs. None of them hit their target, however, as Gabriel enveloped himself in a giant, spiky cocoon and then exploded it, shattering everything.

They all ducked and crouched as they were pelted with debris. Leo felt a strong flare of anger from Gabriel and erected his shield again quickly before the next volley of attacks slammed into it. This time, the force felt even stronger and the concussive impacts knocked the wind out of him, causing the shield to flicker. His friends noticed this and tried to buy time by starting a rapid cascade of individual attacks.

Stella pulled another mass of water out of the pond and fractured it into a thousand small spikes that Meimei launched at Gabriel. He just swatted them away with a hand enlarged massively by his armor.

Ania sent the root of a large maple tree under Gabriel's feet to destabilize the ground where he was standing, but he raised a foot and slammed his heel into it while sending a blast of energy through it. The root caught on fire, which quickly traveled to the tree and began to fill the air with smoke.

Aran found and took command of a mountain lion, sending it racing toward Gabriel. However, he lost it as Ania shoved him out of the way when a branch from the flaming tree nearly fell on his head.

Then, before they could regroup, Gabriel took off in a sprint, running directly at Stella. With a steely glare of a seasoned competitor, she whipped up a waterspout around herself in the pond.

"NO!" Meimei shouted, noticing Gabriel had a concentrated blast charged up in both of his hands that he intended to punch through the water.

"Uhnnnn!" Gabriel grunted as the mountain lion slammed into him suddenly before he could reach Stella. Without any time to charge his armor again, the large cat swiped its claws at him several times while he backpedaled comically away from it and slid through mud that now covered his back and hands. Gabriel yelled something unintelligible and the mountain lion suddenly flew through the air and it landed on its side, knocked unconscious.

The battle descended into a grinding pace, with Gabriel slowly gaining ground while the kids dug deeper and deeper for ideas on how to keep up with him. All of them were covered with burns and cuts. One of Meimei's eyes was swollen shut and Ania's arm was hanging limply at her side, most likely broken.

Leo was panting from exertion as he ran between each of his friends, temporarily boosting their abilities as they had planned, to keep Gabriel off balance. When he shifted over to Aran, he detected a deep sense of confidence despite the fact they were clearly starting to lose the battle badly.

"Stay with me, I need every ounce of control we have to do this…" Aran said through gritted teeth.

"What are you going to do?" Leo asked while focusing on aligning his energy with Aran's.

"You'll see," is all Aran responded with.

The girls began to take the brunt of the attack as Gabriel sensed their defenses crumbling. He kicked a large armored foot at Ania, taking her legs out from under her and she landed hard. She struggled to get up, but Stella yelled "Stay down!" while she tried to draw Gabriel's attacks. She and Meimei double teamed him with a constant barrage of rocks, branches, and ice shards. Stella even created some quicksand that surrounded his legs up to his calves that slowed his movement down considerably.

Gabriel was able to deflect most of what they were throwing at him, but enough made it through that it occupied his full attention. So, he didn't notice the growing sound of buzzing until he felt the first stings in his neck. Almost immediately, spikes of pain erupted all over his face and arms as the bees swarmed over him. He could also feel them working their way under his clothes to reach other parts of his body. He suffered hundreds of stings in less than a minute and his skin quickly began to feel hot and painfully swollen.

"NO! NO! NO!" Gabriel yelled and the kids' eyes grew wide as another cocoon formed around him and the bees disintegrated around him. This time it was different though as it seemed to be much more volatile. The spikes were throbbing like a heartbeat as it steadily grew.

Ania felt herself being lifted up by two strong sets of hands as she was dragged away from the growing energy field. Stella and Meimei noticed what the teachers were doing and each grabbed a leg as they carried Ania to safety behind the screens.

Aran sank to his knees with exhaustion as Leo pulled his energy back carefully. When he was done, he looked across the cavern to see the teachers' and students' petrified faces and yelling for them to run to safety. As if he heard them through his shell, Gabriel's cocoon expanded dramatically, blocking any path that Leo and Aran could take to the screens. Thinking quickly, Leo saw the cavern entrance a short distance away and immediately pulled Aran's arm over his shoulders as they stumbled their way across uneven ground.

They made it through the doorway just before the energy field expanded across it. The spikes surrounding the cocoon pulsed even more erratically, clearly becoming unstable the bigger the field got. Leo realized there was not enough time to get all the way up the stairs to safety, so he wedged Aran in a corner half-way up and formed the thickest shield he could to cover the two of them. He went into a deep meditative state in order to maintain their protection as long as possible and, moments later, Gabriel's energy exploded through the cavern and whipped up the stairs. It lashed at Leo's shield, tearing off layer after layer, which he replenished with every last ounce of energy in his body. When the storm abated, Leo slumped to the floor, unconscious and breathing very shallowly.

✦

"Leo, open your eyes," he heard a voice say. He didn't recognize who it was and he felt terribly weak, so he didn't want to listen.

"We don't have much time. I need you to open your eyes," the voice said more urgently. Leo struggled for a moment and then slowly pulled his eyelids apart. When everything came into focus, he found himself in a dimly lit room, laying on a leather couch, and Maranda was kneeling next to him.

"You! I saw you in the park!" he said, trying to sit up. She put her hand gently on his chest and he relaxed back into the couch.

"Yes," she said, "I've been trying to make contact with you, but it has been very difficult to say the least."

"Why are you trying to contact me? How are you not dead? I mean, everyone thinks you have been dead for years!"

"I know. It had to be this way and I can explain, but that should be done in person."

"What do you mean? We are in person now."

"Not exactly, I can explain that too. I need you to come find me when you are better."

Maranda then looked away suddenly, worry cascading across her face again. She looked back to him and said, "I'm sorry our

203

time is so short. Remember, come find me! I trust you will figure out a way, just trust your instincts!"

Suddenly, Leo was thrust out of the room and into the corridor. The doors flew past him so fast they all blurred together. He saw a bright light growing in his vision and when it surrounded him he found himself in the middle of the cavern. Mr. Novickas' hands were on Leo's chest and his eyes were closed. Gabriel had his hands on Mr. Novickas' shoulders and was staring down at Leo with deep concern.

"Adam, he's awake," Gabriel said with a hoarse voice and Leo's mom came from someplace out of view and began to stroke his hair with tears in her eyes.

"We almost lost you…" she said, her voice quavering.

"We won, right?" he asked.

"Really? That's the first thing on your mind?" she admonished gently.

"Nobody won that battle, Leo," Gabriel interjected. "It was a travesty and something I will be ashamed of for the rest of my life. I am truly sorry for what I did, it has been a long time since I unleashed that kind of power… You all fought so well… It was my pride that led to such a foolhardy action…"

"You need to recuperate, Leo. I'm going to have you go to sleep now. Don't worry, it will be some of the best rest you will ever have. We can talk more about this when you've recovered," Mr. Novickas said gently and, before Leo could begin to protest, his eyes grew heavy and he drifted off.

"Leo! Pick something already!" his dad called from the kitchen as another preview started on the TV. At this point, Leo must have watched at least thirty of them.

"Ahhhh… I can't decide! I don't even really want to watch anything…" Leo responded with annoyance.

"Then get off the couch and do something! Adam said you're fine, so go over to a friend's house or something."

"Fine… You're going to give me a ride?"

"No, I have some things I need to take care of. Just let me know where you'll be and bring your phone."

"Wait… WHAT?! I can walk to a friend's house *by myself*?!" Leo asked half sarcastically and half excitedly.

"Yeah, Adam and Gabriel decided that you all are a pretty potent force together and there's been no sign of the mystery Star Born anyway."

"And you're just telling me this now?!"

"Well, you were asleep for about 36 hours. So, technically this is one of the first things I have said to you since you fully woke up," his dad said, poking fun at Leo.

Leo tried to jump up from the couch and every muscle protested so much that he only managed a slow rise like an old man before falling back into the cushions. "Ugh… I can't move… My body feels like it is filled with lead…"

"Of course it does, you have only eaten instant ramen and fruit snacks today. Here, have some apple," his dad said and left a plate next to him. Leo reached out a snuggy-covered arm, grabbed a slice, and slowly raised it to his mouth. He took a bite and let out a moan of pleasure before shoving the rest of the slice in his mouth. He grabbed another slice and devoured it just as quickly. Soon enough, the plate was clean.

Leo then stood up a little more quickly and started shimmying toward the stairs. His dad gave him a suspicious look and said, "Note to self, no more ramen in the house."

"I wouldn't go that far…" Leo cautioned.

"Fine, but you're cut off for a while."

Realizing it was best to get out of the conversation before he said something that got him in trouble, he made his way up the stairs as quickly as he could manage. When he reached his room, he changed quickly and then found out his friends were exactly where he thought they would be. In short order, he was on his way to Ania's house while working his way through a sandwich his dad handed him on the way out of the house.

It felt so good to be walking around the neighborhood by himself that Leo barely felt the aches and pains that kept his pace to a slow stroll. He wanted to revel in this moment and let his mind wander like it usually did on his walks to meet friends, but he couldn't turn off his brain. It was consumed with one thing, finding Maranda. He had assembled a mental list of potential locations he wanted to check out and it was way longer than what could be covered in an afternoon by himself. He knew he would have to enlist his friends to split up and cover more ground. He just hoped they would still be up for it after what they all went through to get their freedom back.

When he reached Ania's house, Leo went around the side as usual, but it was oddly quiet. Normally he could hear everyone talking loudly from at least a block away, but there was just a circle of empty chairs in the backyard. He checked his phone and saw there were no messages about a change of plans. Frustrated, he sat down in one of the chairs, resigned to waiting for his friends to show up at some point.

He didn't have to wait long, however, because about a minute later everyone poured out of Ania's back door with plates filled with a buffet of frozen foods they had clearly just been heating up.

"LEO!" several of them shouted.

"You're alive!" Aran said cheekily.

"Barely…" Leo replied. "I think it is going to take me weeks to not feel the aftereffects of that battle…"

"Here! These gyoza will cure you! Each one is plus five health!" Ania said, handing him a plate. Unable to pass up a gyoza, Leo gladly accepted it.

"So where are we going to look first?" Meimei asked Leo, clearly not interested in waiting for a slow conversation ramp up.

"You're sure that you all are still up for this? I mean, I totally understand if you don't want to, given everything…" Leo said tentatively.

"Dude, we battled a Star Born for this. Of course we are still up for it!" Stella confirmed what they are all feeling.

"Well, I have some ideas of where she could be. It's a pretty long list, we will probably need to split up," he said, excitement returning to his voice.

"Do we have enough time to savor my freshly baked spanakopita?" Ania asked, using a fake English accent and holding a triangle with her pinky raised.

"But of course. It would only be proper," Leo agreed, badly imitating her accent.

"OK, take us through the list," Meimei said, getting back to business and pulling out a notebook from her backpack.

Leo reeled off a list of twenty possible locations they should check out based on where he thought there would be good hiding places. The group decided four of them were extremely unlikely, but identified seven others he hadn't considered. By the time all the food was gone, they had divided the list based on the proximity of the different locations with one half going to the boys and the other half to the girls. The plan was to notify the other group if they found anything or if there was trouble. Heading out from Ania's house, they walked together for a few blocks before splitting apart.

Leo and Aran headed to the park by the library where Leo had seen Maranda before Gabriel showed up. They did a cursory search around the area over the course of ten minutes, but then agreed they had done a pretty sloppy job and spent another thirty minutes going over every square inch of the park looking for anything out of the ordinary. It was quite unlike both of them because their parents regularly made cracks about their lack of ability to find things. In fact, Aran's mother had been laughing at him for days because he wasn't able to find his tablet and it had been sitting right on the table next to his bed.

Finally satisfied, they hit three smaller locations much more quickly without anything to show for it. They spent the next two hours trekking to four more spots and going over each with a fine-tooth comb. At one point, they thought they had found her hiding spot, but it turned out to be an old fort some kids had constructed in the bushes off the old school trail. With their list getting shorter and no progress to show for it, Leo grew steadily more frustrated. He'd thought a few of the locations were some of the most promising, but clearly his instincts were striking out. As they set out for the next location, Leo's phone erupted loudly with a famous, cheesy pop song, "Hey! I just met you! And this is…"

"Really?" Aran asked him, clearly annoyed with the song choice.

"Hey. My phone, my ringtone," he replied firmly as he lifted it to his ear to answer. Before he had a chance to even say hello, Meimei was already talking fast.

"We think we found something! Come to the cemetery, we're right by the big waterfall."

"Got it. We'll be there in about fifteen minutes," he replied and hung up quickly. "C'mon, they found something," he said to Aran.

They ran as fast as they could, Leo running through his soreness and cursing the fact the girls had found something at a location on the opposite side of town. Arriving at the cemetery and making their way to the spot Meimei described, they were thoroughly hot and suffering with massive cramps in their sides. They looked around for the girls, but couldn't see them anywhere. As Leo took his phone out to call them, they heard, "Hey! This way!" and they saw Stella leaning out from behind a stone Mausoleum and waving her hand to catch their attention.

They walked up to the structure and around the side to where they saw Stella peering out and they found all three of the girls looking through one of the windows.

"Take a look," Meimei said and she stepped back to make room for them. Inside, Leo and Aran saw they struck paydirt. It was Maranda's backpack, with her sleeping bag laid out and a small camp stove set up in the center of the small room.

"This is it! You guys are awesome!" Leo said loudly and the girls told him to quiet down so they don't attract any attention.

"We just have to figure out how to get inside," Ania said.

"Did you try the door?" Aran asked.

"Of course we checked the door. We aren't idiots. There's a chain on it." Ania replied, clearly miffed.

Aran walked around to the front of the mausoleum and glanced around carefully to make sure nobody was watching. Then he looked down at the chain and saw a padlock tucked behind it, but it was not latched. He rotated the body of the lock around and then slid the shackle out from the chain links. He quietly unwrapped the chain from the door handles before opening the door and stepping inside. He waved to the others who were still looking through the window, then he started looking around the room.

"How did you do that? Did you learn to pick locks or something?" Ania asked as she came into the room, genuinely curious.

"I figured if she could get in, so could we. She left the padlock unlatched," he answered matter-of-factly.

As they all crammed themselves into the space and closed the door behind them, they began searching through Maranda's things to get an idea of who she was and why she came back. Leo unzipped the top pocket of the backpack and reached inside. He pulled out the first thing he found and it was her passport. He opened it to the identification page and saw her full name - Maranda Eileen Hastings. Then he flipped through the rest of the book and saw many of the pages filled with stamps from all over the world. England, Kenya, Singapore, Vietnam, Australia, Chile, the list went on.

He began to feel like they were invading her privacy, so he slid the passport back into the pocket and said to the group, "I don't know if we should keep snooping through her stuff."

"You were the one who wanted to search for her. How are we going to find her if we don't look through her stuff?" Meimei asked.

"We could just wait for her to show up here. She has to come back for her stuff sometime, right?" Stella suggested.

"That's actually a good idea..." Meimei admitted.

"Cool! Stakeout!" Aran said. "Can we pick up some food?"

"Uh... I think I am good for at least another day. I don't know if I will be able to look at frozen spring rolls the same way again..." Leo said.

"I could eat," Ania said.

"Yeah, me too," Stella agreed.

"Let's all go down to the market and pick up supplies," Meimei added.

"You all go ahead and I will hang here," Leo said, sitting down on the hillside next to the mausoleum. He smiled to himself as they walked away and he heard them debating the merits of spicy versus regular cheese crunches. As he settled in for a long wait, he felt the familiar chill down his spine and, before he could look around, Maranda sat down quietly next to him.

"They're finally gone!" she said lightly.

"You've been here the entire time?" Leo asked, looking around to see where she could have been hiding.

"Of course, I have been following you all day."

Leo cocked his head to the side in confusion and said, "How come I couldn't feel you at all?"

"Ah, you're right, that's a good skill. I'll teach you that one."

"What do you mean, *teach me*? I already have a teacher and I know almost nothing about you."

"You know you can trust me, right? You can feel it, so you know I am telling the truth. You're such a remarkable Star Born, Leo. I mean, what you are able to do is well beyond what is normal at this point in your training. Honestly, there are probably only about ten other Star Borns in the world who have developed some of the abilities you have learned. People have been searching for someone like you for a long time."

This last comment made Leo very uncomfortable, he remembered the dream he had in the connector with the voices saying they had found the one they were looking for. He fought the urge to be consumed in his thoughts and asked Maranda, "Are you one of those ten?"

"I happen to be, yes," she answered seriously.

"Why have you been searching for me?"

"Because you're in danger."

"I'm so sick of people just saying I am in danger and not explaining what is going on!" Leo exploded suddenly and leapt to his feet. He looked down at Maranda and her eyes were wide with surprise as she alternated between meeting his gaze and looking at his hands. He glanced down and saw his hands were enveloped with armor that looked like what Mr. Novickas described as Maranda's pattern. Embarrassed at his loss of control, he calmed down quickly and sat next to her silently.

"Your pattern matching is amazing…" she said to him.

"So I've been told," he answered impatiently.

"It is one of the oldest and most beautiful abilities a Star Born can master," she said, holding out her left hand to show him it is covered in the turquoise waves of his own pattern.

"You can…" Leo started to say, overcome with surprise and, interestingly, relief.

"Yes, though I learned it a couple years later in my training than you did. It seems only the most sensitive and empathic Star Borns are able to master this ability. You have to truly want to understand another person to be able to match their pattern. There is an aspect of giving up a part of yourself to accept them inside you."

They sat quietly together, each lost in their own thoughts. Then Leo came back into the present with a question he now felt ready to ask, ""How am I in danger?"

"That's going to take a while to explain and we don't have that much time right at this moment. I can feel your friends near the bottom of the hill, can you?"

Leo closed his eyes and reached out to sense for his friends and he could detect the smallest trace of them, but not their exact location. He opened his eyes and sheepishly said, "Kinda…"

"It's OK, you'll get better at that too."

"Fine, just explain it to all of us when they get here," Leo said with conviction.

"Look, I can tell how much you trust your friends, but I would prefer to keep this between us for the time being. I just think it would be safer to keep things simple for now."

"What is with all the secrets?!" Leo pointedly asked. "Ever since I joined the tribe, it has just been secret upon secret upon secret. Can we not just be open and honest for once?!"

"Yeah, I see your point…" Maranda said thoughtfully, taking a moment to consider things further. "OK, how about this, I just need to get you up to speed with a few things and then you can guide me through how we bring your friends into the fold."

"I guess I can live with that… As long as it doesn't take months…" Leo said hesitantly.

"Yeah, I don't want it to take that long either. We will go as quickly as we can since we really don't have any time to waste. We already lost so much these past few weeks where I couldn't make contact with you again. Do you think you could sneak out and meet me tonight so we can get started right away?"

Leo nodded quickly in response, without considering if it was a good idea.

"Good, meet me in the cavern tonight at midnight. OK, I have to go, your friends are almost back. Please don't let them root around in my stuff anymore. Thanks!" Maranda said as she quietly scurried between two bushes behind them and disappeared.

Leo waved at his friends as they came into view and they waved back.

"Any sign of her?" Ania asked when they were speaking instead of yelling distance.

"Nope," Leo replied, feeling the guilty tug in the bottom of his stomach.

"Oh well! Let the stake-out begin!" Aran said enthusiastically.

They all spent the next couple of hours snacking and hanging out, waiting for Maranda to show up. Of course, she never did and eventually they had to disband and head home.

&

That night, Leo was too keyed up to catch a little sleep before he had to meet Maranda. He just kept going over his plan repeatedly, trying to find a mistake he had made that would get him caught. At ten o'clock, he heard his dad head to bed, but he knew his mom was a night owl and sometimes went to sleep way too late. That was why he was relieved to hear her walk up the stairs softly just after eleven o'clock. For the next twenty minutes he stayed very still in bed and listened to all the various creaks and other noises in the house, straining to make sure he didn't hear anything from his parents' room.

Finally satisfied, he slowly slid out of bed and onto the floor where he left dark clothing to change into. Taking great pains to not make a sound, he eventually got completely ready and grabbed his backpack from under his desk. He then crept down the stairs and into the office where he'd unlocked a window earlier, slowly opening it and sliding out onto the small path that ran along the side of his house. When his foot hit the ground, however, the gravel let out a loud crunching sound and Leo froze. His heart pounded so loudly in his ears that he couldn't hear the frog calls that normally filled the air at night.

Calming himself, he listened for any movement in his house

and let himself the rest of the way out of the window, allowing the gravel to make noise as he stood up fully and looked around. He found a narrow band of soil next to the path and gently tip-toed along it until he got to the front of his house. Then he ran through the shadows in the neighbors' front yards, staying away from the street and sidewalk where he would be clearly seen under the lights. He made it to the bookshop much more quickly than normal and was actually early for a change. Walking up to the back door, he opened the panel on the alarm keypad to enter the code Mr. Novickas told him, but he saw the panel was lit up green instead of amber. Maranda must have already been inside.

He opened the door as quietly as he could and then closed it softly, locking it behind him. He then made his way down to the cavern and found it dimly lit with Maranda sitting on the floor cross legged. She opened her eyes and smiled widely.

"Thank you for coming," she said. Then she stood up and walked over to the bookshelves at the side of the room. She gestured for him to follow her and he reached her just as she was pulling a book off the right end of the top shelf. He looked at it and saw the title was "A Detailed History of Medical Procedures Used During the Middle Ages." He was about to ask her why she chose that book, when she reached the back of the shelf where the book used to be. Then he heard a soft click and the bookshelves pushed away from the wall slightly.

"Give me a hand," she said to Leo as she started pushing on the first shelf and it slid along the wall revealing an opening behind it.

"Are you serious?! There's another secret room?!" he said excitedly.

"You have no idea…" she said, giving him a wink. "Come on, keep pushing."

The bookshelves weighed more than Leo expected and they had to push quite hard to move them well out of the way so a large opening in the wall was revealed. Then, as they walked into the room, lights began to turn on revealing a huge space full of all the equipment Mr. Novickas had been using for their training sessions. There were rows and rows of different items he recognized, but even more rows full of items he was completely unfamiliar with. Maranda led him to the back of the room where there was a nice sized open space and two dark tunnels. She sat down on a cushy chair and gestured to a matching one across from it.

"Everything makes so much more sense now…" Leo said.

"Pretty cool, right?"

"Totally…" he said, still looking around. Then he asked, "So, where do those two tunnels lead?"

"I was wondering if you were going to ask me about those. The one on the right leads to something called The Crucible. Before you ask, yes, everything has to be named dramatically."

Leo chuckled a bit with that comment. He wasn't going to ask that, but now that he thought about it, everything did seem to have a dramatic tinge to it.

"It tests a Star Born when they have reached the end of their training," Maranda continued. "There is a series of eight rooms and in each one there is a challenge that can only be solved by a very skilled Star Born. To be successful, you must pass through all eight rooms within an hour. You can take the test as many times as you want, but that time limit is what makes it so hard. Not only that, but some of the challenges change every time. It takes many Star Borns at least 10 tries to complete it. Only a few have completed it in one or two tries. I was training to complete The Crucible when I left."

"OK, so what happened? Why did you disappear?" Leo asked eagerly, leaning forward in his chair.

"Hold your horses, I'll get to that. There are a few things we need to cover first," she responded with a friendly tone. "You asked me before why you are in danger," she continued. "Well, in truth, we are all in danger. Things are happening in the world and there are signs that something big is coming. It's worrying many of us across the tribes, tensions are really high right now."

"That must've been what my parents were talking about a while back…" Leo said and Maranda looked at him in a way that told him he should elaborate. "I woke up one morning and something felt really off in the house. Normally, mornings are when we all are in great moods and talk about our different plans for the day. That morning… I don't know how to explain it. The house felt cold even though it was a bright, sunny day. I came down the stairs quietly and heard my parents arguing about something. I mean… They barely ever argue. It was so weird to hear them like that. When they heard me, they stopped talking suddenly. I asked them what they were talking about and they just played it off as something in the news. I could tell they weren't telling the entire truth though…"

"Yeah… I think you're right… As you know, we Star Borns are extremely sensitive. Sometimes, we can even sense when someone isn't telling the truth because of how they feel to us. That conversation you described is actually what I wanted to talk to you about. Ever since leaving Kensington, I have been traveling around the world and meeting with different Star Borns. Many of us are sensing the same thing, a war is coming. Momentum is building and we have formed a network to do what we can to avoid another Calamity."

"Wait, Gabriel mentioned something about that a while back. What is it?"

"Damn… It has been so long that I forgot you likely haven't learned anything about it yet. I actually didn't know very much about it until I began traveling and now I think it should be required learning for every member of the tribe. It is probably the darkest moment ever in history and something that has set us all back for thousands of years. Even now, we are still struggling to recover from it and that is why we need to do whatever we can to avoid it happening again. We need all the help we can get, so when we heard another Star Born had been discovered here, I knew it was time for me to return. Leo, we need you to join our cause."

"Me? But I haven't even been training for a year. How can I make a difference?"

"Everyone has a chance to make a difference. Even the most average person can help take steps to avoid this. I am not saying you're the chosen one and everything hinges on you. This will take all of us working together as one, unified front."

This spoke to Leo deeply. He had felt how powerful he became when he and his friends acted as a team, combining their individual strengths into something much greater than any one of them could be by themselves. He felt a pull toward Maranda, there was something about her that was so convincing.

"What would I need to do?" he asked.

"In order for you to join us, I am going to start training you to complete the Crucible."

Leo's eyes widened in disbelief even though he knew she was completely serious.

"Yeah… I know how crazy that sounds. I am not going to sugar coat it, this is so dangerous that it approaches utter stupidity. I just don't see any other way around it. If you don't learn those skills the world will be even more dangerous for you."

"This is all just happening so fast…" he said, struggling to wrap his brain around what she was suggesting.

"It's only going to get faster, Leo. You can choose not to do this and I will completely understand. You and I would leave here tonight and probably not see each other again."

"So I have to choose now," he said, already knowing the answer and Maranda nodded her head sympathetically. Leo stood up and spent a while walking around the large antechamber, occasionally picking up an item and then setting it back down carefully. He didn't even notice that he had made his way back to Maranda unconsciously when he heard her ask, "So, you have made a decision?"

"Yes," he answered seriously.

"OK, what is your answer?"

"I just told you. Yes, I will begin training with you."

"Excellent! I am so glad you trust me with this responsibility," she said, completely relieved.

"I didn't say that," Leo cautioned. "I believe everything you have said to me so far, but I need you to be completely open with me from now on or I will immediately stop training with you. The secrets stop here, with us."

"You drive a tough bargain… I'll accept your terms," Maranda responded with a warm grin.

12

A WARNING

L EO LEANED HIS back against the wall just outside his classroom and slowly slid down until the last foot where friction wasn't enough to hold him up anymore and his butt dropped heavily onto the concrete sidewalk. He let out a deep sigh and started to close his eyes, ignoring his rumbling stomach and the lunch he was clutching with his right hand. Before he drifted off to sleep, however, a voice made its way through the fog of fatigue.

"What is with you, Leo?" Caroline asked.

Leo opened his right eye slightly and stared at her for a moment before closing it and letting out an unintelligible, "Mmmph…"

"Leo, you already fell asleep during art class earlier."

"Just give me five minutes…" Leo said, his voice slurring.

"Tell me what's going on. You promised you would, I even have it in writing," Caroline pushed with her voice sounding even more concerned.

The guilty tug he started to feel beat back the fatigue and Leo opened both of his eyes and reached into his lunch, pulling out some carrot sticks and chomping down on one. Caroline sat down across from him, pulled out a sandwich, took a few bites, and waited for Leo to speak. They both sat quietly this way until Leo finished his lunch. He looked at Caroline with bloodshot eyes and said, "I haven't been getting enough sleep."

"Yeah, that's pretty obvious," Caroline affirms with her characteristic smirk.

"It's only temporary, once summer break starts in a couple weeks it will be a lot better," Leo assured her.

"Nope, not good enough," Caroline said firmly. "Why are you not getting enough sleep? It's not like Mr. O'Reilly is assigning a ton of extra work. I mean, he has us watching a movie after lunch."

"I started some new training and it is very physically demanding. Honestly, I thought my training before was hard, but this is a whole different level. I don't know if I can keep up…" Leo admitted, his shoulders slumping forward and his head hanging low.

"Woah… Leo… I thought you were doing that training because it is fun for you. If it's having this effect on you, maybe you should consider whether it's something you still want to do."

"No, I HAVE to do it."

"Why?"

"I made a commitment… it's important."

"More important than your health? Maybe if you tell me more about it, I can help," Caroline volunteered.

"I really think this is temporary and I do want your help. Actually, I want our entire crew's help and was planning on discussing it with you all on the camping trip," Leo assured her.

"You think you can make it that long?"

"Trust me, it's what's keeping me going right now."

❧

That night, Leo was fast asleep when his phone alarm began to buzz under his pillow. His fingers wouldn't listen to him and he fumbled with the phone a couple times before he could get a firm grip and jab the big orange button in the middle of the screen to turn it off. He rolled onto his back and his hands dropped to his sides, then his eyes started to close again before he caught himself and got out of bed quickly while he's still somewhat conscious.

It took him a lot longer than usual to get ready and he was already late by the time he managed to sneak out of the down-stairs window and start on his way to the cavern. He didn't even bother trying to run, knowing he needed to conserve what little energy he had for practicing the first room of The Crucible. It had been weeks and he still wasn't able to advance past it despite all the coaching and advice that Maranda gave him. He could still feel the deep bruise in his shoulder that he sustained the prior week because of the way he landed when he was launched out of the room after a particularly short-lived attempt.

When he arrived in the cavern, Maranda was sitting in the center of the room, meditating as usual. She heard his footsteps and looked down at her watch to check the time. However, when she saw the state he was in, she thought better of what she was about to say and her face softened as she waved for him to come join her. Leo walked slowly to the center of the room, sat down heavily, and then shed his backpack and sweatshirt, leaving them in a heap behind him.

"We're going to do something a bit different today," Maranda began to say.

"Look, I know I am stuck on the first room, but I have a few ideas I want to try out tonight that I think will do the trick," Leo interrupted defensively.

"Don't worry," Maranda said soothingly. "We'll get to that next time. You made me promise to be open with you and I feel it is time that I shared some more information. You have been working so hard and you deserve to understand what we are going to be fighting for."

"OK, I'd like that," Leo said, suddenly feeling much more alert.

"First, I am going to explain something to you and then I am going to show a set of memories. I know that sounds weird, but it will make sense, I promise."

Maranda took a moment to roll her shoulders and rotated her head back and forth a few times to stretch out her neck, then took a few deep cleansing breaths before she began.

"I think you might already know about this first point somewhat, but it is important that you have a full understanding. So, please ask as many questions as you need as I go. OK?"

Leo nodded.

"All Star Borns are connected together by the different copies of The Book of Star Born. I am aware of at least ten copies around the world from my travels and each is identical to the others. They contain the combined learnings of all Star Borns since they were created thousands of years ago."

"That book over there," Leo said pointing to the copy on the desk along the wall, "is thousands of years old?"

"Yes. I know that's hard to believe because there isn't a scratch on it. The knowledge that was used to create it has been lost for a long time, but I believe we might find it somewhere in the book when we have a Star Born who is ready to learn that ability. That's why each copy is so valuable. There used to be many more, but they have been destroyed or lost over the course of time. You'll understand why a bit more after I finish this explanation.

"When I said each copy contains the combined learnings of all Star Borns throughout time, that means the book is constantly being updated as we learn more about our abilities. When you were first initiated and learned to read the book, that is when the connection was established. You are now forever connected to the Book just like every other Star Born who has been initiated before and every one that will be initiated in the future. If you learn a new ability, it will automatically be added to the book."

"It'll just know when I learn something new and update itself? I don't have to do anything?"

"Now that's a good question! Yes, it automatically updates, but many of us feel it is our responsibility to add as much knowledge to the Book as possible. Have you noticed that some sections have a lot of information, with diagrams and detailed instructions, while other sections are brief, maybe a paragraph long?"

"Yes! The visuals are so helpful!" Leo agreed.

"Well, the book does not automatically create those. A Star Born took the time to add to that section so others could learn from it more easily. The short sections are what is automatically created. Still helpful, but not nearly as much as the curated sections. Throughout my travels, I have met so many other Star Borns and some can do amazing things! My teacher in Chile specialized in amplifying Physics and her tribe has made some amazing leaps in science the rest of the world hasn't even dreamed of yet. What is even more important is that she has carefully documented all of what she has learned about amplification in the Book so that others can develop these abilities when they are ready."

"How does it know when we are ready?" Leo asked, his curiosity deepening.

"I'm not entirely sure… Some of that knowledge has been lost over time. What I do know is the Book draws on our combined experiences and knowledge to help it decide."

"Huh…" Leo said, clearly preoccupied.

"What is it?" Maranda asked, sensing his confusion.

"The Book showed me something a while back that seems really advanced and I have no idea why it feels I am ready to learn it. I haven't even told Gabriel about it…" Leo said, trailing off.

"What was it?" Maranda asked, her curiosity piqued.

"It was called The Spider's Web?" Leo answered tentatively.

"That can't be…" Maranda said, her voice just barely above a whisper. Then a bit louder she asked, "Can you show me?"

Leo nodded and they both stood up and walked back out to the Book of Star Born. As Leo reached out his hand to open the Book, Maranda instructed, "Focus your mind on that section and the book should open up directly to that spot."

Leo closed his eyes and thought of the section. He remembered it perfectly, like a clear photograph. He felt the book open and heard the pages flipping quickly. When he opened his eyes, they were both staring at the small section titled, "The Spider's Web."

"You are full of surprises, Leo…" Maranda muttered.

"Why does it want me to learn this now?" Leo asked, pressing the subject.

"Again, I don't know exactly why, but I haven't known the Book to ever be wrong before. You should begin practicing this."

"Has the book shown this to you before?" Leo asked, hoping she could guide him.

Maranda shook her head slowly and said, "Let's get back to it, there's more to explain."

"But I…" Leo began to protest, but Maranda held up her hand and responded in an uncharacteristically firm tone, "I'll come back to this later."

When they were back and seated in the center of the cavern, Maranda continued where she left off, "This next part I am going to explain is a doozy. The Book also creates a link through our subconscious, we call this The Connector."

"That's real?!" Leo blurted out, completely forgetting about what they were just talking about. "I thought it was just my brain working through stuff while I slept!"

"No, I assure you, it is real. You and I saw each other for the first time there. Each of the doors you saw opens to the subconscious mind of a living Star Born or the memories of one who is deceased. I don't know how you found my door so quickly, it must have been one of your many talents. If you remember, when you tried to come inside, you ended up immediately falling into a deep pit, right? That's because you needed me to guide you in. That is the only way you can enter someone's mind."

Leo's face drained of color and he looked down at his fidgeting hands.

"What is it?" she asked with concern.

"I heard something through one of the doors…"

"That is pretty normal. There is always some leakage from our minds into The Connector," Maranda tried to reassure him.

"No… you don't understand… they knew I was there. They're looking for me…"

Maranda didn't say anything in response, instead she just stared at Leo intensely.

"What?" he asked awkwardly.

Maranda finally blinked and said seriously, "It seems we should have had this discussion sooner, but I am glad we're having it now."

This just made Leo feel itchy with anxiety and he asked, "Do we need to do something?"

"Not yet…" she answered carefully. "But what I am about to show you is even more important knowing that others are trying to reach you."

Maranda then reached out and took both of Leo's hands gently. She said, "I'm going to share several memories with you that were given to me by my teacher in Japan."

Leo started to pull his hands back, remembering how it felt when he connected to the Book of Star Born.

She recognized his trepidation and said, "Don't worry, this won't hurt at all."

Leo felt warmth spreading from her hands into his. It was actually a pleasant sensation, similar to how it felt when Mr. Novickas healed him. The warm feeling spread up his arms, to his neck, and then finally around his head.

"Open your eyes now," Maranda instructed and Leo found himself standing in a small park surrounded by a bustling city. It was unlike any place he had seen before with buildings taking forms that he was sure were not possible in the world today. He saw a narrow spire in the distance that was probably much taller than the Eiffel Tower, but without any supports spreading out from its base. The buildings that surrounded the park where he was standing had unique structural details and in some cases twisted together. What was most striking were the intense colors everywhere that seemed to infuse the buildings. He felt like he had to squint to protect his eyes from how bright they were.

The other thing that took him aback was the sight of so many

Earth Borns openly using their powers. He saw one at the far end of the park lifting a heavy block to the roof of a nearby home. Just a few paces from him and Maranda was a small team repairing a broken pipe for the fountain in the center of the park. One was guiding water from the pipe into the fountain while another manufactured a new one and put it in place. He marveled at how comfortable they were with their abilities and how powerful they all seemed to be.

"This was Coreolis," Maranda told him. "It was the heart of civilization during a golden age before The Calamity, when all of humanity was aware of their abilities and when we learned a great deal about them. In fact, most of what you will read in the Book of Star Born was discovered during this time. It lasted for over a millennium."

Leo felt a slight tug from Maranda's hand as she began to walk down a large avenue at one end of the park. As they ambled slowly, Leo was able to get a true understanding of the city's scale. When they crossed streets that met what was now clearly a main thoroughfare, he saw they ran far beyond what his eyes could see. They passed by shops and restaurants. There were produce vendors on several corners, but he didn't recognize any of the bright, delicious-looking fruit.

Without warning, Leo's vision blurred and they were now standing in front of a large iridescent building that he could only assume was some kind of religious institution like a temple or something. As he looked around, the colors reflecting off the structure shifted in rainbow shimmers and he looked at Maranda with a wide smile despite a slight queasiness in his stomach.

"Amazing, isn't it?" she said in answer to the delighted look on his face. "This was called the People's House and it was the center of Coreolis' government. The citizens' elected representatives met here daily to guide their society forward. There were three leaders, one Earth Born, Star Born, and Moon Born, who were selected from all the representatives to guide the decision-making process. They were simply called The Three. No one person could amass too much power, which is why the government was stable for so long.

Again, Leo's vision blurred and when it cleared he realized they were now walking down a hallway inside the People's House. He stopped and put his hands on his knees, feeling woozy and taking deep breaths.

"You OK?" Maranda asked.

"Yeah, I think so. The shifts between memories are a bit jarring…" he confessed.

"I know what you mean, I'll try to let you know when the next one is about to happen. Are you OK to continue?"

Leo stood up and took one last deep breath, then looked at her and nodded his head.

"At the height of this age," Maranda begins again, "two Star Borns emerged as leaders and, in an unprecedented move, decided to share the Star Born seat amongst The Three. Their names were Torrell and Warwick and it was seen as an example of how cooperative society had become. The two of them were also proponents of a new philosophy, called Advancement, in which they proposed that society should come together and focus on advancing the understanding and development of abilities more quickly. The key to achieving this was a new form of communalism that involved a deeper amount of sharing amongst all members of society. Star Born, Moon Born, and Earth Born would all need to combine abilities to achieve this massive leap.

"Countless people joined their movement for a variety of reasons. Most wanted to do their part to make the world a better place, where illnesses and conflict were eliminated. However, their following wasn't big enough to achieve the advancement as they envisioned. Many people held off embracing these beliefs because their leaders believed society wasn't ready for the kind of power that might come with advancement and it would be better to take a slower, measured approach that allowed people to develop abilities at a pace they could handle. This was especially true with the Moon Born community and only a handful of them joined the movement.

"Brace yourself," Maranda said to Leo and he gripped her hand tightly as everything became fuzzy again. This time, he found they were in an ornate room with two men standing in the center and arguing with each other. A number of others were sitting around the perimeter of the room, listening to them and whispering comments to each other.

"What you are suggesting is unconscionable! We cannot force people towards advancement!" shouted the man to their left. Leo noticed he was dressed impeccably in a form-fitting suit. He was simply adorned with a large silver ring on the middle finger of his right hand and earring over his left ear that covers the entire outside edge of his ear. His skin was dark and he had long cords of hair held back with a silver band.

"Torrell, all you are doing is showing weakness and they are capitalizing on it!" the other shouted back. He was slightly taller and dressed in heavy crimson robes with a thick gold chain around his neck carrying a large medallion centered on his chest. He had short, dark hair that was spiked up with a thin mustache and beard framing his mouth.

"We are at our strongest when we willingly come together with a common purpose! This is the foundation of what we started! We just need to take the time to work through their concerns!" Torrell rebutted and he took a few steps forward so that he stood barely a foot away from Warwick.

"They're set in their ways and have made up their minds. I am done waiting for them," Warwick said, lowering his tone to a casual conversation and turning his back on Torrell.

"I can't allow you to do this, Warwick. It will be the end of us and I will go to the council and have you removed," Torrell threatened.

Warwick whirled around and bolts of energy erupted from his hands, arcing across Torrell's unprotected skin, causing him to cry out in agony. Despite this, Torrell managed to charge his armor and swung a huge punch directly at Warwick's face, and he barely had time to get his hands up to protect himself as the blow sent him staggering. Looking at Torrell with intense rage, he clenched his hands tight and began to mutter some words too softly for Leo to hear.

Leo then couldn't believe what he saw next. Thick bands of energy sprouted out of many of the onlookers and connected with Warwick, who directed the full force of the energy right at Torrell in a thick beam. Leo saw the agony on the people's faces as they were slowly drained of their lives and he covered his mouth in horror. He turned his attention to Torrell who tried to resist the onslaught, but the strength of Warwick's attack was too great and he was eventually overwhelmed. He crumpled to the floor and lay motionless on his back.

Warwick muttered softly again and the energy connections slowly dissipated as he walked forward and stood over Torrell briefly. Leo noticed his expression was one of disgust and he quickly turned and strode out of the room. Several people stood up and followed him and Leo looked around the room counting the number of people who were slumped lifeless in their chairs.

Several people who managed to survive rushed over to Torrell, assessing his wounds. Leo watched them as they gently moved scorched clothing out of the way to see the raw burns across his body. Leo heard Torrell's grunts from the pain and knew he was still alive. He saw one of the people who attended to Torrell rush out of the room and then she returned with several others who were clearly healers. As they began to work on Torrell, Maranda said softly, "This was the start of The Calamity," and Leo felt a squeeze from her hand as his vision began to cloud again.

When everything resolved again, Leo found himself standing in the midst of scorched ground cover and tall blackened trunks of a small grouping of trees. He surveyed the area and as far as he could see was just utter devastation. Out of the corner of his eye, Leo detected something coming at him quickly and he turned to see Torrell running full speed toward him. He couldn't help but flinch as Torrell launched himself forward and dove into the soot and brush at his feet. Torell popped up, his face smeared with black streaks and he looked around quickly.

Moments later, members of his unit joined Torrell and Leo noticed they all had the same haggard appearance. As soon as it was clear they were all accounted for, Torrell looked at a small woman with short cropped hair and intricate blue designs running up her arms and appearing above the collar of her shirt. Without saying a word, she shifted into a sitting position and closed her eyes.

Minutes ticked by, each one feeling like an eternity, and they all just watched her patiently. Then, without any warning, she gasped and two others held her up as she almost collapsed while coming out of her trance. Torrell leaned over her and asked urgently, "What happened? Are you OK?"

Leo saw her fight back tears and her face contorted, showing anger and determination. She impatiently shrugged off the support from her friends and got onto her knees. Then she wiped the ground in front of her clear with her left hand. She carefully drew a map of the area and, when she was finished, she spoke with a voice that was clearly hoarse from exertion and breathing in smoke.

"This isn't going to be easy, but I don't see any other way through the battle," she started. "We will need to follow this creek starting here." She pointed to a spot at the base of the hill where they were sheltering.

"As soon as we reach that point, we will be completely exposed. There won't be any safe place to stop until we reach the temple and we will be running between two armies actively attacking each other." She took a moment and rubbed her eyes with the back of her hand in frustration.

"They have some of their most powerful fighters on the front lines. I saw my brother's unit pinned down by the largest Mors vines I have ever seen. The thorns were as big as my middle finger. They were all being torn apart and there wasn't anything they could do to stop it."

She tried to hold back the tears, but lost the effort this time and began to sob. Her friends tried to comfort her, but that just made her cry harder. She let out a low moan, trying to release all the emotions she was feeling and then she heard Torrell's deep voice say, "I can feel what you're going through right now. I know it's excruciating, but there will be time for mourning later. Now there is one thing we can do. Get to that temple. Those Mors vines can only be created because Warwick and his Skein are powering their fighters. We need you to show us the way, Ciara. Can you do that?"

Leo saw Ciara slowly relax and breathe more regularly as she wiped her wet cheeks leaving long muddy marks. Finally, with one more deep, cleansing breath, she continued.

"OK, I think the best bet is to keep to the left side of the creek. That way, it will be our forces who can see us the most and it might provide some minimal cover, especially here and here." She pointed out two bends in the creek.

"This is where the creek dips down lower and it creates a miniature canyon. If we make it past these points…"

"*When* we make it past," a young man to her right corrected her.

"OK, *when* we make it past, we will need to move as fast as possible. I can only think of one way to make it through this last part since it is completely open. Anyone will be able to see us and Warwick has concentrated his forces near the entrance of the temple to protect him. It's just… It means we will have to leave someone behind," Ciara said.

A woman behind her right shoulder who had leaned in to support her said, "We all knew what we were getting into. We joined this unit because it was the best hope for ending the war today. Every one of us would give up our lives to make that happen. Tell us your idea."

Ciara looked at Torrell with wary eyes. "Torrell will need to give Kuba a huge amount of energy right when we reach this point," she jammed her finger into the ground just past the second bend of the creek.

"Then Kuba will need to launch us with all of his strength over Warwick's guard units and Phoebe will have to cushion our fall. Otherwise, we won't arrive at the entrance in any shape to fight Warwick," Ciara finished.

"Seems like a good plan to me," Kuba affirmed.

Torrell stared at Kuba and didn't say anything for several

moments. The rest of the unit knew to stay quiet and let Torrell think. Finally, he said, "You've been with me since the beginning, Kuba. I don't know if I can let you do this. That amount of energy will almost certainly kill you."

Kuba chuckled lightly and said, "I suppose you have a better idea? Of course you'll let me do this because it must be done."

Torrell stood up slowly and Kuba rose with him. Then Torrell reached out, grabbed him by the scruff of the neck, and pulled him in until their foreheads were touching. They didn't say anything to each other and just shared the moment. Finally, Torrell let go, looked around and said, "Ciara, you're in front to guide us and Greyson I want you with her. Kuba and Phoebe, you're in the middle and protected at all costs. I'll be right next to you so we can be ready. Michael, you take up the rear with Leila. Don't let anyone surprise us."

Then Leo and Maranda watched as Torrell and his team ran down the hill away from them. With every step, cracks from dry sticks echoed around them and dust billowed up giving away their movements. They didn't slow down to muffle their steps or even try running between the trees to protect themselves. They just picked the most direct path and ran as fast as possible.

"This is likely going to be very disorienting," Maranda said. "These memories are just snippets of those Torrell passed down personally to only a small group very late in his life."

Leo then found himself watching from Torrell's eyes as the group ran toward the creek Ciara had described. A small group of fighters appeared ahead in the distance and both Ciara and Greyson began to stagger their steps to run in a more unpredictable way. Suddenly, something extremely fast slammed into Greyson, sending him tumbling. Ciara screamed, but didn't stop running.

All Leo could do was stare as Torrell focused on Greyson stepping up unsteadily, clearly injured. Whatever had slammed into him was approaching again and it slammed him flat on his back. Then it stopped and Leo could now see it was actually a fighter who was unsheathing a long blade from a scabbard on his back.

Greyson struggled to get up, spitting out blood and shaking. The fighter then launched himself again at Greyson, who was swaying as if he was about to faint. As the fighter got closer, Greyson stopped shaking suddenly as he set himself. His feet dug into the damp ground and he reached his hands forward like two big claws, one over the other. The fighter tried to slow down, but he couldn't do it quickly enough and Greyson grabbed him by the waist and neck, swinging him over his head and then slamming him into the ground with unimaginable force.

Greyson examined the fighter carefully and nodded with satisfaction before falling to his knees. He coughed several times and then slumped onto his side and watched as his unit disappeared around the bend. Leo felt the same stab of pain in his core as Torrell when the connection to Greyson was cut.

Leo felt another jolt as the surroundings shifted rapidly to the next memory and he realized the group was heading toward a large bend. As they made the turn, the sheer size of Warwick's army in front of them was astounding. There were countless well equipped fighters with crazed looks on their faces. There were cries across the front lines as the group was spotted and Leo saw boulders levitating into the air, large vines growing out of the ground, a tornado forming off to their right, and a horde of insects coalescing almost directly ahead of them.

Warwick's forces could never have expected such a brazen attack from a small team and the firepower they amassed was like bringing a pickaxe instead of a scalpel to perform surgery.

Ciara held her hand up and curled her fingers into a fist. Then Kuba raised both of his arms quickly and the remainder of the unit rose with them. When Kuba swung his arms forward in a dramatic motion, they were all launched over the battlefield, leaving him behind. He collapsed on the ground, having expended every ounce of energy in his body. The army erupted with attacks aimed high above it and the sight was like a dazzling fireworks display. Frustrated cries filled the air when not a single attack found its mark.

As Leo felt the strange exhilaration of flying through the air, the memory began to fade and he found himself on the ground, watching the group dust themselves off from what seemed to be a particularly rough landing. Torrell turned to Phoebe and said, "How close are we?" She lifted her head in a gesture for him to look behind them and then he saw the large, unguarded cave entrance.

"There's nobody here protecting the entrance?" Ciara asked incredulously.

"They must have thought there was no way anyone would be able to make it this far," Torrell replied with a wary voice. "They're probably on their way now and we don't have much time. Let's go," he continued as he headed into the cave.

From Leo's perspective, there really wasn't anything that identified this cave as the entrance to a temple. There were no markings or stones on which countless people had rubbed their hands and smoothed out the ridges. In fact, the entrance was really just a large crack in the side of the mountain. The floor was smooth, with a light coating of dust that barely showed the sign of footsteps.

The group fell into a single file line as the cave narrowed a short way in. It steadily grew dimmer too, the light from outside failing to penetrate into the deeper parts of the cave. Torrell charged his hands and they began to glow and crackle with enough light to see where they were going. The group fell quiet and all they heard was each other's breathing and the scuffling of their feet as they made their way through the passage.

They continued this way for what felt like hours. The passage got brighter as they walked and they came to a large room where the path forked. Torrell didn't hesitate and went immediately to the right. Eventually, they saw a large arch in front of them. This was the first sign that they had reached the temple and the roughly cut stones each had different symbols that were glowing brightly and then dimming in a regular rhythm.

Torrell held up his hand, quietly asking the rest of them to stop while he carefully peered past the arch. Leo leaned over his shoulder and saw there was a large cavern, in the center of which was an altar that was surrounded by ten pedestals. Warwick stood on top of the altar and there was a Star Born on top of each pedestal who was chanting something unintelligible. He also saw power arcing from the priests as they fed Warwick and he concentrated it through a round oculus above him. This was how Warwick was amplifying his army and why they were decimating everyone who had come to oppose them.

This final memory faded as well and Leo felt the cold floor of the cavern underneath him. He opened his eyes to see Maranda staring at him with warmth and care in her eyes.

"That was the last battle of a war that lasted twenty-three years. Countless people died and a great society was destroyed. Torrell was the only one who survived and he did that by imprisoning Warwick in a vial created by skilled Moon Born artisans. The location of that vial is a closely held secret because even today there are people who still believe in Warwick's vision and are working toward bringing it to reality. They would love to find a way to release him so he could lead them again."

Leo blinked a few times and then gently let go of Maranda's hands before he stood up and started walking around in a small circle and shaking out the tightness in his arms and legs.

"This is the war you are trying to avert…" Leo said as he came to the realization and he walked back to stand facing Maranda.

"Yes. To them, the war never ended."

"There's something I don't understand. Since they beat Warwick's armies, why did everything fall apart?" Leo inquired.

"Warwick thought that he could force the world into advancement, but the exact opposite happened. Following the war, people began to believe their abilities were the source of the world's conflicts and humans should avoid using them at all cost. A new movement called Abatement began to spread like wildfire. Torrell and other leaders who believed abilities could still be used for the betterment of society tried to engage in rational arguments with the leaders of the Abatement movement, but they were met with hostility and sometimes violence.

"In the span of nine years following the war, multiple laws were passed to restrict the use of abilities and to even mandate the destruction of anything created by someone who used their abilities. Coreolis was basically torn apart brick by brick and replaced by a sprawling sea of mud huts and open sewers. People were so dependent on their abilities, they had no idea how to create anything without them. Diseases spread and more people died, but it was always blamed on abilities. Large gangs were enlisted to find and kill people using their abilities.

"This is how the tribes were formed. They realized it would not be safe to form a new Coreolis or any kind of large concentration of people. So, they split into small groups and scattered across the world, always trying as much as possible to live far away from other people and making it a priority to preserve the knowledge and study of our abilities. Eventually, that became much harder as the world became more crowded. Tribes began to hide and integrate within communities or cities formed near them. This approach has been very successful for a long time, but sometimes mistakes have been made. You have probably heard of witch trials, right? Some of our people were accused of practicing magic because they got too comfortable with their friends or even family members who did not have or use their abilities.

"That's not the worst example, though. During World War II, the Nazis scoured the world for signs of the tribes so they could exploit their abilities. They investigated every rumor and clue they could get their hands on and were able to find many of the tribes in Europe. Most died resisting them and our communities there are still recovering from those losses today."

"What if they were right?" Leo asked. "Maybe our abilities *are* a source of conflict…"

"No, Leo, you can't think like that. Our abilities have always been a part of us. Would you cut off your right arm because somebody said it is a source of evil? No, of course not!"

"But… The Calamity… All of these wars… I mean…"

"There still would have been wars and conflict even if nobody had any abilities. People are capable of both amazing and horrible things."

"Look at what Warwick did to those people! At least without that kind of power, fewer people die."

"Yes, that was a horrible use of his abilities. However, people have still been able to use knowledge to do catastrophic things. How about the atomic bomb? The same knowledge that can be used to create abundant electricity was also used to destroy two cities in Japan. That had nothing to do with our abilities."

Leo's face shifted from concern to confusion. He walked away from Maranda, circling around the perimeter of the room, finally feeling the fatigue settle in again as the initial jolt of adrenaline from the memory wore off. He tried to process all the doubts and concerns he had felt since the beginning of his training with the new perspective Maranda had provided him. He had to admit, it made a lot of sense, but it was hard to let go of something he had been worried about for this long. He finally stopped, nodded to himself, and walked straight back to Maranda.

"I think you're right," he said definitively to Maranda. "I have to decide what I want to stand for and I can't see how ignoring or suppressing our abilities is the right path. So many times throughout history, people have been forced to hide parts of themselves because society said it was wrong. I'm in, I'll do my part."

Maranda stared at him, her eyes filled with pride, and said, "Good, then you're ready for me to explain a little more to you about what you saw in those memories. When Warwick attacked Torrell, he was using the Spider's Web. Up until that moment, it had only been used a few times for beneficial purposes. Once to eradicate an outbreak of a dangerous illness in an area on the outskirts of Coreolis. Another time was to erect that tall spire you probably saw as I took you through the memory of the city. That ability was an example that Torrell and Warwick used over and over again to advocate that advancement would be good for society. So you see, even things that initially seem to be good can sometimes be twisted into something evil. It all depends on how we teach people to use their abilities. This is at the heart of what we do throughout the tribes now."

"You're telling me this because you think I should still learn to use that ability," Leo said with resignation.

"Yes, because I believe you are someone who would only use it to help people."

"What happens if you're wrong?"

"I'm not. You have a good heart," she said firmly, but also reassuringly. "Warwick thought it was fine to take whatever he needed to achieve his goals. When a Star Born wouldn't willingly join his cause, he would reach into their core and take it. I barely know you, but I already can say with confidence you would never do that."

"How did he do that?" Leo asked, suddenly feeling frigidly cold, goosebumps spreading over his arms, and dreading what the answer may be.

"It's one of the most forbidden acts a Star Born can do. He would connect to them and reach deep inside to where they generate their energy and form their individual pattern. He would pull it out of them and add it to his own core. He did this to countless people and it made him by far the most powerful person in the world. To this day, it is forbidden for a Star Born to reach inside another person."

"*Forbidden*?" Leo asked pointedly.

"Yes, the punishment is immediate expulsion from the tribes. What's going on, Leo? You are looking pretty wound up all of a sudden."

"Gabriel reached inside of me the first day I trained with him," Leo said through clenched teeth. "It was very uncomfortable and I eventually found a way to push him out. He said he was doing it to assess my abilities…"

"Did he touch your core?!" Maranda asked, extreme worry permeating her voice and body.

"No, he was reaching for it when I pushed him out," Leo said quickly, feeling the urge to calm her down.

"This is important, Leo. Are you sure he didn't touch it?"

"Positive," Leo answered definitively.

"OK, good…" Maranda said, taking a deep breath and leaning back, her hands positioned behind her to hold her up. Leo could see small beads of sweat had formed all over her forehead. After a few minutes of silence, Maranda began to speak again.

"There have been rumors in recent years that Gabriel may be an advancement believer. Nobody could imagine that a member of the council could possibly follow that path, but you just confirmed it…" Maranda stared into space, her eyes moving around as she accessed different parts of her brain to think through the problem.

Focusing back on Leo again, she said, "This is a really big deal, I need to go speak to some people. We won't be able to meet again for the next two weeks."

"You need to be back by the camping trip," Leo said assertively.

"What? Why?" Maranda questioned, not understanding his thought process.

"Because you need to be there when I tell my friends everything."

"Uh… I'm not sure that's a good…"

"You promised," Leo said simply.

"Yes, but…"

"You'll be there or I will consider our deal over."

"Fine…" Maranda relented. "I'll be there."

"Good, because I'll need your help explaining this to Caroline."

13

Secrets Revealed

THE WHOLE CREW rushed out of the campsite, speed walking as quickly as they could while trying to not draw any undue attention from the parents. The traffic had been horrendous due to an overturned truck carrying huge pipes that blocked the road for hours, so it had taken an eternity getting to Bodega Bay. Then, Astro stole a piece to one of their tents and they wasted an hour between trying to figure out why they couldn't get the tent to stand up and then searching for the missing piece.

It was tradition to hike out to the beach as soon as possible and, by the time they were ready, most of the day was gone and they were determined to make up for lost time.

"Be back by six o'clock for dinner!" Emily called out to them.

"Got it!" several of them shouted back.

"I mean it! I'll feed your dinner to the dogs if you're late!"

"How does she always see where we're going?" Stella asked the rest of them in amazement.

"I think she slips something in our food to track us," Meimei responded, only half joking.

Leo laughed as he listened to his friends bantering back and forth as they made their way down the trail, but he couldn't really release any of the massive amount of tension in his body. It had been building over the past two weeks while Maranda was away and he continued his sessions with Gabriel. Constantly on alert, he had been thinking about every move he made or word he said to ensure he didn't tip Gabriel off. In the process, his neck and back were now bound up in knots so tight he had barely slept the past few days. Despite all his care, however, he was pretty sure Gabriel had noticed a change in his behavior and all his efforts had probably been wasted.

At the head of the group, he did his best to scan along the trail and then deeper into the thick brush while moving his head as little as possible to avoid the pinches of pain that came with it. About half-way to the beach, he finally saw what he was looking for, a piece of blue ribbon tied to a sapling at the head of a small, overgrown offshoot trail. This was the sign Maranda said she would use to let him know which way they should go. Without a word, Leo turned onto the trail and almost immediately one of his friends questioned what he was doing.

"Uh, wrong way Leo!" Ania called.

"This trail also goes to the beach," Leo replied.

"Yeah, but we never go that way, it takes so much longer."

"I know, but I still think we should go this way. Just trust me, OK?"

The debate immediately stopped and Ania looked frustrated, but she took a few steps onto the trail. It had become an unstated rule that when one of them asked for the group's trust, they should all grant it unconditionally. They had been through a lot together over the past year and in many cases they had to solve problems in ways the others didn't always immediately understand. Trust was not only what held them together as friends, but it was also the foundation for their success as a team.

The group returned to the brisk pace that Leo set, but the chatter was practically nonexistent. While they didn't ask Leo to explain all of the reasons he was leading them this way, there was a feeling of anticipation amongst all of them. That was, except for Caroline, who was in the back singing to herself and happily oblivious while absorbed in a particularly good daydream. Soon, the trail widened enough for the group to start walking together instead of following in a single file line. Meimei pushed to the front to walk with Leo, so she was the first to notice there was another person on the side of the trail in front of them, sitting in the shade of a large tree.

It took her a moment to register that she recognized the person and she dropped her backpack from her shoulders, pulled out two throwing knives from the back pockets of her jeans, and levitated them while she crouched and reached for a large rock in front of her on the trail. Immediately reacting instinctively to Meimei's actions, the rest of the group responded in kind with Ania growing two thick vines of poison oak on either side of the hiker, Stella pulling several spikes of water out of the creek running along the left side of the trail, and Aran surrounding himself with a small flock of what appeared to be very angry finches.

"Woah, woah, woah! Don't hurt her! I can explain everything!" Leo shouted as he jumped in front of them and held out his hands to be able to protect Maranda if they decided to attack, even though he knew she hardly needed the help. He glanced back to take a look at her and saw that she was ready for anything, even though she was still seated calmly under the tree.

"What's going on, Leo?!" Meimei shouted, not lowering her knives yet.

"I can explain everything! Please!" Leo said in desperation. "Remember that day when we went searching for Maranda all together? Well, she kind of found me instead," he continued with a nervous chuckle, trying to break the tension.

"That was weeks ago! Why haven't you told us?!"

"That's what we are trying to do today!"

"Let's hear what they have to say," Aran said to Meimei. Then he looked at Leo and said bluntly, "This better be good."

"HOW… THE… *HELL*… ARE YOU ALL ABLE TO DO THAT?!" Caroline shouted at the top of her lungs and the rest of the group quickly turned around with looks on their faces like they had just been caught stealing.

"Oh, crap…" Aran muttered.

"This is what we were talking about at school a couple weeks ago," Leo said quickly, not missing a beat.

"I thought you were talking about *KARATE*!" Caroline continued to shout.

Maranda finally stood up and walked over to stand next to Leo.

"Look, we're kinda out in the open here. I got here yesterday and unexpectedly found a nice private spot where we can continue this discussion," she said calmly to the group.

"We can trust her, guys," Leo chimed in to reassure them.

"Who the hell is she?!" Caroline yelled again, clearly unable to calm down.

Aran took a few steps over to her and put a hand on her shoulder, "Oh you have no idea the story we're about to tell you…"

Caroline just stared at him, barely able to register what he was saying.

"Follow me," Maranda instructed and the group began to shuffle after her. After going a few hundred yards further down the trail, she walked directly into the brush on the right side and they all followed as she led them around some large bushes and small stands of trees for several minutes. Finally, she stopped in front of a large boulder and ran her hands along the bottom, clearly searching for something.

"Ah, there you are," she said when she found a small crack and reached her index and middle fingers inside. With a soft thud, the rock split in two and slowly opened to reveal a room that was big enough to fit all of them, but just barely. Maranda gestured for them to go in and they all took warry steps inside except for Caroline who hung back, shaking her head.

Leo walked back out and reached for her hand, but she yanked it back quickly.

"No way am I going in there," she said.

"You said you wanted me to tell you everything," he replied calmly.

"This is way too much…" Caroline said, her eyes filling with tears.

"I felt pretty overwhelmed at first too," he admitted. "Just come inside and we will explain. You heard Aran, this is going to be one hell of a story."

"You promise this is safe?" she asked.

"Completely."

The confidence in Leo's voice seemed to convince her and Caroline followed him into the small room. Maranda was the last one in and touched a small square on the wall that caused the rock to seal around them.

Leo looked around the room, noticing the walls emitted a soft glow and his eyes settled on Maranda. He gave her a curious look with a raised eyebrow and she said, "This place is ancient. Whoever made it was really strong, I could feel it when I got close enough. There's no way I would've known it was here otherwise."

"OK, get on with it," Meimei said icily.

Leo opened his mouth to speak, but nothing came out. He had been thinking about how he was going to explain everything to his friends ever since he met Maranda that day in the cemetery. He had even practiced some of it while walking home from training sometimes. Now that everyone was there, staring at him with expectation and anger, his mind was flooded with so much information that he couldn't get a single word out.

"Well, there is a lot to cover and I think we should start at the very beginning so that Caroline can understand. Maybe you all can chime in if we forget anything as we go," Maranda said in her usual calm, warm tone. "Before we do that, I must tell you that Leo has insisted we tell you everything and I asked him to wait. I can tell how angry and hurt each of you are right now and it is my fault. I am truly sorry for that…"

Leo couldn't tell if his friends believed her since his senses were feeling jumbled and unclear. However, he was able to tell just by looking at Caroline that she was barely holding it together. She was biting her nails and had already made it through one whole hand, so he knew they better start explaining before she ran out of fingers.

"So, we all have super powers…" he said to Caroline.

Caroline looked at him incredulously and snapped, "I kinda got that part already."

"Well, not exactly. *Everyone* has super powers. There are all kinds of different abilities and some people are really strong while others have almost none at all. Maybe it would help if we explain what each of us can do."

Leo looked to Ania and gave her a small nod to encourage her to start.

"I guess the best way to describe my ability is that I have the ultimate green thumb," she said in her usual brief and slightly shy tone.

"You're good with plants?" Caroline asked, still not understanding.

"Yeah," Ania answered simply.

"She's not just good with plants," Leo interrupted, dissatisfied with the explanation. "She is amazing with them. You will see what she can do. I mean, I guess you saw what she did with those vines earlier."

"That was you? How did you do that?" Caroline asked with a bit of wonder mixed into the anxiety in her voice.

Ania blushed with embarrassment and said, "It's hard to explain, the plants just feel like a part of me. I can understand what they are able to do, just like I am able to understand how to move my arm."

It looked like Caroline was about to ask a question, but Leo said, "Who wants to go next?" trying to keep things moving. One by one, they each explained their abilities until they got back to Leo.

"What's your specialty?" Caroline asked him, starting to feel more comfortable. "I bet you have something really weird."

In response, Leo decided to direct some of his energy into his hands to show her, but, when he tried, it felt thick and sluggish. He used all of his focus to finally bring out enough to cover his right hand and she saw the bright blue waves cascade over it.

"Woah… You are a human flashlight…" she said sarcastically and everyone erupted in laughter.

"More like the battery for the flashlight," Leo replied, still laughing and feeling some of the tension release in his back finally.

"So, you're saying I have super powers too?" Caroline asked, clearly starting to get excited.

"Technically, yes," Stella answered, but stopped short of elaborating.

Sensing there was more to that answer, Caroline asked, "What aren't you telling me?"

Nobody wanted to be the one to answer her and she looked at each one expectantly, starting to get frustrated. Finally, Meimei spoke up.

"We don't know what your ability is. It should have expressed itself around when you turned twelve like the rest of us, but nobody has been able to detect yours."

"I don't understand…" Caroline said and the good mood started to shift back to confusion and frustration.

"It probably means your abilities are not strong enough to detect," Maranda said gently. "This happens sometimes and you may eventually develop them, but they will likely be relatively weak."

Caroline sat in silence, rubbing her hands on her thighs and staring at her feet. Everyone waited patiently for her to process this, knowing how hard it had been for them to process much of this same information. Leo tried to sense what she was feeling, but she was completely blank. It felt like he was flying blind and he came to the realization of just how important this part of his abilities was for him to navigate the world.

"And you have some kind of power to open rocks like an easter egg?" Caroline asked Maranda out of nowhere, surprising the group.

"Nope, I'm a battery like Leo," she answered with a big smile.

"Huh… guess you guys are pretty common. I personally would've liked to have been like Dr. Doolittle over there," she quipped, gesturing to Aran.

"Hey now…" Leo started to say as if he was offended even though he was just happy that she was joking around with the group.

Everyone started to break into conversations, relieved the stress of sharing their secret with Caroline is finally over. They all took turns explaining more details about what they had learned about the tribes and their abilities, sharing some stories of their training sessions with Mr. Novickas and Gabriel. Caroline marveled at what they were able to do and asked an endless amount of questions.

Looking down at her watch, Stella raised her voice and said, "Guys! We gotta get back to the campsite in twenty minutes or we won't get dinner!"

"Relax," Meimei responded in an uncharacteristically nonchalant way, "my mom can be a bit intense about some things, but she never does it with food. Don't get me wrong, we should get back soon, but we have a little more time to play with and I want to hear Maranda's story."

"Oh yeah! Me too!" Leo jumped in excitedly.

"She hasn't told you?!" Stella exclaimed.

"At least I'm not the only one who's learning something new here," Caroline ribbed.

"Alright, alright, enough of that. Back to Maranda," Leo redirected.

"I hoped I might be able to dodge this bullet today, but it looks like I'm in the hot seat now. Let's get this over with…" Maranda began. "Not long before my abilities expressed themselves, the last Star Born in our tribe passed away. So, like Leo, I started my training with Mr. Novickas at the bookshop. He was a very good teacher, but at some point during my second year of training I moved beyond his knowledge and he reached out to Gabriel to see if there was a Star Born teacher who could come continue my training. It turned out, one of Gabriel's most successful students had just completed the training of another Star Born and was ready to take me on. His name was Sayed and he arrived a couple months later.

"I can still remember what it was like when we first started training together… I mean, I had learned so much already, but he just opened my world to the possibilities of my abilities. There were times where I felt like I could barely keep up with him, but he somehow knew and never pushed me too far.

"We trained together for over five years and it felt like he wasn't just my teacher, but also like the big brother I never had. When it was time for me to train for The Crucible, that closeness helped me handle a level of training I had never experienced before."

"The *what* now?" Aran asked.

"Oh yeah, I guess we haven't covered that yet," Maranda replied. "Think of it as the final exam before Star Born graduation."

"Will we have to do something like that?!" Aran asked, starting to go down a rabbit hole.

"The short answer is yes, but let's not get into that right now, OK? Anyway, Sayed and I had to spend a ton of time together as the training intensity ramped up significantly. He began to guide me through the skills I needed to pass the test and sometimes we would just talk while I rested between attempts.

"I can tell you, he really liked going deep and talking about philosophy and religion. We would get into intense debates just

for fun and to have a distraction. Until one night, we were training really late. I think it must've been one in the morning or
something. I had made it pretty far that day and we were both
excited that I might soon be able to take the test. Sayed was so
amped up and he started talking about how I could soon become
a part of the movement. I had no idea what that meant, but he
insisted I was holding myself back on the final challenge and I
needed to do whatever it took to complete it. He was so wrapped
up in what he was saying, he didn't notice how his words had
hurt me. I was working so hard and his opinion meant a lot to
me, so the idea that I wasn't willing to do what it took made me
upset…"

Maranda grew quiet, as she became lost in her thoughts.
The group waited for her to start again, shifting impatiently and
coughing or clearing their throats to try and nudge her. She
finally looked up slowly, eyes glistening with unshed tears and
began to speak softly.

"He told me that if I didn't have enough power, that I should
take it from someone else. He said that's what he did to complete
The Crucible on his fourth attempt and that he wished he had
done it for his first."

"Wait! You can do that?!" Stella asked in surprise.

"Yes," Maranda confirmed, her voice growing louder and
angrier, "I was floored. Here was this person I thought I knew so
well and he was telling me to take the energy from someone else
in the tribe. Something we both knew meant killing that person.
I couldn't believe he would even suggest such a thing!

"I said I wouldn't do that and there was no way he could
convince me otherwise. He grew angry and started yelling at me,
calling me naive and saying he regretted coming here to train me.
He said that Star Borns like me were why the tribes were stuck

hiding when we should be proud of our abilities and leading the world to greater prosperity.

"Every additional thing he said just made him sound crazier and I had heard enough. So, I decided to leave and started to walk out, but he just followed me. He was scaring me, but I didn't know how to get away from him, so I left the shop and started walking down Solano Avenue. I figured it would be better to stay on a main street at least.

"He kept yelling at me and I kept walking without saying a word. This just made him angrier, calling me soft and weak. Finally, he grabbed my shoulder and spun me around, but I'd had enough. I told him I was done working with him and he should just leave. He looked so crazy in that moment and then his eyes turned cold. He said that I didn't deserve my abilities and that he would relieve me of them.

"Then he grabbed my arm and sent his energy inside me, trying to find my core. I was so consumed by fear and panic, my body was frozen. The feeling of his energy coursing through me, reaching for something that is part of who I am, felt like the deepest violation he could ever commit. I started losing control of my energy, but there was nothing I could do to stop it and suddenly all of it was exploding out of me in one massive blast. I lost consciousness and, when I came to a few minutes later, everything that had been right around us was gone. I mean, completely disintegrated… The sidewalk, garbage can, street sign… Everything on that corner just wasn't there anymore. I looked around and saw the windows for all the shops and cars down several blocks were shattered. Some of the trees had black scorch marks on the side that had been closest to us… I knew then that Sayed was dead…

"I couldn't believe I had the ability to do that and I panicked when I started to hear people coming to see what had happened. I ran away as fast as I could. At the time, I thought Adam would think I was dangerous and send me away. So, I kept running for months, traveling across the world until I found other Star Borns who could explain what had happened and why I had been right to resist."

Maranda had been staring at the floor the entire time she was telling her story, So, when she finished and stopped speaking, she looked around and noticed every single one of them had been listening with rapt attention and were now speechless. She grinned awkwardly and said, "Well, that's my story and it's late. Probably good to stop for today."

When everyone remained quiet, clearly still processing and not sure what to do, Maranda shifted back into teacher mode, saying, "Come find me here tomorrow when you can break away for a while, I will be waiting."

She touched the square on the wall and the entrance opened up again. This snapped the kids out of their almost trance and they finally moved and filed out silently, starting to make their way back to the trail. Maranda walked alongside Leo at the back of the group until they reached the narrow, sandy path.

"Over twenty of the most senior Star Born leaders gathered last week to discuss what you told me..." Maranda said quietly and Leo stopped in his tracks, turning around to face her.

"We have all been troubled by what we have been sensing in the world. In addition, like you, a number of others reported odd experiences in the Connector over the last several months. This kind of disturbance can only be achieved by a strong, coordinated effort. There is just too much evidence pointing at Gabriel for us to ignore."

"If Gabriel is the source of all this, why is he here training me? Don't tell me I'm *that* important…" Leo asked dubiously.

"We think he is here to recruit you. You know how rare Star Borns are and how few are as strong as you and me. He will need to bring as many as he can over to his side and he probably figures it will be easier to do with you since you're young and impressionable."

Leo's face turned red with frustration and started to wind up to defend himself, but Maranda placed her hand gently on his shoulder and said, "You are a kind, generous, and dedicated member of your tribe. I don't think you would ever have willingly joined his side. I am sure he will figure this out soon enough and that means we need to start training you to defend yourself. I don't want you to be caught unprepared like I was if he tries to take your core."

"I won't ever let him reach inside me ever again," Leo said with determination and finality.

Maranda gave his shoulder a squeeze and said with a sad smile, "Tomorrow is an important day, get some rest. I am going to need your help explaining The Calamity and how dangerous Gabriel will be."

With that, they each turned to go their separate ways. Leo saw that Caroline had waited a short ways away and he jogged to catch up to her quickly. As they walked back, Leo finally felt the last of the tension release in his back and, with that, the last part of him holding out on talking to Caroline about everything faded away. He began to tell her everything he had wanted to say since he found out he was a Star Born. Starting slowly, he talked about how scared he was at first and the ways his confidence had grown. As he went on, everything started flowing out of him faster and he dug deeper about how hard it had been for him to keep these big secrets from her.

Caroline listened thoughtfully the entire time, but barely uttered a sound until they were just about back to the campsite and they could hear Emily giving the others ahead of them a hard time. They couldn't help but chuckle a bit to themselves, knowing they were about to get their own share of it. The levity quickly settled back into quiet and they only heard the sound of their footsteps, so Leo noticed right away when Caroline stopped walking and he turned around to see what was up.

"No more secrets," she said firmly to him.

"No more secrets," he repeated back to her.

"I mean it, Leo. You're my best friend and there can't be any more secrets between us."

"I will never keep another secret from you," he said with conviction, knowing how hard a promise that would be to keep.

"Good. I may not have any super powers like you, but I can still make you hurt," she warned him. "Now, let's get some food, it smells *amaaaaazing*. Then maybe later you can answer some more of my questions."

"You have questions? No way." Leo playfully joked and she laughed along with him as they entered the campsite.

Dunk. Scrub. Rinse. Dry. Repeat. The whole crew had settled into a rhythm, cleaning up the entire dinner as penance for getting back so late. They didn't mind though, the food had been everything they were hoping for and more. The flavors of crispy Asian rice lettuce wraps and mexi-dogs were still dancing all over their taste buds. It also helped that the adults had all gone to the beach for an evening fire and the younger siblings were already in bed, so they were left on their own to enjoy each other's company and settle into their usual goofy banter.

"Hey Aran, how many mexi-dogs did you end up eating?" Stella asked.

"Foooooour aaaa leeesss," he answered while letting out a huge yawn.

"Want to try that again?"

"Four at least," he clarified with a guilty grin. "I lost track after the third one…"

"Dude! You're the reason I only got one!" Meimei lamented.

"Hey, you snooze, you lose," he answered without remorse.

They devolved into an extensive debate on camping food etiquette, but eventually all agreed that you just had to go for it when Emily was cooking. Even Meimei conceded that point.

"What is wrong with me?" Leo asked no one in particular as they were finishing up. "I can barely keep my eyes open…"

"Same here," Ania agreed. "Hey Meimei, did your mom tranq us?"

"Wait, where did Caroline go?" Meimei asked.

"Mmmpfff…" they heard from her tent and everyone laughed really hard like it was the funniest thing they have ever heard.

"Oh, we are all done for if we are this punchy…" said Stella.

"Yeah, I'm done fighting it. See ya in the morning and feel free to not wake me," Leo said as he climbed into his tent. He listened to a few of the others talking softly for a little while as he dozed off and the next thing he knew his tent was shaking violently from hands banging on the sides and he heard kids yelling that he needed to get up. He scrambled out of his sleeping bag and unzipped the flap, but his foot caught on the lip of the door and he tumbled out, landing on his back. All of his friends who had been pounding on the tent now gathered around him laughing.

"What the… I thought I said you didn't need to wake me!" Leo said through the fog of confusion and grogginess.

"Well, it's lunchtime and we figured you needed to eat *something* today. We all know how much of a joy you are to be around when you're hungry," Caroline said with every bit of sarcasm she could muster.

"Oh shoot…" Leo responded, worried that he had wasted so much of the day they wouldn't be able to meet with Maranda.

"Don't worry, the parents felt bad that we didn't have much time at the beach yesterday, so they said we could go back this afternoon after we all go on a hike together," Caroline said, clearly reading his mind and Aran reached down to help him up.

After lunch, Meimei's dad, Casey, tried to convince everyone they should hike his favorite trail. Unfortunately for him, everyone remembered the death march he had led them on two years ago and he was quickly vetoed. Instead, they did one of the overlook trails they loved and they had a blast soaking up the beautiful weather and playing games along the way. It wasn't until the kids headed by themselves to the beach, at least that's where their parents thought they were going, and Leo saw Maranda sitting on top of the massive rock that he remembered what they were going to talk about today. While he didn't want to let this ruin his mood, he couldn't help but feel bad for what they were about to tell his friends.

Maranda hopped down and opened up the doorway quickly, then all of them filed in, chatting like it was completely normal to be making their way into a magical room inside a boulder. Maranda and Leo looked at each other as everyone was settling in while continuing their conversations and she nodded to him indicating he should start things off.

"So," Leo said loudly to get their attention, "today we are going to talk about something called The Calamity."

"Ooooo… Are we telling ghost stories? I should have snagged some marshmallows on our way here!" Aran said playfully.

Leo looked at Maranda to say, "You were absolutely right, everyone thinks it sounds dramatic." Maranda waved him off to get him to focus on the task at hand.

"This is going to be more of a history lesson," he said.

"Uh, hello? It's summer, remember?" Aran continued to goof around.

"Just be quiet and listen, there's a lot to cover and not enough time already," Leo said testily and everyone focused on him finally.

"Thousands of years ago, there was a society on this planet that was much more advanced than we are today," Leo began. "Everyone had strong abilities and used them openly, without fear. Honestly, it's hard to describe…"

Leo furrowed his brow, trying to think of the words that would capture what he saw in the memories Maranda showed him. That was when it hit him, they needed to see it for themselves.

"Maranda, can you show them?"

She looked like Leo caught her off guard a bit, but he could tell she was thinking about it carefully.

"I think so…" she said hesitantly.

"Maranda can look into the past?" Caroline asked, confused, but ready to believe anything at this point.

"Not exactly," Maranda replied. "I can show you a couple of memories that were shared with me. I just haven't done it for more than one person at a time, but let's give this a shot. Why don't we have everyone join hands."

Maranda held Meimei and Anla's hands on either side of her and called up the memory in her mind, following the steps she had used before. She bent her pattern to mimic a Neural to better connect with the minds of everyone there and started to feed her energy into the group. However, it felt like she was trying to force it through a tiny hole and everything was getting backed up. She paused for a moment, wiped the sweat off her forehead and tried again with the same result.

"It's not working," she said in frustration to Leo.

"What do you mean?" he asked curiously, but he had a feeling that he knew what was happening to her.

"It feels like my energy is… I can't think of a better word for it… Clogged."

This confirmed what Leo was thinking and he said, "That happened to me yesterday when we were in this room. Maybe there is something about how it is constructed that messes with our abilities?"

Meimei let go of Maranda's hand and pulled out the first thing she could find in her pocket and it was a stick of gum. She tried to levitate it in her hand and it took all of her strength to lift it an inch.

"It's gotta be this room…" she said.

"Well, we can't go outside, we will be completely exposed and unaware if anyone sees us. You'll just have to describe it," Maranda said to Leo.

"Well, I have an idea," he said, not accepting defeat just yet. "What if I amplify you?"

Maranda thought for a moment and said, "It might work, but it's going to be pretty tricky in this room. I guess we can give it a shot, the worst thing that could happen is we all blow up."

"You're not serious," Stella said.

"I could think of worse ways to go," Ania said cheekily.

"Naaa, I'm just messin' with ya," Maranda smiled and then gestured for Leo to come to where she was sitting.

Leo made his way around until he was standing behind her and placed his hands on her shoulders.

"Sense my pattern," she instructed. "I have to bend it in a way you're not used to in order to share memories."

Leo closed his eyes and focused all his attention on trying to understand every last detail of Maranda's pattern. At first, it was very difficult. Whatever was interfering with their abilities was also impacting his senses, even when he was in direct contact with her. The pattern emerged slowly, like it was coming out of a thick fog and he took his time to make sure he understood it fully before he started to bend his own pattern. When he was finally confident that he had it right, he began to share his energy with Maranda and he knew he had it right when he heard her take a deep breath. He had to use every bit of his training to keep the flow steady due to the room's interference.

"OK, quickly everyone, join hands again," Maranda said urgently.

Leo opened his eyes and watched the group as they were pulled into the first memory. It looked as if they had all fallen asleep together, their heads drooped forward and shoulders slumped. Then, after a minute or two, he felt Maranda shift under his hands and everyone's eyes began to flutter open. Leo carefully pulled back his energy and stepped back as the group shook off the disorientation of being back in the present.

"Did it work?" he asked as he sat back down in his spot.

"Coreolis! Are you kidding me?! No wonder you couldn't describe it!" Aran said excitedly.

"How could they do all of that? I mean, they could do so

much more than we can today," Meimei asked, but already kind of knew the answer.

"It was… breathtaking…" Caroline said softly and Leo could see her eyes were glistening with tears. He gave her hand a squeeze and she shook off the emotions, returning to the conversation.

"They did know more," Maranda said gravely and looked at Leo to continue.

"You guys, that was the height of human civilization. Not long after those memories, a huge war erupted and it lasted for decades," Leo continued to explain. The group listened quietly as he spent the next half hour explaining the beginning of The Calamity and how it plunged the world into thousands of years of turmoil and darkness.

"So, wait…" Stella interrupted him as he was about to get into the really difficult stuff and he welcomed the pause. "It sounds as if we have never fully recovered from this…"

"We haven't," Maranda answered bluntly.

"How is that possible?"

"There are lots of different things that have made it difficult to find our way back or to create another golden age," Maranda explained. "The biggest and most dangerous obstacle is Warwick's followers."

"But, he's dead," Meimei said. "How does he still have followers?"

"Not dead. Imprisoned," Maranda corrected her. "The vial keeps him in stasis, so it's as if he's frozen in time. His followers still want to pursue advancement and they believe the only way to help humanity is to pursue it at all cost. They have been working towards this goal ever since The Calamity. Wars, famines, assassinations. Nothing is too horrible, nothing will stand in their way. It is their religion and they are its most devoted followers."

"There's a reason why you came here to tell us this and it isn't only because Leo insisted," Caroline said suspiciously and Maranda suddenly looked stricken.

"You're right…" Maranda said slowly, gathering herself.

Leo stared at her anxiously, wondering what he didn't know and unable to sense anything clearly due to all the interference from the room.

"Originally, I agreed to come here because it was the only way Leo agreed to work with me and support our efforts to fight Warwick's followers," Maranda continued. "But we have come to believe they are about to do something big and we have no idea what it is. We are going to need your help finding out."

"Uh… That's crazy talk. We're just kids," Aran said skeptically.

"True, but you all are in regular contact with the person we think is their leader," Maranda said.

"What?! Who?!" Stella asked anxiously.

"Gabriel," Leo said through gritted teeth, dread filling him quickly because it just dawned on him how much danger he had gotten his friends into.

14

HANDS OFF

"STOP! LET'S START over again!" Maranda said sternly and took a step back, stretching her hands as high as she could reach and then rolling her shoulders to loosen them up.

Without much room to move, Leo just leaned on the cold metal doors to the mausoleum and tossed a baseball-sized energy orb up and down, changing its pattern each time he caught it. They had been practicing tactics for protecting his core for several weeks since they had returned from the Bodega Bay trip and he had become quite adept at two of them. The one they were practicing today was particularly difficult and it just wasn't clicking for him. He had learned early on in his studies that forcing his way through a problem rarely worked and he was confident he would figure it out eventually. Besides, he was supposed to meet Gabriel in thirty minutes for his official training and he was pretty sure they wouldn't figure it out in such a short amount of time.

"How can you be so casual right now?" Maranda asked pointedly.

"Huh?" Leo asked, missing what she said because his mind had been elsewhere.

"Huh? Huh?! Are you taking this seriously?!"

"Of course I am! What's your problem?" Leo asked, confused by Maranda's tone. She had never been this short with him and it made him very uncomfortable.

"This is important and it seems like you're not even trying."

"Look, I got the other techniques just fine, what's so important about this one?"

"The others will work on less skilled Star Borns, but that would never apply to Gabriel. He has skills you have never dreamed of and probably more power than you and I combined," Maranda admonished him.

"Probably because he stole it…" Leo muttered.

"Yeah, you're probably right! That doesn't mean he won't use it against you! When are you going to realize that at some point you're going to have to fight him and you better be ready for that day?"

This hit home for Leo in a way that he had not expected. The past several weeks had been so much fun because all of his different worlds finally joined together. Caroline was a part of all of their activities, his friends knew about and were training with Maranda, and with school out for the summer he was able to balance all of his training without having to forgo sleep. He knew now that he had become too relaxed and his guard was down. Maranda was right to call him out.

Leo caught the energy ball in his hand, squeezed it tightly, and then absorbed it back into his core. "Let's go again," he said soberly.

"Good," Maranda said, noticing the seriousness in Leo's voice and body language. "But first, show me what you can remember from what we covered last week. What are the different ways of protecting your core from Gabriel?"

"I can block him, eject him, or trap him."

"What are the pros and cons of each one?"

"Blocking uses the least amount of energy, but is temporary and will likely only slow him down. Ejecting him is the most effective way to remove the threat, but it uses the most amount of energy and he could still try again if I can't break physical contact with him. Trapping him creates home field advantage and I can find multiple ways to reduce the threat, but he will still be inside me and could potentially find his way to my core."

"Good. What happens if he touches your core?"

"I become marked. He would be able to find me easily in the Connector and would have advanced warning of whatever I want to do before I do it."

"Correct. And finally, what happens if he takes your core?" Maranda asked, but before he could answer she grabbed his hands and immediately reached inside him towards his core.

Leo gasped as his body became rigid. Even though he knew she was going to start another practice round, he still couldn't avoid that reaction each time. He was getting better about regaining his composure quickly though and the internal battle began as he quickly searched for a weakness in her attack. Of course, she had already erected countermeasures that would make blocking or ejecting her more difficult and she was quickly barreling through him to his core. He knew she wanted him to trap her, but he had failed to do that every time he tried. It either took him too long or she spotted the trap a mile away.

A crazy idea occurred to him and he ran with it since he had nothing else to work with and he was sure it would at least be a learning experience. The first thing he did was quickly erect a reasonably strong barrier directly in her path. He visualized it as a tall wall made out of logs, kind of like the way settlers protected themselves hundreds of years ago. It was nothing she wouldn't be able to get through eventually, but at least she couldn't smash through it. It also bought him enough time to construct five other barriers that appeared to be random or haphazard, but they forced her to follow one of the preferred paths he had chosen.

Each time she slammed into another one, she quickly turned and moved down the next path, not realizing that he was narrowing her options each time. Leo continued to work patiently, putting more barriers and decoys in place until finally Maranda moved down the final path he had chosen. She immediately encountered what looked like a partially constructed setup to eject her, but she didn't take the time to check carefully as she barreled through it, shattering the hastily prepared pieces.

To her surprise, however, right behind it was the trap he had laid and she immediately felt like she was stuck in quicksand. The more energy she put into moving through it, the slower her progress became, regardless of the direction she tried. As she stopped to assess her options, Leo struck and used a trick she had inadvertently taught him the prior week during one of these sessions. He surrounded her energy and encapsulated it in a tight cocoon. It was the equivalent of holding a knife to her throat. If she moved, she could harm herself just by touching it and, if he wanted to, it would be fairly easy for him to absorb her energy.

Leo felt the excitement from the moment of triumph. Sensing

she knew that she was beaten, he immediately released her from his trap. She quickly retreated and a moment later they were facing each other, breathing heavily from the effort.

"Well, that was an interesting strategy. How did you come up with it?" Maranda probed as she let go of his hands and leaned back on the hard granite wall behind her.

"You caught me off guard and I had to think on my feet. I guess I just followed my instincts."

"Well, I had no idea what you were doing. At one point, I thought you were just throwing ideas at the wall to see which one might stick. You should trust those instincts more, they are going to help you a lot when the time comes."

Leo tried to savor the victory, but knew the real test would come sooner than he liked and possibly before he was ready. This worry started to take over his thoughts, but before he could go down a rabbit hole, Maranda pulled him back into the present.

"You gotta get moving, I'll see you later at the school," she said.

"Sure… right… yeah… Let's get outta here," he agreed and they packed up their stuff. Leo left first, quickly looking around to see if anyone was nearby. Seeing the coast was clear, he made his way on one of the main paths to the cemetery exit, leaving Maranda the small trail next to the mausoleum.

Leo hurried to the book shop and managed to walk through the back door only a couple minutes late. He was startled when he saw Mr. Novickas there, peering into one of the boxes on a shelf right next to the door. He glanced at his watch and looked down at Leo, "You're kinda cutting it close, aren't ya?"

"Yeah, sorry," Leo said quickly, trying to head to the cavern as quickly as possible to avoid two lectures.

"Don't worry, Gabriel is late, too, and I won't tell him you just got here," Mr. Novickas assured him.

Leo pulled his backpack around and took a long drink from his water bottle as he leaned in the doorway, taking a moment to relax.

"It's kinda been a while since we've spent any time together, how've you been doing lately? I've been hearing rave reviews from Gabriel," Mr. Novickas said warmly.

"All good, I guess. Learning a lot. Definitely glad it's summer, it was tough to juggle everything this past year…"

"I get that for sure… It has certainly been an eventful year. We haven't had one like this in quite a while…" Mr. Novickas trailed off and let the statement hang in the air.

Leo felt the discomfort and wanted to help make it go away as fast as possible, so he said the first thing that comes to mind.

"So, what has Gabriel been saying about our training? He barely gives me any feedback."

"That's the Brits for ya," Mr. Novickas said, trying to commiserate. "Great teachers, but not always the most communicative in the ways Americans like."

"Yeah, the most he has said recently is something like, 'You should practice that one a bit more,' or 'That's good enough, let's move on.'"

This made Mr. Novickas chuckle and say, "Well, he said a whole lot more to me. I probably shouldn't tell you this, but he thinks you're one of the brightest students he's ever taught. In fact, he's impressed with your whole group and wants to bring some other teachers here to work with you all. It's pretty exciting!"

Quite inconveniently, this was when Gabriel decided to arrive. He opened the door widely and looked around, quickly assessing that he was interrupting their conversation.

"Apologies for my tardiness," he said curtly. "Come, Leo, we need to pick up where we left off yesterday since we didn't make it as far as I expected."

Then he strode briskly across the room, brushing past Leo on his way to the office. Mr. Novickas raised his eyebrows and opened his eyes wide while giving Leo a nod to communicate that he now understood what he was saying about Gabriel's feedback style. Leo just grinned and shook his head somewhat ruefully as he turned to follow Gabriel down to the cavern.

After dropping his bag in its usual spot, Leo joined Gabriel where he was waiting in the center of the room. The day before, they had been working on methods for projecting armor so it could do more than just shield him from attacks. He had just figured out how to stretch it across the room to protect someone not immediately next to him when Mr. Novickas had come down to tell Gabriel that he had a phone call. This abruptly ended the training session, so Leo assumed that was where they would start off today.

He powered up his armor around his hands until they were over ten times their normal size and was about to start quickly projecting a disc the size of a super hero's shield around the room when he heard Gabriel say, "I assume you and Adam were talking about our plans to start your training on The Crucible?"

Leo's heart started to pound on the inside of his chest and his ears filled with white noise as he anxiously tried to think of how to navigate this moment.

"The *what*?" he asked, trying to buy at least a little more time to think.

"You don't have to play dumb. I could tell you were having a serious conversation when I arrived and I know how protective Adam is when it comes to you," Gabriel responded less tersely than Leo expected.

"I seriously have no idea what you're talking about," Leo said, adding a little attitude in his voice to better fit how his friends sometimes talk to rude adults.

"What were you talking about then?"

Leo decided the best approach in this situation was to tell the truth. He rolled his eyes and said, "Honestly? You promise you won't get mad at me or Mr. Novickas?"

Gabriel nodded once, staring seriously at him.

"We were talking about how British teachers are very different compared to most teachers here in the U.S. and how you are not somebody who likes to give high-fives."

"What?"

"Yeah… We didn't mean it as an insult. You're just hard to please."

"Huh…" Gabriel uttered and then stared up at the ceiling for a moment before shrugging and continuing, "Worse things have been said about me. So, you're saying you've never heard of the Crucible?"

Leo just stared blankly at Gabriel and shook his head, not trusting himself to talk his way through this lie.

"Ah, well, it's a rather unfortunate name for our highest level of training." Gabriel began with a bright, matter-of fact tone. "While you are still pretty rough around the edges, you have progressed much faster than I could have ever expected. And since I need to return to London at the end of the summer, I want to see if we can start you on this training now."

"Is it dangerous?"

"Not at all for someone like you," Gabriel responded flatteringly.

Leo's blood ran ice cold through his body as he listened to Gabriel blatantly lie to him, but he tried to hold onto his playing dumb routine.

"You're sure I am ready for this?" he asked, testing Gabriel further.

"I wouldn't have brought it up if I didn't think so. That's why I was asking if you were talking about it with Adam. We discussed it last night and he is fully supportive."

This last statement was where Gabriel slipped and Leo was able to sense just how much Gabriel was lying to him. There was much more to this than he was letting on and it was clear something about it was very important to him. He could sense Gabriel exerting immense control over the dense emotional brew of excitement, anxiety, and impatience inside him. This was it, Leo was sure of it. Maranda had said this day would be coming sooner than he would expect and here he was sitting in the moment coming to that realization. It was suddenly all so clear to him, whatever Gabriel had planned, Leo starting his training on the Crucible was an important part of it. Leo was also sure of one other thing, Mr. Novickas had no idea that Gabriel wanted him to start this training.

"Well, wow!" Leo responded, filling himself with pride and feeling honored. He let these emotions wash out of him so that Gabriel could feel them easily and it elicited exactly the response he was going for.

"Yes, this is a very special thing, Leo. I am sorry that I am not more effusive with my praise, but you should know that you're a very gifted Star Born." Gabriel said using all of his charm as a weapon and Leo had to remind himself to guard his real emotions closely. Then Gabriel shifted back to his more serious teacher voice, "I do have to warn you though. This training is one of the most important secrets for Star Borns. You are not permitted to speak of this with anyone, not even your parents."

"OK," Leo readily agreed and then decided to test things a little. "But how come you shared it with Mr. Novickas?"

Gabriel's thin control of his emotions betrayed him again as Leo detected a healthy dose of anger had been added to the brew even though nothing changed on his face or with his body language.

"Adam is a special case and is probably the only non-Star Born in the world who knows about this training," Gabriel said without missing a beat. "He has been a loyal friend and ally to us all these years. Since he has started the training for a number of new Star Borns, it made sense to make him aware of the training in general. However, he does not know any of the details and it should stay that way."

"So… Are we starting today?" Leo asked, having heard enough lies for the day.

"No, I just wanted to speak with you about it today. We can start the training in a couple days, I need to set a few things up first. As I mentioned upstairs, I want to finish what we were working on yesterday."

Leo made a mental note to tell Maranda all about this turn of events when he saw her later that day. Then he charged up his armor again and shot a shield across the room to block an energy orb Gabriel had sneakily formed behind his back and then thrown hard at the ceiling to ricochet it into one of the targets stationed around the room.

Leo walked into the high school gym in the late afternoon expecting to see everyone gathered, but it seemed he was the first one there. The large space echoed with the squeaks from his shoes as he walked across the floor with lines for different sports laid out across it. There was plenty of light to see as the golden afternoon sun streamed through the windows ringing the top of the wall near the ceiling and he couldn't feel anyone else in the building as he stretched out his senses to check that he was alone. He had to admit, this was definitely one of the handiest things Maranda had taught him so far.

Relishing the unfamiliar feeling of being early to training, he decided that he should make things a bit more interesting for when the others started to arrive. So, he found a dark corner at the far end of the space and crouched down right next to the stack of bleachers that had been pushed back against the wall to create more space. He didn't have to wait too long before he felt the familiar itch of Aran arriving, but he would have also heard him a mile away with all the noise he was making.

"Hello?!" Aran called out and Leo stayed quiet as the only response was the echo bouncing back.

Aran set down two animal carriers in the middle of the room and then sat down on the floor with his back to Leo. Grinning to himself, Leo knew exactly what he should do and conjured up a small ball about the size of a grape. It looked milky white and it sparkled as if it was filled with tiny little stars. Leo rolled it across the floor directly at Aran and nailed the distance perfectly as it stopped a few feet behind him. Leo snapped his fingers softly and the ball emitted a loud popping sound and suddenly the room was filled with a dazzling bright light.

Aran leapt to his feet and yelled, "WHAT THE?!" so loudly that his voice cracked badly. He turned around and scanned the room as the light dimmed and small wisps of fog and twinkling light slowly faded. Leo came out laughing so hard he was clutching his stomach.

"You little!" Aran yelled angrily and this just made Leo fall into another fit of laughter.

"I could've hurt you, ya know! That wasn't safe!"

"Oh, come on. It was funny and I saw you didn't open either of those carriers," Leo said while catching his breath.

"Doesn't matter, these guys are only staying in the carriers because I asked them to. I almost let them loose and they would've torn their way out and come looking for you," Aran said seriously, but Leo could tell he was mostly calmed down and not really angry at him.

"Whatcha got in there?" he asked Aran.

"I thought you'd never ask!" Aran said, winding up to be super nerdy about his animals. "This one on the left is an ocelot and his name is Bernie. The other one is a young cougar named Evelyn. I borrowed them for training today."

Leo knelt down to take a look at both of them and he could see what Aran meant about them being able to tear their way out of the carriers. Then it occurred to him, there was no way that Aran could have carried them here.

"Uh, Aran," Leo said hesitantly. "Don't tell me you just strolled through town with two medium-sized cats."

"No, no, no… I'm not an idiot. They met me here and then I put them in the carriers. That's why I am late, these guys are heavy!"

"And, how did they know to meet you here?"

"Well, I gave them directions, of course."

"You can just give them directions and they'll listen to you?"

"C'mon," Aran said matter-of-factly, "you know how good I am with cats."

"If they'll listen to you so well, why did you put them in the carriers?

"I didn't want to make everyone nervous. I figured this was the best way to introduce everyone. Speaking of which, where is everyone?"

"Just you and me so far."

"And me!" they heard Ania call from the hallway. "Can you guys come give me a hand?"

Leo and Aran came over and saw Ania had two medium-sized duffel bags sitting on the floor next to her and her face was flushed with exertion. Leo bent over to pick one up and immediately realized just how heavy it was as he strained to sling it over his shoulder.

"What do you have in here, rocks?" he asked.

"Plants, dork," she shot back.

"How many plants did you need to bring?" Aran asked as he lifted the other duffel and they all started walking back into the gym.

"Well, I wasn't sure what we were going to be practicing so I wanted to be prepared."

"Did you have to bring the entire greenhouse with you, though?"

"Shut it," was all she said and that ended the discussion.

Caroline, Stella, and Meimei arrived a few minutes later and, for once, Maranda was the one who arrived late. When she walked in, she had her large backpack loaded up with all of her stuff and everyone gave her confused looks.

"It's not what you think," she said as she set her stuff down. "I just got caught by one of the groundskeepers as I was sneaking back into the mausoleum. He was actually pretty cool and said he wouldn't tell anyone about it. I just had to pack up and leave right away."

"Ugh… That stinks!" Stella said. "Where are you going to stay?"

"Well, I'll just crash here for a couple nights since we know the maintenance schedule thanks to Meimei's brother. I'll use that time to find my next landing spot."

Seeing the group's concerns were addressed, Maranda got down to business, "Shall we get started? I think we can still fit in a good amount of work in the next two hours before the sun sets."

"Actually, I have something we should discuss," Leo spoke up.

"Whadaya got?" Maranda said casually, sitting on the floor and leaning on her backpack.

"It's starting. Gabriel wants me to start training on the Crucible."

"Why do you think something is starting? Maranda has already started you on the Crucible, right?" Caroline asked.

"Yes, but he really shouldn't be starting it yet. We began his training because Leo will need many of the skills he will learn from it, but it's very dangerous and really shouldn't be started until he has four or five years of training under his belt. Leo's right. The fact that Gabriel has decided to start the training now means something big is coming."

"It's not just that," Leo built on what Maranda covered. "He made a mistake and there were gaps in his defenses. I could sense how important it is that I start the training now. He needs me to do it for some reason and I could sense how much he wanted me to agree to it. He used all of his charm on me… I had to force myself not to vomit."

"Leo! You didn't…" Maranda started to chastise him.

"No, you would be very proud of me. I concealed my true feelings and fed him what he was hoping for," he interrupted her and she quickly relaxed.

"So, you're going to start the training with him?" Caroline

started the questioning again, clearly skeptical this was a good idea.

"Well, I don't see how I can avoid it," Leo answered.

"If you're going to do it, then how do we help?" she pushed further.

"I don't know if you can…" he replied, starting to feel the weight of this burden.

"No," Caroline replied simply.

"What do you mean, no?"

"We are all in this together. Nobody faces these challenges alone," she said as if she was in charge now and, looking around at the rest of the group, it was clear she actually was in charge.

"We will need to start sneaking into the cavern to train on the Crucible again," Maranda said, thinking out loud.

"Here come the late nights…" Leo lamented.

"I think you all could definitely help," Maranda continued, ignoring Leo's complaining. "You won't be able to go in with him, but we could set up some challenges that would prepare him for each room and you all could practice with him. Actually, this might be a better approach for our training than we had originally planned…"

Maranda stood up and started pacing around the group, sometimes muttering to herself. After a couple of minutes waiting, the rest of the group decided to do a little planning of their own and discussed how they would be able to sneak out for these training sessions.

"OK, I think I have an idea figured out," Maranda finally said, turning toward them.

"Great, we have figured out how to get everyone to the cavern secretly," Caroline replied.

"Perfect, do you want to go first or shall I?"

"Our plan is actually kinda simple, as most of the best plans are," Caroline offered. "We're going to ask for weekly sleepovers in the cavern. It's a safe place, so the parents won't be worried at all and we won't all be in one of our houses annoying them, so they will probably agree to it. I'll have to sneak out, but my parents are deep sleepers. It shouldn't be a problem."

"You're right, that's actually pretty elegant in its simplicity," Maranda said approvingly.

"Your turn," Caroline prompted.

"We're going to make Leo into Gabriel's star pupil," Maranda began. "We will train him on each room before he starts it with Gabriel. We've already gone pretty far with the first one anyway."

"You mean I am not being launched out of the room as far as when I started?" Leo interjected.

"Stop being such a Debbie Downer," Maranda chided. "You are familiar with the overall challenge of the room and have made progress in learning it. I think we can set up some equipment from the stash in the cavern to help you make more rapid progress than just throwing you into the room repeatedly. We won't make it so you pass through each room right away because Gabriel will become suspicious of that. You'll just make much faster progress than the average challenger."

"There's more to this, right?" Caroline prodded Maranda again.

"Yes. If Gabriel is approaching Leo, I am willing to bet he will start approaching the rest of you as well."

A memory then popped into Leo's head and he blurted out, "Oh my g-… How could I have forgotten to tell you all this?! Mr. Novickas said Gabriel is thinking of bringing other teachers here to start training with the rest of you!"

"And there you have it," Maranda said with satisfaction.

"This is when you all will become the eyes and ears for the rest of us. I hate to ask so much of you… This shouldn't be something that young people take on…"

"We've got this," Aran said, uncharacteristically with simple confidence and no bravado.

"Yeah, we are in all the way," Stella added and Meimei and Ania nodded their agreement.

"There's just one more thing," Maranda said, looking over to Leo. "and you're not going to like this part."

Leo furrowed his brow in confusion, not following her train of thought.

"Part of our training will need to include you all learning to use the Spider's Web."

"Nope! Veto!" Leo yelled immediately and began to stand up, but he felt the gentle pressure of Caroline's hand on his shoulder. He sat back down even though every part of him still screamed that he needed to run out of there as fast as possible.

"Sounds like what you're proposing is pretty dangerous," Caroline said as she kept her hand on Leo's shoulder protectively.

"It can be in the hands of the wrong person, but that's not Leo," Maranda said with confidence.

"How about we give it a shot? If it doesn't feel right, we stop," Caroline said quietly to Leo.

He didn't move a muscle for a few moments as he struggled with his thoughts. Somehow he knew Maranda was right about this and he would have to face his fears. Finally, he gave a slight nod and looked up at Maranda.

"OK, with that settled, let's get a little practice in," Maranda said and the group got up, thankful for the distraction from all the thoughts that had started weighing on them.

❧

"Wow! That looked really good, guys!" Caroline called out from behind the Moon Born screens by the cavern wall. The group had just completed a complex maneuver where Leo had to amplify their respective abilities in rapid succession without being in physical contact with them. Several targets were in various stages of disarray from the attacks the team inflicted upon them. Stella directed a stream of water at one that was still smoldering.

"Not bad!" Maranda agreed. "Ania, that was an interesting use of dandelions to create a cloud to obscure the vision of your opponents. Meimei, really nice work with those blades, but don't forget you can use all the things in the room to accomplish a goal. Leo, you lost your focus while amplifying Stella and she compensated well, but that would be costly in a real fight."

"Really?!" Leo said, taking objection from her comments. "That was good! My shifts were solid that time!"

"Yeah, yeah…" Aran disregarded Leo's comments. "What about me? I mean, look at those two targets!" Aran gestured towards a mound of insulation that used to be a couple targets a few yards away from him.

"Where are my manners?" Maranda said and she strode across the cavern toward Aran. Then passed him and knelt down to scratch Evelyn behind her ears. She let out a large purr and Aran threw up his hands in exasperation.

"What's next?" Meimei asked as they all converged at the side of the room.

"Can we do some more practice with the strangler vines?" Ania asked eagerly.

"Leo needs to go back in," Caroline said and he looked at her with surprise, as if she'd betrayed him.

"What?" she said in response to his look.

"We've only been working on this challenge for a couple hours," Leo began to make his argument.

"She's right and you know it," Stella said to him.

Leo looked up at the ceiling in frustration. He had been dreading going back into the first room since they all met in the gym a couple days ago. It felt like an exercise in futility since everything happened so fast in there. He could barely keep up with the conditions and there was no way to learn a pattern because the room changed each time he tried it. The goal of the first room was to demonstrate many different ways to use armor for defense and offense. However, there were a myriad of options to choose from and he invariably chose the one that would get him launched out of the room.

Now that he was going to have to go train in there even more with Gabriel, he felt like he wanted to maximize the time he was able to work with his friends. Especially since the first thing Gabriel did after he informed Leo about the training was to cancel the Friday group sessions.

"You could practice the Spider's Web instead," Caroline offered.

"I'll take the Crucible," Leo responded quickly, knowing that was exactly what she was going for.

Leo walked through the rows of shelves outside the entrance to the Crucible and then paused, staring at the dark tunnel that obscured a door at its end. He didn't feel anxiety or trepidation, he was just sick of not being good at something. He had been able to grasp so much of what had been thrown at him before this and his struggles had started to affect his confidence. He thought about the last two attempts and ran through what he could have done differently, but he got distracted when he heard Maranda's slow quiet steps approaching.

"Stop thinking and just use your instincts like we discussed," she said.

"That was different, I just had to focus on you," he protested.

"You just amplified four strong Earth Borns to destroy as many targets in less than two minutes."

"I see your point…" Leo conceded.

"Just go in there and do your best. Nobody is expecting perfection," she encouraged.

"Yeah, I'm just looking forward to seeing what it looks like when you get ejected," Aran said brightly.

"Dude, you ruined their moment," Stella said.

"Well, we were all thinking that, right?" he retorted and Ania nodded her head in agreement.

While this back and forth was going on, most of them didn't notice Leo walking quietly down the tunnel. As usual, once he was inside, he was greeted with complete darkness. It only took a few seconds for a green light to appear in the center of the room. This was his target and he started moving toward it slowly, careful to stay on guard for the defenses that would soon erupt all around him. He made it about half-way to the target before he heard the sound of a large amount of air being displaced behind him. He whirled around while creating a large wall of energy just in time to block a giant mallet that would have sent him flying through the air if he had been a second slower.

Leo didn't take a moment to think because he could already sense several attacks coming from either side of him. However, with such a little amount of light emanating from the target and his glowing hands, he couldn't get a fix on anything. In the gaps between attacks, he decided to take a risk and experiment with a new idea he had thought of, but never tried before. He rapidly created dodgeball-sized globes of energy that were super soft and squishy like water balloons, and threw them as hard as he could at different spots on the ceiling. Each one immediately spread out and stuck to where it landed, creating enough light that Leo could now see most of the room well enough. With the additional light, he also saw that he was about to get pummeled by another large mallet coming from his left.

He only had enough time to wrap his arm in armor and brace for the impact. So, when it came, he found himself with the familiar sensation of flying through the air and then landing hard on his right side. He knew he still was in the game when he landed, so he immediately rolled a few feet back to his left and pushed himself to his feet as fast as he could. He saw weighted ropes flying through the air toward his legs and he swung out a long whip of energy, lashing it to the first mallet and then retracting the energy back into him so that he was now intentionally flying back to his starting point in the room. He watched the ropes miss him by a lot, but he felt the sting of high-velocity bean bags graze his back and thighs.

He decided it was now or never, so he coiled himself into a crouch and then set out toward the target like a sprinter launching out of the blocks for a race. This triggered a flurry of attacks and the air thickened with projectiles as he got closer to his goal. While he ran, he sent shields out of his hands, legs, and even his back, to parry as much as he could before anything got too close to him. In the heat of the moment, time felt like it slowed down and he marveled at the pandemonium around him. When he was a few yards away from the glowing green target, he noticed it was sur-rounded by something shimmery like a small pond. He decided to throw caution to the wind again and lept through the air, reaching for it like he was swinging from vine to vine in a jungle.

Just as his index finger grazed the target, however, he felt something wrap around his right ankle and yank him back so that he landed on his stomach. He looked behind him and saw some sort of tentacle had emerged from the liquid he was trying to avoid. Undaunted, Leo swung out the whip of energy again, wrapping it around the target and he found himself transformed into the rope in a game of tug of war. The tentacle increased the pull on his ankle and another emerged to wrap around his waist. All of Leo's energy went into holding onto the thin rope of energy he had wrapped around the target, but he could already tell that he simply wasn't strong enough to hold out for much longer.

In a final act of desperation, Leo channeled some of his remaining energy into the tentacles, hoping this would shock them into releasing him. He watched as the energy traveled down them and into the pool with no discernible effect. Then he saw the energy travel back up through them, smacking back into his body and causing him to lose his grip. The tentacles began to push him across the floor to the door and Leo struggled, reaching for anything he could get his hands on and coming up empty.

He rolled onto his back and looked up to see the open door and he covered his head as he was pushed out of the room. He skidded across the floor and came to a hard stop against the side of one of the couches. Letting out a loud groan, he pushed off the couch and slowly got up so he was kneeling on the floor and shook his head to clear it.

"He must've done pretty well that time, he didn't fly through the air," Caroline said.

"That's true and it was also the longest he has ever lasted in there," Maranda concurred.

"I got a finger on it!" Leo said looking up at the group with a lopsided grin.

"Nice job!" Maranda congratulated him and reached out a hand to help him to his feet. "What got you this time?"

"Tentacles," Leo answered as if it was the most ordinary thing.

"Oh, I'm about to start working with some marine animals. I can ask my teacher to hook us up with some octopuses or squids to practice with if you like," Aran offered.

"No, these weren't animal tentacles. They came out of some kind of shimmery liquid."

"Sounds like a Moon Born reflector pool," Maranda said.

"OK, wanna explain that one a bit more?" Meimei asked.

"They're actually used pretty often to protect things," Maranda explained. "The concept is simple, too. The more you use your abilities, the more the pool reflects that back at you. The easiest way to deal with them is to use your abilities as little as possible. Another option is to use your abilities and then run away as quickly as possible. The range of a pool is pretty limited, probably only twenty or thirty yards."

"Well, that explains it," Leo confirmed. "Shall I try again?"

"You *want* to go again?" Caroline asked.

"Yeah, that time it felt like things started to click into place."

"Alright, go for it," Maranda encouraged him. "Caroline, why don't you stay here and keep an eye on him while I work on some drills with the others in the cavern."

"Sounds like a plan," Caroline agreed.

❧

"GAH! I thought I had it that time!" Leo said as he stood back up and adjusted his clothes.

"Leo, set realistic expectations for yourself. That was just your second time in the Crucible. Tell me what you experienced," Gabriel coached.

"The whole floor was covered in a few inches of water. The first time I used my abilities, I got shocked pretty badly. So, I figured I needed to get out of the water and I found some platforms that I could move between. Each one had a defender though and the one closest to the target happened to catch me as I landed. I slipped off and didn't recover fast enough before I got ejected by one of those big mallets."

"OK, well, those were reasonable adjustments you made. We've talked about checking your surroundings before making a move, though. Seems like you are learning that lesson again the hard way," Gabriel said impatiently.

Leo quickly masked his anger and reminded himself of the real goal here. He was confident he would have reached the target during that attempt, but knew he couldn't be successful that quickly without drawing suspicion.

"Again," Gabriel ordered.

"You want me to go back in right away?" Leo asked incredulously and for a moment he was worried that he might have gone too far because Gabriel shot him with a steely glare.

"I have learned it is best to strike while the iron is hot. You were close that time, so it would be a good idea to go back in there as soon as possible. You can take a break if you need one," Gabriel said, using the teacher voice he so rarely pulled out for their sessions. Leo already knew he wasn't really being offered a break. It was another one of Gabriel's tests to determine just how hungry and ambitious Leo could be. He shot Gabriel a look of his own and then turned around, walking determinedly back down the tunnel.

This time, it felt like the Crucible was giving him exactly what he wanted because it immediately started an all out onslaught against him. Every single kind of attack he had experienced so far from all his attempts, all at the same time. He let out a loud battle cry as multiple strikes pounded his armor and he proceeded to battle back, smashing his shields and weapons through the fray to create a path. It was slow going and exhausting, but it was a huge release to do some damage after all the frustration he had been experiencing. He made steady progress, leaving a trail of destruction behind him, until he reached the far end of the room where the target was hanging from a chain in the ceiling.

He reached out, wrapped his fingers around the target, and yanked down hard. The attacks ceased just as quickly as they started and a door opened up in the floor in front of him. Not sure he was supposed to solve the first room so quickly, he decided he didn't really care and began to pick his way back through the mess toward the entrance. When he emerged, Gabriel looked up in surprise and Leo thought he even saw a smile flash across his face. It disappeared quickly and was replaced by Gabriel's normal annoyed look.

"What are you doing back out here?" he asked Leo pointedly.

"I solved the room. Isn't that what you wanted me to do?"

"Yes, but why did you come back out and not move onto the second room?"

"You said you wanted me to solve the first room and I did that," Leo responded with some swagger and then he sat down heavily on one of the couches, letting out a satisfied sigh. He could feel Gabriel staring at him intensely, but he didn't respond. He just sat there with his head resting on the back of the couch, pretending like he was thinking of something more important.

"I like the confidence," Gabriel said finally and Leo thought he could detect a feeling of pride as well. "Let's see more of that tomorrow. We can call it a day for now."

✄

Meimei stood in the center of the cavern surrounded by a variety of sharp objects that were orbiting around her in a complex pattern that resembled a three dimensional star with its points undulating to a silent rhythm. Without moving a muscle, the tips of each point broke off and flew at a variety of targets arrayed around the room. Each buried itself deep in the center of its mark and was joined by five more of its friends in rapid succession. In less than a minute, only about a dozen objects remained in the air around Meimei and her friends erupted in applause from behind the protective barriers.

"When did you learn to do that?!" Stella asked her excitedly.

"Late last week I started to get the hang of it. My new teacher… I mean *Gabriel's spy*, Rania, taught me. She got into a huge argument with Leslie about it. I mean, they were *shouting* at each other. Leslie said they shouldn't be teaching a technique this violent to kids, but somehow Rania trumped her. It's definitely a hard one to learn, but it looks so cool!"

"What did I miss?" Leo said as he walked into the cavern from the storage area, rubbing his left shoulder and wincing.

"Meimei was showing us something she learned last week while we took a break," Maranda answered and then asked, "Back so soon?"

"I'm stuck…" was all Leo could say.

"Really? You were on such a good run in the prior rooms and those are all pretty hard. I mean this one doesn't even change each time, you just have to move as fast as you can."

"I know, it just isn't clicking…"

"We've been practicing similar stuff with the team and you were going quite fast. This shouldn't be that hard."

"I KNOW! I'm already frustrated! I don't need you telling me how good I am supposed to be at this one!" Leo erupted, unable to keep his temper in check.

"OK… OK…" Maranda said, holding up her hands in peace. "I was just surprised, but everyone has a different experience with the Crucible. I mean, I got really stuck on the second to last room because it was all about exerting as much power as you can. I barely got past it and that was why Sayed tried to get me to steal energy from someone else for the final test…"

"Sorry, I know you're just trying to help and I really should be good at this…" Leo started to say and then hung his head as he walked further into the cavern. Everyone waited patiently for him to continue and after reaching some invisible mark he turned around and started back up.

"I mean, each of the rooms is hard in its own way and I have no idea how anyone can complete all of them in an hour, but each has felt like a puzzle to solve and I just needed to learn the trick. This one feels like there is no trick, I just need to go faster than is humanly possible."

"Trust me, you'll get it, I've seen you go plenty fast in training," Caroline assured him and Maranda nodded in agreement.

"I'll tell ya what. We've been so focused on staying one step ahead of your training with Gabriel, I think you have been spending a bit too much time in those rooms. How about we change things up a bit for the rest of the evening?" Maranda offered.

The group looked excitedly to one another and that was all the answer she needed. She stood up and walked into the storage room. The group heard her move something heavy and then there was a loud click. Water began to emerge from the cracks between the large stones covering the floor and the group sprung up quickly. Maranda came back into the cavern and strode toward the center, gesturing for them to join her.

"OK, I think we can all agree that was a pretty cool technique that Meimei demonstrated earlier, right?"

Everyone nodded, not sure where she was going with this train of thought.

"Here's a puzzle for you to figure out. Help her do it again, but with three times as many objects."

"What?! I definitely am not ready for that!" Meimei exclaimed, her voice even cracking a bit with anxiety.

"AND," Maranda continued, raising her voice to cut through the murmurs in the group, "I want all the objects to be made of ice."

"You've gotta be kidding me…" Stella said under her breath.

"I'll be over at the couches if you need anything. Don't worry about me, I have a good book to read," Maranda said cheerily and she walked away.

The group spent the next hour trying and failing to solve Maranda's challenge. Stella attempted to make the requisite number of ice objects, but couldn't even create the same amount that Meimei had used earlier. Then, when Meimei tried to combine the ice objects with the metal ones to test things out, it was an utter disaster and both she and Stella got nicked several times on their arms and legs.

"Maybe you should try amplifying them," Aran suggested to Leo.

"Both at the same time?" Leo asked skeptically and Aran gave him a shrug that clearly said something like, "It's worth a shot?"

Leo made his way around the protective screens and headed over to Meimei and Stella.

"I know Maranda likes to give us tough challenges, but this is ridiculous," Stella lamented when Leo arrived.

"I'm going to try to amplify both of you," Leo responded.

"You learned how to do that?" Meimei asked, clearly concerned.

"Well, no, but there is a first time for everything, right?" he said, willing himself to believe his own words.

Neither Meimei nor Stella had a good response, so they both turned around and he placed a hand in the center of each of their backs. He closed his eyes and tried to split his pattern into two so he could align safely. He did everything he could to stay focused and almost succeeded several times, but inevitably the patterns began to merge.

He felt his friends shift and fidget with impatience, but he didn't want to give up just yet. He decided to try one last time and went into a deep, trancelike meditative state. He visualized the patterns of two of his closest friends and held them in each of his hands. He allowed those patterns to melt into his hands and then up his arms, until he felt like each was possessed by a distinctly different person. He slowly added his own energy into his hands and, somewhere in his consciousness, he registered a slight intake of air from them as the energy flowed into Meimei and Stella. He didn't exit his meditation or open his eyes, he just continued to feel his two friends use his energy until he could sense they had stopped. Only then did he pull everything back and open his eyes.

Meimei and Stella turned around and he looked at them with expectant eyes, hopeful it worked. Meimei shook her head and said, "It definitely helped, we were able to make a huge leap in creating the objects and then arraying them, but it wasn't enough energy to go further."

Then they heard another set of splashing footsteps and turned to see who was coming. It was Caroline stomping confidently over and getting her jeans thoroughly soaked in the process.

"OK, you had your chance to try it your way," she said pointedly to Leo with a penetrating stare. "Now, stop fooling around and do it the right way."

Leo met her stare and knew she meant it was time to practice the Spider's Web. He wanted to be mad at her, but he knew she was right. He also knew being tricked into practicing a technique that made him uncomfortable was probably the only way to get him to try it. Recognizing he had gone through this thought process in his head, Caroline waved for Aran and Ania to come out and then said confidently to him, "You got this."

She began to walk back just as Aran and Ania joined the group and Aran asked, "So what's up?"

"Spider's Web," is all Meimei said in response.

"Ohhh…" Aran said slowly with wide eyes.

"Better to be the web than the fly caught in it, right?" Ania said in her own optimistic way.

"I'm going to take things slow," Leo said, making sure his nervousness didn't come out in his voice. "Just stay patient while I figure things out. There aren't detailed instructions on how to do this in the book."

Leo nodded his head upward at Meimei and Stella, asking them to turn around and then said, "Aran, Ania, put a hand on my shoulders please." He felt the weight as they followed his instructions and then he placed his hands back on Meimei and Stella's backs.

He returned to his deep meditative state, except this time, in addition to the two patterns he held in his hands, there were two more on his shoulders. He tried to let them melt into his body like before, but when they traveled into his arms and touched each other he struggled to keep them separate and distinct. It felt as if the patterns *wanted* to merge. He tried over and over again, but no matter what he did, the patterns either dissolved or started to merge.

Finally, in a moment of frustration, he thought, "Fine! Go ahead and merge if that's what you want!" He grabbed all of the patterns roughly and smooshed them together. They all began to swirl and combine as they hovered in a lumpy ball in front of him. Staring at it, he felt an inexplicable and growing urge to add his pattern to it as well. Giving in to the urge, he reached out to hold the mass and began to add his own energy to it. The ball swirled faster and faster, streaks of light and dark colors appeared and, in an odd moment of clarity, he thought it looked somewhat like Jupiter without the big red spot.

"Oh… my…" he heard Stella say and he opened his eyes to see a chaotic scene unfolding around them. Shards of ice were flying all around them, but in no recognizable pattern. A big clump of them slammed into the ceiling and it shattered into a rain of sharp particles that fell down on the group, sending little stings across the parts of them not covered by clothes.

He heard Aran let out a grunt of pain and the anxiety he had been holding at bay finally broke through his defenses. He closed his eyes and returned to his visualization of their combined abilities. Without thinking, he reached into the swirling ball and it immediately shattered, the different patterns flying away from him. He felt a force slam into his chest and found himself flying through the air and then landing hard on the stone floor of the cavern, water splashing around him. He quickly rolled onto his side, pushing up on his elbow to check on everyone else, and he saw all of them in a similar state lying several feet from where they had been and slowly getting up.

Leo heard splashing behind him and Caroline shouting, "That was great!"

He got up quickly, turned to face her, and yelled, "Are you kidding me?!"

"No way! That was epic! You definitely dialed up the power that time," she continued ebulliently.

"Wha… How… I can't even…" Leo stammered.

"She's right Leo, I could feel how much better that was," Stella said.

"Yeah, we should try again," Meimei agreed.

"Were you all not seeing what I was seeing?!" Leo finally got out.

"Yeah, it was a little messy, but I just wasn't ready. The amplification came faster than I expected and I struggled to adjust to it. Maybe if you go a bit slower this time we can maintain more control," Meimei counseled.

Leo looked around and he could tell all of his friends were on the same page. Everything inside him told him they shouldn't try again, but he couldn't help but be swayed by their earnest desire to keep going.

"Come on, Leo. You only launched us a few feet at the end there. I'm sure you can do better than that," Aran joked and the others started to giggle.

"Fine," Leo relented, "but if anything doesn't feel right, we are stopping."

"Super! Let me just get out of the blast radius first," Caroline said with a wink and turned around to trudge back behind the screens.

The group then came back together and assumed the same positions as before. Taking his time to calm himself, Leo felt the meditation begin to do its work with his muscles relaxing and his mind growing less cluttered with anxious thoughts. When he felt ready, he visualized the patterns again and this time allowed them to merge together into the lumpy ball like before. Instead of just throwing his pattern to the mix, however, he added it slowly and he could tell this was where he misstepped before. The ball grew smoother and, instead of spinning wildly, the patterns coalesced into a new, unique pattern. This just felt right to Leo and he directed this new combined pattern into Meimei and Stella.

A short while later, he heard Caroline yell, "MARANDA! YOU BETTER COME!"

Suddenly concerned, Leo opened his eyes and had to blink several times before he believed what he was seeing. The five of them were surrounded by a thick, moving screen of ice. In fact, there was so much ice, gaps only appeared in a predictable pattern as it shifted around them occasionally.

"EXCELLENT WORK!" they heard Maranda call out and they took this as a cue to shut things down. The ice started to melt, producing a cold rain shower in the cavern, and Leo worked to pull back the combined energy and separate the patterns carefully. When he was done, he turned around and looked at his friends.

"Everyone OK?" he asked.

"My turn!" Ania called out right away. "I want to grow a forest of crazy plants in here!"

Half in relief and half in excitement, Leo said, "Why not?"

"Good idea," Maranda agreed and then added with a sly grin, "Except this time, create the connection without making physical contact."

It was the next day and Leo was back in the Crucible for the third time for his training session with Gabriel. He had become adept at the first four rooms, completing them faster and faster each time. So when he entered the first room, it only took him about ten minutes to navigate his way through the gauntlet of attacks, blocking, dodging, and parrying constantly. He reached the target and quickly jumped through the door that opened up in the floor, sliding down a chute to the second room.

The transition between these two rooms always felt pretty abrupt to him because it involved shifting from the high energy effort of deflecting constant attacks to the detailed focus and control of navigating an energy orb the size of a marble through a narrow maze in the floor without touching any walls and avoiding moving obstacles. He often thought this must be some early version of Pac Man. It took him over twenty minutes to complete this room, but he was proud of himself because he was now able to complete the maze consistently on his first try. Once he reached the end of the maze, it split apart to create an opening a couple yards wide and he jumped into it to reach the third room.

This was where he thanked his lucky stars for having met Maranda and her insistence on developing his sensitivity. It was another pitch black room, but he could not use any of his abilities. He was almost positive the entire floor was covered in a Moon Born reflector pool because the first two times he attempted it, he felt something like those tentacles grab and yank him back to the entrance. The goal of this room was sensing the attacks and evading them while also using those same senses to find the hidden target. This room was often his most inconsistent since it once only took him three minutes to find the target. This time, however, he spent fifteen minutes and it involved him having to find a small opening located low on a wall he couldn't see and crawl through it. When he grabbed the target in this room, he held on tight as it pulled him up through an opening in the ceiling to reach the fourth room.

The transition this time was not nearly as abrupt as earlier rooms. When he was set down on the floor, he was in a dim room with a single glowing orb in the middle and a doorway on the opposite end. It took him over five attempts to even figure out what to do in this room and he had pleaded with Maranda to give him a hint that never came. One of his experiments finally worked when he realized he could connect with the orb and feed it some of his energy. When he did this, the door would open based on the amount of energy he provided. The real challenge was that he needed to maintain absolute focus on feeding the energy while making his way to the door. If his mind wandered even a fraction, the door would slam shut again. On the bright side, he was never ejected from this room, he was just stuck there until he succeeded. Since he had already been focusing in the prior room to heighten his senses, he was already prepared for this next task and was able to complete it in just a few minutes.

However, when he reached the fifth room, all of his confidence faded away as he ran quickly to a corner and planted his back in it. Almost immediately, small darts resembling sparrows, but glowing a sinister red color, started flying at him in the same pattern they always followed. He began generating energy balls as quickly as he could and threw them at the darts, not even waiting to watch them disintegrate as he focused on the next one. The only trick he had learned to navigate this room so far was that he could limit the directions the darts came from if he had a wall to his back. It only helped a little bit, though, since they arrived at a furious pace. He was able to consistently last about ten minutes in the room before he had to start making his way towards the center to reach two large targets on opposing walls. And this was when he inevitably missed a dart. As soon as it made contact with him, it disappeared and the floor shifted down at an extreme angle. He lost his footing and slid down into another chute that ejected him once again into the storage room.

When he landed, Leo laid on his back and didn't move. He was sure that if he did, Gabriel was just going to tell him to get up and start again. He just couldn't do that yet and hoped that if he stayed as still as possible it would give him enough time to rest a bit. Unfortunately, he heard the clicks of Gabriel's fancy leather boots as he approached. Once he was standing over Leo, he just said, "Get up."

Leo sighed deeply and then slowly stood, eventually facing Gabriel and looking up at his stern face.

"Failed again?" Gabriel said tauntingly, as if he wanted to pick a fight.

"I'll get it eventually, I just need some more time to figure it out," Leo responded, not wanting to take the bait.

"Time?" Gabriel asked skeptically. "You've run out of time."

"What is that supposed to mean?" Leo asked angrily, unable to hold it back.

"I thought you were someone who only comes around once every few generations, Leo. I really did. But then I found out you've been lying to me and all this amazing progress is only because you had a great deal of help."

This caught Leo so off guard that a fear response erupted inside him instantly and he was not fast enough to conceal it.

"See? That is how I know." Gabriel said, shaking his head in disappointment. "You can't even maintain simple control over your emotions. It tells me everything I need to know. You are a liar and cannot be trusted."

The intensity of the interaction brought Leo clarity and focus. Instead of panicking, he knew exactly how he wanted to navigate this moment. So, he responded calmly, "I learned it all from you, Gabriel. You are such a great teacher, how could I not have picked up a few tips on secrets and lying from you?"

Gabriel glared at him with intense rage, no longer bothering to conceal his emotions. Leo just stared back calmly, even smugly, despite the fact that he could feel the danger growing.

"Who is the Star Born you have been working with?" Gabriel demanded.

"I have no idea what you're talking about," Leo said to try and buy a little time.

"You and whomever you have been working with were sloppy. Stop this pathetic dance and cooperate with me right now. It might just save your life."

"I knew the real you would come out eventually. I was just wondering when the death threats would start," Leo spat back, trying to guess just how hard to push.

Without any warning or indication, Gabriel's hand shot out and grabbed Leo's shoulder.

"Enough of this," he growled and Leo felt Gabriel reach inside of him.

This development was not a surprise to Leo and, while he was petrified to be battling for his life with the most powerful Star Born in the world, he was prepared to defend himself. He was also counting on the fact that Gabriel would not be expecting this. He quickly erected a number of barriers, trying to lure Gabriel into a trap like he had done successfully against Maranda.

However, Gabriel smashed through one with ease and his arrogant voice reverberated inside Leo's mind, "Whatever you have learned to protect yourself will be of no use. I have faced far more impressive Star Borns than you."

"Well, I guess there's no advantage of surprise," Leo thought to himself, but didn't dwell for more than a second. He already knew he would need to use Gabriel's cockiness to his advantage.

If Gabriel wanted to roll through his defenses like a juggernaut, why not let him?

Leo worked quickly and deliberately, erecting a massive array of barriers and traps all around his core. Predictably, Gabriel barreled straight through them, taking the shortest path to his goal. These countermeasures were not set up to stop him, however, just slow him down and distract him. He finished the last of his preparations and then, like a hockey team pulling the goalie late in a game, he abandoned the defense of his own core and made his way carefully through his defenses to arrive behind Gabriel.

Being so close to his prize, Gabriel didn't even sense Leo's presence behind him. He simply continued to bash and destroy, watching with satisfaction as each of Leo's carefully placed defenses disintegrates. He pulled back to execute a particularly violent ram and was completely surprised when he felt a sudden, sharp tug as Leo quickly dragged him out of his body. Gabriel struggled and fought with everything he had to hang on, but Leo's grip was solid and he had enough momentum to successfully eject him.

Back in the outside world, Gabriel paused to get his bearings, but Leo knew he didn't have a second to spare. Picturing the doorway to the stairs in the cavern, he focused all of his attention on using Gabriel's energy to travel to that point. Not realizing what was happening, Gabriel tried to strike again and reached out to grab Leo's wrist, but it closed in on air as Leo arrived at his destination.

It had been a while since he last practiced traveling and Leo felt a bit queasy, but he immediately started running up the stairs when he heard Gabriel let out a loud roar of frustration and anger. Loud bangs from shelves toppling made their way into the cavern as Gabriel tore through the storage room after him. When Leo reached the top of the stairs, he barreled into Mr. Novickas' office and, as he grabbed the knob to the door leading to the store, he decided to take a risk and quickly laid an energy net across the floor. This simple trap might be what helped him get away safely.

Leo continued his flight through the store, accidentally running into one of the employees with a stack of books they were putting on the shelves, but he was too panicked to notice who it was. Finally reaching the front of the store he heard a huge bang from behind Mr. Novickas' office door and another loud yell from Gabriel. He instinctively turned back to look, but then fought the urge to stay frozen in that spot and whirled around back to the front door. Yanking it open as hard as he could, he caught a glimpse of Mr. Novickas behind the front counter looking surprised and scared.

"He's coming!" Leo shouted because it was the only thing echoing through his mind. Then he tore out of the shop, running as fast as he could down the sidewalk.

15

Reunited

LEO WAS LITERALLY running on autopilot, not paying attention to where he was going. He just wanted to stay as far ahead of Gabriel as possible. Stretching out his senses, he knew Gabriel was not that far behind and it felt like he was gaining ground. Maranda would want him to conceal himself and hide and, he had to admit, the thought of that was really appealing right then. Deep down inside, however, he was sure that would only postpone the inevitable. No matter what, he knew a fight was coming and he would need all the help he could get.

His legs burning with the effort of running for so long, Leo thought back to when he first met Maranda and the strong pull he felt when she put out her beacon. He had to face facts, he couldn't run forever and he had already decided not to hide, so the only other option was to call for help. Putting out a beacon, however, would make him visible to *everyone*, not just the people he picked. Without any better options available, he decided to go for it and showered the entire area with a call for help. Like a sonar ping, he felt just how many people who had received his call reflecting back and the number was astounding.

With that done, he took a moment to register where he was and realized he knew this street well. There was a trail in the middle of the block that led directly down to the cemetery that he took all the time as a shortcut. Since he knew the cemetery like the back of his hand, he rationalized it was probably one of the best places to make his stand. So, he pushed a little harder and sprinted, taking a hard turn down the trail. When he reached the cemetery, he ran directly for the mausoleum where Maranda had been hiding. Arriving at the ornate wrought iron doors, he saw a brand new lock hanging from a rather robust looking chain and realized he probably couldn't get inside without making a huge racket. Instead, he ran around the side and huddled in a dark shadow at the back corner of the structure.

He didn't have to wait long before he felt Gabriel arrive, his rage sending jagged waves of emotion almost as strong as the beacon he put out. Leo hoped quietly to himself that if people were hesitant to come to his aid when he called, this might convince them.

"Even a boring, average Star Born like you should know there is no way to hide from me!" Gabriel yelled and a headstone erupted in a spray of rock and dust a short distance from the mausoleum.

"If you really wanted to hide, you should have stopped letting the whole world know where you are!" he called out and another stone exploded on the other side of the building.

"Dammit!" Leo muttered angrily, chastising himself and hastily turning off his beacon.

Leo then thought to himself, "I'd rather go down fighting,"

and pushed himself up the wall he was leaning against. The normal sounds of life disappeared and all he could hear was his shirt dragging slowly and catching on the rough stone. He took a couple of steps to turn around the corner and paused. Shaking off the fear and doubt, he drew his shoulders back hoping this helped him project some confidence and strode out into the open. He saw Gabriel a short distance away and was struck by just how much he had transformed from the cool, dapper man he had first met many months ago. Now, his hair was wild, sticking out at odd angles and plastered to his sweaty face. His perfect outfit was singed and torn in parts and Leo noticed he had lost one of his boots. Hunched over and breathing hard, Gabriel looked like a bull ready to charge.

"That wasn't very nice what you did," Leo yelled at Gabriel, trying to stall for time.

"You don't deserve your gifts," Gabriel seethed. "Just give up now and let your powers serve a higher cause."

"And what would that be? Advancement?"

Leo saw his words have an immediate impact on Gabriel, his fingers twitching and his head cocked to the side.

"You are full of surprises today…"

"What did you hope to gain from coming here to train me?" Leo asked, seeing whether Gabriel would reveal his plan like a villain in a movie. Instead, he formed a large, dense energy orb and chucked it at Leo. Swatting it away with his left arm encased in thick armor, Leo still felt the impact stinging his arm as the ball smacked into a tree and splintered off a large branch.

Gabriel sent three more energy orbs flying and Leo traveled a safe distance away up the hill behind him.

"What a lovely ability that is. I have never heard of a Star Born being able to teleport… Maybe there is a little something interesting about you… Nevertheless, I look forward to trying it out when I have absorbed your core," Gabriel taunted.

Then, the real fight began with Gabriel encasing himself in his spiky, green armor and launching an array of energy projectiles. Leo felt small pieces of rock scratch the right side of his face as another gravestone shattered next to him before he could cover himself with armor. The time for talking was clearly over and Leo engaged in an intense back and forth with Gabriel. Each of them hurled energy attacks at the other, most missing by inches as each dodged or parried at the last minute.

Leo traveled behind Gabriel who whirled around, ready with a spike of energy that he aimed directly at Leo's head. He dropped to the ground and felt the crackling of the spike as it grazed the tips of his hair. Gabriel lunged at Leo with armor encased hands raised high above him, bringing them down like a sledgehammer to crush Leo. He rolled out of the way as Gabriel left a huge dent in the asphalt where Leo had just been kneeling.

Leo traveled as far as he dared, trying to create some distance since a close quarters fight was clearly not in his best interests. When he appeared far up the hillside in a familiar hide and seek spot from his childhood, he was relieved that Gabriel couldn't see him and also that he could sense his friends were close.

"Go ahead and keep hiding, Leo!" Gabriel called out. "I'll just take care of your friends first!"

Without thinking, Leo's next move surprised both him and Gabriel. He traveled to within inches of Gabriel, grabbed onto two spikes in his armor, and delivered a huge jolt of energy into it. Gabriel flew through the air for twenty or thirty yards and landed hard in the chain link fence at the bottom edge of the cemetery. Leo was pushed back several feet from the force of the blow he delivered, but managed to stay upright.

He stared at Gabriel, ready and waiting for whatever would happen next and he saw the armor shrink and flicker momentarily, before expanding again to full strength. The fence rattled loudly as Gabriel pushed against it, trying to stand. Leo didn't hesitate and cast another energy net over him, entangling his limbs. Gabriel let out an avalanche of British expletives that Leo was only barely familiar with, stretching out the net and slowly breaking it apart.

Leo prepared to chuck another cannonball at him when he noticed the foxtails growing in thick clumps all along the fence were starting to envelop Gabriel's legs. Stretching his senses out again, he felt Ania's familiar pattern and quickly amplified her. He watched all of the plants around Gabriel grow rapidly and thicken to encapsulate him in a tough shell. Picking up signs of movement in his peripheral vision, he turned to see Ania and Meimei running up the hill just below them and was relieved to finally not be fighting this battle alone.

"Thanks for coming," Leo greeted them while keeping his eye on Gabriel's temporary prison.

"Of course! I mean, we felt you needed us" Meimei said, clearly wondering how Leo did that.

"So guys, I think that will only hold Mr. Fancy Pants a little longer. I can feel the plants are starting to die. He's cooking them from the inside…" Ania cautioned them.

"Do we do the sensible thing and run while we can?" Meimei asked sarcastically.

"We need to buy some time for the others to get here," Leo said warily.

A large crack opened up running from the top to the center of Gabriel's forced cocoon and they were hit with the strong smell of burning green wood like a poorly constructed campfire. Their training kicked into gear and the three of them immediately backed up and spread out widely. With a loud tearing sound, the layers of roots, vines, leaves, and grass finally gave way into two halves and Gabriel stepped back onto the wide asphalt drive looking barely human. Whatever he decided to do to make his way out of several feet of dense material had taken a hefty toll. Most of his exposed skin was red and raw and he no longer had hair on the left side of his head where only a little bit of his ear remained.

Nothing needed to be said because they knew what they needed to do, immediately launching a full assault on Gabriel with everything they had. Meimei embedded a throwing knife into his right thigh and he didn't even respond, barely uttering a grunt from the impact. Ania ran to a nearby tree and placed both hands on a large root that swelled, breaking the pavement all the way to Gabriel and wrapping tightly around his arms and torso. Leo generated a whip of energy and wrapped it around his legs, pulling it tight to keep him as immobile as possible. Still Gabriel did nothing in response, he just continued to stare directly at Leo with pure hatred in his eyes.

"So, uh, what do we do now?" Meimei asked them with a sinking sensation, levitating a handful of knives from the open backpack at her feet for good measure.

"This doesn't make sense…" Leo said through gritted teeth as he pulled tightly on the thick cord of energy in his hands.

Gabriel pulled his thin lips back into a wide smile and began to chuckle, sending shivers down their spines. Something big was coming, but Leo couldn't figure out what it would be. He decided to take the opportunity to do a simple focusing exercise to calm his mind. The noise from competing thoughts died down in his head and only then was he able to sense at least twenty strong

Earth Borns flowing into the cemetery. None of their patterns were familiar to Leo and he quickly deduced they were all coming to help Gabriel.

"His people are coming!" Leo shouted just before Gabriel sent a huge burst of energy up the root Ania was directing and through his whip. They were both thrown back, tumbling through the air. Ania landed hard in the grass at the base of a large pond with a waterfall feeding it and didn't stir. Leo's back slammed into a large gravestone and he struggled to take a breath from the wind being completely knocked out of him.

Meimei fired off a burst of knives, trying to hit as many parts of Gabriel as she could reach, but he threw up a large shield that knocked them out of the air and sent them clattering to the ground. Then he used the shield like a bulldozer and ran at her full force, slamming it into her and pinning her against a tree.

Leo continued to struggle to take breaths and leaned against the stone, watching a small group of Gabriel's followers arrive and approach him. Gabriel pulled the knife out of his leg and Leo watched as one of the newcomers put a hand on his shoulder. Gabriel's skin calmed from an angry red into a more healthy color, though the scars remained.

"Kill those two," he said, gesturing towards Ania and releasing Meimei to a woman who looked like she had been in the middle of jogging when she was called and a man with thick glasses wearing a sweater vest branded with some tech company's logo. They each grabbed an arm as she slumped down, unconscious, and started dragging her toward a more secluded spot. Then he pointed at Leo and said, "Bring him over to me so we can get this over with."

Leo felt himself rise off the ground and he started to glide toward the small group clustered around Gabriel. He recognized

Meimei's new teacher, Rania, and knew she was the one moving him. As he got closer, Gabriel reached out a newly scarred hand, hungry to reconnect with Leo and finish what he started before. Leo doubted he would survive a second round against Gabriel, but he started preparing himself when he felt raindrops hit his cheek and arms. He looked up to see a column of water stretching from the pond and positioned directly over the heads of Gabriel's group. Leo braced himself and watched as the mass of water, algae, and mud smashed down on top of them, and he immediately dropped from midair, landing in a wobbly crouch.

Without hesitation, he scrambled back up the hill toward where he had seen Gabriel's minions dragging Meimei when he heard the full battle erupt. Members of the tribe were flowing into the cemetery from every entrance and attacking Gabriel and his followers. He saw his father rapidly pull a huge cube of earth from beneath several people he didn't recognize, launching them high into the air. Not stopping to see their fate, he came around a dense thicket, expecting to see Meimei unconscious on the ground. To his surprise, he found the jogger lady and tech guy lying there with a small trickle of blood coming from each of their temples where Meimei had clearly hit them with two rocks. Their patterns were shaky and weak. Meimei was nowhere in sight, but Leo discerned her pattern amongst all the people in the cemetery and he knew she was still alive.

So, Leo ran back into the open to rejoin the fight and he was met with complete pandemonium. Gravestones were being thrown at clusters of combatants from both sides. Leo saw Aran directing his new favorite cats, Bernie and Evelyn, along with a flock of wild turkeys at an opposing Caretaker commanding some geese and several dogs. His mother and Stella were sending a dwindling supply of water from the pond to a Cinder who was trying to start a fire on the hillside. And when he looked up, he found Meimei along with her teacher, Leslie, hovering over the makeshift battlefield launching and redirecting a swarm of projectiles back and forth against a dripping and filthy Rania.

He knew he must find Gabriel as quickly as possible. If they stop him, they stop the entire battle. It took him less than a minute to find his target in the middle of the fray, locked in a dizzying bout with Casey, Meimei's father. He ran toward them, witnessing Gabriel launching attacks at an amazingly fast pace, and he couldn't help but think this was what he needed to learn to pass the fifth room of the Crucible. Of course, Gabriel had to move that fast because Casey was a blur, constantly shifting directions and barely in one spot for more than a second.

Leo was almost there and he tried to power up his armor, but he felt his reserves had been depleted and he couldn't spare the energy. Forgoing the protection, he charged up two dense energy orbs and was about to hurl one when Gabriel caught Casey in his shoulder, sending him spinning hard into a large tree.

"NO!" Leo shouted as he chucked both orbs as hard as he could at Gabriel. They made shuddering impacts on his shield, which flickered briefly and Leo created two more. Before he could throw them, however, a dazzling golden octagon flew through the air and wedged itself into Gabriel's shield. The shield started to fluctuate erratically and then exploded in a cloud of green and gold particles that faded away quickly, leaving Gabriel defenseless. Leo already knew who it was, but he relished the look of utter surprise on Gabriel's face when Maranda appeared.

"You…" Gabriel growled deeply.

Maranda didn't waste time with the chatter and she had arrived fresh to the fight, so she launched one of the most inventive attacks Leo had ever seen. She threw two handfuls of small, spiky objects that resembled very sharp jax that surrounded him. One caught on the front of his blazer and it stuck there, starting to grow bigger at an astronomical rate. Gabriel grabbed at it, trying to pull it off him as fast as possible. When he finally succeeded, it exploded spectacularly, with the force of the blast slamming him into three more. These jax attached to him as well and started to expand like balloons being filled by helium. He tore off his blazer, throwing it as far as he could and it created a large fireworks display while disrupting several nearby fights momentarily.

Not interested in giving Gabriel any time to collect himself, Maranda created a large hook with a sharp anchor that she threw like a javelin, catching him around the waist and pinning him to the ground. Leo marveled at the variety of ways she could configure her energy and he would have loved to just watch her work, but instead he took the opportunity to throw the two energy orbs he had been holding and watched them crash into Gabriel's leg and arm. Upon impact Leo heard a loud snap from Gabriel's arm and then he emitted a loud groan that was so satisfying to hear.

They pressed their attack and Gabriel hobbled backward, dodging as much as he could, but unable to return fire. They were close to having him pinned down against the fence he had been trapped against earlier, when Leo caught sight of Caroline running up the hill from the main entrance. His eyes grew wide with panic and he yelled, "GET BACK!" Maranda followed his gaze and was similarly shocked.

Gabriel followed where they were looking and decided to strike, sending a long energy spike directly at Caroline's chest. Leo looked on in horror, knowing there was nothing he could do as Caroline raised her hands in panic. The spike hit the center of her palm and the most curious thing happened as the air around Caroline rippled and the spike was torn apart by the disturbance.

She stared down at her chest, amazed that she wasn't impaled and then looked at Maranda and Leo, mouthing the words, "What the…"

"It can't be…" Gabriel said doubtfully and sent two more spikes at her. This time she met both confidently, holding up her hands like she could command a speeding truck to slam on its brakes and sending huge ripples of air out at them. Again, they all watched the spikes tear apart.

Leo, ignoring the battle raging around him, stared at her, seeing her mind at work as she looked down at her hands in wonder. Then she turned her attention to the chaos around them and settled on the frenetic battle going on in the sky. She sent another blast of rippling waves at Rania who immediately tumbled to the ground with all of the objects she was controlling, landing in a messy heap.

Maranda turned back to confront Gabriel again and saw him limping down the drive as quickly as he could, trying to escape along with about ten others who had fallen back with him. She and several members of the tribe started to run after them until they heard Mr. Novickas' booming voice yell, "STOP!" They all turned toward the sound of his voice and saw him waving for them to regroup around him. They all looked at each other and, while hesitant to give up the fight, they slowly jogged back.

Leo and his friends gathered together and then headed over as a group over to where Mr. Novickas and the others had clustered. They heard him giving instructions to different members of the tribe to clean up the cemetery as quickly as possible in order to erase the evidence of the battle. Different Physics were lifting up gravestones and moving them back into place. Leo saw his father stitching some of the gravestones together so they looked as if nothing happened to them. His mother was moving whatever water she could find splashed around the site back into the pond.

As they got close, they saw Mr. Novickas was now kneeling over someone on the ground, tending to their wounds. Caroline was the first to see who it was and quickly grabbed ahold of Meimei's hand, squeezing it as she gasped when she saw her father on the ground, covered in sweat, and clearly in a lot of pain. Mr. Novickas looked up at the sound and saw their group shoulder to shoulder in a small arc, watching him work. When he noticed Caroline standing with them, he raised an eyebrow and looked over to Leo, saying gruffly, "I could use your help."

Leo knew what he was asking for and came around to rest his hand on a shoulder, adding some energy to speed Casey's healing process. They watched as the severe burn on his shoulder from where Gabriel winged him started to mend itself until there was no trace of it. Casey let out a restorative sigh and looked up at them, nodding his thanks and moving out of the way for the next injured person to receive treatment. Leo felt a swell of pride in his chest, knowing his abilities were being used for something good.

They healed a handful of the most severely injured people, including Rania and another of Gabriel's followers who were both promptly restrained and taken away. Then Mr. Novickas stood up slowly and Leo stepped back to join his friends.

"What the hell happened here?" he said, clearly directing the question to Leo.

"Well…" Leo started to answer before he was interrupted.

"I should probably do the explaining," Maranda said, coming from behind several others who had been assisting with the injured people.

Mr. Novickas' eyes grew wide and his mouth opened in surprise. Then, very quickly, his eyes filled with tears. He started to fidget, his hand running through his hair and smoothing out his clothes, trying to process that he was not seeing a ghost. This was Maranda standing alive and well in front of him, years after they had "buried" her. Leo heard gasps and whispers from other members of the tribe.

"I know… I'm sorry…" Maranda began to say, also overwhelmed with emotion and her voice was shaking so badly that she could barely say those words.

"We should go," George said quietly, hesitant to intrude on the moment, but the urgency to disperse was clear since they heard police sirens getting closer.

"Right… Yes…" Mr. Novickas said, gathering himself quickly. "Everyone! We need to hightail it out of here! Take different routes and meet back at my shop after closing!"

Then he turned back to George and said, "Can you ask Camille to help erase this?"

"Got it," George responded. Then he and Caroline started to run out of the cemetery.

With that, he turned his back on Maranda, Leo, and his friends, making his way up the hill to one of the narrow paths. Leo's mom came over and took his hand and then his father joined them as they started to walk out the back entrance like they had just been taking an afternoon stroll. The others joined their families and quickly scattered until it was just Maranda looking around and feeling like she had been cast adrift. She rubbed her arm, feeling goosebumps forming from a cool breeze that had started to blow with late afternoon and the sun starting to set slowly. Finally, the growing din outside the cemetery spurred her to move and she ran to an overgrown path that led the exact opposite direction to the one Mr. Novickas took.

&

As they are walking home, Leo's parents engaged in the normal family chit-chat. Discussing what to cook for dinner, weekend plans, making a list of back to school items for Leo. He was struck by how normal they could act when everyone had just been in a massive battle. There were enemies somewhere nearby and they were trying to decide if they wanted to have rice or couscous with dinner? It just felt wrong.

As soon as the front door closed behind them, however, talk immediately stopped and his parents walked quickly into the kitchen. His father reached into a high cabinet, grabbing several water bottles and starting to fill them. His mother turned to the living room, pulled the furniture off the rug, and then rolled it up to reveal a large trap door that Leo had no idea was there. She lifted up the door and gestured for Leo to come over as she started pulling out several boxes and a large duffel bag that clearly weighed a ton.

"Go to the garage and put this stuff in the back of the car. Then take a quick shower and get dressed in the camping clothes we bought you earlier in the summer," she instructed. Leo knew he just needed to listen and do what he was told, so he picked up the duffel first and lugged it out to the car.

Once he finished loading the car, he made his way upstairs and stripped off his clothes as he walked across his room to the bathroom. He made the water hotter than normal and stood under the running water, trying to let the day wash off him. Fatigue set in as he tried to process everything that happened. He had gone toe to toe with one of the most powerful Star Borns and lived to tell the tale. His friends did brilliantly while battling a force of people with extensive training to use their abilities in a fight. Caroline is a Moon Born! With that last thought, he opened his eyes in astonishment, forgetting he was washing his face, and the soap stung his eyes.

Realizing his quick shower was turning into an epically long one, Leo rinsed off and toweled dry. It took him several more minutes rummaging through his drawers to find the camping clothes and then put them on. So, he was in a big rush when he finally swung open his door quickly to run downstairs. His parents were in the kitchen waiting for him and his mom pushed a steaming mug of soup across the counter to him.

"I'm not hungry," he said, the fatigue now just making him want to flop down on the couch and sleep for several days.

"Emily dropped it off while you were in the shower, you should have some," she coaxed.

That was all Leo needed to hear and he took a big sip, feeling it coat the inside of his mouth and then warm his body as it traveled down to his stomach. He took another gulp and he felt the fog lift from his body.

"How does she make such amazing food? I mean, it always seems to make me feel better," Leo commented.

"Well, she's a Chem," his dad commented as if Leo should have known this already.

"Huh?"

"I swear, they spend so much time teaching you about your own abilities, but nothing about others?!" his mother lamented.

"She has the ability to combine the chemical properties of different things to create new substances. She focuses on food, but she has also done some very interesting things with medicines," his father clarified.

"So you're saying this food is designed to make me feel better?"

"Exactly. In fact, she designed it specifically for you to replenish your energy. She's been working on it all summer long. It should sharpen your mind and reflexes for at least twenty-four hours."

"Wow, I'd gladly have some of this every day," Leo said as he downed the rest of the soup.

"Be careful what you wish for," his dad warned him.

"We should go," his mom said, breaking the brief respite and they all gathered the items set out on the counter and made their way to the car.

They piled in and pulled out of the garage, setting off on a roundabout route to the bookshop. Everything felt different to Leo, his senses were heightened and he felt all the different families settling into quiet evenings in their homes. Not his or his friends' families, though. They were all headed to a secret meeting in a hidden cavern to talk about what happened this afternoon and what they would do next. It was not lost on him that many of the people there would be looking to him for explanations that he wasn't entirely comfortable giving.

His mom pulled in behind the shop and Leo and his dad took out the boxes and duffel bag. She then went to park the car a few blocks away so as to not arouse suspicions. They knocked on the back door and George greeted them and said, "You guys can go into the shop for a few minutes, Adam is having a conversation downstairs."

They passed through the storage room and office, heading to the front of the store. Mr. Novickas had pulled all the shades for the front windows down, making the space feel much smaller. Maranda was sitting at the front counter behind the cash register, spinning the silver ring she always wore on the thumb of her right hand. She looked up to see Leo approaching and gave him a weary smile with red rimmed eyes. Clearly, the reunion had not been going smoothly.

Leo was at a loss for what to say. There was so much he wanted to talk about with her, but it didn't seem to be the right time for any of it. The silence started to build a gulf between the two of them and he anxiously ran through idea after idea in his head, discarding each one almost as quickly as he came up with it. So, it was a relief when Mr. Novickas walked down the aisle stretching between his office and the front counter.

"Ben, Amy," he said and just nodded his head. As if some silent conversation had occurred, they each picked up a box and Mr. Novickas took the duffel. Then they filed back towards his office, likely to go down to the cavern.

A few minutes later, more people started arriving in the bookshop from the back door. Each of his friends and their families appeared with short intervals between them and they all clustered around the front counter, replaying moments from the fight in the cemetery and asking each other questions. Maranda quietly listened for the most part, occasionally smiling when someone said something funny. It continued this way for a while until Aran ignored social norms as usual and asked the question everyone is thinking.

"So what's up with you, Maranda?"

She pushed herself back from the counter, surprised at the directness of the question and stuttered a bit, searching for a way out of answering the question.

"C'mon, it's us," he prodded.

Maranda's shoulders slumped as she gave up trying to dodge the question and a tear ran down her right cheek as she took a deep breath to start answering his question.

"You all know Adam and I were very close, right?" she began

and the group all nodded. "Well, I haven't told any of you this…" she looked at Leo briefly before continuing, "but my dad died when I was pretty young. This was well before when I found out I am a Star Born. Adam was always there for my family when I was growing up and… he became like a father to me. When I started training with him, that bond just got stronger. So, when he thought I was dead, something broke inside him…"

She paused to wipe another tear from her cheek.

"He was never this careful or conservative when I was growing up. I mean, think about it, he's someone who can heal himself and others easily if they get hurt. Why not take a risk if you're going to learn something from it? Once I was gone, he couldn't bear losing a single member of the tribe if he could help it."

"That makes so much sense…" Stella said softly.

"Well, anyway, I know there's a part of him that is overjoyed that I am alive. There's just also a bigger part of him right now that is deeply hurt that I didn't find a way to let him know sooner… It's going to take some time for us to heal from that…"

"We can help. We will talk to him, help him understand," Leo offered.

"No, this is between us and we will make it better together. Anyway, we will have much more to talk about shortly. Adam and I have only talked a little bit about Gabriel, but he is taking it very seriously. He has already consulted the Council."

"That's a good thing, right?" Meimei asked.

"I think so, but we will need to take action as soon as possible. Every minute that goes by is a gift to Gabriel and his followers," Maranda cautioned.

"Everyone! If you would please make your way downstairs!" they heard George call from the back of the room.

Maranda stood up, raised her eyebrows, and said, "Here we go…"

The group slowly funneled through Mr. Novickas' office and down the stairs to the cavern. When they stepped through the entrance, they saw many more people had arrived and the room was crowded and warm. The din from the voices was loud, but there was a pause as people saw Maranda, Leo, and the rest of their group walk in. They found a small area of open floor near the center of the cavern and sat down together, unclear what was supposed to happen next.

The flow from the stairs began to slow and finally George came down and nodded to Mr. Novickas who was standing off to the side with a woman Leo and his friends had never seen before. They weaved their way through the dense clusters of people towards the center of the room and the conversations trailed off, replaced by the sound of shuffling bodies easing to sit on the floor.

Mr. Novickas looked at the woman and said softly, "If you would, please."

She nodded and closed her eyes. Then she took a deep breath, opened her mouth wide and an inky, black fog came out. It spread out quickly across the room, its tendrils reaching for people's noses and mouths. Some seemed to be unfazed by this and actively took deep breaths, letting the fog in willingly. Others were clearly uncomfortable or scared and tried to prevent it, shutting their eyes and placing their hands tight over their noses and mouths. Nobody could hold their breath forever, however, and one-by-one they each eventually let the blackness in.

Leo and his friends looked at each other anxiously, but they tried to follow the lead of the people who were relaxed and they breathed in the fog with small, tentative gulps. It didn't have any taste or smell to it and it barely had any substance, so it felt like they were breathing normal air. As soon as Leo had several breaths in his lungs, he started to feel something in his mind. It was searching for something as memories and thoughts flowed into his consciousness faster than he could handle. It was so uncomfortable that he started to fight it, trying to use the techniques that Maranda had taught him to protect his core and realizing this was an entirely different connection.

He eventually gave up and let it do whatever it wanted, trying to watch what it found like a never ending string of home movies playing just for him. After several minutes, it slowed down and eventually stopped entirely. He felt like he had to cough badly and others around the room started to let out deep chested hacks, releasing big puffs of fog with each one. Leo coughed uncontrollably for a minute or so until his lungs felt raw and tired. He took a few deep, cleansing breaths and looked around to see that almost everyone else had recovered as well.

"I'm sorry about that, but it was necessary," Adam said in his deep voice that easily carried around the room. He placed his hand on the shoulder of the woman next to him and continued.

"Some of you know Margot. She is the head of the Sacramento tribe and has thankfully come to join us this evening to discuss something very important. You all may have noticed leaders and members from other tribes in the area. We are thankful all of them are with us today as well." He gestured to several men and women around the room who each nodded their head in recognition.

"For those unfamiliar with Margot's abilities, she is a Reader and is able to search your memories and thoughts. Normally, we try to avoid using her abilities this way, but we had to be absolutely sure that everyone here is trustworthy."

He turned to Margot and she said in a clear, soft voice, "We are safe amongst our friends and family here."

Clearly relieved, Mr. Novickas turned and scanned the group around him, finding Maranda. He reached out his hand, asking for her to join him, and she got up slowly. Taking hesitating steps, she picked her way the short distance through the crowd, a few people reached up to offer her a hand to steady herself along the way.

When she reached the center of the room, Mr. Novickas took her hand and pulled her closer, turning her to face him. He bent forward, placing his forehead on hers, and she began to cry softly.

"It is such a blessing that you are back with us again…" he said.

"I'm… so sorry…" she struggled to get out, trying and failing to gain control of her emotions.

"Shh… It's OK… I'm not angry. I could never be angry with you. You're the closest thing I have ever had to a child of my own," he consoled her and started to cry with her.

Everyone watched quietly, letting the two of them have their moment, not wanting to disrupt something so special. After a few more whispered words that couldn't be overheard, Mr. Novickas stood up straight again and asked her clearly so everyone could hear, "We need your help to understand what happened today."

Maranda nodded her head, wiping away the tears from her cheeks, and said, "Of course."

"OK, good. Then let's start with the hardest question first. It is one that I believe we already know the answer to, but I have to ask it anyway. Is Gabriel a follower of Warwick?"

"Yes," Maranda said clearly and confidently. Talk immediately erupted around the room and Mr. Novickas raised his hand to ask for quiet. When the voices died down, Maranda continued.

"We believe he has been amassing a large group of followers around the world."

"We?" a voice from off to the right asked and the group turned to see it was one of the local tribal leaders who had been introduced before.

"Yes, I should explain. Since I… left… I have been traveling quite a bit and have met a number of Star Borns who have been tracking the changes many of you have been noticing in the world. It has not been random and the frequency is increasing, suggesting something big is coming. We did not know the source of these changes for a long time, but earlier this year we received a clue from one of the members of the tribe here in Kensington."

"You have been in contact with one of our members?" Mr. Novickas asked her with surprise and concern.

Maranda looked quickly at Leo and his stomach flipped anxiously, but he nodded his head to answer the question he knew she was asking with her eyes.

"Yes," she answered Mr. Novickas' question. "Leo and I first made contact in the Connector and then I came here to meet him in person."

Another, smaller, eruption of chatter spread around the room. Leo could tell it was largely members of their tribe and primarily the parents. His mind jumped to how he was going to explain all of this to them and what kind of trouble they might be in.

"Leo!" Mr. Novickas called out, breaking through the increasingly outlandish ideas of how he was expecting to be punished. He stood up slowly and raised a hand meekly.

"Leo, please join us," Mr. Novickas instructed and Leo immediately complied, hopping in between the small gaps of open floor space.

Turning to Leo when he reached the open area in the center

of the cavern, he asked more gently than Leo expected, "Do you understand what Maranda is saying?"

"Yes," Leo answered softly.

"You understand how significant this is?"

"Yes…" he said quietly again and then he couldn't hold back his next thoughts. "I'm so sorry I didn't tell you sooner, Mr. Novickas! It is such a big deal and we wanted to be sure! I mean…"

"It's OK. It's OK," Mr. Novickas said, placing his hands on Leo's shoulders to calm him down. "First off, call me Adam from now on," he said to Leo and then turned to look at his friends. "In fact, this goes for all of our young members here tonight. We fought in a battle shoulder-to-shoulder today. It was such a brave thing to do and, on behalf of all the leaders here tonight, I would like to express our gratitude."

Leo felt a huge upwelling of pride and looked over to his friends who, he could tell, felt the same way.

"Now I need to ask you, and please share as many details as possible, why do you think Gabriel is a follower of Warwick?"

"Well, it wasn't any one thing at first, there were a lot of different things he said and did that just didn't seem right," Leo began.

Before he could continue his thought, Mrs. Beacher, one of the tribal elders interrupted him and said, "Acting strangely is hardly a reason to charge someone with such a serious offense. He's just a kid and is easily impressionable. With all due respect, I don't believe Maranda is a liar, but possibly she is jumping to conclusions too quickly and has convinced Leo to support this theory?"

Leo's face grew hot from anger and embarrassment. How could they discount his experiences, just because he wasn't an adult yet?

"An accusation like this could lead to war!" another person called out.

"Gabriel is a well respected leader, he should have a chance to defend himself!" Leo heard someone call from behind him.

The chorus of voices began to pick up and Adam held up his hands trying to bring back some order. Leo looked over to Maranda and she shook her head, acknowledging this was not going well at all.

"He tried to take my core!" he shouted at the top of his lungs suddenly and the commotion died down, replaced by worried whispers.

"What did you say?" Adam asked, not believing his ears.

"That was the cause of the battle today! He found out I had been training with another Star Born. I mean, he didn't know it was Maranda, but we must have accidentally left some clues and he confronted me. When I wouldn't answer his questions, he said that I didn't deserve my abilities and grabbed me. He reached inside and tried to take my core!"

Leo felt jittery with all the adrenaline coursing through him from sharing something that felt so violating in front of a huge group. The voices erupted around them again and he heard snippets of conversations. Some had clearly been swayed, saying things like, "that's forbidden" and "he should be imprisoned." Others still seemed to be skeptical, saying "it's probably a lie" and "this is a serious accusation for a child to make." He looked over at Maranda again and saw the steely, determined look on her face.

"For the second time!" she added, raising her voice above the din around them.

"WHAT?!" Adam yelled, turning toward Leo and Maranda with intense fury in his eyes. All the conversations immediately ceased as everyone focused back on the three of them.

"It was during my first training session with him," Leo started with a shaky voice.

"Why didn't you tell me?" Adam asked, the fury in his voice replaced with guilt and sorrow.

"Part of me knew it was wrong and I was able to eject him before he reached my core, not that I knew that was what was happening at the time. He said it was just an assessment and made it sound like it was a normal part of his process. I doubted myself… I mean, he is on the Council and I was still so new to all of this… I thought… I don't know what I thought anymore…"

"Adam, there is no way this *boy* could have stood up to a Star Born like Gabriel if he wanted to take his core," Mrs. Beacher spoke up again.

"Now see here, I trust Leo and do not believe there is any reason he would lie to us," Adam rebutted angrily.

"I think your judgment is being clouded by your feelings for them," she pushed harder with her skepticism.

"How much more evidence do you need?!" Casey shouted at her. "We were there! Gabriel and his people attacked us! He almost killed me! This shouldn't even be a debate."

Several parents and other adults who had been at the battle in the cemetery called out their agreement. Many people were now nodding their heads in agreement and Leo could tell the tide was shifting in their favor.

"I can put this to rest," Margot said in her calm soft voice, appearing next to Adam.

Adam stroked his chin, debating options in his head. Failing to come up with anything better, he turned to Leo and said, "It's your choice, Leo. I can't force you to let her read you."

He didn't hesitate, "I have nothing to hide." Then, repeating what Maranda said earlier, he looked at Mrs. Beacher and said,

"Every minute we spend debating this is a gift to Gabriel and his followers." She just crossed her arms and stared stubbornly back at him.

Leo turned to face Margot and she looked at him with a kind smile while taking both his hands. She closed her eyes and took a breath, then concentrated wisps of black fog curled out of her nose and mouth. For the second time that night, Leo inhaled and let her into his mind. Except this time, he decided to guide her directly to his memory from hours earlier where Gabriel committed one of the most violating acts for a Star Born. He felt Margot take her time, watching the memories leading up to Gabriel reaching inside him until Leo ejected him. Then she watched them again, carefully stopping at various points to understand from his perspective how the event unfolded. She also went beyond when he ejected Gabriel and completely stopped when Leo traveled across the cavern.

"What was that? Is there a memory missing there?" Margot asked, but the words ringed out in his head, not his ears.

Leo didn't know how he was supposed to respond, so he tried to just think the word, "No."

"That doesn't make sense. You were next to Gabriel one moment and then all the way over at the stairs. That isn't possible," she stated and Leo felt uncomfortable from her skepticism.

He had said he had nothing to hide, so Leo told her the whole truth, "I traveled there using my abilities. It isn't a common one for Star Borns and it probably saved me today."

Leo felt Margot accept his explanation silently and then she continued to search through his mind, but she wasn't looking at his memories anymore. The sensation became somewhat uncomfortable, as if she was prodding different parts of his personality and character to see if he was trustworthy. He felt extreme emotional swings when she pushed on parts of his mind. Thankfully, it only lasted for a minute or so before he started to cough the fog out again. Margot waited patiently for him to catch his breath and then spoke loudly for everyone to hear.

"Leo is being completely honest. Gabriel attempted to take his core and he successfully defended himself. It is admirable that someone so young was able to stand up to such an evil act."

"But… something like this is unheard of…" he heard Mrs. Beacher continue plaintively, but Margot's words held more weight and several people sitting close by shushed her gently until she finally stopped trying.

"Now that we have evidence of Gabriel's actions," Adam began to move on, "we need to understand why he came here."

Maranda pulled on his shoulder and he leaned down to let her whisper in his ear.

He pulled back in astonishment and said loudly, "You can't be serious! How do you even know where it is?!"

Maranda pushed up on her tiptoes to whisper in his ear again, but several people called out that the conversation should be had in the open for everyone to hear.

"Yes, yes, I agree!" Adam responded impatiently. "Maranda believes Gabriel is here for the vial."

Many people couldn't help but gasp. Small groups furiously debated the troubling piece of information. It took over ten minutes of Adam walking around and asking everyone to quiet down before enough people began to comply so they could continue the discussion.

"Maranda," Adam began again, "only the Council knows where the vial is kept. Why do you think Gabriel is here for it?"

"More people than you are aware of know the location of the vial and Gabriel is on the Council, so he definitely knows where it is. The fact that he is here and has brought such a large group of his followers with him means he is going after a big prize. Nothing would be bigger than the vial."

Adam, along with most of the room, struggled to process this information and Maranda decided to press for action.

"He is either already on his way to the temple or soon will be," she said. "We need to organize ourselves and try to beat him there. It may be our only chance."

People started to respond to her saying, "We're not ready!" and "We should consult with other tribes!"

Then Leo heard his dad's voice from across the room, "Adam, we shouldn't be allowed to know where the vial is kept. It is the most important secret for our people. You should consult the Council."

This seemed to help Adam make up his mind and he shook his head slowly. Then he turned to face Ben and said, "I understand your concern, but I think Maranda is right. Gabriel is… I mean was… a member of the Council. That means he is one of the keepers of that secret. If he is going to take the vial, it is more important that we try to stop him."

Ben's shoulders relaxed with acceptance and he sat back down waiting to hear what should happen next.

"I also do not think we can tell the Council of these events yet." Adam continued. "If Gabriel has been enlisting followers around the world, there is a chance there may be more on the Council. We will need to be very careful about who we trust for the time being."

He turned to Margot who was still standing nearby.

"How many Readers do you know we can absolutely trust?" he asked her.

"I can think of at least twenty off the top of my head,

probably more. However, I am not sure I like what you're think-ing of doing…"

"I know, Margot… This is a difficult moment for our people. I will never ask you or anyone else to read someone against their will, but we need to find a way to start rooting this cancer out."

Satisfied with his response, Margot said, "I'll see what I can do." Then she made her way out of the cavern.

"Alright, everyone, it's late and I think it is time to bring this meeting to a close. If my fellow leaders can wait for me upstairs, I would appreciate it." Then he turned to Leo and his friends and said, "I would like you all to stay as well, along with your parents and teachers."

Adam then stepped away and walked around, having short conversations with different members of the tribe and helping George control the flow of the crowd as it slowly made its way out of the bookshop discreetly.

16

RACING TO THE PAST

LEO JOINED HIS friends and they fidgeted and talked uncomfortably for a while, not sure why they were asked to stay. Leo tried to form an energy ball to distract himself, but he couldn't summon it. He let out a frustrated huff and was about to complain to everyone when he noticed Caroline standing right next to him.

"Hey, can you turn off your Moon Born mojo for a little while? I can't even do the simplest thing with my abilities when you're standing next to me," he said playfully.

"You can't use your powers near me? But I'm not even doing anything."

"You know, it's probably because you haven't learned how to control your abilities yet," Aran chimed in. "I was accidentally using my abilities for a while before I got the hang of turning them off and on. You must be stuck in the on position right now."

"You know, that actually makes a lot of sense…" Caroline replied, clearly getting lost in her thoughts.

"Since you can basically block our abilities, how were we even able to practice with you around?" Stella wondered aloud.

"I was always behind those screens. They must block my abilities too." Caroline answered. Clearly this was what she had been thinking about and it made complete sense, too.

Their parents and teachers gathered around them when the room was almost empty and the kids grew quieter, listening for clues on what would happen next. Maranda walked over lightly and mussed Leo's hair and he wondered how she could be so carefree in this moment. Then he thought about it and realized most of the weight she had been carrying for so long had just been lifted off her shoulders. So what if Gabriel was racing to release a tyrant back into the world, she was back with her tribe. He chuckles to himself at this thought and Maranda shot him a look, wondering what he was thinking about.

After the last stragglers left the cavern, Adam walked back over to the group and they all formed a large circle instinctively.

"Alright, given we have no idea where Gabriel is and he could have a sizable head start on us," Adam began, "I think we should have three groups set out for the temple. This way, we can be more confident that at least one of them will make it there in time."

"OK, who do you want on the teams?" Leo's mom asked.

"Everyone here along with a few others I just spoke to. We will need you all to leave immediately."

"You're just talking about the adults here, right?" Emily asked him.

"I'm afraid not and I know this is a big ask. We simply haven't been preparing anyone for battle and your kids are the only ones with recent experience. Maranda has been training them herself and it seems they are an amazing team. Honestly, I think they are our best hope in this situation."

"Well, not our daughter," Camille interjected. "We just discovered her abilities today. There's no way she is prepared for anything like this. I mean…" she started to get teary, "How could we ask her to do something so dangerous?"

Caroline was usually a big goofball, but when she got frustrated she could be known to explode, so her friends braced themselves for a big argument. However, Caroline placed her hand gently on her mom's shoulder and said, "I have been at every single training with them for months. I know how they think and I can help them." Then she turned to Adam and asked, "How many other Moon Borns do you have for this?"

"Well, I know a few of the tribes have experienced Moon Born members, but it will take at least an hour if not longer to get them here."

This hardened Caroline's resolve. She looked at her mother and said earnestly, " I can't let everyone I care about go into harm's way without some kind of protection. I saw what I could do today and I know it can make a difference. Let me be there for them… Please…"

Her mom's tears fell freely from both pride and fear, but she managed to nod her head. Her dad, George, pulled her over into a tight hug and Leo heard him whisper to her how proud he was.

"Is everyone in agreement?" Adam confirmed and he looked to each person as they answered with a simple "yes."

"OK, then we must move quickly from this moment on. We're all going to the Yosemite Valley, the temple entrance is at the base of Half Dome. It is where the Calamity ended and Warwick has been imprisoned there ever since. Only a secret keeper can find the entrance, so I will make Casey and Maranda keepers when we are done here. I'm going to divide up the groups to make sure there are complementary abilities on each one.

"Josh," he turned to Aran's dad, "you, Aran, Stella, Jennifer, and Justin will all be coming with me. Nikki, the leader of the Oakland tribe, will give us an initial lift. We'll need you to carry us the rest of the way."

"You got it," Josh answered and twirled his index finger, creating a miniature tornado that dissipated as soon as he stopped.

"Casey," Adam continued, "Meimei, Leo, Amy, Ben, Caroline, Camille, and George will be with you. I'm sure you can figure out a way to get there quickly."

Casey simply nodded and stepped away from the group to speak with Emily quietly.

"Maranda, you will have Ania and her parents, Chris and Hannah, with you along with a member of Margot's tribe, Petra, to join you. She's a Tempestus and is rather gifted with creating fast moving storms, so I think she will be very helpful in our efforts. I expect her to be here shortly, Margot sent for her when she left.

"I know you all understand what you will face when you get there. They will be ruthless in their pursuit of the vial. You must not hold back, it will take every ounce of your combined efforts to defeat them. The one bit of good news I can give you is the vial can only be opened by a Moon Born and they must give up their own life to do so. However, we cannot rely on that to stop them and you will need to protect Caroline. They know she is a Moon Born because of her display in the cemetery and may try to take her to open the vial. The best case scenario is that we reach the vial first. If that happens, get it out of there as fast as possible."

Adam stopped talking and looked to Ben who knelt down

and opened up one of the boxes Leo loaded into the car earlier. He took out a small cloth bag and handed it to Adam who reached inside and pulled out a handful of simple, silver rings. He gave one to each of them and, as they placed them on their fingers, the rings let out a bright light and shrank onto their fingers. Eventually each one faded away, leaving a faint line where they used to be.

After inspecting his hand thoroughly, Leo looked at the group and each person had a sheen surrounding them.

"We are the only ones who can see the glow around us," Ben said. "This will allow us to see each other even in darkness and hopefully will make sure we don't mistake one of us for one of them. It will also allow some limited communication, but only from the person holding this ring," and he handed a small box to Adam.

"Casey? Maranda? Can you join me over here please?" Adam asked as he took a few steps away from the group. They came together and joined hands, forming a small triangle. Adam chanted several words over and over that were not any language they had heard before. He stopped abruptly, then looked at them both, and said, "There, that's done. You'll now be able to find the entrance."

He then walked over to Ben and knelt down, unzipping the duffel and rooted around inside.

"Ah, there it is… Leo!" he called out.

Leo turned and walked over quickly as Adam pulled out something that looked like a shirt at first and then once it was unfolded it resembled something more like a medieval tunic. It was iridescent like the buildings in Coreolis, changing colors as it swayed slightly in Adam's hands.

"Here, put it on," he instructed Leo.

Leo took it and pulled it over his head, sliding both arms through the large holes. It fell down to Leo's ankles and it draped over him like a large mumu.

"Uh, it doesn't fit," Leo said and he started to take it off.

"Hold on, give it a second," Adam said impatiently.

Leo looked down at the fabric, feeling uncomfortable and slightly embarrassed. Then he noticed the bottom of it starting to lift up higher. The sleeves were also narrowing and shortening, his fingertips peeked out and then his whole hands were finally fully visible.

"There, that should do it," Adams said with satisfaction and, Leo had to admit, it fit perfectly now.

"Thanks? What is this for?" Leo asked tentatively.

"That's something our tribe has cared for across many generations. It is something specifically for Star Borns and it should help you focus your abilities. Don't ask me how it works, I have no idea, but we're going to need all the help we can get today."

Leo looked down at the duffel and asked, "You got any other good stuff in there?"

Adam zipped it closed and shook his head, saying, "There is nothing else that's good and I pray we don't have to use what's left in this bag."

On that note, he stood up, slung the bag over his shoulder and signaled his group to follow him out of the cavern. Leo joined his group and saw Casey finishing a bar and Emily handing him another one while they started walking out of the cavern together. While the soup he had earlier was energizing, it wasn't that filling and his stomach rumbled loudly.

"You don't want to eat one of those," Meimei said to him, smiling. "They are concentrated calories. My dad burns so much fuel when he moves at full speed that my mom developed those to make sure he can function after a lot of exertion. If you tried to eat one, you'd probably feel like you have a massive brick in your stomach and you wouldn't sleep for a few days."

"Don't worry, I have a few things to send you off with that should do the trick," Emily assured him with a wink.

They all quickly headed to their cars and Ben drove them to Meimei's house so fast that Amy gripped the door handle tightly and took deep breaths. As soon as they arrived, Leo jumped out of the car as quickly as possible and hurried away from it.

"You think that was fast? You ain't seen nothin' yet," his dad told him, following close behind.

They walked down the driveway and saw Casey emerging from the crawl space below their house, hauling out something that looked like a huge net crafted with thick climbing rope. It was very heavy and the rest of them pitched in to get it spread out fully. Emily and Meimei came out the back gate carrying fully loaded hiking backpacks and a bunch of windbreakers.

"You're gunna want to wear one of these," Meimei said as she passed them out to Leo and his parents. Caroline and her parents were already wearing them.

Emily opened one of the packs and handed Leo something wrapped in aluminum foil. "Here," she said, "my kids call this mana. It's not the tastiest thing I make, but it has helped them survive many of the hikes Casey takes us on."

Casey looked up at her with a "who me?" look on his face and it made Leo grin. He was glad they could still joke around given what they are setting out to do that night.

"OK, folks, let's get this show on the road," Casey said. "If you all wouldn't mind stepping into the net, that would be appreciated."

He and Meimei moved around to position each of them

carefully. When everything was just right, Meimei came over to stand next to Leo in the center of the net while Casey walked off, standing just off the front edge.

"I'm going to need a little help for this next part," Meimei said quietly to Leo and he caught her drift easily. He instantly aligned his pattern with hers and started to feed her energy slowly. Realizing how much easier the process was, he had a greater appreciation for the tunic Adam had given him.

"Just a few quick notes for everyone before we set off," Casey said, sounding like a tour director. "We're going to be moving extremely fast, so please keep everything inside the net at all times. We're going to look pretty conspicuous in this contraption, so, Camille, do you think you can make us invisible to onlookers?"

"Oh, that's easy, I learned that in my first year of training as a kid," she said confidently and Caroline looked at her mom in astonishment. "Honey, I'm sorry, we haven't had a chance to talk much yet. I'm a Conjurer. While Readers are able to know what people are thinking and feeling, I am able to plant ideas in people's heads, make them believe things, mess with their senses. All those kinds of things."

"And she doesn't need any of that creepy fog to do it," George said playfully.

Leo felt Meimei's draw on his energy change and the net rose up and formed itself around everyone, guiding each person to a sitting position in a seat that was molded specifically for them. The net then began to hover about three or four feet off the ground. Meimei looped one of her hands through the netting next to her and others followed her lead. A long section of net stretched straight out from their feet towards Casey and he ducked in through a large loop.

"I want you and our daughter back here safe and sound, do you hear me? I may not have abilities that will help in a battle, but I won't stand for either of you doing something crazy," Emily warned him. This made Casey smile widely and he pulled her into a tight hug in acknowledgement. Then he pulled away from her and repositioned himself, hooking two hefty carabiners at the end of the net to a thick leather belt around his waist. He leaned forward and they were pressed into their seats when Casey accelerated quickly out of the driveway and down the street.

Leo's dad was right, they were moving much faster than even the fanciest sports cars and the world around them was a blur. The wind buffeted them, his eyes were watering, and he found it difficult to breathe. After a short while he acclimated and was able to fish out the mana Emily gave him and took large bites to help fuel the steady flow of energy Meimei needed. Her eyes were closed tightly to help her concentrate and keep everything stable, but Leo saw a bead of sweat trickle down the side of her face and then dry quickly in the wind.

It wasn't long before they left the densely populated areas behind them and the dark silhouettes of mountains grew in front of them. At this rate, they would likely arrive in less than an hour. A few minutes later, the road angled upward and Leo felt a painful twinge. He searched inside himself, trying to find the source of the pain when another jolt hit him and he was able to trace it to Meimei. He felt the climb was straining her past her limits and she was starting to weaken. As soon as he made that diagnosis, she let out a soft groan and the net dropped in the air by about a foot. Some of the parents whispered urgently to each other, preparing for what they would do if she couldn't continue.

However, between the soup and the mana, Leo had plenty of energy to spare and he increased the feed to her significantly.

Her face relaxed and then her eyes opened. She looked at him and quietly mouthed "thank you." Then the net rose up again in time for the ride to get even more challenging.

At this speed, the twists and the turns on the road were crazier than any roller coaster ride they had ever been on. Casey didn't seem to slow down and, as he went around switchbacks, Meimei had to focus hard to keep the net close behind him rather than swinging into mountain sides or out over cliffs. Caroline turned green from motion sickness and George leaned in close to speak in her ear to help her through it.

The road started to become more level and then, soon after they sped past the entrance and visitor center, they descended into the valley. Leo noticed Casey's pace change as he decelerated. The wind around them became much more tolerable and the roar in their ears died down to a softer whoosh.

They reached the valley floor and Casey quickly navigated them past the clusters of camp sites toward their destination. Leo felt Camille scanning around them, working hard to erase the image of their bizarre setup from anyone who happened to be awake or any enemies who were on the lookout. He read her pattern quickly and gave her a little boost to help her efforts. Her eyes opened wide for a moment and she looked at him, then nodded and got back to work with her increased range.

Casey continued to move them forward at a much more modest pace, being cautious and not wanting to find themselves in an ambush. He left the road and weaved through the terrain as best as he could, relying on Meimei to watch carefully and adjust their position constantly. Half Dome emerged in front of them and the sheer white rock looked bright from the moonlight reflecting off of it. Leo also noticed a cluster of glowing blobs near its base and he pointed them out to the group. Casey accelerated his pace a bit and the blobs resolved into the human forms of Adam's group in a defensive arc in front of a large, narrow crack.

Adam raised his hand in greeting as they arrived and Casey pulled up alongside him, unhooking himself from the net. Meimei slowly lowered them and let the net fall to the ground. They all stepped out carefully and Caroline ran behind a tree, finally emptying the contents of her stomach.

"I don't know how we beat them here, but we did," Adam told them.

"I was sure we would be running headlong into a battle when we arrived," Casey said, his mouth full with another energy bar.

"This is the entrance?" Ben asked skeptically, scanning the large crack in front of him.

"Yes. Keepers know how to open it. You could spend a lot of time examining it carefully and not find the mechanism," Adam said.

"So, what do we do now?" Caroline asked, wiping her mouth with the back of her hand.

"We wait," Adam answered simply.

As if on cue, Leo felt a huge surge in energy behind him and he whirled around to see where it was coming from. Caroline reacted instinctively to Leo's movement and she raised her hands above her head, creating a rippling dome around them just as a huge energy orb came flying out of the darkness in front of them. It slammed into Caroline's dome and ricocheted off into some trees that immediately erupted in fire.

Adam clenched his fist and yelled, "Keep them away from the entrance at all costs!" his voice echoing in everyone's heads through the connection created by the rings.

Then, Leo's heart sank as Gabriel strode out into the open with dozens of followers close behind him.

17

DAVID VS. GOLIATH

EVERYONE FELT A large, concussive thud in their chests as another massive energy ball pounded into Caroline's shield and caromed off, creating another small blaze. The Cinder from the earlier battle ran forward and stoked the flames, making them climb and spread to start a larger forest fire. A pair of twin Physics started to pelt the shield with rocks and branches, but they fell out of the air before they even reached within a foot of it.

Two men and a woman ran out from behind Gabriel and they transformed before everyone's eyes, heads stretching and elongating into large jaws of a wolf and fur growing rapidly all over their new faces. Their hands twisted into four-fingered talons, with three inch long claws. Letting out grotesque bellows, they ran directly at the shield and the group just stared in disbelief as these nightmarish monsters barreled toward them.

The woman reached the shield first and immediately let out

a scream in agony as her body transformed back to its normal form in an uncontrolled manner. She was only half-way through before she collapsed on the ground, writhing from the pain of her bones not matching up and there was nothing she could do to correct it. The two transformed men witnessed this and tried to shift their momentum to avoid a similar fate. One of them successfully curved away, barely skirting the shield and running back to Gabriel's army. The other slipped on the loose ground and his feet slid out from under him as he flew through the shield and began his own agonizing process of rapid transformation. He and the woman passed out from the trauma after a minute. George and Ben, dragged them back, and tied them up with pieces of the large net they'd arrived on.

Gabriel held up his hand as several more came forward to try their luck. He shook his head, acknowledging their attacks had no chance of success. Then he leaned over and said something to a small, weaselly-looking man standing next to him, who promptly scurried back into the crowd behind him.

In the meantime, Amy ran to the edge of the shield and tried to stretch out her abilities to reach the creek running nearby to put out the flames, but nothing happened. She tried again and it felt like her abilities were just gone. She turned back to the group, at a loss for what to do. Adam looked at her soberly and gestured with his head at Caroline, standing as still as a statue holding up the protective roof over them.

"They can't use their abilities and neither can we," he said to all of them.

They turned back toward Gabriel's forces, wondering if a stalemate was the best possible outcome they could hope for, when they saw a ripple through the group as if something very large was making its way through. A few seconds later, one of the largest human beings they had ever seen stepped out into the clearing between them, just a few paces away from Gabriel.

"What the heck is that?!" Aran shouted.

"A Heavy," George responded from behind him. "He's a kind of Biologic like these Chimeras we have back here. The difference is where they are able to alter their bodies to take on animal properties, he's just all muscle."

Leo stared at this behemoth and recognized some of his facial features. That tiny man had just transformed himself into a giant.

"What makes him think he'll do any better than they did?" Ania asked.

"No idea…" Ben answered honestly.

The Heavy gave them a smarmy smile and then opened his hand to reveal a massive rock the size of an exercise ball. He tossed it up and down like a baseball, taunting them with it, and their eyes grew wide in recognition of what he intended to do. When the rock landed in his palm again, he held it tightly, cocked his arm back, then unleashed it with a powerful and smooth throw. It flew through the air, making a loud hiss as it pierced the shield like it was not even there and slammed into the wall behind them. Everyone was pelted with small and medium-sized rocks as it exploded above their heads.

They crouched, covering their heads from the debris except for Caroline, who kept the shield above them despite the large gash in her thigh from a chunk that tore through her jeans. When they looked back out again, they saw the Heavy standing there with that same creepy smile and tossing another rock, this one even bigger than the last. He was staring at Caroline and, instead of taunting them, he just hurled it straight at her. Leo could only stare in horror, too far away to help her and unable to do anything with the shield inhibiting his abilities. Caroline saw it coming too and the protective dome flickered as her concentration wavered in the face of a deadly projectile. This might not have been enough of an opening for most people, but it was plenty of time for Casey as he sprinted and moved her out of harm's way.

Another spray of rock and dust pelted them from behind and then there was a lull as everyone took stock and both sides noticed the barrier was gone. Leo heard each beat of his heart pounding in his ears and realized he was holding his breath. His senses erupted with the feeling of aggression and violence right before a loud battlecry burst from Gabriel's forces.

Ben pulled up a thick wall of soil and rock from the ground surrounding them, but they all knew it was a very temporary measure. Adam immediately started barking out orders in rapid succession.

"Camille, get as many people away from here as possible, we can't have a massacre of innocents," he started and she winked out of sight without a word.

"Stella, get those fires out, they're trying to pin us down. Justin, you're on their Cinder. See if you can put him out."

Justin and Stella ran over to the section of wall closest to the fires and stared back, waiting for their moment. The wall was taking a pounding and cracks were starting to emerge in a concentrated spot near the center. They all knew that was probably where the Heavy was focusing his efforts.

"Jenny, you know what we need you to do." She cracked her neck and kicked off her shoes. Then Leo and his friends stared on, slack jawed as she started to grow, her muscles inflating dramatically, becoming even bigger than Gabriel's Heavy. She stepped forward to the rapidly spreading cracks in the wall and shook out her limbs, getting ready for a brawl.

"The rest of you, try to take as many of them out as possible. We need time, as much of it as you can get us. Hopefully the others will get here soon to help."

Then he turned to Leo, "I need you close to me. They're going to come at us hard and I am going to need to keep everyone functioning as much as possible."

Two flaming logs flew over the top of the wall and smashed into the mountain. Sparks cascaded down on their heads, but Josh pulled them into a compact sphere and stifled the flames.

"Ben, it's now or never!" Adam called out.

Leo's dad reached down like he was grabbing something and quickly rose up like he was pulling an invisible carpet with his hands. In unison with his actions, the wall transformed into something resembling a wave and it crashed down on the first several rows of combatants. In its wake, bodies were submerged, arms and legs sticking out at random angles and wiggling as their owners struggled to extract themselves.

The rest of Gabriel's forces didn't bother to help their comrades, they immediately started attacking. Pandemonium ensued, making the earlier battle in the cemetery seem like a schoolyard squabble. Jennifer and the other Heavy slammed into each other like two sumo wrestlers, grabbing and pulling at each other while looking for an advantage. Everyone around them scrambled away to avoid being trampled.

Leo looked around to see where he could help and he noticed the third Chimera barreling toward his mom. She pulled spikes of water from a bladder slung across her back and threw them into the air for Meimei to launch at him, but he was much too agile and easily dodged as he got closer. Leo threw caution to the wind and amplified his mom with a large amount of energy. Her shoulders relaxed, accepting the energy and immediately putting it to use.

Something glittering in the dark where Gabriel's army came from caught Leo's eye, but he didn't have time to figure out what it was because he heard a howl as the hellish creature leapt toward his mom. He could hardly look, but he didn't dare to close his eyes and risk taking away that lifeline to her. He then took a deep breath, getting ready to call Adam to help heal her, when the glittering object grew in his field of vision. It was a huge sphere of water that enveloped the Chimera and then, just as quickly, turned to solid ice. They stared for a moment at him frozen in mid-pounce as the ice sphere thumped down to the ground.

His mom looked back to him in thanks, but he could already tell the trouble had shifted to Meimei. She was now levitating off the ground a few feet in a pitched battle with the twin Physics. They were surrounded by a sea of ugly looking implements that they were firing in rapid succession at Meimei. She was completely focused on fending them off, unable to counter attack.

"MOM!" Leo called and pointed at Meimei.

She turned to see where he was looking and didn't hesitate for a moment, tearing off a large, round chunk of ice that Meimei immediately grabbed to serve as a barrier. Chunks of ice splintered off as the twins tried to batter their way through to Meimei. Leo created a long energy whip and swung it at the closer of the two twins, wrapping it around her ankle. She screamed from the burns that blistered all over her skin around the whip and he started to pull on it to separate her from her sister. They both hurled implements at Leo, but everything simply bounced off the armor he formed around himself. With plenty of energy reserves, he didn't hold anything back.

Leo shifted the amplification from his mother to Meimei who reached toward the large boulder that she was hovering next to. It rose out of the ground, clumps of dirt falling off its bottom, and then she swung both of her arms toward the twins. The boulder hurdled toward them, just as Leo pulled back his whip and released the twin's ankle. While suddenly free, they had no time to react as the boulder slammed into them. Leo, Meimei, and Amy all looked away as the boulder lost momentum and dropped to the ground, rolling for about thirty yards before stopping.

It was at this point, with the fighting raging around him and not in the line of fire, that he realized there hadn't been a single energy attack against them. He looked around frantically for Gabriel and didn't see him anywhere in the fray. Panicking, Leo whirled around, looking behind them toward the large crack that marked the temple entrance and he saw Gabriel and two others crouched at the bottom of it. He was reaching inside the crack, his arm buried inside up to his bicep as he strained to reach something.

"He's at the entrance!" Leo shouted and pointed briefly before yanking back his arm in agony as he felt large claws tear three deep gashes down his arm. He turned quickly to see a large mountain lion next to him. It crouched, preparing to pounce on Leo. He stumbled backward, his mind wild and unfocused in a cloud of fear, preparing to run. Then somebody placed their hand on the large cat's head, scratching it behind an ear. He looked up, expecting to see its Caretaker, but instead found Caroline standing there. The mountain lion's eyes grew unfocused for a moment and then it glanced between Leo and Caroline, clearly frightened. They had no idea what it would do next, holding their breath and not wanting to make any sudden moves. Then the cat turned suddenly and bounded away as quickly as possible.

Feeling blood dripping down his arm and covering his hand, he pulled it close and cradled it across his stomach. He looked back up to where he last saw Gabriel and saw the crack had widened enough to let two people walk through comfortably. He and his minions were nowhere in sight.

"Find Adam! Tell him Gabriel is inside!" Leo said to Caroline and she immediately ran off.

Leo started to jog toward the entrance when he felt Aran's familiar pattern tinged with fear and panic. He followed it and looked down at the clearing that was once packed with combatants, which had now thinned out significantly. Jennifer had subdued the Heavy and was wielding two large trees as clubs, helping his father deal with a group of mixed Elementals. Stella had most of the fires out, but Justin had been joined by Josh and they were still battling with the Cinder.

He finally found Aran and George at the edge of the clearing trying to defend themselves against two of Gabriel's followers who were riding on the backs of machines that resembled giant spiders. At the end of the front legs were sharp blades that were thrusting at them. He could also tell they were barely holding on, cuts covering their arms and legs. There were several nasty gashes on their faces, one dripping into George's eye.

Many wounded animals were laying around them, casualties from their failed attempts to defend the two Caretakers. Leo took off at a sprint and formed a dense sphere of energy about the size of a bowling ball. Using his good arm, he hurled it at the closer machine as hard as he could without missing a step and he watched with satisfaction as it sheared off a back leg. The machine teetered for a moment, but then righted itself quickly and turned toward Leo.

He quickly amplified George and Aran as he powered up his armor, creating two large energy blades that ran from his hands down to his elbows. He planted his feet and waited as the machine and its pilot scurried toward him at a fast clip. He had just enough time to think, "Man, I hate spiders…" before it arrived swinging its front arms down on him from above. He brought his arms up to block the attack and was surprised when his blades barely made a scratch in the metal. They descended into a bizarre form of hand to hand combat, clangs ringing out as the pilot tried to skewer Leo.

He rushed forward and then slid under the machine, thrusting the blades up into its abdomen and finding a weak spot. The damaged electronics sparked and motors whirred loudly in the openings he created, but he had to move quickly to avoid being squashed from the pilot spreading out all the arms quickly and slamming the core of the machine down on him.

Emerging behind the machine, Leo heard several loud roars and was then hit with a powerful funk of large animals before three gargantuan grizzly bears emerged from different places around the clearing and barreled toward George and Aran. The pilot of the other spider machine realized what was happening before Leo could put things together and started to backpedal the machine as fast as it would go. It was just not fast enough and the bears arrived, tearing the limbs off the machine and then dragging the pilot into the forest with them.

Leo looked up at the back of the pilot who had also just witnessed his comrade's demise and was about to launch back into the fight when several large lightning bolts rained down on various parts of the clearing. One of them slammed directly into the pilot and the machine exploded into small pieces. The blast and shards hit Leo's armor and sent him flying backwards through the air for several yards. He landed hard on his back and tumbled another yard or so into a large blackberry bush. He scrambled out of it before his armor set it on fire, thankful that it protected him from the thorns.

When he emerged, a drastically changing situation was unfolding. Maranda's group had arrived and it had started to turn the tide. Petra's lightning had scorched several groups who were now either injured and unable to fight or running away. Leo saw Maranda running to help his dad and Jennifer finish off the last of the Elementals. Ania had subdued the Caretaker who had attacked him earlier and Meimei was fending off two large vultures trying to attack Ania.

Leo also saw a stream of Gabriel's fighters flowing toward the temple entrance. Hannah, with flames surrounding her hands, and Chris, now covered in what appeared to be diamond encrusted skin, were running to intercept them. He started to run towards the entrance to join them when Aran and George appeared alongside him, looking pretty banged up, but clearly ready for more.

An actual firefight erupted at the entrance as Hannah scorched her way through anyone trying to make it through. Chris ran directly into the flames and Gabriel's followers fell like dominoes as he barreled his way through them. Leo, Aran, and George arrived and were about to dive into the fray when he heard Adam's voice behind him yell out, "Let them handle it!"

Leo turned around, staring at Adam in confusion.

"They are more than capable of handling the dregs of Gabriel's forces. We need you and the rest of your friends to go in after him," Adam explained. Then he held the ring up to his mouth and the blue stone in the center glowed brightly.

"Maranda, Ania, Meimei, and Stella," Adam said in a normal voice, but it echoed loudly in everyone's head. "Make your way to the entrance as quickly as possible. The rest of you, mop things up."

Adam then looked down at Leo and noticed his injuries. Leo glanced at the gashes on his arm, the blood still flowing slowly out of them, and he felt light headed. He stumbled backward a few steps and Aran steadied him.

"Let's have a look at that," Adam said, placing his hands on Leo's arm. The familiar warm sensation wrapped around it and he watched as the wounds closed quickly and then sealed over with new, pink skin.

"That'll have to do for now," he said to Leo and then turned to Aran. "Let's get you and George fixed up quickly as well."

By the time he was done, Maranda, Meimei, Ania, and Stella had all arrived, winded and miraculously with only minor injuries. Caroline ran up a minute later and said to Adam, "Casey is taking care of it." He nodded with a grave look on his face and turned to the group.

"This is the only way into the temple," he told them, pointing at the door. "There may be other ways out that I don't know about. Gabriel has been in there for a while, I am sure he's found the vial by now. I also recognized some of his followers who followed him in and they are *very* strong. You have faced Gabriel before and know what you're walking into. Last chance, everyone. If you're not up for this, nobody will blame you."

Without a word, they all turned around and headed toward the entrance.

"Caroline, not you," Adam said.

"What?! Why?!" she shouted and everyone turned back around.

"I told you this before. He needs a Moon Born to open that vial. You haven't been trained and we can't risk you being captured," he said firmly.

Caroline threw up her hands in frustration and said, "I can help! I mean, you saw how I can protect them and I figured out how to not block their abilities when I'm near!"

Adam crossed his arms and shook his head.

"She comes or I don't go," Meimei said quietly.

"Yeah, same here," Ania agreed.

"Me too," Stella, Aran, and Leo said in quick succession.

"Kids, listen…" Adam started to say.

"Don't call us kids and talk down to us now after you have asked us to go in and fight Gabriel," Leo snapped, unable to hold back. "She's been with us every step as we prepared for this. She's coming."

With that, they all turned back around and headed toward the entrance. Adam, taken aback, tried to muster a response. Maranda looked at him and just shook her head to tell him to let it go. Then she followed the group in.

The sounds from the fighting outside died down very quickly and soon all they heard was each other's breathing and the sound of their footsteps on the smooth rock floor. They stayed on their guard as they winded their way down the corridor, but there were no signs of Gabriel's group except for the soft glow of lanterns they left behind for their comrades to follow. They hurried, moving quickly around a large bend, and found themselves in the large room from the memory Maranda showed them. The space felt smaller than they expected, about the size of a classroom at their school with the two different tunnels on the opposite side.

Leo suddenly heard the sound of his mother screaming in pain. He looked around in panic and yelled, "MOM?!"

He heard her call back, "LEO! HELP US! WE NEED YOU!"

Leo turned around to run back out and he heard his father call out, "HURRY! We can't hold out for much longer!"

He tried to start running, but he tripped over Ania who was huddled on the floor, rocking back and forth with her hands covering her ears. He tried to get up, but Aran ran into him as he smacked his hands all over his body, trying to get something off him that Leo couldn't see. He didn't care about anything else but getting to his parents and he shoved Aran aside as he tried to make a path back to the corridor.

All of a sudden, everything was quiet again and Leo and his friends stared at each other in bewilderment. He heard a groan and turned toward it to see Caroline standing over a slender man who had collapsed on the floor. She was holding a rock at her side and glared down at him, clearly ready to deliver another blow..

"Conjurer," she said flatly. "I was in back when he started messing with everyone and I started to play along like I was scared of something. When he revealed himself, I ran right at him and blocked his abilities. Then I hit him with this." She held up the rock and then dropped it on the ground seeing he was not going to recover soon.

"Nice work," Maranda said, getting up and dusting herself off casually like they had only been taking a short break. "Let's get moving. Leo, now would be a good time to start concealing your pattern so Gabriel or one of the other Star Borns with him doesn't detect you as we get closer."

Leo focused intently for a moment and Maranda nodded at him when she sensed this pattern had disappeared.

The group then gathered in front of the two tunnels and Maranda didn't hesitate, "Leo, Meimei, and Ania go right. The rest of us will go left."

Nobody questioned, they just set out on their respective paths. Feeling the urgency and ignoring the risk of being heard, they ran and soon came to the large arch with symbols etched in the stones. Pausing to examine it, things became even more familiar and Leo recognized the symbol carved into the capstone.

"Connection…" he said softly, trying to look around and read the other symbols, but not making any headway.

"What?" Ania asked.

"That one," Leo pointed to the center of the arch. "It means connection."

"Really? I don't recognize that one. This one looks like the symbol for life," she replied. Leo bent down to get a closer look, but it didn't make any more sense to him.

"Guys, this one over here looks like the symbol for time," Meimei added. "It must be a mix of different symbols that match our types…"

Leo reached out to the symbol for energy that was right above the one Ania pointed out and traced a finger along the lines. It began to glow along with several other stones that Leo recognized as Star Born symbols. He took his hand away and the glow slowly faded away.

A blood curdling scream echoed toward them and they all startled, looking at each other while trying to recognize if it was one of their friends.

"Bloody hell!" they heard Gabriel yell following the scream. "Nobody else touch it!"

"They've found it!" Meimei whispered urgently.

"But they haven't figured out how to take it yet…" Leo finished her thought.

"Well, what are we waiting for? Let's stop them before they do," Ania said, snapping them into action.

She led the way as they crouched and entered an enormous cavern that was at least three times larger than the one they trained in. As they scanned around, they saw the large pedestal that rose high above the floor and Gabriel's group circled around something, probably the vial, on the altar in the middle. Right next to the pedestal was a wall of boulders and debris they didn't recognize from the memory.

Ania looked at Leo and Meimei in confusion and after a moment Meimei's face lit up in recognition.

"That probably happened as a part of the huge cave-in when Warwick was imprisoned. The other half of the cavern must have been closed off." she said.

Before they could distract themselves further, Gabriel and his followers erupted into a heated argument, completely oblivious to the arrival of Leo and his friends.

"I don't recognize any of them except for Gabriel and Rania," Meimei said.

"The one over there is Harland…" Ania said with loathing. "I can't wait to take him out…"

"How do you know that guy?" Leo asked.

"Gabriel's teacher for me… He has no business being a verdant. He doesn't care about living things, he just cares about what they can do for him…"

"So what do we do?" Meimei asked them. "I don't know if we can take them by ourselves."

"Umm… probably not," Leo agreed.

"Yeah we can. We have the element of surprise," Ania said with resolve.

Before Leo or Meimei could respond, they heard a "Pssst!" from behind them and they turned to see the other half of their group with Maranda in the front.

Leo, Meimei, and Ania made their way back to the arch and joined the others in the corridor. Without waiting for the obvious question, Aran answered, "The other path was blocked. Looks like there was a cave-in or something."

"Yeah, we saw the other side of the cavern collapsed," Leo confirmed.

"So what is going on?" Maranda asked urgently.

"They are all gathered on the big pedestal on the far side of a huge cavern. We think the vial is on an altar there. They haven't figured out how to take it yet," Leo briefed them quickly.

"Well, let's go stop them," Maranda said with resolve.

"That's what I said," Ania responded with annoyance at her thunder being stolen.

"So, what's the game plan?" Stella asked.

"Can we skip the game plan and just go wreak havoc for once?" Ania asked.

"You know what? I think that's exactly what we should do," Meimei agreed.

"Really?" Ania asked, not expecting the unlikely ally.

"Well, you all will change any game plan I came up with as soon as they start fighting back. Might as well go for the havoc," Maranda added.

"Yes!" Ania said excitedly and reached into a pouch tied at her side. She pulled out a handful of seeds and told the group with a maniacal grin, "I've been looking forward to using these."

She started to head back into the cavern, then turned to Leo and said, "Little help?"

He knew exactly what she was looking for and he amplified her significantly.

"That's the stuff," she said with satisfaction and then ran in. The others streamed in behind her, watching what she was doing and prepared to start creatively riffing off her plan. She rushed straight to the base of the pedestal and then cut to the right at the last minute, tossing two of the seeds along the way. Plants erupted out of the wall and floor growing to enormous size. One had bright red berries and nasty looking thorns, the other looked like an immense tree with large apple-like fruit. One of Gabriel's followers was distracted by the movement in the corner of her eye, but it was too late as the thorns enveloped her and she was pulled into the heart of the plant. She screamed loudly from the cuts and stabs she received while struggling to get out.

The rest of Gabriel's group was now completely aware of their arrival and Ania ran back to Meimei and said between gasps of air while pointing at the large tree, "Nick… as many… branches… on that one… as you can!"

Meimei didn't hesitate and started sending the knives hovering around her directly at the tree. They sliced at the bark rapidly, creating thick milky trails of sap in their wake, and the tree grew even more. The branches reached toward the group on the pedestal and Harland urgently grabbed for one of his comrades as a branch came close, not noticing another branch arriving on the opposite side of him. A wide trail of sap rubbed against the right side of his face, painting his cheek and neck, and some also splattering his eye. His skin erupted into bright blisters and he screamed in agony touching his face.

"Those daggers are potent now," Ania said to Meimei. "Have fun!"

Meimei grinned and started sending the knives at the rest of the combatants and then all hell really broke loose. It turned out the two followers standing closest to Gabriel were also Star Borns and they launched a flurry of attacks. Leo instinctively started to rapidly travel around the cavern, appearing just in time to intercept the energy attacks with a large, fortified shield.

Aran knelt at the side of the room, near the base of the pedestal and opened up his backpack. A raccoon popped out and scurried around the rocky base and was quickly out of sight.

Aran then sat down and stared into space as if in a trance. An Elemental high up on the platform, reached high above and a stalactite formed on the ceiling. This captured Caroline's attention and she immediately reacted, sending a rippling wave directly at the Elemental, catching him by surprise. The sudden loss of his abilities caused the stalactite to shatter into large chunks and several hit the Elemental, knocking him off the pedestal. He landed hard on the cavern floor and didn't move.

With the Elemental separated from the group, there was now a clear view of the vial and Caroline felt a powerful connection to it. She was frozen in place, unable to move or focus, just consumed by her need to hold the vial. She could see Gabriel was also intensely focused on it, completely ignoring the fight raging around him. He brought his glowing hands close to it and they faded as soon as he was within several inches of the vial.

In the meantime, Maranda launched a counterattack that Leo recognized as a Flicker. Hundreds of small energy charges about the size of a firefly were emitted from all over her body. They swarmed around Gabriel and his followers, stinging and distracting them, but not doing much damage. It created enough of an opening for Leo to amplify Stella who extracted water seeping down the walls of the cavern and converted it into a spikey ball. She hurled it toward the top of the pedestal, not aiming for anyone specifically and got lucky as it slammed into a powerful air Elemental who was defending the group from Meimei and Ania's attacks.

The distraction was also enough for Aran's raccoon to climb up to the altar. Caroline continued to stare as it reached its tiny hands toward the vial in a careful, almost human-like way. Gabriel swept a glowing arm in a wide arc in front of him and the remnants of the Flicker suddenly winked out. He looked back to the vial, saw the raccoon about to grab it, and yelled, "I don't think so!" swinging his arm down like a bludgeon. With its heightened senses, the animal leapt away, scurrying down the backside of the pedestal. Gabriel sent several more attacks after it, but quickly turned his attention back to the vial.

He placed his hands on the two Star Borns next to him and his entire body started to glow brightly while they both sank down to their knees. He removed his hands and then reached toward the vial, stopping about a foot away. Strands of light started to flow out of his fingertips and they swirled around the vial. As more strands emerged and joined together, they created a glowing egg around the vial. Suddenly, Caroline's connection to the vial was broken and she returned to the present, trying to process what happened.

The two Star Borns got back on their feet and started hurling energy attacks at the group as quickly as they could. Leo continued to protect his friends as they struggled out of the way. Rocks splintered and pelted them with debris, stinging their arms and backs. Caroline sent a concentrated wave directly at a woman as she was about to hurl a deadly looking energy orb at Ania. It hit her mid-throw and the orb flew directly into the large tree Ania had grown, lighting a number of branches on fire. The smoke reached the man at the side of Gabriel first and he began to cough and gag, holding his throat as he fell down to his knees and struggled to breathe.

Gabriel's concentration was broken for a moment and he saw the smoke and his dying follower. He reached out quickly and touched the egg he created, but nothing happened. Then he boldly grabbed the glowing egg and jumped down the back side of the pedestal, out of sight. The woman followed him, leaving just Leo and his friends alive or conscious in the cavern. The smoke was starting to fill the space and Ania yelled, "We can't breathe that stuff!"

Everyone ran for the arch, except for Aran who remained seated at the base of the pedestal. Maranda looked at Leo and he saw the panic in her eyes.

"I'll get Aran! Just get the rest of them out!" he shouted, then traveled directly next to Aran. Leo tried to get him to stand up, but he was too heavy. Making his thousandth risky call of the day, he knelt in front of his friend, held his hands, and visualized the arch. They traveled together and emerged where he planned, thankfully as separate and whole people, and Maranda was waiting there for him. The smoke was now thick in the cavern and reaching toward them, so Maranda reached down to pull Aran over her shoulder like a fireman. She struggled briefly as she adjusted to the load and then moved as fast as her legs would allow her down the corridor to the exit. Leo followed close behind, helping to steady her whenever she lost her balance.

Stumbling out of the entrance, Chris and George caught Maranda and Aran before they crashed to the ground. Adam looked desperately at Leo and asked, "What happened? Did you get it?!"

Leo shook his head and responded urgently, "Did Gabriel come out this way?"

"No, we haven't seen him," Adam answered with a mix of dejection and anxiety. Then he held up his ring and said, "Casey, bring it now."

Before the words stopped ringing in their heads, Casey appeared next to Adam with the duffel. Adam slung it over his shoulder and started to walk towards the entrance.

"What are you doing?! You can't go in there, the smoke will kill you!" Leo shouted.

Adam looked over his shoulder and said, "I will be able to heal myself long enough to get this close enough to Gabriel before he escapes. It's our last chance."

"He's already gone," Aran slurred, coming out of his trance and everyone turned to look at him.

"What do you mean, gone?" Adam asked tersely.

"I followed him out another passageway that led to the other side of the mountain," Aran responded a bit more clearly. "There were people waiting for him there. One of them was an air Elemental and he carried Gabriel away. The rest split up and are taking trails away from here."

"How do you know this?" Adam continued to interrogate him.

"Sneaky," Aran answered.

"Sure, you're sneaky, but you're here and saying they are on the other side of the mountain."

"Sneaky is my raccoon," George said. "We have been practicing direct control with him because he seems to not mind it as much as other animals."

"I asked him to follow one of the groups," Aran told George.

"That was a good idea," George said, patting him on the shoulder.

"So, what do we do now?" Leo asked.

"We'll need to call for a Gathering," Adam said heavily.

18

A GATHERING AND A DEPARTURE

"Have you heard anything?" Aran asked Leo as they settled into the sun on the grass in Leo's backyard.

"Not a peep..." Leo answered sullenly.

"Not even from Maranda?" Aran asked in surprise.

"Trust me, I asked her. She just said things were complicated and I needed to stay out of the Connector for the time being. That it still wasn't safe."

"But it's been weeks!" Aran lamented. "We were out there, risking our lives, the least they could do is keep us in the loop."

"Not even us elders have any idea what is going on," Amy said as she came up from around the back of the deck with a watering can.

"Oh... Hey, Amy... Didn't know you were there..." Aran said awkwardly and she just raised an eyebrow and gave him a knowing smile as she headed back inside.

"So, it's our last week before school starts up again. What should we do?" Leo changed the subject.

"Don't remind me…" Aran said, still sullen. "We barely got a real summer with all the training we did."

"Don't say that," Leo chided. "You liked the training. We all did."

"True…" Aran said, grinning sheepishly.

Aran then sat up quickly, looked at Leo seriously, and yelled, "Boba!"

"When the craving calls, you have to answer," Leo admitted and they got up quickly, heading through the house and out the front door to go to the shops and get their favorite bubble tea.

When they arrived, Meimei and Stella were outside, already sipping through the large straws of their drinks. They waved when they saw Leo and Aran.

"You felt the call too, I see," Aran said when they were closer and they both held up their arms to say, "Of course!"

After getting their drinks, Leo and Aran pulled two heavy metal chairs over to Meimei and Stella's table, making a loud racket that caused some grumbling from an older couple sitting nearby. Nobody said anything at first, they just savored their drinks and felt the warmth of a truly nice summer day.

"Have any of you talked to Caroline?" Stella asked, ending the peaceful moment.

"I saw her a couple days ago at Zachary's. She was there with her parents for dinner. It was… weird…" Aran answered.

"I tried to hang out with her last week, but she never answered my messages," Meimei added.

"Yeah, something's up," Leo confirmed. "I walked over to her house yesterday and her mom said she wasn't up for hanging out.

She had this look on her face like when we were keeping Caroline in the dark about the tribe."

"What do you think it could be?" Stella wondered aloud.

"She's been this way since the temple," Leo said, trying to piece together clues.

"Huh… Did you notice anything then?" Meimei joined in the investigation.

"Honestly, I was just focused on not dying," Stella said and they all nodded, acknowledging there wasn't enough information to solve the riddle.

Silence settled over the group again, the only sounds coming from the straws trying to find the last bits of liquid in their cups until several of their phones buzzed in their pockets. Leo pulled his out and looked at the screen. His heart started to race when he saw it was a message from Maranda.

"Cavern in fifteen minutes," was all it said.

Leo looked to his friends and they gazed back at each other in excitement and trepidation.

"What?!" Aran asked since he didn't have a phone.

"We're supposed to meet at the cavern in fifteen minutes," Meimei answered.

"Says who?" Aran asked for more details.

"Maranda," Leo replied.

"Really? My mom messaged me," Stella said.

"Yeah, it was my dad who sent the message," Meimei added.

"Well, it sounds like we might finally find something out," Leo said excitedly and he got up to head to the cavern immediately, even though it was only a short walk away.

⁓

Bounding down the stairs to the cavern, Leo and his friends

found Adam, Maranda, and their parents already there and looking very serious. Maranda stepped away from the group and jogged over to them with a big smile on her face and gave each of them a warm hug to greet them.

"What happened at the Gathering," Leo asked, getting straight to the point.

"We should probably wait for everyone to get here before we cover that," Maranda answered. Then seeing the consternation on all their faces, she added, "Don't worry, all your questions will be answered. Why don't you all go hang out on the couches in the storage chamber."

They all walked as slowly as possible toward the open passageway, the bookcases having already been moved over, trying to pick up snippets of conversation from the adults. All they heard were updates about their tribe for Adam since he had been away. Reaching the chamber, they decided to walk down the aisles and explore everything stored in there, instead of making their way directly to the couches.

"Huh… wonder what this is for," Aran said as he picked up a staff with a spiked metal ball at the end.

"Man… it's heavy!" he noted and handed it over to Leo.

As soon as Leo's hand touched it, the weapon began to glow brightly and the metal ball spun rapidly, creating electric arcs around it.

"Perhaps you should put that down…" Meimei suggested and Leo agreed, handing it back to Aran so he could put it where he found it.

They found several more curious items, but decided not to touch them for the time being. When they reached the end of the shelves, they saw Ania sitting there writing in a small journal. Her legs were covered in dirt and grime and she was in her biking gear.

She noticed them taking in her appearance and said, "I don't want to hear anything from you guys. My mom and dad sent me straight here when I got back from my ride. They wouldn't even give me time to take a shower."

"I wouldn't have noticed if you hadn't pointed it out. Remember, I hang out with animals all day long," Aran joked and the rest of the group laughed loudly. Ania squinted her eyes as she decided how to respond and Aran was relieved when she started laughing along with the group.

They all began to speculate what they were going to find out from Adam and Maranda until they heard soft steps walking toward them. They all turned to see Caroline emerging from the closest aisle, her arms crossed in front of her like she felt it was too cold, her head hanging low, staring at her feet. She looked up at the group and extracted one of her hands from the tight knot across her chest to give them a small wave, but she stopped walking toward them.

Everyone stared at her for a moment before raining warm greetings down on her. She flinched slightly at the loud and excited "CAROLINE!" coming from Meimei and Stella as well as the "WAZZZAAAAP?!" from Aran. Leo walked around behind her and pushed her to join the group and she took hesitating steps, resisting his push. Reaching the couches, Ania pulled her down to sit with them and everyone settled back down.

"So, what's going on?" Leo asked, still in an impatient state and not willing to wait for pleasantries to be exchanged.

"Leo!" Meimei snapped at him, trying to steer away from the tough conversation.

"No, we all promised we would not hide anything from each other and this counts. We want to be there for her, so it's legit to ask her what's bothering her. Something clearly is," he responded, gesturing at her.

Caroline shifted uncomfortably and looked around before relenting and taking a deep breath to speak.

"Something happened in the temple," Caroline started.

"I knew…" Leo started to interrupt before Meimei shot him a look and he decided to listen this time.

After a short pause to collect herself again, Caroline continued, "In the middle of the fighting, I got a clear view of the vial and… I can't explain it… It had a power over me. I couldn't move, talk, or anything. I was locked onto it and nothing else around me mattered."

Her eyes filled with tears and she reached up a sleeve to wipe them away. Stella came over to rub her back and comfort her.

"Warwick can control me from inside the vial… I just know it! I almost risked everything by being there with you guys… What if he had commanded me to let him out?!" she said urgently, her voice shaking from all the pent up emotions flowing out of her.

"You can't be sure that is what happened," Leo responded, but not as confidently as he intended.

"See?! You're not sure about that! I can hear it in your voice!" Caroline snapped.

"Wait…" Leo said, trying to fix things, but was interrupted.

"I couldn't help but overhear what you all are talking about and I think I can help," a woman standing at the end of the aisle Caroline had emerged from said. Everyone turned quickly to look at her and saw she was dressed in an intricately patterned blue dress with a golden shawl wrapped around her shoulders. She looked stylish and also wise. They could also tell she was older than their parents, but couldn't place her age.

Nobody said a word, so she continued, "My name is Rebecca

and I am very pleased to meet you all. I am especially excited to meet you, Caroline, since I have heard so much about you."

Caroline looked confused and pointed at herself to make sure Rebecca was talking about her.

"Yes, you," Rebecca answered. "Perhaps I should introduce myself a bit more. It will help when I explain what happened in the temple."

She walked over to the opposite couch and Aran moved over to make room for her to sit. She smiled a thank you and continued, "I am the High Chief of the Moon Born and have traveled a long way to see you. It has been a while since we had a powerful Moon Born found in the tribes and usually we can sense and find them much earlier than this. But interesting things happen all the time and we always learn from them when they do. Now, with that out of the way, I think you all can agree that I am well qualified to explain things, right?"

Rebecca looked at everyone and each one nodded in turn. Then she looked warmly at Caroline, who responded with some relief, "OK… yeah… I would really like to know what you think, actually."

"Caroline, you are a raw, untrained Moon Born," Rebecca began. "You have no knowledge of your abilities, nor do you understand our history or traditions. However, even without all of this knowledge, you still have a deep connection to our people and our ways. It is built into how we have grown and evolved over millennia. The problem is, when you don't have the context, it is hard to understand what is happening when you start experiencing the full impact of your abilities.

"That is what is happening, mind you. You are starting to feel the impact and it is only going to get stronger. You will need a guide as you enter this phase and, I will not lie, it will be difficult. However, it doesn't have to be painful or traumatic. In fact, it should be enlightening. For instance, did you know what this means?"

Rebecca pulled out the large plate that Caroline decorated on her birthday from a satchel that had been concealed underneath her shawl and showed it to Caroline.

"That's just some pattern I saw when I was younger and I tried to copy it," Caroline said, dismissing the connection.

"No, it is not just some pattern, my dear," Rebecca corrected her. "Patterns are holy to the Moon Born and this one has particular significance. It symbolizes balance and the cycle of life. I'm sorry I cannot explain this in more detail with your friends around. It is one of the things that we only share with our own. Suffice it to say, you would not have seen this anywhere before and it came to you because you have the ability to become a very gifted Moon Born."

Caroline's friends tried not to stare at her, but they couldn't help themselves. They sat and gawked, waiting for her to say something, but nothing came. She just stared at the plate intensely.

"So, let's get to what you experienced in the temple, shall we?" Rebecca continued and Caroline still didn't reply. "I heard you say you saw the vial and felt an intense connection and attraction to it, is that right?"

Caroline didn't waiver, she just remained fixated on the plate.

The timber of Rebecca's voice changed when she said, "I need you to hear me now." Caroline blinked a few times and looked up at Rebecca with a startled expression on her face. Rebecca put the plate away in her bag again and smiled at Caroline.

"Was that kind of what you felt in the temple?" she asked and Caroline nodded energetically, her throat suddenly dry and unable to make a sound.

"It wasn't Warwick you were connected to. It was your people. Our patterns are powerful and a deep part of who we are. That's what you were connected to in the temple and it was completely natural. If you start your training, we can help you control that connection and understand it better."

Tears rolled down Caroline's cheeks again and Rebecca got up and crossed over to her, kneeling and wiping the tears away.

"I hope this is a relief to you," she said to Caroline.

"You have no idea…" Caroline answered.

"I'm sorry to interrupt," Adam said, "but I think it's time for us to discuss some things."

The spell of the moment was broken and everyone looked around, remembering why they were there. Meimei was the first to stand up and start walking back toward the cavern, following Adam's lead. The rest of them got up slowly and made their way, too.

Emerging from the chamber, Caroline saw her parents and ran to them, giving each a tight hug. Camille immediately got teary as George knelt down and hugged Caroline tightly again. Rebecca came over and gave each a warm greeting as if she had known them for many years, even though they were just meeting for the first time.

Adam gestured for everyone to have a seat on the floor and each of the families came together and formed small pods to listen. Maranda came around and sat next to Adam, forming their own family unit again.

"I'm sorry it has taken so long to let you all know what will happen now that Gabriel and his followers have the vial. As I am sure you can appreciate, we needed to take extraordinary precautions given the circumstances and we needed to deliberate on the best course of action. There were… let's just say, a variety of opinions. However, we were able to come to an agreement thanks to Maranda and her network of Star Borns around the world, as well as Aran's fast thinking at the temple.

Aran looked around, surprised to be called out.

"Yes, you, Aran," Adam continued. "If you hadn't thought to follow Gabriel from the temple, we would not have been able to intercept so many of his followers. They have yielded a great deal of information that has allowed us to find a number of senior leaders of their movement in our midst. I am sad to say, it was not a small number…

"These are tough times and we must pull together. That is what we decided at the Gathering. As you know, we were not exactly prepared for this, so we need to do some work to get ready for the struggle ahead. That is why we have decided to form five special schools around the world that will start educating our youth to have a greater connection to our history and abilities."

Leo looked at Maranda and she met his gaze with an excited look.

"These schools will be staffed by a rotating set of teachers who will guide your studies. This will be a bit of a learning experience for them as well because, as you know, we normally train new members of the tribe just in their own area of abilities. However, you all have shown us there is a significant benefit to training together. So, each school will be a mix of Earth Born, Star Born, and…" Adam cleared his throat as he glared at Rebecca, "a small number of Moon Born."

"For now…" Rebecca added serenely.

"Right… For now…" Adam accepted. "You all will be headed to one of these schools together in a few weeks since we are still working out some of the details."

"Wait! You're saying we don't have to go to middle school?!" Aran interrupted excitedly and Josh shushed him impatiently.

"Well, you'll still be studying many of the things you would have learned in middle school," Adam broke the news to him, "but you will also be studying your abilities along with other students from around the world."

"Won't it look weird that we are suddenly all disappearing from school?" Stella asked.

"Well, let's just say there will be an unfortunate issue with your school so that all the students will need to be split up into other schools. You all will just have an opportunity to attend one not in the area," Adam explained.

"All of us?" Leo asked, sensing not all of the details were being shared.

"Well, not exactly…" Adam answered with hesitation.

"Caroline will be coming to study in a special school for new Moon Borns," Rebecca interjected. "That is, if she wants to."

"What if I want to stay with my friends?" Caroline asked.

"I'm sorry, given the strength of your abilities, we will not have the capacity to guide your development in these new schools yet," Adam answered, clearly unhappy with his own explanation.

"There will be a time when you will be able to reunite with your friends, but for now the best place for you to develop is in our school," Rebecca explained.

Caroline and her friends didn't love this twist, but none of them saw any way around it. They just sat silently, their parents feeling the weight of their emotions.

"Rebecca has assured me that no Moon Born will support Gabriel's effort to set Warwick free," Adam started up again. "This means we have some time to plan for a fight we expect to take a long time to win. And mark my words, we do intend to win it. While you all are developing your abilities, we will be laying the groundwork to find the vial before they are able to open it. In the event that is not successful, it is our hope you all will join our cause and fight alongside us to keep Warwick from unleashing chaos on our world."

"Ok, so it is our choice to attend these schools?" Ania asked.

"Yes," Adam answered simply.

"Well, I'm in then," she said.

"Me too," said Stella.

"Yeah, I wanna go," said Aran.

"You're not leaving me behind," Meimei added.

They all looked at Leo who remained quiet, staring at his hands. They all waited for him to say something, the tension building with each heartbeat he stayed silent. When it was becoming nearly unbearable for everyone, he finally spoke up.

"I made a vow to share everything with my friends," Leo said, "I don't see how I can keep that vow if you separate Caroline from us. If she doesn't come with us, I don't think I can go."

"Wait a sec, honey…" his mom began to say before Caroline interrupted.

"I need to go on this journey, Leo… I can feel it…" she said. "You won't be breaking your promise to me and this won't be forever."

She looked at Rebecca who just smiled warmly back.

"You need to go," she said to Leo.

"But…" he started to counter.

"You know it's the right thing to do," she pushed harder and he knew she was right.

After thinking quietly for a few moments, he said, "OK, I'm in." Then the tension in the group released and Adam smiled at him encouragingly.

"Well, I guess we will give you some time to say your good-byes then," Adam said, starting to get up. The group looked at each other in confusion, not understanding what he meant.

"Caroline will start her travels to our school immediately," Rebecca clarified. "Unfortunately, there is only one Wayfairer available for the next several months. She will be needed to take Caroline since I have more business to attend to following the Gathering."

"It's OK, guys," Caroline reassured them. "I've been watching you all for so long now. I'm ready to start on my path. Honestly, the sooner, the better."

Her parents came over and they had a tight group hug, then George handed her a large bag and they stepped away with the other parents who gave them hugs to comfort them.

Caroline's friends gathered around her and for once they were all at a loss for words, but, as usual, Aran was the first to say something.

"So... I guess we'll see ya when we see ya?" he said and Caroline smiled nervously. He gave her a hug and then peeled off, walking over to stand with Maranda.

"Damn, girl, you've got some guts. Give 'em hell," Ania said, punching her lightly in the shoulder and then joining Aran.

"If you ever need anything, we'll be there for you," Stella said earnestly, then gave her a brief hug before moving away quickly, wiping her eyes.

"Try to stay outta trouble," Meimei said with a smile and gave Caroline a fist bump, leaving Leo by himself with one of his oldest and closest friends.

They shuffled their feet awkwardly for a moment, not sure what else to say to one another. Then Leo let his thoughts flow out of him.

"We've always faced stuff together..." he said.

"And we will again," Caroline assured him.

"But it won't be the same..."

"Yeah… you're right."

"This sucks…"

Caroline let out one of her large, characteristic guffaws and said, "Totally."

"Friends forever?" he asked.

"Always," she answered and wrapped him up into a tight hug. Then she stepped back and walked over to Rebecca who was standing by the cavern entrance. A moment later, they were up the stairs and out of sight.

ACKNOWLEDGEMENTS

This book would not have been possible without the support and editing prowess of my partner in life and all things, Amy Draemel. It is very difficult to express just how critical she was throughout the writing process. We have a pretty busy life with activities for our children and then working full time, so just the gift of time to write has been amazing.

I would also like to thank a very supportive community of friends and family who have read the book, provided feedback, and generally made me feel so great about embarking on this creative process. To all of you who have been there for me throughout the creation of this book, thank you!

Finally, to our children and their friends, thank you for being an inspiration to this book through many backyard sessions of Dungeons and Dragons. Who would've thought it could lead to something like this?

ABOUT THE AUTHOR

Ben Barry lives in the Bay Area with his family. He discovered his love of storytelling while putting his kids to bed and making up fantastical tales on the fly. As they grew older, the stories became more complex and he began writing them down to feed their voracious reading appetites. Now Ben carves out some time every week to capture his imagination in words.